Berman's Wolves
By
Gretchen S. B.

Acknowledgments

I wanted to thank everyone who helped me get this manuscript into a book. Thank you to my very patient Beta reader, for reading this story a handful of pages at a time for the better part of a year, unedited. Also, I need to give a written hug to all my friends and family who continue to encourage me to reach for my dream of becoming a full time author. Lastly comes ‘He who must not be tagged.’ Though he hates to be mentioned, he deserves credit for all his support.

Prologue

June 2012, Graduation Day

Winter quarter of 2010 changed my life forever, though I had no idea at the time. I was plugging along, getting my business degree dreaming and dreading the day I would graduate and join the real world.

That day is here now and I find the completion of my college years much less daunting than it was two years ago. After all I have been through over the past few years, graduation seems more like a drop in the bucket than the life altering event it is supposed to be.

My roommate, Lyra bought me this journal as a graduation gift. She knows the nightmares that wake me several nights a week. She sits up with me in silence when the memories of what was done to us won't let me rest. She knows I worry about what I will do now that I will not have her empathetic presence with me. That is why she bought me this journal. She herself has her own demons that stare her in the face at night. She told me time and time again that her journal is sometimes the only thing that stops her from losing her mind. So she bought me one almost identical to her own and told me to fill it.

"Start from the beginning" she said. "You can tell it anything and everything. But start with the madman that ruined your peace of mind."

So here it is. The story of how my life was changed by someone I still have never met. A new instructor was hired at Pacific Northwest University, where I attend. I am told the Chemistry department was thrilled with their new hire. Doctor Nicholas Berman was in his mid-sixties and had worked with organizations all over the world. Once hired, a meeting was scheduled to gain student feedback.

Berman apparently won over many of the students by saying, “After years of experiments it was time for simple research and reflection.” He was unanimously accepted. Students found him captivating and candid. Little did they know it was all a front for a more sinister agenda. Seniors fought to be on his research team. It wouldn't be until May that the school's folly would come back to bite them.

Berman, as it turned out had been performing human experiments at the school under the noses of the administration. How they could have missed this was beyond me. But after all the lawsuits that ensued I bet they will never be so careless again! Over the decades he'd all but perfected his research in undocumented trials. He fooled those at Pacific Northwest University as well as two other neighboring Universities. This is one of the baffling parts for me, he gained positions at three local universities, all under different names and false backgrounds. How did no one catch this sooner!

He was at Pacific Northwest University that horrible night in May but webcams kept him in contact with the labs at the other two schools. His calculations turned out to be off just slightly, but the assistants at the other schools copied exactly. To this day no one can ever convince me that those calculations were anything but intentional! I do not care what the government investigation says, Berman knew what he was doing! The chemicals hit the air, affecting every living soul in the science buildings and through the opened windows to any person within a quarter mile.

At Pacific, it hit those of us studying in the library. At Southern West, it seeped into the Students Union Building, where a charity rock concert and an interdenominational Christian group were held. The University of the Peninsula, is much smaller than the other schools so everything on campus was closed down.

I still remember that night as if it were yesterday. Lyra, Justin and I were sprawled out on one of the large group work tables. Lyra and Justin were exchanging resources for the final papers they had for their shared lit class. I was trying desperately to cram as much stats as I could into my head for my final the next Monday.

I remember Lyra looked up first. She had gone dead silent and her expression of horror is burned into my brain.

"Get under the table!"

It was a loud whisper but Justin and I didn't question it. We dove. Not two seconds later there was a boom that shook the building, something you won't see in the official reports, book and papers slide on to the floor. I could hear my heart in my ears. I looked at lyra and grabbed her hand, the rest of my body was frozen.

She looked me in the eyes as we heard people downstairs start coughing.

"Hold your breath as long as you can!"

Justin and I nodded. We had no idea what was going on, what was about to happen to us. I just remember the terror and the deep seeded knowledge that something very bad was happening.

Seconds later the panicking people around us were coughing and running downstairs. My lungs started to burn. Then people began collapsing. I squeezed Lyra's hand, but she didn't squeeze back. She couldn't comfort me in those moments because there was no comfort to give. I knew something was wrong with the air. But I was starting to see those black spots.

Then I heard Justin gasp. I looked over, my eyes watering, fear roaring through me. He grabbed hold of both Lyra's and my other hands. I couldn't help it, as the cries and struggling in the library started to quiet my lungs screamed for breath and I gave in. Air filled my lungs and my body screamed with relief.

At first nothing happened. Then my lungs began to itch. I started to cough and distantly I could hear Justin coughing with me. My lungs began to burn. Then I blacked out. The whole thing could not have even been five minute but it seemed like so much longer.

The government took control while we were out, locking down the campuses and quarantining those affected. Every one of the five hundred and twelve students were removed and bussed to a facility east of Seattle. All that time two-thirds of us, myself included were still unconscious. Everything I know about the transport is what I heard from Lyra and others.

Lyra came to still in the library, but there were men in hazmat suits around her. Her body was a giant nerve ball of pain. I was lucky enough to have been out for this period. There were about fifty of us, that I have talked to who woke while the poison was still changing our bodies. All of them have said it was the most painful thing they ever felt in their lives.

She told me later that she was not even aware she had been screaming until a hazmat suit walked up to her and gave her a shot. To this day she does not know what was in it, but it brought the pain to a tolerable level.

She told me that when they started moving all of us to the 'more secure location' she would not let them separate the three of us. They told her she couldn't go with us because she was conscience and we were not. She never went in to details on how, but eventually she won and was able to travel with us.

When I woke up, three hours after I passes out, Lyra was standing next to the cot I was in, crying and gripping my hand. Lyra rarely ever cries, so that scared me, once the relief of us both being alive passed.

"Tell me." It was all I could get out, my voice hoarse.

The fear started to creep back, growing like a weed. Lyra explained to me what she had learned. That it was an experiment gone wrong. She told me about how we had gotten there and that she had overheard several doctors talking about possible genetic mutations. That Berman disappeared in all the pain and confusion. Government officials were interrogating the fourteen research assistants. None of the students were admitting to having knowledge of Berman's whereabouts. What little notes the government found mentioned something about Berman's goal to create 'Werewolves'. The scientists suspected that somehow Berman figured out how to create the mythical creature with the use of modern medicine.

Lyra paused before looking passed me. "Justin seems to be fine. But we won't know for sure until he wakes up. While I waited for you to wake up I looked around and noticed something." Her breathing shuddered then and her grip on my hand tightened. "Seth and Jack were in the library too. They were downstairs."

My heart broke. Jack and Seth were our friends. We had known them as long as we had known Justin.

"Where are they?"

She tilted her and motioning behind her and to the left. "About three rows that way."

My eyes became glassy. "Are they okay?"

Her breath hitched. "I don't know. They're still sleeping."

"We can't leave them here."

Her eyes steeled and seemed to dry instantly. Her whole body changed before my eyes. "We won't."

She made sure we didn't. When the doctors cleared me to be moved to the waiting area Lyra fought vigorously. She made sure all of the doctors and staff knew we were not leaving that room until Justin, Jack and Seth were awake.

Hours passed after the five of us were cleared and moved to the waiting area. The tension skyrocketed as the scientists began breaking people up and sending them to other parts of the facility. I lost it. The emotional toll hit me like a truck. Lyra hugged me to shield me from the room and let me cry into her shoulder. I couldn't be separated from my friends. I didn't know how I could cope without them.

Then I heard Lyra's voice in my ear. Her word was not meant for me. I knew that as soon as my brain processed it.

"Taylor."

I knew by her voice that she was looking at her cousin's best friend. They grew up together, almost like siblings. I felt her stiffen a second later as a gruff voice told the five of us we were being moved. I swear she stopped breathing before there was a whispered, "No."

As we moved I looked over my shoulder, sure enough I there was Taylor standing maybe twenty feet away, at a dead stop. Watching us leave with anger in his eyes.

We were taken to a room with nine other people already in it and were left there for another hour waiting to hear our fate.

The government assigned us into groups known as 'packs' to make us easier to handle. As it turned out, a psychologist on the program stated we would probably be more willing to go along if they kept us in the groups we clung to in the waiting room.

In the months after the incident, two downtown Seattle office buildings were built for individual packs to use as offices. Putting all of us in one place made it easier for the scientists keep tabs.

Over the next year, we were put through tests and training programs. Those in charge tried to figure out how to best use us. We were Werewolves struggling to get our bodies under control. So we knew little more than they did about what we would be capable of.

After the first year, disputes broke out among the scientists about how to proceed with the program. While they fought, most of us graduated and began to organize ourselves.

Fast forward another year and it was my turn to graduate, along with my entire pack actually. None of us are sure what to do now, but at least none of us have to do it alone.

Chapter 1

Lyra knew the Weres who jumped her were members of pack L, former lab assistants of Berman's from Pacific Northwest University. They hadn't tried to negotiate this time, but had simply jumped her as she turned the corner on her way home from the off-leash dog park in her neighborhood.

As soon as she smelled her attackers approaching, she turned to Hazel and pretended to have lost her cell phone. Hazel hadn't questioned it, just taken Fizgig's leash from Lyra's outstretched hand and continued walking to Lyra's apartment.

Lyra double-timed it toward the park. She knew her attackers would follow. All she needed was enough distance between them and Hazel. Lyra loved Hazel like family, but the other woman was not a fighter. Hazel would try, but she would only be hurt or used against Lyra. It didn't really help matters that Hazel and Lyra knew all of each other's secrets. In Lyra's case some of those secrets could get them killed.

Lyra knew leading the attackers away from Hazel and the dogs was her best and only option. As the outskirts of the forested trail closed in around her, Lyra spun and braced herself for the attack. She could smell the malicious intent like rotting meat rolling off of them. She had one advantage: they didn't know how well she could fight. Growing up in a predominantly male social group, Lyra had honed her skills. They thought girls were weak. They would underestimate her. Lyra gave a small grin as the three Weres came into view around the bend.

Lyra posed as if she'd been caught off-guard and was helpless, widening her eyes and shrinking away in horror. The tallest guy headed toward her. Lyra counted, waiting until the last second when his arms stretched out to grab her. She roundhouse-kicked him in the head. The Were crumpled. Weres could take and dole out major damage and Lyra was stronger than most. The blow landed perfectly, and he'd be out of commission for a few minutes.

The other two men didn't make the same mistake; they rushed her. Lyra backed up. She needed more room than the thin nature trail provided. She was able to get one punch in to the guy on her left before the other man grabbed her.

Panic began to rise as a strong arm banded around her throat. Screaming to herself, she pushed the panic aside. She struggled to remember the course of action for this type of attack. Using the heel of her shoe, she stomped on her attacker's foot. Inwardly she swore as she connected with a boot—she couldn't do any damage that way. His arm tightened, and she knew he meant for her to lose consciousness. That would be bad. She felt the loss of breath acutely and Lyra knew she had maybe thirty seconds to get out of the hold before she was incapacitated.

She gave one swift kick behind her as she dug both her thumbs at her throat to relieve the pressure. Her kick hit true and her attacker cried out as her heel connected with groin.

She felt the man back up and she moved the opposite direction, scanning for the Were she'd punched in the stomach. She didn't see him, not at first, but what she did see made her curse.

Two of her larger packmates, Ryan and Cole, stood nearby. At Cole's feet was the missing attacker. Ryan dropped the other man, the one who had been choking her, to the ground. All three attackers were unconscious and bleeding. Lyra might be strong and fast, but both Cole and Ryan were leagues beyond her.

Both men were watching her now. Ryan was staring at her neck in fury. Lyra knew it was red, but there was not much she could do about it. It would clear up within five minutes. Accelerated healing was a plus of being a Werewolf.

Cole found his voice first. He was six-foot-six and built like a house; the Samoan was already intimidating without being a Werewolf. Cole kept his hair cut close to his head. He was the largest and strongest in the pack, but he wasn't Alpha material despite his physical qualifications. Cole was too laid back and quick to smile, but when someone was threatened, he could be incredibly dangerous.

"What's going on, Lyra?"

His voice held a threat, but Lyra knew it wasn't for her. Cole was far too overprotective for that. Normally she would lie, say she had no idea, but pack L had actually attacked her this time and she couldn't keep this to herself anymore.

Lyra looked at each of them in turn. "To be totally honest, I'm not entirely sure."

Ryan folded his arms over his chest as he opened his mouth, but Lyra held up a hand to stop him. She didn't know why, but Ryan always had a knack for knowing when she was lying. He didn't always call her on it but he made sure she was aware of it.

"What I do know is that a few days ago two members of pack L approached me on my way to work. They told me they had a deal to offer me. They wanted me to switch packs, and I don't mean switch teams for the coming soccer season, I mean, actual packs."

Both men stiffened. Lyra could feel the outrage rolling off of them. Weres were intensely loyal to their packs. Those from stable packs would never think of leaving their packmates. Lyra took a deep breath and continued.

"I told them where they could put their offer and walked away. Apparently they don't take rejection well."

Lyra saw Ryan's lip twitch, but he wouldn't admit his amusement. Ryan prided himself on his stoicism. Ryan was six-foot-three. His light brown hair was shaggy but short and he had pale greenish yellow eyes. He could seem pretty intimidating, but standing next to Cole he almost looked small.

"Was there any preamble to the attack? You knew they were coming. Don't try to deny it. You don't come to this park without your dogs."

Sometimes Lyra hated that Ryan was so observant. She couldn't help her glare.

"I smelled them coming. Hazel and I were walking the dogs back home. I told Hazel I had dropped my phone. She's at my place by now. I doubled back; I didn't want to endanger her or the dogs."

Ryan watched her a moment. He was the Second in their pack, which gave him some authority. Only Jack, their Alpha, had authority over him.

"Do Hazel or Jack know about these encounters?"

Lyra fidgeted. She didn't want to worry anyone; she didn't see the point in sharing things that would only cause panic. She hadn't even told her cousin Graham, and they were incredibly close.

Ryan read her silence. "I see." He turned to Cole. "They'll attack her again, and come with reinforcements. We should watch her."

Cole nodded once. "Agreed."

Lyra opened her mouth to protest, but closed it again. She knew full well they were right, but she hated the idea of being babysat. Plus the last thing she wanted was for this to get back to Jack. Jack was a good friend of hers, had been for years but he was a worrier and he had enough on his plate right now.

"Twelve hour shifts? I'll take tonight and you relieve me in the morning. If they get the idea that Lyra is protected, they should back off long enough for us to figure out what it is they want with her." The authority in Ryan's voice prevented any argument.

Cole nodded again before motioning to the three unconscious men. "What about them?"

Ryan seemed to think about it a moment, then smiled. "Payphone, anonymous 911 call. Three men mugging a girl. A good Samaritan came along to help her. You saw the whole thing and the three guys are just lying here unconscious. Without an actual witness, the police probably won't hold them, but it will delay these guys a while."

Cole gave Ryan a matching smile before jogging off toward the main area of the park. Several seconds went by before Ryan looked over to Lyra again.

"I don't want you arguing with me about this. You need someone with you. Don't try and lose either of us or anything else you might think of." There was a pause. "I assume you'll be wanting me to keep this from Jack?"

Lyra just held her breath. This was the moment of truth. Ryan could theoretically be their Alpha, but for some reason he had stepped aside for Jack. He was a good Second but every once in a while his real dominant nature peeked out. Lyra hoped this was one of those times.

"I won't mention it to him as long as you play by my rules. Right now it's not a big enough problem to bother him with."

Lyra heard what wasn't said. If Ryan thought the situation worsening, he would bring Jack in and Jack would be pissed. But then, if Jack knew all the information Lyra kept from him he'd kill her, figuratively that is. Exhaling slowly, she agreed to Ryan's terms.

He unfolded his hands and slid them into the pockets of his jeans. "All right then, go home before Hazel starts to get suspicious and comes looking for you. You call me the moment she leaves. I'll come over straight from Cole's."

Lyra didn't respond, just headed back home. Everything had changed in the last ten minutes. She was trusting others with her safety. Lyra didn't do that, but she had no choice this time. Ryan would never back down. Any other pack member Lyra could have convinced to leave matters alone, but Ryan would never buy it. Lyra didn't know what she was going to do. She had her suspicions as to why pack L wanted her, but she couldn't exactly question her contacts with Cole and Ryan around. Lyra shook her head clear; she couldn't give Hazel any indication something was wrong. Everything had to appear normal. Lyra snorted. Nothing had been normal in years.

Chapter 2

The noise was getting too loud for Lyra, Jack could tell. Jack had always been better at reading his litter mate than anyone else.

Litter mate was a term used for those in a person's pack who were close before Berman's experiment. He and four others in his pack had attended to high school together. They had gone their separate ways in college, running into each other from time to time. When they saw each other in quarantine, they banded together. They were then placed in Pacific Northwest University's pack F with nine others. Before pack training, Jack had never met any of the other nine, but now he trusted them explicitly.

Jack gave a worried glance toward Lyra as the volume in the room went higher. Today was negotiating day for the next year of soccer. All the packs played on soccer teams. Soccer had been the one recreational sport they could all play. Strength varied vastly from one Were to another, which left most contact sports out of the question. The only two sports left to them had been soccer and ultimate Frisbee. The latter had been unanimously banned due to too many dog jokes. They couldn't play in an average league, so a Were soccer league had been formed a year and a half before. It was a way for all of them to stay in contact with each other.

There were enough packs to form three divisions within their league. PNWU pack F played in the PNWU/UP division. Since some of the packs were smaller than could field a team, negotiation day had been scheduled before fall season began. Jack's pack didn't need extra teammates, nor did anyone want to trade to another team for the year. Despite that, as Alpha, Jack, along with every pack Alpha in the division, had to attend any kind of multi-pack meeting. So while PNWU/UP Weres hollered back and forth at each other, Jack and his Second sat at their packs' desk and only responded when something was directed at them.

The two schools shared a twenty-storey building which held offices for all sixteen packs. There was one entire floor in the building used for multi-pack business. It contained a circle of labeled desks for the representatives, one for each pack. Not all packs had Alphas, which caused struggles within the packs and the group at large as well. That's why each desk was labeled. Jack never knew who the representatives would be for some of the other packs.

Trading negotiations were never pleasant, which was why they agreed to only do it once a year.

Lyra hated crowds and too much noise, even before the accident had improved her hearing, and yet every time there was a multi-pack meeting, she was determined to go with him. One time early on, he deliberately hadn't told her about a meeting to save her the discomfort. She had been furious with him and attacked him, pinning him to the floor while he was still in shock and made him promise never go without her again.

She had come to every meeting since, in wolf form. She never sat in when he or Ryan couldn't make it; she just lay behind them. Jack noticed over the years that two male wolves did the same thing, one in pack J and one in pack M. When Jack mentioned it to either Alpha, both stated it didn't matter what they said, but that their wolf accompanied them anyway.

A couple months ago before each meeting, Ryan had taken to grabbing one of the two large yellow ottomans from pack F's seventh floor office and bringing it downstairs to the second floor, multi-pack meeting room. Jack had been surprised the first time, but grateful the other man thought to make the meeting less distressing on their packmate. No doubt Ryan picked up on her discomfort, but never brought it up. The gesture made Jack respect his Second even more. Ryan had been a stranger to Jack before quarantine, but now he couldn't think of a better Second.

Ryan was four inches taller than Jack and built like a football player; he had played before having to quit after becoming a Werewolf. His enhanced abilities were too obvious an advantage. Ryan wasn't much of a talker. The only people Jack saw him hold conversations with were three other packmates, were the twins: Sadie and Syrus, and Cole, who also played football for PNWU.

As two packs on the other side of the room began a shouting match, Jack nudged Ryan under the table and gestured behind them at Lyra. The salty-grey female wolf was curled up as tight as she could on top of the ottoman. If you didn't know her well, there would be no indication she was uncomfortable. Anyone in pack F, however, would know better. The two men exchanged glances. Without further communication, Jack and Ryan moved their chairs farther apart and Ryan got up to stand in front of the ottoman. Jack knew he was the only one outside of Lyra who heard Ryan speak.

"I'm going to lift you and bring you closer, okay?"

When Lyra just continued to watch him, Ryan picked up the ottoman, with her still on it and moved it just behind the two chairs. As Ryan sat back down, Jack put his hand in Lyra's fur. The ottoman was shorter than the desk so no one could see Lyra except those on either side.

Jack heard the Alpha to his left clear his throat loud enough to get Jack and Ryan's attention. Packs arranged their own tables, so they were not in any real order. Jack made sure the four tables closest to him were Alphas he felt he could trust.

The man to his left was Mathew, Alpha of pack J. Jack looked over and saw the man giving a small smile and nodding at Lyra. Before Jack could say anything, Mathew, with his hand by his side, pointed under his desk. Then he gestured at the desk to his left, which housed pack M. Jack gave a small smile back. Mathew was telling him the other two wolves at the meeting were curled up under the desks, hiding from the growing noise. Jack was sure the wolves were thankful the desks were enclosed on three sides.

"Enough!" The room went silent as the Alpha two tables to the right stood.

Finn was the one pack leader that could get everyone's attention. pack A's Alpha had been the post-grad running the advanced chemistry lab in PNWU's science building across the floor from Berman. The man had finished his doctorate and was to start teaching at PNWU next month. His pack was made up of the twelve students in the advanced chemistry lab. Finn was six-foot-four and slightly on the thin side but still had a strong presence. His dark red hair was short but not short enough to hide the slight curl. Finn used to need contacts but the accident had fixed his eyes.

Finn waited a beat before continuing. "This is utterly ridiculous! It is not like this is the end of the world. We have been here an hour already. How many teams are set?" Jack and eight others raised their hands.

"Figures," said pack D's Alpha, Grant, who sat to the right of Ryan.

Ryan grunted his agreement. The last three teams were run by packs without Alphas.

"Fine," Finn continued. "All the wolves that want to switch teams stand in the middle of the circle." He paused as twenty people moved. "Okay, now go touch the table of the open team you want to play for."

All but five people touched a table.

One of the last five, a guy Jack didn't know, spoke up. "We don't care. We just refuse to be on the same team as pack P."

There was a groan from half the room as the four members of pack P started shouting.

This same thing happened at every multi-pack meeting. Packs O and P were the two packs from University of the Peninsula. The five students happened to be working on a biology project at the time of the accident refused to work in any way with the four guys who made up Berman's lab team.

While the other ten lab assistants hadn't known too much about the research Berman had been doing, UP was where the government found the majority of Berman's notes. While no one really trusted any of the three lab teams, the Weres from PNWU and SWU accepted them as part of the pack structure. Pack O hated all fourteen lab aids.

Finn sighed. "Fine, two of you go there and two of you go there." Finn pointed at two teams that were short players. This left pack P with the PNWU pack L, and they would only have nine players all year.

It was pack L's female rep that spoke next. "We're short. From the looks of it, we need another defender."

Normally trades happened toward the beginning of the meeting. At this point no one would want to trade with the Alpha-less team. Especially one made up of all lab assistants, and Jack wasn't sure that had ever happened before. They might not outwardly exclude the PNWU assistants, but Jack didn't know a single Alpha that would loan one of their packmates to all of them.

Finn gave the girl a blank stare. "I believe we are finished now. The fact that no one leapt in to trade you shows that clearly."

As Finn sat back down the girl spoke again.

She was looking at Jack's side of the room. "We don't want a trade. We want pack F to give us Lyra. Having a star defender will more than make up for us being shorted like this." She was smirking, sure she would get her way.

Before she finished talking, both Jack and Ryan were on their feet. Jack's anger spiked at the insult, there was no way he would just give out one of his packmates. Jack could feel Lyra crouching on the ottoman behind him and Ryan. Lyra was an intensely loyal person, and even if he ordered her to another team she wouldn't go. It was almost as if she physically couldn't.

Ryan was growling an answer before Jack opened up his mouth. "Do not insult us. We do not offer up our packmates to anyone."

When Ryan wanted to he could be the most intimidating person Jack had ever met. The woman automatically backed down, as even she knew who she couldn't beat in a fight, and Ryan would have made it a fight. It was why he made such a strong Second.

Both Jack and Ryan sat in unison, still watching the female rep across the room. It wasn't until Jack put his hand back in Lyra's fur that he felt her body vibrating. Then he heard the faint growl. Ryan must have heard it too; Jack wasn't aware the other Were's hearing was that good, because the other man put his hand on Lyra's lower back and made a light shushing noise to comfort her, all without moving his gaze.

Jack wasn't the only one to notice it; the two wolves were up from under the desks and watching both Lyra and the woman across the room. Lyra was still growling as she leaned forward to make herself seen over the desk. Her eyes bored furiously into the other woman. Jack suddenly had the inkling he was missing something. Lyra was more of the 'ignore them until they are a threat' school of thought. It was unlike her to make this blatant a scene. Jack's hand curled into the fur at the back of Lyra's neck in warning. He was going to find out what had her so spooked, but later. Pack business was not something you confronted in front of outsiders.

Finn spoke as if nothing happened. "All right then, the teams stand as they are now, meeting adjourned. See everyone on the fields next week."

People everywhere stood milling about or headed for the elevators or stairs. The stairs across the room led down to the entry floor, while the elevators behind them led to the floors of the pack offices. There was a staircase by the elevators, but it only went up. All four of the elevators and the stairs required thumbprint verification by every person who entered, unless they were in Wolf form, then there was voice verification instead. The program pumped a lot of money into the security of the pack office buildings.

Jack looked at his two packmates and let go of Lyra's fur. "What's going on, Lyra?" He whispered.

He didn't get any kind of answer. Lyra stood still, fixated on something across the room. She was watching the lab assistants as they grabbed their belongings and bee-lined for the stairs, all strategically not looking over at the still growling Lyra.

Once all nine had disappeared down the stairs Lyra stopped growling and hopped off the ottoman, looking up at Jack as if nothing had happened.

Ryan picked up the ottoman, and glanced down at Lyra, who sat on the floor, continuing to look up at Jack.

"Fine, we'll discuss it upstairs then." Jack searched his mind for anything he might have missed as he led the way toward the elevators.

They were followed in by the members of pack J and pack M. It was a good thing three of them were in wolf form, as the nine of them wouldn't have a fit on the elevator with the ottoman. Jack knew this for a fact, as some of his packmates tried to see what combination for people and objects could fit on the elevators. The far elevator still had dents along half the wall.

Everyone verified their identities one by one. These security features made it impossible for unknown people to reach any of the upper floors. Sometimes Jack thought it was good to have government funding.

Mathew glanced between Jack and pack M's Alpha, Bishop. "I believe the nine of us need to talk."

Both he and Bishop nodded.

Jack pushed the button for the seventh floor. "Okay, let's go to my pack's lounge. We have the best furniture."

Victor, Bishop's Second snorted. "I know, how the hell did that happen."

Jack shrugged. It had been Hazel who picked out the furniture. Hazel had a knack when it came to homemaking and if memory served him right, she had dragged Lyra along with her in an effort to create an interest in such things. Lyra had hated it.

Jack really wanted to speak to his littermate about what happened. Lyra could be irritable at times, but she was always careful at the multi-pack meetings. He wanted to know if pack L's request bothered her that much, or had she believed he might hand her over? Jack really wanted answers, but knew he had to be diplomatic and find out what the other Alpha wanted first.

As the elevator doors opened into the entryway, Jack heard Mason, Mathew's second, snort.

"What the hell is with the sign?"

Jack sighed as they got off the elevator. Syrus, one of the packmates who 'tested' the elevators, thought it would be funny to name their floor and every time Jack, Ryan, or Jack's littermate Seth, took the sign down, a cruder one would appear in its place. So they gave up trying to stop Syrus and in return he toned down the signs. Every other month or so a new one would appear above the door, giving a new name. This month THE DEN OF INIQUITY was scrolled in red dripping letters on a black sign.

Jack leaned closer to Ryan. "I hate that he has two English degrees."

Ryan only grunted.

As Jack moved forward to give handprint verification at the door, he spoke over his shoulder. "One of our packmates thinks he's funny. We've learned that to ignore it is the only way not to encourage it."

Victor responded. "Last time I was up here it said Den of Antiquity and had graphics on it…"

Jack sighed again as the door opened. That had been one of the cruder signs. "Yeah, he changes it regularly."

Jack felt rather than saw Lyra brush past him and into the front room his pack made in to a lounge. To the left of the door was a decent-sized kitchen stocked pretty regularly with both food and booze. Though Jack didn't really drink, some of the pack were, in his opinion, bordering on alcoholics. It didn't help that his other male littermate Justin was a bartender. Jack made it clear that Justin was in charge of stocking the alcohol. They pretty much took turns on everything else.

His litter made sure there were baking supplies continuously stocked. Lyra would fidget when agitated, she always had. Hazel tried to explain it to him, but it wasn't until quarantine that Jack had really seen it. Lyra rarely sat still the entire six hours they were detained. She had always been tugging on her clothing or tapping her fingers on her leg. She just seemed to build up energy when she got worked up and it was better for all of them if she had an outlet. For whatever reason, baking seemed to work the best. So to prevent irritation and outbursts, they kept the kitchen stocked and every once in a while there would be a table full of treats.

The kitchen had a six-stool bar separating it from three, four-person cherry wood tables. On the wall in between the tables was the door to his office, where all the pack paperwork was stored.

Across from the door, taking up the rest of the room was the actual lounge. From the looks of it, Hazel had rearranged the furniture, again. Five dark brown leather chairs sat in a circle around a square coffee table, with the other yellow ottoman on the far side. There was an obvious gap in the circle where Ryan had gotten the ottoman from. In the far corner was a big screen television with a matching maroon leather couch, love seat, and two huge chairs. There were small light wood end tables between each. To his right were three cream pull-out couches, just in case someone needed a place to crash, set in a semi-circle facing the wall.

They used to have a foosball table but it was the cause of too many fist fights, so Jack made Syrus get rid of it. Jack could see the three tie-dye bean bag chairs had been thrown into the far right corner. Hazel hated them, which was the only reason they appeared in the first place. Every few months a new one would appear and no one was admitting to buying them.

On the far right wall were three doors. The farthest one was the men's bathroom, with a sign on the door that read, 'Water Closet'. The closest door was the women's bathroom, with a matching sign that read 'Powder Room'. The middle door was a utility closet that held everything from movies to towels; its sign had huge letters reading, 'Middle Earth'. The last sign kept getting vandalized and removed, yet it kept reappearing.

Jack motioned toward the circle of leather chairs as Ryan moved in to put down the ottoman. As everyone but Ryan and Lyra found seats Victor looked around the room.

"Wasn't this furniture different a few weeks ago too?"

Jack nodded as the other man plopped onto the ottoman next to Bishop's chair.

"Yes, but Hazel has a thing with furniture. She can't have it one way for too long, something about wasting space."

Mathew changed the subject before anyone could say anything else. "I think this discussion needs to be done with everyone in human form."

Jack looked over his shoulder to see Lyra already changing in the kitchen. Ryan was sitting on the stool across from her. The change from one form to the other had been painful at first, until the body got used to it. It had taken months before he could change smoothly. It took even longer to change while wearing clothes and a good number of the wolves in their pack could barely make a smooth transition, let alone maintain clothing. Jack himself could keep boxers on while changing and that was it. Lyra never seemed to have a problem. He had never seen her changes be anything but smooth and she was always fully clothed in whatever she had been wearing to begin with.

Within a minute, all three wolves changed and Jack noticed the two male wolves changed just as smoothly as Lyra; no one in his pack was as smooth as Lyra. Apparently he wasn't the only one who noticed because Mathew was watching Lyra and nodding grimly.

"That's what I thought."

Jack heard a cupboard close and he knew this evening there would be a counter full of sweets for the pack. Jack made a mental note to talk with his littermate as soon as their guests were gone.

Ryan cleared his throat, drawing attention away from Lyra. "Can I get anyone something to eat or drink?"

Jack cursed himself. As Alpha it was his job to offer refreshments to guests. If Ryan hadn't done it to take eyes off Lyra, Jack would have forgotten altogether. As several of the other wolves asked for something to drink, Jack watched Lyra, assessing how upset she was.

Her back was to him but he could see the tense set to her shoulders. Her dark brown hair lay in the thick braid that fell to the bottom of her shoulder blades. Her five-foot-seven body stretched as she reached for something on a top shelf. As if she heard his thoughts Lyra turned her head from her homemade cookbook and gave him her profile. Lyra was very pale, her eyes were almond shaped and hazel. They were her most striking feature. She always seemed to be looking right through people, seeing things they didn't want her to see.

She looked at him with a blank face for a few beats before giving him her back again. She and Hazel could hold entire conversations without saying a word; they had always been like that, as far back as he could remember, and this was one of the times Jack wished he could do that as well.

Ryan must have understood Lyra's mood, because when he finished getting drinks he sat back down on the same stool as before with a beer in one hand, turned toward the circle of chairs. Jack knew his Second was keeping an eye on Lyra, just in case. He appreciated that as he turned his attention back to their guests.

Everyone seemed to be waiting on Mathew, who took the silence as a cue.

"I think we have a problem. Pack L has been sniffing around my pack lately and I didn't know why until a week ago, when Dylan approached me." Mathew gestured toward the blond who had been in wolf form. "He told me several pack L members had been approaching him about switching packs, even if just for this soccer season. Not to join their team, but their pack."

Jack heard the pantry open behind him, the squeak it made told Jack it had been opened faster than necessary. No one would catch it unless they were pack F and he wasn't going to give it away by looking behind him. As Jack listened to Mathew he kept one ear on Lyra, monitoring her mood. Not that he didn't trust Ryan to handle Lyra if she got angry, as Ryan could very easily overpower her, but Jack would rather handle it himself.

"When Dylan refused, they started trying to use incentives to convince him to change his mind." Mathew frowned.

Jack heard a bag flop down on the counter. Interesting.

"It wasn't until it had gone on for two weeks," Mathew paused and glanced at Dylan.

He was obviously not happy with the other man's decision to wait on informing his Alpha. Dylan met the glance with eye contact; it was a dominant wolf backing his decision.

"That I heard about it. So I bribed some of my government contacts and I received some very interesting information. I wanted to test my hunch, but today's meeting may have proved me right without me having to ask. When the pack L rep tried to snatch Lyra, it all but solidified my theory."

The oven banged shut.

"I was wondering if Lyra had been receiving such attention from pack L?" Mathew switched his gaze to Jack as he asked his question.

There was silence as all attention went to Jack. He was about to say no, but as a mixing bowl banged into the sink he rethought his answer.

He hadn't seen much of her for the last couple of weeks, but he didn't think much of it. Lyra was a manuscript screener so she spent a lot of time alone. He felt things click into place and began to get angry. Not only had she been keeping things from him, her Alpha, but she was being threatened.

As Jack slowly turned in his seat, all eyes shifted to Lyra, who was scrubbing at a blue mixing bowl for dear life. She was facing away from them so she could easily pretend to not know what was going on, but Jack knew she was aware of every sound in the room and was blatantly ignoring them all.

After about five seconds, Jack was surprised to hear Ryan speak softly to Lyra. "Lyra, answer Mathew."

Jack found himself wondering how Ryan could know about this and he didn't.

Lyra huffed and turned off the water. Swirling around, she put one hand on her waist and the other on the bar. She looked directly at Mathew. Lyra was one of the few non-Alphas Jack knew of that would look Alphas in the eye and stare them down. As if they couldn't maim her in an instant. Not that Jack or Ryan would ever allow that, but still, Lyra was not strong enough to be challenging Alphas.

"No, Mathew, I have not been approached by pack L and offered incentives to switch packs." Her voice dripped with disdain and when she finished she whirled back to the sink.

Jack was turning back around when he heard Ryan's low voice. "Lyra, if you don't, I will."

Jack was trying to work through the confusion to say something as Lyra spun back to Ryan faster then Jack had ever seen her move. She was furious and inches away from Ryan's face.

"Drop it, wolf boy."

The tension between them was so thick Jack could practically see it and Ryan continued to stare back at her with a blank expression. Jack was so surprised he wasn't sure what to think. Lyra was someone people went out of their way not to fight with, and Ryan, who never got into a fight with any of their packmates, was clearly picking a fight.

Ryan kept eye contact with Lyra while speaking to the rest of the group. "Lyra was approached by pack L twice, which she refused in her own biting sarcastic way. They skipped the incentives and went straight to the threats. And by threats I mean cornering her and attempting to kidnap her. Cole and I have been trading off watching her over the past week, after the first time a group of them jumped her."

Jack saw red and dug his hands into the arms of his chair. "The first time? Exactly how many times has this happened?"

For a moment Jack thought there wouldn't be an answer, which brought him dangerously close to the boiling point.

Then Lyra punched Ryan in the chest hard enough for it to have caused damage to a regular human. Ryan just grunted and jerked back with the force, keeping himself seated by grabbing the counter.

"Three." She sighed as she leaned back and shifted her gaze to Jack. Her eyes were so sad and resigned Jack felt his temper lower.

"Why didn't you tell me this?" Jack asked, as a littermate instead of an Alpha.

She started playing with the end of her braid. "I didn't *tell* anyone. Ryan and Cole happened by as I was fighting people off and Ryan recruited Cole because he lives in the apartment complex next to mine. The two of them have been stalking me since. I told them castration was in order if they told anyone else."

There was silence for almost a full minute.

"Though I have not experienced what Lyra has, my dealings with L are similar to Dylan's."

Jack turned to the light-brown haired man sitting on the floor nest to Victor.

Bishop rubbed between his eyes. "Of course you have, and how long has this been going on, Taylor?"

The other man shrugged. "About three weeks, but it was nothing worth noting. I didn't think anything of it until the meeting today. After Karissa's strange request of the F pack, I decided I would broach the subject with you after the meeting, but this happened first."

The man's tone was serious but light, as if it really had not occurred to him to tell Bishop. It made Jack feel better not being the only one out of the loop.

Mathew waited a handful of seconds before filling the silence. "There are four Weres from SWU they are also trying to recruit. In talking with my contacts over there, I heard similar stories about all four men. Strange that the only female gets different treatment. Is that on purpose or coincidence?"

Jack thought about it and Lyra had probably pissed someone off but he wasn't going to say that out loud.

When no one answered, Mathew continued. "My contacts in the government project tell me all seven of these wolves' training files were flagged and pulled for a separate study before they disappeared altogether. None of my contacts knew where they had gone. This sudden attention makes me believe pack L knows something about those missing files."

Mason spoke. "I know everyone's probably thinking this but all five of the lab assistants are in that pack."

The silence continued, except this time Lyra was taking something out of the oven and the smell of vanilla hit Jack's senses.

There was a slapping sound that brought everyone's attention back to reality. "Don't touch that! I'm not done with it yet."

By Lyra's laughing tone, Jack knew Ryan had tried to reach for whatever just came out of the oven. Lyra's tone told him Ryan was probably trying to get back on her good side by making her laugh. Jack was relieved to hear it working.

"I want to switch packs, better furniture…better food…" Victor wasn't taking his eyes off of whatever was on the counter as he spoke, swiftly moving toward the kitchen. Jack turned to see Victor plop down on the stool next to Ryan. Lyra eyed them both suspiciously before moving the tray farther away and placing something else in the oven.

"Yeah, but she hits hard."

Lyra narrowed her eyes to slits and glared at Ryan, but there wasn't any real malice to it. Then she rolled her neck from shoulder to shoulder. "It was for training." She exhaled heavily.

Jack heard Bishop from behind him, "What was for training?"

"The flagged files."

Jack felt his breathing stop as he stood. "You knew your file had been pulled?"

She looked at him, then the two wolves in question behind him. "Didn't you?"

Jack turned to see Dylan shake his head and Taylor answered, "No Lyra, we didn't."

She stood there, one arm leaning on the bar, her expression confused. Jack knew that face. Lyra's mind was moving a mile a minute scrambling to find the answer she was looking for.

"Why would they tell me and not you?"

No one said anything as all eyes continued to be on Lyra.

"Do you know who the other four males are?" This from Mathew.

Lyra shook her head slowly as her other hand went to her braid. "I only know one of them. The other three names I didn't recognize. There was Graham. The males I didn't know were Kipling, Reed, and Boone."

Jack could see her mind still working to find answers. He walked toward her until he was standing two feet from his littermate. "Do you know why you were flagged?" he asked and watched something move through her eyes. Panic.

"Maybe."

The answer was so quiet Jack was sure the other men had to strain to hear it. Jack watched her. Anyone else he wouldn't have to ask, they would just tell him. As her Alpha, in theory, she answered to him, but Lyra was great at bending rules and finding loopholes.

Jack gave her a look that asked for the information instead of demanding it. "Lyra, I'm assuming we need to know why the files were flagged."

He was giving her an out and they both knew it. He couldn't help it, seeing Lyra this uncomfortable made Jack feel like a jerk. They both also knew that since he gave her the out she was more likely to tell him what he wanted to know. Lyra would see anything else as chickening out.

Lyra watched him a second, looking for a way around answering before she closed her eyes and sighed, stepping back in to the kitchen with both hands on the tail of her braid.

"I was flagged because I'm a very good liar and one of the trainers realized I had been lying on the training tests."

Jack folded his arms and leaned against the side of the bar, trying to work out the best wording. He knew he had to tread lightly.

Ryan beat him to it. "How can you cheat on the training tests?"

Lyra sighed. "Like this."

Before the words left her mouth, she was in the air. Before Jack could blink, Lyra had vaulted the bar, tackled Ryan and had the other man pinned to the ground with claws at his throat. To say Jack was shocked would be an understatement.

Lyra was one of the weakest in his pack, even though she had a temper. He was sure her temper would cause problems because she was all bark and little bite, but apparently he was very wrong.

Jack had never seen someone change only part of their body before either, but her hand was perfectly normal, except for its long sharp claws.

She was looking down sadly at Ryan. “Please don’t try me, it will only emphasize my point.”

Ryan looked just as shocked as Jack felt, but part of Ryan’s expression showed complete faith that Lyra wouldn’t hurt him. If the situations were switched, Jack wouldn’t have been so sure.

Lyra looked over to where the other men were now all standing with identical shocked expressions. “I assume you two could do that as well?”

Jack watched as Dylan and Taylor exchanged worried glances before nodding slowly. Victor cursed.

Lyra continued but she was only looking at Jack from where she was perched on Ryan’s stomach. “They wanted to match like with like. To reorganize the packs, put fast with fast, strong with strong. They just didn’t count on pack bonds being so sturdy.” She smirked.

“So why has your file disappeared?” That was from Ryan, who still hadn’t moved from under Lyra.

She stretched her legs and got up as she answered. “That I have no idea about.”

Leaning over, Lyra reached down to offer Ryan help up. Jack filed away that although he didn’t need the help, Ryan took her hand and held onto it a beat longer than necessary. Lyra didn’t seem to notice. She headed back into the kitchen and started putting ingredients into a mixing bowl.

“How long ago were you approached about this?” Dylan asked warily.

Lyra didn’t even turn around. “Two months ago.”

Jack turned his attention to Ryan as the other man banged his almost empty beer bottle on the bar. “That’s why you went missing for a week?”

Lyra didn’t answer, but she didn’t need to.

How had Jack missed Lyra disappearing for a whole week? He searched his memory but couldn’t find the answer.

"Why was I not told about this? Any of this?" Jack was on edge. He shouldn't have been in the dark about something this important.

If word got out that he didn't even know when his own littermate went missing, other dominant wolves could jockey for his position. His pack was one of the strongest. Where would they be if another Alpha tried to take control?

"It's not like I could tell you squat if I'm missing."

Two cups of sugar banged against the side of the mixing bowl and Jack knew Lyra was right back to being angry, which was fine with him. He was starting to itch for a fight.

"By the time I got back, I had it handled and I was pretty sure no one noticed I had been gone."

With that she glanced over her shoulder at Ryan before grabbing a stick of butter and turning away from the group. Jack was so frustrated with Lyra he wasn't sure he could talk to her anymore without yelling.

So he turned his anger to Ryan. "So why didn't you tell me any of this?" Ryan gave him full eye contact as he finished his beer.

He didn't respond until he set the empty bottle on the counter. "I had my suspicions something might have happened. For me not to see her for a week isn't strange, but I didn't even hear about her threatening anyone and there were no baked goods for two weeks. I'm kinda surprised you *didn't* notice. I just remembered one of the first things you told about your littermates was that Lyra needed her space and liked to be left alone. So I figured if something happened, you handled it. As for pack L, I had her protected so there was no reason to worry anyone else. It is my job as Second to handle some things so the Alpha doesn't have to do it all."

Ryan got up, put his bottle in the recycling bin and grabbed another beer from the refrigerator. As he opened the new bottle, Ryan leaned against the counter so he was on the other side of the sink from Lyra. Jack fumed as he watched his packmates. Lyra was ignoring him after hiding things from him. Ryan was watching Jack right back, leaning between Jack and Lyra, nursing his beer. The man was deliberately putting himself between Jack and his littermate.

In the first couple of months, some of the scientists noticed in packs where female made up less than forty percent of the pack, the males were exponentially more protective of their female packmates.

It made Jack wonder if that was why Ryan felt he needed to protect Lyra from Jack. Ryan was every inch a dominant wolf, and Jack knew in that moment Ryan could just as easily be the Alpha of pack F. That thought was both worrisome and comforting.

Mathew coughed to gain everyone's attention. Jack turned his head but kept an eye on Ryan.

Lyra moved to take something else out of the oven and Ryan took his eyes off Jack to watch her. Only then did Jack turn to the other Alpha.

"Don't worry, Jack, we would never let anyone take your pack from you. Most of us will fight to keep what stability we have."

Bishop nodded in agreement. If Ryan was paying attention, he would know that the other big dogs were in Jack's corner. Jack was somewhat relieved but he didn't want to be the weakest link.

Bishop seemed to understand. "We are all having problems Jack. Even if it has been more than a year since we got ourselves this organized, we were all thrown into this. It's a social hierarchy no one is used to.

"I myself have a packmate that wanders off for long periods of time and I have absolutely no idea where he goes. I have another that still can't easily transition from one form to another. Plus I have to deal with Victor, and every day I do not kill him is probably positive."

Bishop's lips twitched before he continued. "Our packs are stable because our packmates want stability. I can fully understand why your littermate would choose to hide these things from you. She's knows she's strong enough to handle it on her own. That leaves you open to concentrate on something else. Which I'm sure is why this is the first I've heard of it as well."

Jack knew what the other man was saying made sense and to a certain extent he even agreed with part of it. He just didn't see things the same way. If someone threatened one of his pack they threatened the whole pack.

Mathew moved out of the circle of chairs, closely followed by Mason and Dylan. "I propose an idea we should think about for a few days. I think we can all agree something bad is coming our way and it's best we prepare for it."

There were several nods in agreement and Lyra finally turned around to watch Mathew with a skeptical look.

"I think we should gather the packs we trust and form an, oh I hate this term, alliance. We draw up an agreement--because I know we have to have law students somewhere--that states come to each other's aid if something should happen. All of the Alphas would be equal and we could have a council, like the multi-pack meetings, to get things decided. If things stabilize over the next few years than maybe all the packs could be with us."

Lyra interjected, "You mean all forty packs don't you?" When Mathew nodded, Lyra shook her head. "I never took you for such an optimist, Mathew."

Mathew gave a small chuckle. "I have to, Lyra, or I'd go crazy."

Lyra watched him a few more seconds before turning back to what she had been doing.

Bishop moved to stand so he could see Mathew's face. "And who exactly do you propose for this agreement?"

Mathew started counting on his fingers. "There would be us three of course. I was also thinking packs A, D, and I…"

Bishop cut him off. "Why I? Almost nothing is known about their pack."

Jack agreed. He trusted the other two Alphas. pack I had two joint Alphas instead of an Alpha and a Second. One was male and one was female that was all he knew.

"I had a chance to communicate with both Alphas and they have a good rein on their pack, much better than any of us. I trust them enough to meet with them about it. I also think we should consider SWU packs B, C, T, and X. I know the Alphas or the Seconds for all four of these packs and I trust them."

There was quiet while Bishop and Jack thought the idea out. Jack didn't know any wolves from SWU and had only seen a few in passing. Mathew had connections all over the place, which made Jack a little suspicious of the other Alpha's motives.

Then Jack had a thought. He turned to Ryan and Lyra. Both were the type of people who could be in a room and follow every conversation in it. If they heard anything good or bad they would tell him and their character judgment he did trust, even if he was currently pissed at them.

Ryan was still watching him but his face was blank; it was the face he gave when they were in public. He was back to being the Second that took in everything and said little. Lyra was milling around in the kitchen, putting her baking in plastic containers. Jack knew they were both listening.

"Either of you know those packs?"

A plastic lid snapped shut as he got a response. "I would trust pack C. The others I've not heard anything that you would find useful to this particular topic."

"Why pack C?" Jack didn't know why he wanted to know so badly, but under the current circumstances he wanted to be absolutely sure he got all the information before he gave Mathew any kind of answer.

"It's Graham's pack, he's the Second." Out of the corner of his eye, Jack saw Mathew nod.

"Why trust Graham? Because his file was flagged like yours?" Jack knew his voice held a bite.

She turned, both hands on her waist. "No moron, because he's Graham."

When Jack just continued to stare at her, she rolled her eyes impatiently.

"Use your memory, littermate. Graham also begrudgingly goes by the name Hammy."

The last word clicked. One of Lyra's numerous cousins. She called him Hammy and he hated it but let Lyra call him that anyway. How had he gotten stuck in this Werewolf mess?

As if she was reading his mind again, she shrugged and looked at whatever was in front of her on the counter.

"He was at the rock concert, one of the techies."

Jack turned back to Mathew, who watched him patiently.

"It seems like a good idea but I want to talk it over with my pack first. Since this agreement would include all of us."

Mathew nodded and turned to Bishop.

The other man was looking at his Second, contemplating, but after almost a minute he turned to everyone else. "I agree with Jack. I need to discuss it with my pack. I will be able to get back to you the day after tomorrow."

Mathew nodded again. "Very well, both of you can get hold of me on Monday, so that way you have all weekend to think it over." Mathew bowed his head to both Jack and Bishop. "I'm headed upstairs; I have some pack issues I have to handle." He rolled his eyes; clearly they were issues he didn't think were his problem.

As the wolves of pack J headed out the door, Lyra shoved a plastic container at Dylan's chest. He grabbed the container and gave Lyra a huge grin that made Jack knock a few years off Dylan's age.

"Thanks," Dylan said as he beamed at her.

Lyra just narrowed her eyes. "Bring back the container when you guys are finished."

The male wolf nodded and he followed his Alpha out the door.

Bishop bowed to Jack as he passed him, then smiled and nodded to Ryan and Lyra.

Victor stopped in front of the kitchen and put his hands out to Lyra, who ignored him.

"Oh come on, Lyra, the other box is for us."

Continuing to ignore Victor, she reached across the bar and handed the container to Taylor. "Thank you, my lady."

Lyra gave him a lopsided smile. "Just don't let Vicky here have the container. He doesn't share well."

Jack watched Taylor's lips twitch. "Of course not, my lady."

Taylor headed out the door with Victor following after him, trying to strike a deal.

After the others left, Ryan dove across Lyra and straightened back up with a handful of cookies. Lyra burst out laughing.

Ryan swallowed the cookie he inhaled and gave her an innocent face. "What?"

She laughed harder.

"What? I'm hungry and I've been smelling these forever. At least I waited until the others were gone."

As Lyra tried to control herself, Jack sat down on one of the stools and watched. There was some aspect he couldn't put his finger on that made this not quite normal behavior for these two.

Shaking his thoughts away, Jack looked directly at Lyra. "So how much danger are you in, really?"

Jack watched as Lyra dropped her hand and her smile faded. He hated to be the one to do that. Lyra had so rarely laughed since becoming a Werewolf.

Her face was serious and calm when she answered. At least she wasn't angry. His own anger lowered in response.

"Honestly, I'm fine. I probably wouldn't have been able to fend them off the last two times if one of the two boys hadn't been there. Ryan and Cole are the strongest Weres we have, and I couldn't be in better hands, but we have to figure this out soon because I'm starting to miss my alone time. No offense, Ryan."

Lyra glanced at Ryan, who nodded because his mouth was full of brownie. Jack watched her, trying to figure out if she was telling the truth.

"I would never let anything happen to her, or anyone in our pack."

Jack knew Ryan meant it and there wasn't anything Jack could do about the problem right now.

Sighing, he looked Lyra directly in the eyes. "I'm telling you now I'm a little pissed about this. You should have told me. Even if it was just to keep me in the loop. We have bigger things on our plate right now, but I want to discuss this and I don't want this kind of thing happening again."

There was silence. Jack could tell Lyra was deciding whether she was going to be offended or not, after a few beats she seemed to give up.

"I don't appreciate you scolding me. That pisses *me* off. We will be having a discussion and in that discussion we will decide whether you trust me or if you really think I'm too fragile to function." She blinked at him.

Jack knew if they kept this up they would be screaming at each other soon. He loved Lyra dearly but they could push each other's buttons like no one else.

Luckily Ryan stepped in by grabbing an entire plate of brownies.

Lyra, effectively distracted, slapped their packmate. "Put that down!"

Ryan grinned before setting the plate on the counter next to him and grabbing another brownie. Lyra shook her head and moved the plate farther away from him.

"Well." She put her hands on her waist. "Ryan, you can either leave my kitchen or help me make dinner. Or am I wrong in thinking you're going to call a pack meeting tonight?" She looked at Jack waiting for him to contradict her.

Jack shook his head. “No you’re not wrong.”

“It’s about four now. When were you thinking?”

Jack shoved his hands in his pockets and tried not to openly laugh at his littermate. It wasn’t intentional, but Lyra was using her ‘mom voice’. Jack knew she’d get mad if he pointed it out and right now mad was something they were both trying to avoid.

“Seven good for you?”

She gave him a look that said she didn’t think he was funny. Jack turned away and headed for his office.

As he entered, he heard Ryan. “What can I do to help?”

Jack hid his face behind the closing door as he heard Lyra’s response. “Stop eating everything, for starters!”

Chapter 3

Lyra gave him her keys and sent him on food errands. Ryan was instructed to get the big cooking trays from her apartment so she could bake enough lasagna for the whole pack, as well as garlic bread and various other ingredients from the store. Ryan couldn't help his smile when he thought about the she-wolf. She was so much softer than everyone, including her littermates, thought she was.

Jack had been angry with both of them, which was why Ryan stayed between them. He knew it hurt Lyra to have their Alpha angry with her, but this alliance might make things easier, the whole safety in numbers thing. Ryan shook his head. It was almost the identical thought he'd had when the scientists divided them up in quarantine.

Back then, Ryan had only really known the twins, as they had grown up down the street from him. The military personnel had escorted all of the wolves into designated rooms. They were to wait until the 'program managers' came to explain what the government planned for them. He and the twins were put in an empty room. Minutes later, came the four Health Science Majors: Cole, Adam, Liam, and Kelly. Next came the two guys who had been checking out movies from the media center: Bruce and Felix. Out of those six, Ryan had only known Cole because the Samoan played football with him. They gave each other surprised nods when Cole walked in.

Last was Jack, and his littermates. Justin walked in first. Checking out the room and moving to a corner away from everyone else, Seth had been right behind him. Then came the girls. Ryan had been struck by Lyra's scent. His new Were abilities were on the fritz, but her scent came to him loud and clear.

Her base scent, everyone's unique identifier, mingled with passion fruit. After he smelled her, he tried to scent out which of the two girls possessed the intoxicating smell, but he couldn't work it out from across the room. The girls were walking side by side, Hazel's arm wrapped around Lyra's as if Hazel was afraid of what would happen if Lyra left her side. Lyra checked out the room more thoroughly than Justin. She looked at every face and when Ryan made eye contact with her, his body stirred, which surprised him under the circumstances.

Right behind them had been Jack, obviously asserting himself and taking the rear in case something happened.

After about ten minutes, Ryan's attention was taken from his whispered conversation with Sadie and Syrus to where the two girls were, about twenty feet away. Lyra was leaning and Hazel was trying to pull her back up.

"I said, what are you doing?" That had been Hazel.

"No, I heard you I just thought everyone would know sitting down when they saw it."

Hazel tugged on Lyra's arm in an attempt to pull her back up.

Hazel said the next part quietly, but with their improved hearing, everyone in the room heard it. "You don't know any of these people. They could be dangerous."

Lyra snorted and wrenched her arm away from Hazel with little effort. Lyra walked past the boys and took in everyone in the room. Jack tried calling her back to their little corner, but she only glared at him.

"Hello everyone. I just want to ask, is anyone evil? I ask this because thanks to the good doctor we are all dangerous. So does anyone really feel like picking a fight?"

Ryan and Syrus exchanged amused glances.

When no one answered Lyra continued. "Fine, I'm Lyra and now that everyone knows me I'm sitting myself down on the floor and resting while I can because this whole zoo is just unorganized enough to guarantee nothing." When she finished she walked back and flopped on to the floor, leaned against the wall and closed her eyes.

Syrus quietly laughed. "I like her. She makes this interesting."

Sadie rolled her eyes at her brother.

Lyra's movement to the center of the room had shifted her scent so Ryan could identify it as hers. He had been practically addicted ever since.

Now he stood outside her apartment, preparing to go in. He had never set foot in there before last week. Since then, Ryan had slept here every night and it was killing him. Opening the door, Ryan was engulfed with Lyra's scent. Before he could stop himself, he inhaled deeply. Over the past week her scent had clung to his clothes and skin, making it hard to sleep even when he was at his own apartment. He knew he could shower and get rid of it, but he didn't want to. Ryan loved the way her scent mingled with his soap from a shower hours before.

Getting control of himself, Ryan shut the door behind him and concentrated on the welcome he was getting from Lyra's two dogs. He bent down to pat both dogs on the head. At first they hadn't liked him but now they seemed used to him. The first dog was a Rottweiler named Mogwai, after the creature from the Gremlin movies. The second dog was a something Mountain Dog named Fizgig from an eighties movie Ryan had never heard of. The latter dog was huge, his back hit Ryan at the hip. After paying attention to the dogs for a few moments, Ryan straightened back up and moved toward Lyra's kitchen to get the trays she needed.

Syrus and Sadie had been making fun of Ryan over the years about his feelings for Lyra. It wasn't so much that he had feelings for her, it was how strong they were, yet he did nothing about them.

Ryan was not sure how to proceed when it came to Lyra. Normally he would just ask her out, but given their situation that might not be the best idea. Ryan knew of three couples before and right after the accident. The scientists studied the couples to see if being Werewolves changed anything. Two of the three drifted apart; the third was much stronger and the scientists were baffled by it. Ryan didn't know what baffled the scientists, since he knew next to nothing about the training files. He just remembered all the extra attention. Ryan did not want to be the reason Lyra received more attention. He decided a year ago to not make a move until he was absolutely positive it was something they both really wanted.

Until today, he hadn't even known how developed she was. Ryan had barely seen her coming. She was much stronger than they thought but she only admitted to being fast. The whole situation was a little strange to Ryan. But with her on top of him, he couldn't think straight. He knew she wouldn't hurt him but it took all his effort not to flip her over. Ryan had always been a dominant guy, but since meeting Lyra he felt more need to assert that dominance from time to time.

Shaking his head clear, Ryan left Lyra's apartment, trays under his arm. He just needed to stay clear-headed until this whole pack L situation was settled, then he was going to sit Lyra down for a talk. Ryan needed to understand exactly what was going on with her.

Chapter 4

The entire pack had shown up by seven, but that didn't surprise Jack. The combination of trouble and the promise of food guaranteed his pack would come running. Jack had been thinking for hours and he still wasn't sure what to tell them. At times like this, Jack really wished he had not agreed to become Alpha of pack F.

Not that he would have backed down from the nomination. In the later days of training, the trainers and scientists were not around as much. As pack F had been leaving the training facility for their monthly tests, their trainer Dr. Gibbons told them they needed to choose a team lead before next month's tests. They went back to their newly furnished pack office to discuss it. The pack had been settling in when Lyra plopped down onto Hazel's lap, her legs dangling off the leather arm rest.

"I nominate Jack." She said it with trust and confidence as she smiled at him from across the room.

Jack had been surprised, as he had never known Lyra to follow anybody, let alone willingly pick a leader. Hazel quickly seconded and Justin chimed in from the kitchen his agreement.

Seth nodded from a bar stool. "Yeah, I'd be okay with that."

There had been silence for a moment before Liam directed his question at Lyra. "Why? Shouldn't our leader be the strongest among us?"

Lyra shook her head. "No, a good leader should be in the high middle. That way someone can take him if he gets uppity, but at the same time he's relatively good at everything. For the most part, Jack is pretty calm, that's something we should have in a leader." Then she had grinned. "In an Alpha."

There had been some debate but after half an hour he was made Alpha. They never actually asked if he wanted the position. Shaking his head, Jack tried to concentrate on the present.

While trying to sort out his thoughts Jack watched his packmates from his office. Lyra was still in the kitchen. She was finishing up four massive salad bowls and watching the oven as if she could miss the timer going off.

With her in the kitchen was Justin, fixing drinks and checking on the liquor supply. Justin was six-foot-one and had been almost scrawny before becoming a Were. Now he had filled out to be more toned than anything else. His shaggy black hair always seemed to be in his eyes, which didn't seem to bother him. Justin was quiet when not in his element, but behind the bar or with the pack he was outgoing and mischievous. He and Syrus had taken an instant liking to each other.

As soon as Justin had walked in the door fifteen minutes ago, Lyra grinned, gave a giggly squeal, and removed her shoes. Justin grinned back and toed his off as well. The two of them had a routine that Jack did not understand. Every time both of them were in the kitchen for a stretch of time, they would slide on the linoleum in their socks and slam into each other. It wasn't light either they would try to knock the other off balance, or in some cases out of the kitchen. Justin had slammed Lyra into the refrigerator hard enough for it to bang against the wall several times over the past two years.

Jack watched as Lyra was reaching for the fridge and Justin slammed into her, sending her out of the kitchen. Lyra started laughing, shoved him out of her way, and opened the fridge.

They wouldn't let anyone else play. Justin would growl and one of them would kick the third person out of the kitchen. Some of the males in the pack would wrestle around and wail on each other with the same playful attitude but outside of Lyra and Justin, the play-fighting didn't involve the females.

Sitting at the bar were Ryan and Hazel. Ryan was watching the two in the kitchen and sipping his beer. Hazel was laughing at her two littermates over her glass of red wine.

Hazel was the shortest in the pack at five-foot-four. She had medium blond hair the same length as Lyra's. Hazel had a curvy figure. Jack and his packmates were constantly warning off guys that found themselves attracted to her big smile and generous chest. Hazel had striking blue eyes and a dazzling smile. She could possibly be the most social person Jack ever met. Where Ryan and Lyra knew about people Hazel probably associated with them at one time or another. Justin joked it was Hazel's goal to hold a conversation with every Werewolf there was.

Sadie, Syrus and Cole were playing a card game Jack couldn't see. They were in what Hazel informed him was the 'conversation circle', the circle of chairs and ottomans. Every once in a while there would be a curse or a sound of triumph as all three of them dove toward the table, followed by a slap.

Sadie was closest to Jack but her back was to him. She was the same height as Lyra, but model-thin and she never seemed to gain muscle. She had straight inky black hair that reached her waist and large brown eyes. Both she and her brother had natural tans due to American Indian ancestors. Sadie was the pack member Jack knew the least about. She wasn't shy but didn't share much about herself. Jack knew she was studying to be a veterinarian but not much beyond that.

On her the right was pack F's practical joker. Syrus and his sister had a very striking resemblance but were not quite identical. Syrus was six foot with a lithe built. Until earlier today, Syrus was the pack's fastest runner. Syrus kept his hair shoulder length and back in a leather strap. Syrus spent most of the time joking around, which Jack supposed he would have to as a middle school English teacher.

To Syrus's right sat Cole. The large Samoan had a huge grin on his face. Syrus joked that Cole sometimes resembled a laughing Buddha statue.

When Jack looked all the way across the room, he saw the last six members of his pack cheering over something on the Wii. Both Kelly and Felix were standing so Jack's view of the television was blocked. From the looks of it, Kelly was kicking Felix's butt. The other four guys were scattered on the furniture and the floor.

Before Jack could decide which group to join, he smelled Lyra pulling lasagna out of the oven.

It was followed by Kelly yelling, "FOOD!"

The game was off and the six guys were bee-lining for the kitchen.

Lyra pointed her spatula as the other three joined the group. "Oh no you don't. It has to cool. So set the tables and sit your butts down."

Syrus saluted Lyra before grabbing a salad bowl.

Adam grabbed another and grinned at Lyra. "Yes, mom."

A cookie went flying and missed his head as he ducked at the last second.

Justin dove after it. "NO! COOKIE!"

When he reached it, Justin shoved it in his mouth as everyone began settling down into their seats.

When everyone was seated, with Justin and Ryan at the bar, Jack and Lyra exchanged glances.

Lyra shrugged before turning back to the trays of lasagna. "It's your show, Jack."

Jack sighed and moved to stand close to the kitchen entrance so everyone could see him easily. Jack didn't have to get anyone's attention; all eyes were already on him.

"I want to go over some of the pack business. First I want to know if anyone is having issues with other packs?"

Jack watched most of his packmates tense and exchange glances. They knew Jack wouldn't ask if there weren't problems.

He saw Cole look to Ryan, who mouthed 'no'.

Cole raised an eyebrow but didn't say anything; instead he looked back at the twins and Liam, who sat at his table. When no one answered, Jack was relieved but frustrated.

"Pack L has been causing problems with several packs both here and at SWU."

Out of the corner of his eye, Jack watched as Lyra put slabs of lasagna on the plates for Justin and Ryan to hand out.

"There have been threats and bribes. Since no one knows their agenda, we need to protect ourselves. Some of the other Alphas and I sat down earlier today and talked about it. When everyone's finished eating we need to decide if we want to go with that plan or create one of our own. Either way, we need to implement something."

Jack waited a beat before moving to sit down. He could felt the tension he just created and the worry flowing from his packmates.

Lyra sat down next to Justin at the bar. As Jack passed her, she commented loud enough for everyone to hear. "Buzz kill, see if I ever cook nice for you again."

Jack thought she was serious until Seth piped up. "Jack, if you ruined a good meal for me, so help me I will beat you within an inch of your life."

The tension in the room lowered greatly. Jack glanced at Lyra, who was watching him expectantly over her huge green mug. Jack smiled and inclined his head. He had screwed up by talking shop before everyone had eaten and Lyra, in her own way, had bailed him out. Lyra's lips turned up a fraction before she turned back to her plate.

Though the mood lightened as the meal went on, by the time the plates were cleared, tension was rising again. With everyone done with dinner, the pack spread out all over the furniture, or in Syrus, Justin and Kelly's case, the floor.

Each of the three had taken a beanbag chair. While Kelly was sitting in his, Syrus and Justin were using theirs as pillows.

Adam and Cole had dragged most of the furniture to the right of the bar, only after promising Hazel they would put everything back. Jack grabbed a stool and set it about five feet from the front wall, facing the group.

Syrus and Justin somehow made it their goal to take up as much room as possible, making it so all the couches and chairs had to be in a semi-circle around them.

Ryan and Lyra were still at the bar but Lyra moved to the stool next to Ryan.

Jack took a deep breath. "Here is what I learned at my meeting with the Alphas of Packs M and J. Pack L has been watching seven Weres, three from PNWU and four from SWU. These seven Weres all had their training files flagged and pulled a month or two ago. We were informed these files were flagged because they were the seven fastest Weres in the project." Several people looked at Syrus, who turned to look inquisitively at Jack.

"The trainers told you they were pulling a Pack F file?" Seth's voice was filled with suspicion.

Seth was the most solemn of Jack's littermates. He did not smile often; generally, it was just a small half smile. Seth also had one of the driest senses of humor Jack had ever heard. Lyra seemed to be the only person who could tell when he was joking. Seth had dark blond hair that brushed his collar. He had grown up on his family's ranch until he was seventeen. His parents moved him and his two little brothers to the western half of the state.

Seth was sitting on the love seat with his arm resting on Hazel's shoulder. Hazel was a cuddle bug, and their littermates just got used to Hazel snuggling up with them especially when she nervous or scared.

Jack looked at Seth as he answered the question. "No, before today I had not heard any of this. Apparently the trainers wanted to reorganize the packs, putting similarities together."

There were several angry outbursts from the pack.

Jack held up his arm to quiet them. "My understanding is that no one knew their files had been pulled except one, who they actually brought in to start retraining."

With that, he glanced at Lyra, he was proud of her for standing with her pack against the trainers, even if she had hidden it from him.

Ryan subtly moved his right forearm so it was touching Lyra from wrist to elbow. Jack wouldn't have noticed if he hadn't been looking for it. Ryan was staring at his beer giving a blank face to world. Jack appreciated Ryan trying to comfort Lyra.

Hazel broke the silence, her eyes shooting daggers at Lyra. "Is that why you went missing for a week? You told me it was no big deal. After five days without word, I storm over to your apartment and you answer the door with a bruised face and a limp. You looked me in the eye and told me it was no big deal. This is not no big deal, Lyra!" Hazel was almost shouting.

The entire room pulsed with anger.

Jack fought to keep himself from blowing up; he took a few seconds to concentrate on breathing. Jack looked over to see Ryan's body had tensed and his jaw clenched but other than those extremely small changes Ryan appeared unaffected by the news that the trainers had beaten Lyra.

Lyra looked up from her mug. Her gaze moved over Jack, making sure he knew she was including him in her anger, before locking with Hazel's.

"I'm so glad to see I have friends that can keep a secret. Friends I can trust not to blow things out of proportion. Friends who will share with the entire pack things that no one can do anything about and will only make people more upset."

Hazel looked away. Lyra was furious. Jack could see it in her eyes and hear it in the smooth even tone of her voice. Most of all Jack could smell it; the scent of Lyra's intense anger swept through the room. Jack wasn't good with differentiating scents but this was obvious.

"She did the right thing." Attention snapped back to Jack.

Jack could feel the pack looking at him but his full attention was on Lyra. "There was nothing any of us could have done to help her after the fact. It isn't right for us to take our anger out on her after she chose to come back to us. After what she went through, we wouldn't want her to regret her decision."

Jack gave Lyra a soft smile. She pressed her lips together before turning her back to him. Jack watched as Ryan turned his back to the pack so he could rest his head on Lyra's shoulder. The other man was whispering in Lyra's ear, but no one else could hear it.

Not sure if it was the best idea, Jack continued to explain the situation to his pack, He started with Lyra's file being pulled and finished by mentioning the other Weres Pack L was after.

Jack watched the pack get angry on Lyra's behalf, knowing it was about to get worse. "With Lyra, they didn't bribe her as they did the others. They have been threatening her and on several occasions attacked her."

Jack watched as the pack practically ignited with anger.

"Luckily Ryan and Cole have been taking shifts the past week so someone is always with her. Now whether she likes it or not, that is going to continue until we stop whatever is going on. I'm throwing myself into the rotation, that way Cole and Ryan get a break."

It was hard to make out any one voice as the others chimed in to volunteer. Jack nodded his approval and looked over to see Lyra rolling her eyes. Jack knew there were several sexist comments roaming about her head. He was careful to hide the relief he felt that Ryan had been able to cheer her up.

"We can set up the actual schedule later. There is one more part to this whole thing, so you can sit back down."

Jack paused as everyone settled. Hazel snuggled in closer to Seth.

"Mathew suggested we form a multi-pack alliance with not only his pack but Packs A, D, I, and M. Also with SWU Packs B, C, T, and X. I only know the Alphas from A, D, J and M, I trust them. Lyra's cousin is the second to SWU pack C and she says we can trust them. I want to know what everyone knows about the other four packs."

Bruce shifted in the dark brown leather chair he was sitting in. Bruce was six-foot-one and built solidly. Bruce had been overweight when training started, but had lost most of the fat. His medium brown hair layered to hit his chin. He had the palest blue eyes Jack had ever seen. Bruce worked as a tech for a theatre in Seattle. His boyfriend of three years, Keegan, was the only non-Were Pack F informed about what they were. The discussion to do so lasted two months before the whole pack backed the decision to bring Keegan into the loop.

"I know a couple people in Pack X. They all seem pretty stable. But I want to remind you we don't know the Alphas you mentioned. Since most of us don't go to the multi-pack meetings. You say you trust them which is cool, but I'd like to know who they are just the same."

Jack heard mumbles of agreement.

"Sure, Pack A's Alpha is Finn. Tall red-headed guy, he was teaching the lab course at the time of the experiment."

There were several nods; Finn was kind of hard to miss.

"Pack D's Alpha is Grant. Grant is about six feet tall, with black curly hair. He is snarky and sarcastic but also ruthless. He's the one who had the rich and powerful father trying to get him out of quarantine."

Jack knew by adding the last part everyone in the room would know who Grant was. Grant's father had made a huge scene.

Jack almost missed the exchanged glances between Hazel and Lyra; if he hadn't been paying attention to Lyra out of the corner of his eye, he would not have caught it. Jack found himself wondering what the exchange meant.

Syrus swung his legs so he could sit up. Giving up all pretense of relaxing, "Wasn't he the one who told his father to go home because he was making a bad situation worse?"

Jack nodded. Syrus put the yelling match nicely.

Before Jack could continue, Felix cleared his throat. Felix had sandy blond hair just long enough to be in his eyes. He was six-foot-one, lanky and shy. Felix slumped his shoulders normally as if trying to appear shorter. He did something with designing video games. It had only been in the last nine months or so that Felix opened up to anyone outside of Bruce.

"I know Pack I pretty well."

When the entire pack looked at him, Felix slouched further into his leather chair, but he continued speaking, which surprised Jack.

"They are the pack with one male Alpha and one female Alpha. They also each have a second in case of emergency."

That was news to Jack.

"There are sixteen wolves, making it the biggest pack. They are half male and half female which is why they came up with the two Alpha. They feel with a group that size, one person should not represent all of them. Several of the pack, including the male Alpha, are people I've worked with so I've seen how they run things. They are incredibly stable and efficient. I think they would be a good ally but a hard enemy."

There was silence for a moment; there always was when Felix spoke more than two sentences.

"Okay then Pack I is one we can trust," Jack nodded to Felix, who sat up a little straighter.

"The last two pack Alphas I know are Mathew and Bishop. Mathew is the mastermind of this whole scheme. Mathew has light brown short hair and a lean build. I assume most of you know or have heard about Mathew because for some reason the man has connections to every being on the planet."

Sadie snorted but didn't say anything.

"The last is Bishop, Pack M's Alpha. Bishop is very quiet and watchful. He has very short black hair and is about six-foot-three. Bishop looks about five years older than he is and though Pack M has only eleven Weres, they seem like more when they are all together. Those are the ones I know so how about the other two we have not mentioned yet, B and T?"

Liam smacked Kelly in the chest. "Hey Kell, what about that dude you met at the trainer's seminar last month. Name began with an O, wasn't he from SWU Pack B?"

As attention turned to Kelly, he stared up at the ceiling in thought. Kelly was bleach blond with a dark tan. At five-foot-ten he was the shortest male in the pack, however, he was very muscular. The female packmates called him a 'pretty boy'. Kelly was constantly razzed about the female clients giving him more attention than the other fitness trainers he worked with.

"Yeah Otto, he grew up in Germany. He's a huge blonde, tan dude. Yeah he was Pack B."

Jack couldn't rationalize trusting the all of pack B based on a one-time meeting with one member.

Sighing, Jack looked back to Kelly. "Do you think they are trustworthy?"

Kelly shrugged, "I don't know enough about the pack to say for certain. Yeah, I liked Otto and would go out to drinks with the guy but that doesn't mean I would trust the pack he belongs to with the safety of mine."

Jack nodded, he agreed completely. That was exactly what they were discussing, who to trust with their pack's safety. The pack went silent; Jack could tell there was no way they were going to agree with this idea on so little information.

There were several minutes of silence before Sadie spoke up, flipping her raven hair over one shoulder. "May I make a suggestion?"

She raised one thin eyebrow at Jack.

Jack nodded.

"I'm sure the others meeting right now are in the same place we are. Don't trust what you don't know. I suggest a tryout of sorts, a group of the Alphas and seconds in question, and in our case Lyra, because we all know she won't let you do this without her."

Sadie elegantly gestured to Lyra at the bar, whose eyes narrowed warily. Jack could tell Lyra was not sure whether the comment was a dig or not.

"They travel to each pack office to do a meet and greet. That way we know who we are agreeing to go to bed with. If you visit one each night, you could have it all done in about two weeks and we would all have a stronger grasp on the situation."

Syrus smirked up at his twin and agreed.

Jack straightened on his stool as Death Cab for Cutie began to play, his ringtone. Lyra grabbed his phone from where it sat on the bar and chucked it at him.

Jack caught it and read the display. It was Bishop. Holding up his pointer finger, Jack stayed on the stool, knowing about a third of his pack could hear both sides of the conversation no matter where Jack stood in the room.

"What's up, Bishop?"

Jack could hear two people arguing in the background.

"Jack, I do not foresee Mathew's plan working. Though some of my pack thinks it is a good idea, the majority disagree. You must love how distrustful we all are."

Jack grunted before speaking. "One of my packmates may have come up with a workable idea, can you hold on a sec while I confirm?"

Jack could hear the curiosity in Bishop's voice. "By all means."

Jack put the phone against his chest knowing full well Bishop could still hear him. "Okay gang, show of hands who would like to try Sadie's idea?"

Everyone but Syrus raised their hand.

Syrus grinned up from the floor. “I just want to be contrary.”

Jack rolled his eyes as he put the phone back to his ear.

“So here is the idea, Bishop. Every night for about two weeks, us Alphas travel from pack office to pack office meeting with everyone on their own turf. That way each pack will get to see exactly what they are getting into.”

There was silence for a moment, Jack could almost hear Bishop’s wheels turning.

“All thirty or so of us?” Bishop automatically included the wolves like Lyra, Dylan and Taylor.

Jack found himself nodding as he answered. “Yup.”

There was silence again, but longer this time. “Fascinating, that might work. Hold on a moment while I run this by my people.”

As Jack waited, he could hear Bishop explaining the new idea to his pack, and as he listened Jack could make out some of the comments, mostly Victor's.

Some of Pack F seemed to have lost interest in waiting and migrated to the kitchen for more cookies and drink refills. After almost ten minutes, Bishop got back on the phone.

“Congratulate your packmate for me; they might have just saved Mathew’s alliance. Would you like to tell him the good news or should I?”

Jack felt himself smile. “I’ll tell him. It sounds like you have an argument over there.”

Jack heard the shouting get louder.

Bishop sighed into the phone. “Yes and it’s your fault, we inherited your foosball table. I know now why you were so hasty to rid yourself of it.”

Jack groaned in commiseration. “I’ll see you later this week.”

There was a thump through the phone as well as the ceiling. Pack M was on the floor right above Pack F.

All of Jack’s pack looked up and Jack heard Bishop through the phone. “Oh for the love of… I must go Jack.” Then the phone clicked.

Jack looked at Syrus, who only grinned wider. Bishop only had one female in his pack, which meant all that testosterone regularly caused problems. Jack had no doubt Syrus had given the foosball table to Pack M for that exact reason. Jack shook his head as there was another thud. Most of the pack looked at Jack questioningly.

"Apparently they are the ones who Syrus gave our foosball table to."

Lyra and Hazel burst out laughing and Seth gave a light chuckle. Syrus bowed from where he sat on the floor.

Justin gave what he and Lyra called a 'golf clap', "Five points dude, five points."

Jack shook his head again, he knew Justin and Syrus had some sort of prank point system but had no idea how it worked.

"Pack M agreed with Sadie's idea. So I'm going to call Mathew and let him know our terms to this agreement."

When no one made any snarky comments, Jack called Mathew.

The other man picked up after the fourth ring. "Jack, I did not expect a call so soon. Do you have bad news for me?" Despite the question Mathew's tone was light.

Jack explained Sadie's idea to Mathew and Pack M's agreement with it.

"I like it. It would instill more confidence in the idea. I would assume you pack would go first since it was your idea." When Jack didn't have an answer, Mathew continued. "Okay, give me about an hour to get hold of the other Alphas. I will get back to you with the final verdict. How does eight o'clock Sunday sound?"

Jack put his hand over the phone and looked out at his packmates. "How is the day after tomorrow, eight PM for everyone?"

There were a few verbal agreements but mostly nods from those stuffing their faces in the kitchen. All the sweets Lyra had made today would be gone in the next ten minutes, Jack was sure of it.

Taking his hand off the phone Jack answered Mathew. "That's fine with us."

Mathew let out a breath. "Great. I'll text you in an hour or so to confirm or reschedule."

Jack cracked his stiff neck; it was going to be a long few weeks. "That's fine, talk to you later Mathew."

Mathew said something that sounded like a 'yup' before hanging up.

"Is the meeting done?" Justin asked as he stood up.

Jack slid off the stool as he answered. "Yeah, but Mathew is going to confirm the date and time with me after he talks with the other Alphas. So we won't know for sure for another hour."

Justin nodded as he helped Hazel arrange the furniture. After exchanging glances, Cole and Adam pitched in.

Lyra smirked and leaning around Ryan's back, watched the furniture be moved.

"Hon, you do realize all that furniture is going to have to be moved for Sunday, right? I mean this setup sucks for the pack's first date."

Hazel glanced at Lyra. Then hands on hips, looked around before exhaling heavily. "Dang it!"

Hazel batted her big blue eyes at the three guys helping her. "Boys, you'll help me put the furniture in a better arrangement for Sunday won't you?"

All three of them looked at her warily, they knew they were being sucked in and weren't sure how to get out.

Adam folded his arms over his chest. "What? Now?"

Adam possessed dark auburn hair with a full beard. He was six-foot-five and burly. Adam looked and carried himself like a woodsman who could pick a fight at any minute. But was larger than life with a huge heart and upbeat personality. His goal when he finished med school was to become a pediatrician.

Lyra had once compared Adam to a house pet. He looked all intimidating until he tried to cuddle. Adam had laughed and barked at her. Lyra jumped about a foot. Since then Adam would bark on occasion to startle Lyra.

Hazel nodded as if to say 'duh'. "Of course now, I'm not giving you time to get out of it."

She grinned as they gave her a frustrated huff. Jack tried desperately not to laugh, as he knew if he did he would get roped in to helping as well. Ryan was trying to cover his own laugh with a cough.

Justin turned his attention to Lyra, who was still leaning around Ryan with a huge grin on her face. Justin simply flicked up his middle finger and Lyra giggled. Justin lowered his finger and turned back to Hazel, who was debating furniture arrangements.

Ryan shook his head as the corners of his mouth twitched. "That was cruel, Lyra."

Lyra grinned over her tea mug. "But oh so funny and it's going to keep me entertained for a good hour, if not longer."

Jack looked over to where Hazel had now recruited Kelly, Seth, and Liam to help rearrange the room. Jack heard Lyra softly cackle to herself as she spun on the stool to face the room, blatantly watching the show. Jack went and grabbed a pen and pad of paper from his office.

When he came back, Ryan had been recruited and the last four holdouts were pretending to be absorbed in a card game at one of the tables. Jack sat to Lyra's left and began writing out a schedule for keeping tabs on her.

Curiosity tugged at him. "How are you holding up, seriously?"

Lyra continued to watch the mayhem Hazel was creating over her mug.

For a second Jack didn't think she would answer, but she did, speaking into her mug.

"I'll be fine, Jack. You know me. I make a habit of landing on my feet."

She was clearly making an effort not to snap at him so he spent a few seconds trying to word the next part properly.

"If Ryan hadn't been there when they jumped you the first time, would you have come to me?" Jack tried to make it sound like the answer didn't matter, but neither of them were fooled.

Lyra tilted her head, an unconscious gesture she did when really thinking about something. "Yes, I think I would have."

She started to frown.

"But something about today, I don't know, it was more of a declaration of intention. I definitely would have brought it up if Mathew hadn't."

The frown stayed in place as she watched the furniture being moved. Jack knew she wasn't really seeing the room but was trying to piece everything together in her head.

The next question was more from Jack's curiosity than anything else. He wasn't even sure Lyra would have an answer.

"Why did you lie on your training tests? What made you think it was a good idea?"

Lyra sighed but continued to watch Hazel and her helpers.

"During the second part of quarantine after they initially split us in packs, before initial fitness testing I heard some of the trainers talking outside our room. I just sat on the floor, eyes closed and used my new improved hearing to make out what they were saying. They were talking about shifting the initial groups, even back then, organizing us by skill. They thought it would be a better use of our abilities.

"When we did our first few stamina tests, I realized I was faster and could run longer. So instead of letting the trainers know this, I ran with the bulk of the pack and made sure I finished with low to mediocre scores. I would just watch and when three others dropped back I would too, pretending to be tired. It took me a few months to perfect it. I didn't want to get separated from you guys, and faking the test scores seemed like the best way to do it. Evidently I didn't do a good enough job."

Jack turned his head so he could see more of Lyra. "How did they find out?"

Lyra shrugged. "I have no idea. I just wasn't as good as I thought."

Jack very much doubted that. He really wanted to know how they had figured her out. But if Lyra didn't know, odds were no one else did either.

Jack's last question wasn't really was any of his business but Lyra was his littermate and that pushed him to ask, even if it got him in trouble.

"Lyra, is there something going on between you and Ryan?"

This time Lyra actually turned to look at him while her mug stayed where it was.

"What?"

The shock on her face and in her voice answered Jack's question.

Apparently Jack was seeing things that weren't there.

"Never mind, my bad."

Lyra continued to blink at Jack. "Where an earth did you get that idea?"

Jack gave the paper in front of him his full attention. "He was just awfully protective of you today."

Jack went for the slightly dumbed down version of how he had come to such a now ridiculous conclusion.

Lyra continued to gape at Jack. "Of course he was. Ryan is male and one of his female packmates was threatened. Can you say you would do any different in his place?"

Jack didn't even have to think about it. No, he would not. Had he not been Alpha he probably would have done the same thing.

"I probably would have yelled at you more."

Lyra snorted as she turned back to her mug and her eyes returned to the main part of the room. "Trust me, there has been plenty of that. Ryan just yelled when we were alone."

For a second Jack thought Lyra was going to elaborate. When she just continued to watch their packmates, he didn't try to reengage her. The last part was a dig he knew he deserved and Lyra was just reminding him.

About an hour later, Jack got Mathew's text confirming Sunday night. The furniture sat in a color-coded half-circle taking up most of the room. The circle would only seat about twenty people. Hazel explained that Sunday night they could move the bar stools and dining chairs to add eighteen more places. Jack didn't have the heart to tell her they would probably still be a seat or two short. The last thing he wanted was her bringing in more furniture.

The pack was spread out among the furniture.

Jack cleared his throat to get everyone's attention. "Okay, we are on for Sunday and I've got the schedule down. If you can't make one of your times, swap with someone and write it in on the master schedule up in my office, that way I always know who is with Lyra."

Jack waved the master copy above his head and saw Lyra sneer. Smiling, Jack headed to his office to tack the paper up on his board.

As he walked through the door and reached for a tack he heard Lyra announce, "I'm not cooking dinner on Sunday so fend for yourselves."

Jack chuckled at the grumbling. Coming back out of his office, he walked to the bar to stand in front of Lyra. Ryan sat on the stool next to her with his left arm stretched out on the counter behind her.

As pack members started to head out, Jack turned to Ryan. "Hope you don't mind that I put you for tonight. I figured you were already planning on it."

Ryan smiled. "Not at all, Lyra and I rented movies. Though I find it strange she picked an action movie."

Lyra hopped off her stool to rinse her cup out. “Hey, I love action movies and I didn’t get to see this one in theaters. Sappy movies are something I watch with Hazel, not big, macho football players.” Lyra deepened her voice as she said the last part.

Jack couldn’t help his snicker. “Yeah but did you check out her movie collection?”

Ryan shook his head but gave Jack a questioning look.

“Yeah, check it out when you get back to her place. She has a vast amount of chick flicks and a frightening amount of movies like Bring it On, Mr. Nanny. A slew of sixties beach movies, and some horrible movies I never even heard of before.”

Jack watched a dish towel come flying at his head. He caught it and looked up to see Ryan laughing and Lyra glaring.

“Those are great movies, you just have no taste.”

Jack tossed the dish towel back at her. “Right.”

As Jack turned to leave, he stopped and glanced over his shoulder. “I’m the one relieving you in the morning. Since I know how late Lyra sleeps in, I’ll see you about ten-thirty.”

Ryan stood up. “No, you’re going to want to be there at eight-thirty.”

That got Jack’s full attention. “What?”

Ryan nodded. “Yup. Eight-thirty or one-thirty, your choice.”

“Oh bring workout gear, with pants not shorts,” Lyra said as she started piling dishes in the dishwasher.

Jack had a sinking feeling about what he was about to get himself into.

The next morning Jack was at Lyra’s apartment at eight-twenty, wearing black sweat pants and a black tank. It was early for a night owl like Lyra, so Jack stopped at the Starbucks a block down from Lyra’s complex. He had been flattered when the barista checked him out as she rang him up. Jack knew he wasn’t buff but he had enough lean muscle, evidently, to be worth a good long look.

Jack knocked on the door with his left hand since the right was holding the coffee carrier. He smiled as he heard Mogwai and Fizgig bounding for the door. Lyra had trained them not to bark every time someone was at the door, but the two hundred pounds of dog were not exactly quiet when they ran.

Ryan opened the door. He gave one look at the Starbucks cups before moving the door wide enough for Jack to walk through. Jack ignored the dogs until he set the drinks down on Lyra's kitchen counter. Once the drinks were safe, he looked down at the two excited dogs.

Mogwai the Rottwieler and Fizgig the Bernese Mountain Dog were both familiar with Jack, so their large bodies were wiggling in welcome. Jack made sure to pet them both at the same time. If one thought they were getting shafted they would nudge the offender's body with their head and that little nudge could shove a person off balance. Jack learned this the hard way when Fizgig had nudged him hard enough he ended up on the floor.

After a minute or two Jack felt it was safe to look up at Ryan. The other man stood a few feet away with his arms across his chest, his face a pleasant blank. Ryan wore a black ribbed tank and black work out pants.

"Morning, Ryan."

Ryan turned to face Jack and the dogs, nodding. "Morning, Jack. I see the boys have you well trained."

Jack patted each dog on the side and stood up. Thumping them lightly was a sign the person was done petting them. Or at least that was the theory. They would obey Lyra, but everyone else had a fifty-fifty shot of being knocked over. It looked like the boys were in a kind mood today because they wandered off down the hall toward Lyra's room.

"Let's just say I've been knocked over one too many times not to give the dogs their due."

Ryan's lips twitched.

Jack grabbed one of the coffees from the holder. "I didn't know what you liked so I went with a mocha. I figured it was a safe bet. Where is Lyra?"

Ryan took the cup from Jack. "Thanks, man. Lyra is in the back, changing."

Lyra's apartment had a good-sized main room in the front. The left side of the room had two dark red leather chairs and a matching couch between them. Behind the couch were three large dark wood bookcases. In front of the couch was a glass coffee table. Against the same wall as the front door were the TV and all the other electronics. The left wall had the sliding glass door that led out to the balcony.

On the right side of the room was the kitchen and dining nook. The kitchen took up three-quarters of the space. A three-foot counter separated it from where a cherry wood table sat with four matching chairs. Across the room from the front door was a short hallway with one door on each side and one at the end. The door to the left was the bathroom, the one to the right was the hall closet and at the end of the hall was Lyra's bedroom.

Lyra walked into the hall, trailed by her two dogs. She wore a black sleeveless long women's workout top, with a short, black, un-zipped hoodie and black clingy workout pants that stopped mid-calf.

She stopped and gave a girlie gasp when she noticed the Starbucks. Lyra launched herself at Jack and he braced himself as she threw her arms around him. Jack couldn't stop the chuckle. No matter how many times Lyra flung herself at him for a hug, Jack smiled every time.

As Lyra squeezed and let go, Ryan cleared his throat.

"Well, that was…interesting."

Lyra ignored him and watched avidly as Jack handed her a cup. She sniffed it and gave Jack a face full of childlike joy. "Aromatherapy coffee. I love you." Lyra continued to grin at Jack as she took a sip.

Ryan moved so he was standing next to both Jack and Lyra. "What did you do to her, Jack? It's almost scary."

Jack smiled and grabbed his double white chocolate mocha. "She loves the smell of a cinnamon dolce latte, it makes her happy."

Ryan looked from Jack to Lyra. "It's like crack."

Lyra narrowed her eyes at Ryan but the effect was somewhat diminished by the peaceful smile on her face and the Starbucks cup under her nose. Jack smiled. He was glad he knew his littermate's coffee quirks.

Sighing deeply, Lyra moved the cup to so it leaned against her shoulder. "As nice as this is, we need to head out."

Lyra moved to grab something from the other side of the couch and Ryan grabbed a long, thin black bag. He slung the bag's strap over his shoulder so it lay vertically across his back. When Lyra stood back up she had an identical bag, but put the strap diagonally across her chest. Lyra balanced her coffee and zipped up her hoodie as she started walking back toward Jack.

"Everyone ready?"

Jack looked from Lyra to Ryan. "Am I missing something here?"

Lyra smiled and patted Jack's shoulder before heading out the door.

About two blocks south of Lyra's north Seattle apartment, she gave a little giggle. Jack knew that giggle and was almost afraid to ask.

"What, Lyra?" Jack sighed.

Lyra grinned from where she walked between him and Ryan. "We must look ridiculous! In all black workout gear holding Starbucks cups. I was just thinking about how funny we must look, all matching."

Jack thought about it a second and groaned. Lyra was right.

Ryan pointed a finger at Lyra and away from his Starbucks cup. "I'll have you know we are all wearing different styles of workout gear."

Jack scoffed. "Give it a rest, Ryan. We match. Just be grateful we have a girl with us so it doesn't seem as weird." Then Jack turned slightly to Lyra. "And don't you dare speed up!"

Lyra giggled in reply, telling Jack that had been exactly what she was thinking. The rest of their walk was spent quietly sipping their coffees.

Jack was momentarily taken aback when they reached their destination. It was a three storey building with The North Seattle Group Fitness Center in thick block letters. As Jack walked in, he put two and two together. Lyra had been working on her certification to become a yoga instructor at the end of college. Since Lyra was not the biggest fan of people, Jack had never understood her interest, but he was happy for her that she reached her goal.

Jack watched Lyra bee-line for the long reception desk that took up most of the right wall. The entry room was painted a pale blue and had a small food and beverage stand off the left side of the room with about a dozen tall two and four person tables in a semi-circle around it. With fifteen minutes until nine, according to the clock on the wall behind the stand, there were a good thirty to forty people milling around, ranging in age from late teens to late fifties. Straight ahead of them was the staircase heading up with the elevator next to it. Several community boards were scattered on all four walls. There was a thin gap at the far side of the reception desk's four foot counter, so employees could get behind it. It also led to a door in the corner with an 'Employees Only' sign over it.

Jack kept in step with Ryan as he looked around the lobby. Both of them reached the counter in time to hear Lyra greet the receptionist.

"Good morning, Rachel."

Rachel appeared to be in her mid-to-late sixties and wore her silvery white hair in a pixie cut. She seemed to be in great shape for her age.

"Good morning, Lyra dear. What can I do for you?"

Lyra continued to smile at the older woman as she held up two fingers. "Two things, first am I covering for anyone today?"

Rachel nodded and began skimming a clipboard. "Yes sweetie, I think you are…Oh here it is can you take Amber's two o'clock class?"

Lyra lifted an eyebrow. "What is it?" She sounded like she already knew.

Rachel gave Lyra an apologetic smile. "Cycling."

Lyra dropped her empty cup loudly on the counter. "Oh for goodness sake, Rachel, fine, but tell her this is the last time. If she doesn't want to teach the class then she shouldn't offer it."

Rachel gave a gossipy laugh before grabbing the empty coffee cup and throwing it under the counter, where Jack assumed there was a trash can.

"You know as well as I do, she's gotten herself in enough hot water as it is."

Lyra sighed and yanked on her braid before speaking. "The second thing is I have a guest with me today." Lyra waved over her shoulder to where Jack and Ryan stood. Jack raised his hand and smiled as Rachel gave him an appraising look.

Rachel didn't speak until she was rooting through a drawer. "Lyra dear, why is it you always have such attractive young men with you. You seem to be collecting them now, if you can count two as a collection, which I do."

Lyra rolled her eyes and snatched the paperwork from Rachel. Turning, Lyra handed the papers to Jack. "Read and fill these out." As he moved up to the counter a pen appeared in front of him.

"Rachel, don't go stroking egos after I put in such an effort to keep them in check."

Rachel tittered as she moved a few feet down the reception desk to help a teenage couple. Lyra put her hand on Jack's left forearm to get his attention. When Jack looked up, she smiled.

"I'm going to snag my mail and paycheck. As soon as you're done filling out the paperwork, just reach over and put it on the inner counter. Rachel will take care of it. Ryan, you know which studio we are in." Then she was off walking and around the counter and through the employee door.

After filling out the paperwork, Jack placed it on the inner counter and turned to Ryan. The other man gestured to the stairs. People were making their way to the stairs and elevator. The stairs were wide enough for five adults to walk abreast. So it was no problem for Jack and his Second to climb the stairs in unison.

"I take it you're here regularly."

Ryan nodded. "Twice a week for a year. It pays for me to be flexible. When I made a comment about it to Lyra once, she offered to let me sit in on her yoga class. I really enjoyed it. There are three different yoga instructors here, and Lyra is definitely the best for what I'm looking for. I pay the monthly membership instead of by class so I can come in whenever I feel like it."

Jack was surprised he never heard any of this before, but Ryan and he don't talk much outside of pack business.

"So what's with the cycling thing?"

Ryan grunted as they walked in to the third studio door on the right side of the hallway. "Grab a mat." Ryan said as they passed a rack of them on their way to the far corner of the room.

Jack pulled a purple one off the stack. When they reached the corner, Ryan pulled out and unrolled his black mat vertically in front of himself. Jack did the same.

Ryan didn't answer until they had removed their shoes and were sitting on their mats.

"Lyra hates cycling. She says no matter how much she does it, cycling always kicks her butt. I don't know why she decided to get certified in it, but she did. The girl, Amber, I guess is really flaky, this will be the fifth class Lyra has stepped in for. The classes here go in thirteen-week spans, twelve classes then a one week break before new classes start. Amber showed up for the first two weeks and hasn't showed since. Lyra and an older lady are the only other people certified to teach it and the older lady doesn't work weekends, so that leaves Lyra."

Jack shook his head. "That sucks."

Ryan grunted.

When Lyra walked into the room, the twenty or so students went quiet. It turned out Ryan put them in the back corner of the room, which Jack was grateful of since he knew next to nothing about yoga.

Lyra pulled her bag off. "Oh come on guys, you don't have to go dead silent just because I walked into the room."

There were several laughs as Lyra jerked her dark blue mat in mid air to unroll it, so it was horizontal as opposed to the students. She removed her shoes and walked over to a niche in the side wall that held controls to the sound system.

Since conversation had not picked back up Lyra spoke as she changed the CD. "Fine, if no one is going to talk, I will. How about some chanting this morning, nothing says yoga like chanting."

There were a number of boos and hisses at the suggestion, and Lyra smiled.

"Good to see you haven't lost your communication skills. Henry, will you close the door for me please."

A tall gentleman, who looked to be about seventy, moved toward the door. Jack took a deep breathe and prepared himself to be totally lost.

At the end of the fifty-minute class, Jack had a slight sweat going. About a fourth of the class stayed while everyone else shuffled out of the studio. Jack had found out during the class that it was a beginner course, which explained the large age span. After clicking off the music Lyra made her way toward Jack and Ryan. But every few steps, she would be stopped by one student or another.

Jack took the opportunity to talk to Ryan. "So that was a beginning course."

Ryan nodded.

Jack cracked his neck. "What's up next?"

Ryan smiled and turned to look at Jack. "Intermediate."

Jack cursed.

Lyra happened to make it over just in time to hear him. "What's wrong?"

Ryan smirked and stretched his arms. "Just told Jack what class was next."

Lyra smiled and her eyes softened. "Jack, you can go hang downstairs. You don't have to stay up here through every class I have. After this class is beginners again, followed by another intermediate. We can go get a light snack for an hour before I sub for the cycling class."

Jack shook his head; he knew he could do this, and male pride would not let him bow out.

Lyra continued to watch him. "You sure?"

Jack nodded.

Lyra turned to Ryan. "Since Jack's here today, are you still sticking around?"

Ryan folded his arms and looked down at Lyra. "Absolutely, I told you whenever you had to step in and teach the cycling class I'd stick around, as moral support."

Lyra smiled widely up at Ryan. Someone in the doorway called for Lyra, and Jack guessed it was another instructor. Before Jack knew what was happening, Lyra grabbed Ryan's upper arm to use as leverage and gave Ryan a kiss on the cheek.

"Thank you, Ryan," she said before walking toward the woman in the doorway.

Jack knew Lyra hadn't been flirting, but he'd never seen her do that before. He watched Ryan. Surprise and a few other emotions filled the other man's face for a second or two before Ryan blanked it. That told Jack it was not a common occurrence for Ryan either. Then Jack understood.

"You have feelings for her don't you?"

Ryan kept his face blank and didn't answer, just watched Lyra talk with the woman at the door.

"You know the blank face is answer enough. Do you realize she has no idea?"

Ryan shifted his gaze to Jack, looking him straight in the eyes. It would have been intimidating had Jack been anyone other than Alpha.

"Don't worry, Ryan, I have no intention of telling her. I know better than to mess with Lyra's love life."

Ryan relaxed, but only a fraction before turning his attention back to Lyra. Jack filed away this information as something to watch. The scientists tended to pay extra attention to Weres who dated other Weres and that was attention no one wanted. As a littermate, Jack wanted protect Lyra from getting hurt, even if he did like Ryan.

Jack looked over in time see Lyra give slashing motions with both her hands. The other woman folded her arms.

"I wish I could hear what was going on."

Jack had the urge to storm over and handle the problem so Lyra wouldn't be so upset. He knew that was not a good way to handle things so he stayed put. The other woman spoke and Lyra got more agitated.

Ryan grunted, then said in an imitation of a female smoker's voice, "Look, it needs to be filled. It's only for a month." Then in Ryan's voice but with Lyra's mannerisms and tone, "What and no one thought to ask this sooner? I have another job, Lidie, one that's full-time."

Jack raised his eyebrows at Ryan as the other man switched voices again.

"It's not like your other job has set hours, this will."

Jack held up his hand to interrupt Ryan. "How in the hell can you hear that?"

Ryan answered without taking his attention off the two women. "Practice, you pick up one string of conversation and zone in on it."

Jack continued to watch Ryan. "Yeah, but I can't ever hear them."

Ryan shrugged. "The abilities manifest in everyone differently, remember?"

Jack went back to watching to two women as Lyra, fuming, spun away from the other woman and headed back toward him and Ryan. Jack knew the conversation had ended badly.

Before Lyra even opened her mouth, Ryan stepped in. "So they fired Amber, huh? How many classes do they want you to cover?"

Lyra glared up at Ryan. "You know it's rude when you do that right?"

Ryan shrugged.

Jack didn't even pretend to be surprised that Lyra knew Ryan had heard her entire conversation.

Lyra rolled her neck and sighed. "Five including cycling. The others are twice a week step aerobics classes."

Ryan winced. "I don't want to take step classes."

A laugh burst from Lyra's mouth. "No one is making you, Ryan."

Jack took the moment to interrupt. "Why didn't you decline?"

Lyra smiled a little. "They need someone to cover the classes and I can do it, but Lidie tried to force it on me. I told her if she could come back in an hour and ask nicely with an apology then maybe I would bail her out."

Jack folded his arms. "You sure that was a wise idea?"

Lyra laughed as she headed back to the front of the studio. "We'll see, won't we?"

Jack sighed. That was Lyra, determined to live life by her own rules and sometimes she let her mouth get the better of her. He hoped she hadn't just cost herself a job she so obviously loved.

The rest of the yoga classes passed without much of a hitch. Jack had some trouble keeping up in the first intermediate class, but the second set of classes were easier. It helped that he and Ryan were at the back, so Jack didn't worry too much about looking like an idiot. Though Lyra often would straighten Jack up a bit more than she did her other students. Lyra tried to come talk to them in between classes but people needed her attention for one thing or another. Lidie never came back. Ryan had been quiet, not saying more than two words together.

Now that the yoga classes were over, Jack was positive he could conquer the cycling class. The three of them were sitting at one of the tall tables in the lobby. Lyra bought Jack a twelve-ounce strawberry banana smoothie. When he tried to question her about food, she smirked at him over her own shake.

"Only if you want to puke."

The three of them sat in a companionable silence for about fifteen minutes until Lyra started humming the theme from Jaws. Jack followed her gaze and saw Lidie, who was probably still in college, and another woman of about forty walking toward them. For a split second Jack worried for Lyra, then he saw Lyra and Ryan's expressions.

Ryan's words were barely audible. Jack wouldn't have heard them if he had normal hearing.

"Someone went for backup and got themselves in trouble."

As the two women reached the table, Jack could see the older woman was frustrated and Lidie appeared chastised. Lidie spoke first, looking at Lyra.

"Can we talk to you Lyra?"

Lyra shook her head. "This is my lunch and I'm hanging out with my friends. So you either talk while I drink or wait until I'm on company time."

Jack sighed. That was a Werewolf for you; assert dominance to assure you have the upper hand. Jack watched as the older woman fold her arms and look expectantly at Lidie. When the younger woman didn't say anything, the older woman spoke.

"It serves you right, Lidie. You are not her boss. It was unbelievably rude to command her to take your friend's classes. As if you had that authority. Plus you did it in front of students which just made the whole situation worse. Don't get huffy because she refuses to use her time off. You started this in a public forum so deal with your own mess."

Jack exchanged glances with Ryan before taking a closer look at the two women. Jack knocked another year or two off Lidie's age and began to see the resemblance between the two women. Jack would put money on them being mother and daughter.

Lidie's shoulders slumped even more, definitely a teenager. "I'm sorry, Lyra. I was wrong to tell you you had to take Amber's classes. We would greatly appreciate if you would take over those classes since otherwise they would have to be canceled."

Jack saw Lidie's mother was clearly unhappy with that apology and was about to say so when Lyra stepped in.

"Fine, I'll do it. One the condition that I don't get stuck with the cycling."

The older woman jumped in before Lidie could cause problems. "Deal. Come on, Lidie."

With that the two women walked back through the employee doorway, Lidie getting chastised the entire way.

Jack turned back to see Ryan holding up his hand for a high five.

"Nice job, Lyra! Way to dodge the bullet there."

Jack raised an eyebrow at Lyra, and she smiled.

"I was supposed to teach cycling next session."

Jack shook his head and smiled but didn't say anything.

"So how long do I have you for, Jack?"

Jack looked over to see Lyra watching him, politely waiting for his answer. Ryan, on the other hand, stiffened as if offended. Jack looked back at Lyra so he wouldn't draw her attention to Ryan's reaction.

"Seven. After that you get Seth all night, followed by Adam in the morning. It should be Justin tomorrow night and beyond that I don't remember. If you copied down the schedule like I suggested, you wouldn't have to quiz me."

Lyra continued, totally unaffected by Jack scolding her. "But that's not as much fun, Jack. I can't believe you gave Saturday night to Seth. What were you thinking?" Lyra was grinning at Jack and he didn't know why.

Quickly he searched his brain, then he remembered with a groan. "No, under no circumstances are you two to go over to Hazel or Chelsea's places, you hear me."

Lyra grinned wider. Jack was about to threaten his littermate when Ryan's curiosity got the better of him.

"Why can't they go to Hazel's?"

Jack gave Lyra a glare before answering. "Hazel and four of her college friends, one of whom Lyra is friends with, Chelsea, have a standing movie night twice a month. When Chelsea hosts, she picks at least one horror movie. Hazel does not respond well to horror movies. A few months ago Seth heard Hazel trying to get Lyra to go with her, because if Lyra is there making snarky comments the whole movie it is hard to be afraid of. After Hazel left, Seth started making fun of Lyra for not going and they somehow got the idea to play a prank on the girls watching the movies. I'll just say by the end of the night my phone was ringing and I spent the next three nights on Hazel's futon. It didn't matter that I called Lyra the same night and made her and Seth confess, Hazel was still out of her mind. Lyra and Seth still maintain it was a brilliant idea."

Lyra just continued to grin with mischievous glee.

"Why she ever forgave you two I don't know."

Lyra continued to smile. "She claims some day she will get revenge, silly Hazel."

Ryan was trying to hold back a laugh and only half succeeded. "That's terrible, Lyra."

Lyra just continued to smile.

Jack pointed his finger at her. "I mean it, Lyra, don't go scaring the crap out of Hazel again. I will…do…something about it."

Still Lyra smiled as she sipped from her straw. Jack cursed his own stupidity and sincerely hoped he wouldn't get a frightened call from Hazel tonight.

The cycling class had been a killer, just as Lyra predicted. Lyra encouraged Jack beforehand to pedal as fast as he could without bringing attention to his Were stamina. She told Jack if he wasn't sweating fifteen minutes in than he would stick out in the crowded class. Jack had been a little worried, but once the class got going he didn't need to. He may have stamina but his body still was not used to that type of workout. Jack usually did weights and that was it. If nothing else this day proved to Jack that he needed to vary his workout routine.

The three of them were finally back at Lyra's apartment. Ryan, it was obvious, or at least to Jack, was trying to think of a reason to stick around. Lyra wasn't helping the poor male any.

As soon as they closed the door Lyra turned to Jack. "I'm ordering Chinese from down the street, then I'm jumping in the shower before it gets here. What do you want?"

Ryan's face blanked, which Jack found just as telling as an emotion would have been. Lyra held out a menu and Jack began skimming it. Lyra took off her bag and jacket, throwing them both on the couch.

"I can pay for the food while you're in the shower, because there is no way I want to hang around you in sweats all day."

Jack snuck a glance a Ryan. The other man's eyes widened at her last comment.

As quickly as he could, Jack filled Ryan in, hoping it would calm the other male down. The last thing Jack wanted was to get in a fight with Ryan. If Ryan had become possessive over Lyra, which sometimes happened with male Weres and the women they had feelings for, Jack might not have a choice.

"All of our litter have clothing stored at each other's homes, just in case. So Lyra has a change of my clothes, Justin's, Seth's and Hazel's."

Jack watched as Ryan got hold of himself, more because Ryan realized he was reaching a brink than because of what Jack said. Jack yelled several choice words in his head. What had gotten into Ryan? If things were always like this, Jack would have definitely noticed. Ryan nodded and gave a clipped goodbye before grabbing a brown duffel bag and leaving.

Jack looked to Lyra, whose face was a mix of confusion and concern. Jack knew she wanted to help Ryan but had no idea what was going on.

"How long has he been acting like that?"

Lyra tore her attention from the front door to blink at Jack. "Only the last two, maybe three, days. He's so agitated and if I try to comfort him he only becomes more so. When we were watching movies last night he wouldn't even sit on the couch with me. It's weird. Do you know what's going on?"

Jack couldn't lie to Lyra. One, because he tried very hard to not lie to his littermates, and two, Lyra was pretty dang close to being a human lie detector.

"I have an idea, but I'm not going to share it with you until I'm sure."

It wasn't exactly a lie; Lyra tilted her head and watched Jack for a second before gesturing back to the menu in his hand.

"Pick something."

Jack was relieved she didn't press him.

Jack enjoyed being clean. He always liked the smell of the soaps his female littermates used. It was nice to have one of those familiar comforting scents on his skin. Jack sat on the right side of the couch flipping through the channels as Lyra finished dishing out their food.

"What do you want to drink, Jack?"

Jack answered without taking his eyes off the On Demand screen. "Water's fine."

There was more noise from the kitchen as Jack settled on a TV show he had never heard of but Lyra had marked as one of her favorites. It was something about a fake psychic who worked with the cops.

The next few hours went by with little to no talking. After four episodes of the detective show Lyra stated she was going to work a little and had gone over to her dining table with a good sized manuscript. While she worked, Jack flipped through the channels. There was a knock at the door at five-to-seven. Lyra ushered Seth in.

Seth cleared his throat. "So what's on the agenda tonight littermate? I heard there was a movie night."

Jack shot a look at Seth. "No, absolutely not! No scaring Hazel you hear me!" Jack had a sneaking suspicion nothing he could say would move Seth from the idea if the other man was truly set on it.

"Actually there is a marathon of the newest season of Project Runway tonight; technically I think it already started." Lyra moved to the TV to flick through the channels.

Seth dropped his dark duffel bag and went to stand next to her.

Jack looked at his littermates for a beat; he heard Lyra mention this show before. Lyra was a borderline TV addict and Jack couldn't believe some of the garbage she watched on a regular basis.

"Wait, Seth you're seriously interested in watching a reality show all night?"

Seth shrugged but didn't look away from the screen. "Sure, it's amazing what some of these people say to the camera. Not to mention when they stress out, crash and burn. It's like watching a car wreck without the physical injury."

Jack was not quite sure how he felt about that, so he decided the safest course of action would be to leave. As Jack reached for the door, he heard two feminine male voices yelling from the TV. Jack turned to see both Lyra and Seth with their eyes glued to the screen.

"Bye guys, I'll see you tomorrow."

All he got in return was a grunt from Seth and a wave from Lyra. Shaking his head, Jack let himself out.

Chapter 4

Seth showered first, that way if Adam showed up early he would be the one to answer the door. It wasn't that Lyra couldn't answer her own door, but Seth didn't like the idea of her answering the door in her PJs. Lyra's sleepwear for the most part did not cover much. Last night she donned a pale pink, figure-hugging top that reached the bottom of her hips. Then a matching pair of snug shorts only three inches longer than the top. Even though Lyra had no problem going to the door in such attire, Seth couldn't find it in him to be comfortable with it.

Plus, finishing first meant he got to make breakfast. Seth knew Lyra loved cooking, but he felt it was only fair others cooked for her every once in a while. Seth knew she really did appreciate the gesture even though they both knew she was a better cook. After looking around the fridge, Seth decided omelets would be his best bet

Seth turned on the coffee pot and enjoyed the sound and smell of it brewing. Lyra had a fancy complicated coffee machine next to the coffee pot, but Seth wasn't touching it. On the other side she had half a dozen large flavor bottles with pumps on top. If Lyra wanted something other than plain coffee she would have to make it herself. Seth grew up on black coffee. The only reason he knew as much as he did about fancier coffee was due to Lyra and Hazel. The two of them, mostly Hazel, had been hell-bent on educating him. Seth just felt anything other than black coffee was just too fussy. Whenever he was with the girls at a Starbucks, Seth couldn't help the scowl when he heard others ordering complicated drinks. That much attention to detail over something as meaningless as a coffee was absurd.

Seth heard the knock at the front door at ten after ten. Seth took a second to flip the omelet he was working on before walking to the door.

Adam stood in the hall with a large grin on his face and a black messenger bag hanging from his left shoulder. Adam was one of the biggest men Seth had ever come across. Adam's family were loggers for five generations before Adam's father married Adam's mother and quit to move closer to Seattle.

Seth nodded and stood back so Adam could walk through the door. Adam strode in and set his bag down by the bar and leaned on the counter, eyeing the food Seth had been making. As Seth closed the door he heard Lyra come into the room closely followed by her two giant dogs.

"Puppy! How are you today?"

Seth snorted as he turned to see Lyra grinning at Adam as she walked to the coffee pot. Seth had no idea why Lyra insisted on calling a guy as big as Adam 'puppy' or why it didn't seem to bother him.

Adam grinned back at Lyra as she began pumping mocha flavoring into her very large sky-blue coffee mug.

"I'm fine, Lyra, but I would be better if I could convince someone to feed me."

Seth snorted again as he removed the omelet from the skillet to a plate and handed it to Lyra. "There is no doubt in my mind that you ate before coming over here."

By the time Seth finished making his omelet, Adam was sitting at the table across from Lyra with a mug of black coffee in front of him, and Lyra was about halfway through her food and on a second cup of coffee. Refilling his own mug, Seth sat between Adam and Lyra.

They were silent a few seconds before Adam looked up from his mug. "How did you find out they flagged your file? I mean why did they tell you and not the other six?"

Seth had been wondering along those same lines, but refrained from asking because he noticed Lyra really didn't want to discuss it and her friendship was more important to him than quenching his curiosity. Seth knew if Lyra was comfortable talking about any of this, it wouldn't be for quite a while. But it had been hard and frankly he was glad Adam was the one to crack.

Lyra sighed and stabbed at her omelet but didn't look at either him or Adam. Seth didn't think she was upset about the question, just tired of thinking about the experience.

"Think about it, Adam. What's the best way to get Werewolf males to do what you want them to do? Use a female. I was a bargaining chip. The scientists were going to use me as leverage, convince the males to agree to reassignment. They were betting on the males coming to protect me as a group instead of leaving me to deal with training alone. Really think about it, what would you have done if the scientists put you in that position?"

Seth nodded. It wouldn't have mattered if the female was not pack. Those six males would have gone in voluntarily in a heartbeat to protect one of their own.

"I would have volunteered but I would cause hell while I was there. Jack made it seem like the males were never told, though." Adam remained solemn, almost angry while he spoke.

Lyra continued to stab at her food. "The scientists didn't get the chance. I made it too difficult for them to keep me. They didn't want to outright injure me, so it limited their resources. When I exhibited no such reservations, they let me go instead of let me continue to injure them as well as myself. When I realized they were not willing to do any real damage, I fought back hard enough that it became impossible for them to keep that stance."

Seth could understand Lyra's idea was a good one and he was somewhat proud of her for implementing it to get herself out without help. But a large part of him greatly disliked the whole thing. Seth hated the idea that his littermate had been injured and he hated even more that she had done it to herself. Seth wanted to get his hands on the scientists very badly.

Seth noticed Adam looking at him, his face still solemn. "Though I am extremely glad Lyra fought her way back to us. I can't help but wonder what exactly is going on. Why now? Why change tactics? The program was a positive thing to all of us in the beginning before we began to rule ourselves."

Seth felt the weight of Adam's questions. In the silence that followed Seth knew all three of them were trying to find an answer and coming up blank. Whatever was happening, he was sure the Weres were in for a hard time and hopefully they were strong enough to get themselves through.

Chapter 5

By the time Jack made his way to the pack office it was almost seven. He walked in to see about half the pack already there. Lyra was in the kitchen, working on what appeared to be some type of circular chocolate desserts. There were four large serving platters of various baked goods. Jack knew for a fact there were not enough ingredients in the kitchen to make all that. Lyra must have gone shopping to feed the army coming over in an hour.

Adam sat on one of the stools. Papers and books were spread out across the counter. He was concentrating on his notes. Though Adam was not looking at Lyra, Jack was sure if something were to happen the other man would be on top of it.

Syrus and Sadie sat cross-legged on the floor in front of the coffee table where Hazel's conversation circle had been. Between them was the pack's chess board. Chess was one of the few things, for some reason, Syrus took seriously. With the two of them, a game could last for hours. Jack hoped they would be able to wrap it up in time for the meeting.

Bruce had crashed on one of the cream couches. There was a notebook on the floor in front of him. Bruce must have been asleep a while because someone had taken out a black throw blanket and covered him.

ESPN played on the TV but the sound was turned way down so as not to wake Bruce. Kelly, Liam, and Cole were camped out in the beanbag chairs in front of it. Their conversation consisted of occasional loud whispers.

It all seemed pretty normal to Jack, or at least normal enough. He sat down on a stool three over from Adam, and smiled as Lyra glanced over at him.

"Hey Lyra, how was your day?" Jack made his tone light in hopes Lyra wouldn't notice he was feeling out her mood.

She put some finishing touches on something and turned to give him her full attention. "It was great. Today was shopping day. It was nice to have someone to wander Pike Place with, checking out all the specialty foods. You know Adam never had those little doughnuts?" She paused long enough to make a face of disbelief. "It also helped to have an extra set of hands. I bought a lot of extra stuff since I don't want our guests finishing off our food."

Jack took another look at the platters.

Lyra followed Jack's gaze and laughed. "Don't worry, Jack. I've got five large pies and three cakes and two more trays sitting in the fridge. There are two trays in the oven right now and I still have some things waiting to go in. There will be plenty." Lyra's smile was reassuring.

Jack was glad she thought ahead and baked for the meeting. He hadn't even thought about offering food. Mostly he was glad she was in such a good mood. So he didn't spoil it by telling her she probably cooked too much.

Justin walked through the front door, followed closely by Ryan. Both assessed the room before walking over to the kitchen. Justin plopped down on the stool next to Jack and waved at Jack, then at Lyra with a smile on his face. Lyra waved back before opening the oven and looking in. Ryan, on the other hand, grabbed a beer from the fridge, opened the bottle and leaned against the closed door.

Justin leaned over the counter, looking into the oven as Lyra pulled out a tray of fat cinnamon rolls.

"Oh, pulling out all the stops are we. So what can I eat?"

Lyra put the tray on top of the oven and removed a second one of cinnamon rolls. It wasn't until she slid two new trays in, these filled with peanut butter cookies, that she answered Justin.

"None of it. Nothing gets eaten until everyone arrives. That way everyone has an equal chance of getting hurt trying to get to the food."

Justin sat back on the stool and gave Lyra his best pout. Lyra didn't seem fazed. She began putting things in a mixing bowl.

Ryan took a long drag of his beer before speaking. "Need any help?"

Jack saw Justin was as surprised as he was by Ryan's question. It wasn't that Ryan was inconsiderate, just that no one offered to help Lyra because she preferred to do everything herself.

Lyra didn't seem to find the question strange because there was no surprise or confusion to her tone. "You can grab the eggs out of the fridge for me. Other than that I'm good, thanks."

Ryan nodded and pulled the fridge open, grabbing a carton and laying it down on the counter next to Lyra. He was standing directly behind her and stayed for a beat. Jack worried whether he should step in. One of the last things the pack needed was for its Second to be distracted by hormones. Lyra smiled and thanked him.

Ryan simply nodded before leaving the kitchen and heading over to join the group watching TV.

Jack felt Justin nudge his arm. When Jack looked at his littermate the other man's face held suspicious confusion. Jack shrugged, he wasn't about to say anything.

Adam leaned around Justin to get Jack's attention. When both were looking at him, Adam pointed from the fridge to Lyra then tilted his head in question.

Justin mouthed, 'No Clue'.

Adam waited a beat before shaking his head and going back to his book.

Jack reminded himself to keep an eye on Ryan tonight.

Hazel came through the door a few seconds later with a huge smile on her face. "Good evening, everyone!" she bubbled as she plopped down on the stool next to Justin. Hazel was almost beaming, but then even a moderate smile from Hazel looked like she was beaming.

Justin looked from Hazel to Jack with a raised eyebrow. Jack shrugged, he had no idea why their littermate was so chipper.

"Is it some kinda girl holiday that I'm not aware of?"

Jack tried not to laugh. Justin just couldn't keep quiet.

Both Lyra and Hazel deliberately ignored Justin.

Lyra leaned against the oven, wiping her hands on a yellow cloth towel, staring Hazel in the eyes. After a few seconds the two women seemed to have held an entire conversation.

Lyra's eyebrows raised and one side of her mouth quirked up. "Really?"

Hazel just nodded as an answer, still grinning.

"But what about the other thing?" Lyra waved her right arm as if gesturing to something.

Hazel shrugged, but her grin dimmed slightly.

Lyra watched the other woman a moment. "Huh." Then she turned back to the trays cooling on the stove.

Jack had no idea what any of that meant. Looking at Justin's expression, Jack was glad he wasn't alone. Moving his attention back to Hazel, Jack noticed she seemed somewhat deflated. He wondered what about Lyra's questions made Hazel's mood change.

Before Jack could dwell on that, Justin jumped in.

"Lyra, you broke Hazel." Then he poked Hazel repeatedly in the arm.

She swatted at him, trying to appear irritated. "Quit that." She was trying not to smile.

Jack could always count on Justin to improve the girls' moods.

There was a knock at the office door. The entire pack went silent. Bruce had woken up from the sound and all of them were looking at the door.

When no one got up to answer it, Jack heard Ryan snort. "It's just Bishop and his crew." Then he got up and started across the room to the front door.

Jack got up to stand beside Ryan as the other man reached the door. "How do you know that?"

Ryan took a long drag from his beer before grabbing the door knob. "I heard Victor in the hall trying to call dibs on one of the leather chairs."

Jack didn't even bother trying to fathom how Ryan heard that through a wall and across the room. Jack simply turned as Ryan opened the door. Ryan positioned himself so he was behind the door and Jack was in the doorway so people would see the Alpha as the door opened. It was an unspoken power play, to get to the pack you had to get past Jack first.

Sure enough, standing in the hallway was Bishop, Victor, and Taylor. Bishop inclined his head to Jack and Jack returned the gesture. Bishop wore a charcoal grey three-piece suit. His short black hair was styled. He looked like he was headed to a law firm instead of a pack office. Both Victor and Taylor were in suits as well. Jack had a suspicion Bishop did this to make other Alphas uncomfortable.

Jack moved aside so the three of them could come in. Both Bishop and Victor stepped in and did a quick scan of the room. Taylor, meanwhile, went straight to the kitchen and held the now empty plastic container out to Lyra.

Taylor bowed with the container out between them. "Thank you, my lady. Believe me when I say there was much arguing over the contents of this container. I personally made sure it was cleaned before returning it to you."

Lyra rolled her eyes but smiled as she took it from him.

Once the container left his hands, Taylor straightened up and in a sweeping gesture swiped a brownie off a nearby cooling rack. His actions causing several exclamations.

Lyra went back to what she had been doing before Pack M's representatives entered. Without turning, she addressed Taylor in a light tone. "Don't think I didn't see that coming, Taylor, and have no delusions that I'll let you do it again."

Taylor grinned at Lyra's back. "Wouldn't dream of it, my lady."

As the three members of Pack M settled in to chairs Syrus got up from were he sat on the floor and moved to stand in front of Taylor. "How the hell did you do that?"

Taylor had taken off his coat and was straightening his shirt sleeves. "Do what?"

Syrus blinked at the other man and folded his arms over his chest. "No seriously. She would have bruised any of us."

Jack noticed several other packmates listening for an answer.

Taylor laced his fingers together and looked up at Syrus. "Years of practice."

Syrus continued to watch the other man, waiting for a more complete answer. Then he looked at Lyra's back. "What makes him so special?" When an answer didn't come, Syrus gave a huff and went back to the chess game.

Bishop nodded to Jack from the leather chair he sat in, between Taylor and Victor. Jack nodded back as he made his way to the other man. Jack shoved his hands in the front pockets of his jeans as he stared down at Bishop.

"You ready for this, Jack?"

Jack was somewhat surprised at Bishop's question, though the tone was even and pleasant, the question alone told Jack that Bishop worried about the outcome of Mathew's master plan.

Jack sighed. "As ready as I'm going to get."

Bishop nodded.

Victor snorted. "Like any of us could actually be ready for any of this."

Jack fully agreed with Victor's statement, but he knew better than to make his agreement known. Jack knew he had to appear in control for his packmates. It was important they have confidence he was able to take care of them. Showing any sign of weakness now would worry his pack and make them weak. Jack understood how strong his pack needed to be if this alliance was to work. They certainly were not strong enough on their own.

For the next fifteen minutes there was a steady stream of arrivals. There was an anxious tension in the room no one was mentioning. People were pretty quiet until the arrival of Pack D.

Once he walked in, Grant scanned the room. His gaze locked on Lyra and he smiled. Grant walked over to one of the empty areas on the bar.

Jack tensed and spared a glance at Ryan, who stood to Jack's left. Ryan's face was blank but his eyes could have burned a hole through Grant's head. Jack prepared to jump in if needed. Lyra turned, she and Grant locked in a staring contest. Lyra looked annoyed while Grant seemed amused.

Justin spoke as he moved to stand shoulder to shoulder with Lyra. "What can I get you, Grant?"

The other man smirked and spoke without breaking eye contact. "Irish Whisky, please."

Hazel sat up a little straighter and Ryan tensed further. Jack had no idea why his packmates were reacting this way. Justin looked from Grant to Lyra. When Jack saw the bottle Justin pulled out, it clicked. Only one person drank that stuff: Lyra. Jack took a deep breath. This was not good.

There was a knock at the door and Jack turned to Ryan. "We are both answering that."

Ryan slowly turned to face Jack. His face blank but his eyes were burning. Jack knew Ryan would keep his thoughts to himself. There was a beat as they stared at each other then Ryan turned and opened the door.

Before Jack could get a good look at the two people in the hall the male, about six-foot-two, barreled past him. The man was fast enough that all Jack and Ryan could do was watch as he shot though the kitchen, scooped up Lyra and proceeded to twirl in circles, surrounding her in a bear hug. Lyra had given an initial squeal of shock, but quickly squeezed the large man back.

"You'll have to excuse my Second. He does this every time. He's very attached to his cousin." The low female voice came from beside Jack.

It was Graham, Jack relaxed. Ryan must have come to the same conclusion because Jack heard him exhale. But that also could have been because Grant wandered off after Graham swooped in.

Jack turned to the woman next to him. She was about five-foot-six, with shoulder length brown hair and large pale blue eyes. She was pretty.

Jack put out his hand. “Jack Hastings.”

The woman smiled and took it. “Rachel Morrison, Alpha of Pack C. Obviously that is my second, Graham.”

Jack didn’t know why but he already liked this woman, he could tell she would be someone he could trust. After a few seconds, Jack looked up to see Graham put Lyra down and begin introducing himself to Seth, and Justin. Hazel must already know him because she was demanding a hug.

By eight-fifteen everyone was present. Most were seated in the pre-moved furniture. Jack pulled one of the bar stools and moved to sit in front of the kitchen, right next to the side of the bar. From here he could see the entire room. Jack could lean on the counter if he wanted but somehow he knew that would be a sign of weakness.

The room was dead silent. Even Justin was completely serious, sitting on the floor leaning against the arms of the couches their packmates sat in. Ryan remained standing until he looked about the room, then the fact he was the only one standing seemed to make him uncomfortable. He moved to the stool on the other side of Lyra. He stilled just a moment before picking the stool up and maneuvering his way through the furniture so he could be next to Jack. Ryan knew as Second he needed to help the strong showing by backing the Alpha.

Mathew broke the silence. "Well Jack, this is your turf. How would you like to run this?"

Jack knew the other man was right, but he sure didn't want to be the one to set the standard. Jack glanced at his pack. Both Hazel and Lyra smiled encouragingly at him. His pack knew how important it was he be the one to speak, to show his authority over his pack. Then he caught Seth trying to bail Jack out. Seth had a flat hand against his chest then turned his wrist so that his hand was palm up. Jack shook his head, he should have thought of that on his own, he was more nervous than he thought.

"Introductions would be best. We'll start at the far side and work our way over. Give some information about your pack. That way we get a grasp on how it is run and what the pack members are like."

As if he couldn't hold it in any longer, Victor laughed. "Yes, we want to know all the latest gossip. Who is on the outs with who? Is there really going to be another Terminator movie?"

About a third of the room laughed.

One of the Weres Jack didn't know yelled, "Yes!"

Bishop rolled his eyes to the ceiling.

Victor put out his hand and Taylor slapped a bill into the other man's palm.

Jack wasn't sure he wanted to know, but it shattered a good amount of tension in the room. The two women on the end inclined their heads in unison. Jack thought it was a little creepy. They were both light brunettes, each with a braid halfway down their back. The one who spoke was shorter, maybe five-foot-three. The other was about five-foot-ten. Both were thin but athletic.

"I am Cassandra, Alpha to Pack X. This is my Second, Nina. We are the pack made up of the bands playing at SWU. There are thirteen of us in total. Our third band mate, Maria, then two five-person bands. We have six females in total. I am told that's unusual for the PNWU packs. As for our pack life, we travel a lot as a group so our office is more of a place to crash. Borderline pigsty in comparison to this place. Do not expect anything other than soda and booze from us."

Jack felt a sense of pride from that statement. He was proud of his pack. There were several mumbles of agreement from the majority of the Alphas. That surprised Jack. What had they done with the money given to them?

Victor was dangling a cinnamon twist above his mouth. "Don't expect this from anyone. They are the only pack I know with a resident baker." Then the twist plopped into his mouth.

Syrus leaned forward on the couch. "No she isn't, and no you can't have her or borrow her for parties." He leaned back again.

Sadie rolled her eyes and smacked him.

Then a brownie smacked him in the head.

Justin grabbed it before it hit the floor. "Dude, score." Then shoved the entire thing in his mouth.

It was borderline chaos for a second. Half the room was talking at once, no one mentioning any serious topics. Graham held his arms up in the air and clapped twice at his cousin across the room. Another brownie went flying. It took four tries before one was not intercepted.

People were getting up to fill their plastic plates. The mood was light and for that moment Jack knew this plan could succeed. If everyone wasn't so bent on avoiding the reason they were all here. Sighing, he knew they had to get on track.

He stood and used his best authoritative voice. "Okay, let's get back to business. Some of us do have to work tomorrow."

There was some grumbling and people went back to their seats. Another brownie smacked Syrus in the face, but this time he caught it before Justin could. Jack turned to Lyra, who was giggling.

"Lyra, please stop throwing food at people." He was trying to sound serious and failing.

She just grinned at him before a brownie was launched in his direction. Lyra burst out laughing. Hazel had done it, but she didn't have the best arm. Ryan caught it before it hit his shirt. Ryan lifted his eyebrows at the women before taking a bite.

Victor waved a hand in the air. "You see why I like it down here better, they're more fun and the have food and nice things. Bishop, why don't we have nice things?"

Bishop gave his Second a droll stare. Mathew coughed.

Shaking his head, Jack turned to the next pack and motioned for them to speak.

They were made up of two men and one woman. The taller man spoke. "My name is Charlie. I am Alpha to Pack T. This is my Second and wife Marissa. With us is one of our packmates, Boone."

There was a good amount of mumbling around the room. Most people knew about the Were couple that survived training. But very few people knew who they were. On top of that they had one of the males whose file was pulled. Apparently that story was already circulating.

Charlie waited until the murmuring died down to continue. "Most of our pack is from the Vancouver area. As a general rule we spend most of our time outdoors. We don't usually make appearances. I'm sure by all the muttering you all know why we would choose to make ourselves scarce. We thought about it and seeing as how our pack is only nine, it would be nice to have a wider base of trust."

The woman, Marissa, put her hand on Charlie's thigh. It was one of those comforting gestures. The two of them had a harder time in some ways than anyone else.

After waiting a beat, the next Alpha leaned forward to gain the group’s attention. He was about six-two with almost black hair. With him on the leather couch were two men with light brown hair.

"I am Reginald, but please, please call me Reggie. I am the Alpha for SWU Pack B. I have two Seconds, both are here." He gestured to each man as he said their name. "This is James and Dean. No that's not a joke, those are actually their birth names. We are the other large SWU pack with thirteen. We make up about half of the students that were at the Christian student group. Please don't worry, we are not the ultra-conservative group. We just switched them days because they had an event that night. The irony is not lost on us, by the way.”

Grant waited a beat before speaking. "My name is Grant. I am Alpha of PNWU Pack D. This is my Second, also James, but he goes by Jay. Our pack is twelve members strong. Since we're sharing, we were a sociology study group in the meeting room of the library. We're on the eleventh floor and at any given time there are at least two of us up there. I'm starting to wonder if my pack actually have homes."

There were several snickers, as apparently Pack F wasn't the only one that spent most of their time together.

"We actually have two doctors in residence in our pack, so whether this alliance idea comes through or not, at least all of you now know where medical attention can be found."

That surprised Jack. Grant didn't really strike him as the 'volunteer to help others' type. It made him think more of the other man. Before the next Alpha could speak, Jack's attention was drawn to Lyra, who jumped and gasped.

Not a second later 'Hail to the Chief' began to play. Jack knew that was a family member's ring. As she was pulling it out of her pocket, Grant's phone began to play 'It's hard out here for a Pimp'. From Rachel's reaction, Jack knew it was probably something bad.

Lyra didn’t even look at her phone. She and Graham looked at each other, eyes wide. Graham went straight out the door while Lyra maneuvered her way around some furniture.

The first thing she said when she put her ear to the phone was, “Hold on a sec.” Once she was out the door, Jack turned back to see his pack exchanging worried glances. Jack looked at Rachel, they made eye contact for a moment, neither of them liked the situation.

Oddly enough it was Grant that broke the silence. "They are cousins." He was making sure to encompass the entire room as he spoke.

Jack felt more than saw Ryan stiffen.

"It is most likely a family emergency of some kind."

There were several understanding murmurs. Jack was curious how exactly Grant knew that?

There were a few minutes of idle chatter, as if everyone decided to take a break until the situation in the hallway was resolved.

Jack turned to Ryan. "Can you hear what is going on out there?"

Ryan shook his head, smiling. "No, both of them walked into the elevator before discussing whatever the problem was."

"How did Grant know they are related? He walked away before Graham introduced himself."

Ryan shrugged. "Good hearing."

The pack office door opened and the room went quiet. Graham gave a cross between a salute and a wave to Rachel. Lyra brushed passed her cousin. She looked worried. She walked into the room with all eyes glued to her, even a confused look from her cousin. Lyra had her hands folded in front of her and her head tilted down when she stopped facing Jack. To the rest of the room she was being incredibly submissive to her Alpha. But she was giving Jack direct eye contact, though no one but Jack and Ryan could see that the look on her face was definitely not submissive.

"Jack, there is a family issue Graham and I must go to attend to."

It took Jack a moment to realize that to the rest of the room she sounded like she was asking permission. Jack had not been aware Lyra could play political games that well. Keeping the surprise off his face, Jack nodded.

"Very well, call me when things are finished and I will get you up to speed."

Lyra inclined her head a little lower, but still managed to keep eye contact, before turning and with Graham walked out the door.

A big part of Jack wanted to go with Lyra, to help with whatever put worry in her eyes but he knew he couldn't. Instead he turned and motioned to Finn. The tall man stood up, making most of the room crane their necks.

"My name is Finn I am Alpha for Pack A here at PNWU. My Second here is Ben. My pack is made up of the students in the lab at the time of the incident. Though we are a larger pack we are organized, pretty much what you would expect from a pack of science geeks." Finn's lips twitched into a tiny smile as he sat down.

Jack wasn't sure he had ever heard the other man make a joke before.

The Pack I Alphas exchanged glances before the male Alpha spoke. "My name is Rafael and this is my co-Alpha Gina. We are part of Pack I. Our pack is sixteen strong. Eight of each sex. We therefore decided two leaders could represent the needs of the group better than one. We each have a Second, though they are not with us tonight. My second is Robin and Gina's Second is Kane. I believe we are the largest of all forty packs."

As Rafael finished, Jack noticed the SWU Alphas exchanging glances. Apparently they could not imagine having a pack that size. Jack could relate. He loved his pack but fourteen Weres was a lot to handle.

Next was Rachel. She gave the group a sly smile. "I have a feeling I'll be one of the few Alphas people remember tonight, seeing as my Second, Graham has ditched me." There were a few chuckles. Despite being alone in a room full of strangers, Rachel seemed at ease.

"My name is Rachel and I am the Alpha to Pack C as SWU. We, I suppose, are a small pack, at ten people, six of which are female. We make up the techies from the concert."

She smiled again and turned to Mathew who was seated next to her on an ottoman.

Mathew smiled back and shrugged. "Most of you already know me, I'm Mathew, Alpha to PNWU Pack J. My Second Mason is with me as is one of our packmates Dylan. My pack was just a random matching of people in the library but considering that, we get alone quite well." He shrugged again, at a loss of what else to say.

Bishop turned to his left so the other Alphas could see his face. Jack knew Bishop trusted Pack F, which was why he turned away from them. As far as Bishop was concerned this was an audition for the SWU packs, not the PNWU ones.

"I am Bishop, this is my Second, Victor."

Victor took the opportunity to give the entire room a beauty pageant wave. Syrus matched him until his sister punched him in the stomach. Bishop ignored the lot of them.

"I am the Alpha of pack M. With us today is a packmate, Taylor." Then he leaned back in his chair.

Jack wasn't sure he wanted to let his packmates introduce themselves so he piped up just as he saw Syrus open his mouth.

"Thank you for coming. As Mathew already said, my name is Jack."

He lifted his right arm toward Ryan. "This is my Second, Ryan. And that group over there from next to Taylor over is the rest of Pack F. Much like Pack J, we are four smaller groups thrown together in quarantine."

There was a moment of quiet as introductions were absorbed, and Jack knew, at least for him, it was going to be a struggle to remember all these names. Cracking his neck, Jack turned to Mathew.

"Okay Mathew, how about telling us exactly what it is you have in mind."

Mathew shifted in his chair. "Well, to start with, I know seven out of ten of us have been experiencing the same problems with PNWU's Pack L."

There were some mumbles and exchanged looks, Jack notices his packmates simmer a little at the reminder.

"It also looks like six out of the seven of those who are Pack L's focus are with us today."

There were more glances.

"Okay I take it back, before the family phone calls, we had six of the seven here."

Cassandra swiped her braid back over her shoulder. "Kipling would have been here but his band had a gig that could not be canceled on short notice. He will be at the meeting for Pack M Tuesday."

The room was so quiet Jack could hear people breathing. Finn leaned forward, looking the Alphas he knew in the eyes.

"What exactly are we discussing here, Mathew?"

Mathew sighed, momentarily looking tired. "The entire story was not told to me until Friday. Apparently the scientists wanted to rearrange the packs."

There was a burst of sound as most of the room, did everything from standing to screaming.

Jack knew of one solution. He looked over at Seth. The other man nodded once before letting out a high pitched whistle. After the initial yelps and cursed the room shut up. Most of Pack F reached over to smack Seth.

Mathew continued. "Thank you for that..." He looked at Seth expectantly.

"Seth."

Mathew nodded. "Seth. Anyway, the scientist took the final training files and decided we could be best used if they put us in packs with those possessing similar abilities, fast with fast, weak with weak, et cetera. They started two months ago by kidnapping the fastest female Were there is. They did this with the idea that the six males would come without struggle because they would not leave the female alone. Overall, it's a good plan. The female however, they underestimated, and she somehow managed to get away. I believe they had her for a week."

Grant interrupted Mathew. Turning in his chair to look directly at the other man, his expression surprised. "Lyra is the fastest female Were there is? Since when?"

That made Jack angry, but more than that he wanted to know how Grant knew Lyra. As far as Jack knew, Lyra didn't socialize with other packs, yet this was the second outside Were that seemed to know her.

Adam answered Grant, and his tone didn't seem very happy. "She lied on the endurance tests. She purposefully appeared slower than she was. We have no idea how they figured her out."

Grant stared off as he leaned back in his chair. Jack really wanted to know what the other Alpha was thinking.

Mathew pushed on. "It seems when the scientists failed, for some reason or another, Pack L took over. They have been bribing and vaguely threatening those seven wolves. With the female again they acted differently. My understanding is they physically attacked her on several occasions."

There were more disgruntled murmurs.

"Her packmates however have been helping her fight them off. But these instances got me to thinking, those of us that can be trusted should join together just in case they put more effort in to separating us."

When he finished, the packs were whispering amounts themselves. This time no one tried to call the meeting back to order, at least not for several minutes. Jack wasn't sure where to go from here. As the conversations died down, Ryan spoke so the room could hear him.

"I have an idea. Let's have a kind of Q and A. The resident pack asks questions first. Then questions can be asked of the resident pack."

There seemed to be a general agreement. Hastily Ryan stepped in with the first question.

"Of the Alphas and Seconds, how long have you known about the advances being made by Pack L?"

It was obvious some of them didn't want to answer, but Jack agreed with the question. Jack wanted to know how many packmates thought like Ryan, Cole and especially Lyra.

Mathew started. "Exactly one week today."

Bishop cleared his throat, Jack could tell he was unhappy about his answer. "Friday."

Charlie shifted and looked Boone in the eyes. After a staring contest for about ten seconds, Charlie looked at the group at large, frowning. "About forty minutes ago."

Cassandra whipped her braid again. "Matthew told me. I plan to kick Kipling's butt for not telling me." She didn't seem very pleased either.

Rachel crossed her arms. "Thursday, but I have a sneaking suspicion Graham did not know about his cousin." Her lip twitched slightly but her eyes stayed dark.

Reggie sighed. "Yesterday, but I had been hoping it had been an isolated incident."

The room was quiet again.

Hazel leaned forward on to her elbow. "What are your pack dynamics like? I know that sounds trivial, but if the pack dynamics are different enough we might not be compatible as a group. It would be harder to find middle ground to base all this on."

Jack was surprised; that angle had not occurred to him.

Bishop answered first. "We are a lot like you and Mathew's packs are. There is camaraderie that would not be there otherwise. We might not always get along but we always look out for each other. There is no true outsider. Loners yes, outsiders no."

When no one else answered, Hazel looked around the room. "What, that's it? One answer? You mean to tell me all of us run the same way?"

Rachel tilted her head. "Perhaps that is why we are all successful. The system is not perfect but we manage just fine."

There were maybe a dozen more questions over the next hour, two of which were disregarded because despite what Syrus, Justin, and Victor thought, it was not important to know everyone's favorite kind of cheese. In to the second half Grant asked one that made Jack more suspicious of the other man.

"So what type of Alpha is Jack? I want to know if all our styles are compatible and as his pack, you're the ones to know."

It wasn't the question that tipped Jack off, it was Hazel's jumped in response.

"Jack is a good Alpha, Grant. He would always come to the rescue if he knew we needed him."

The two of them stared at each other and Grant narrowed his eyes. If Hazel's phone hadn't gone off Jack had no idea what would have happened.

Jack knew that ring, but he didn't say anything as Hazel picked it up and walked toward his office. When Hazel got her new phone, Lyra snatched it and gone through all the ring tones to pick one for whenever she called. Lyra spent a half hour doing this, that's how he knew 'Flight of the Bumblebee' meant Lyra was calling. Jack was somewhat annoyed he hadn't gotten a call.

The questions went on without Hazel.

Jack noticed the moment Ryan stiffened beside him. Jack turned enough so only Ryan would hear him.

"What?"

Ryan leaned in. "Lyra just told Hazel not to say anything because I could hear her and odds were others could too."

Now Jack was baffled. "You could hear Lyra?"

Ryan smiled. "No, I just heard Hazel say there was no way my hearing was that good. But after that Hazel hasn't said much."

Jack thought about that a moment, what could have happened?

After another few minutes, Hazel joined the group again. Several people in Pack F were eyeing her.

When there was a lull, she spoke directly to Rachel. "I've been instructed to tell you that you probably will not see your Second for a day or two."

Rachel just nodded once.

After that the meeting slowly wound down and within the next half hour people began to leave. At ten-thirty it was just Pack F left in the office, sprawled all over the furniture or in Syrus's case, the floor.

After several halfhearted attempts, Jack finally got his pack back on topic. "So are we in or out?"

At first no one answered.

"In," rumbled Adam.

"Yeah." Bruce sighed.

Several verbal and non-verbal agreements later, Jack texted Mathew telling him was in.

No one seemed ready to move.

Justin swung so he was upside down on his leather chair. "Ugh, I have to be at work in twelve hours."

There were several grumbles telling Justin to shut up.

A few seconds later, Syrus spoke from the floor. "So what did Lyra have to say?"

Hazel didn't speak for a few seconds, as if weighing her answers. "She wanted to tell me they were okay and she might not be around for the next few of these meetings and asked if I would go in her place."

There was more silence, thicker this time.

Ryan shifted, folding his arms. "Why does she want you to go?"

Jack knew Ryan didn't mean it the way it sounded, he hoped Hazel did too.

"Because neither of you think like her and she wants to know what happens. I'm the closest she has to getting the perspective she would from going herself. Plus I'm a girl."

"What does that mean?" Ryan sounded both confused and frustrated.

"You bring a girl with you and you look more diplomatic. You're better representing your pack because both sexes are present."

Jack never thought of that and he would put money on it being Lyra's idea.

"How is her family?" This from Sadie, concern threading through her voice.

Hazel smiled. "They're all fine now, just dealing with the backlash. One of her uncles has a broken arm but other than that there's just minor injuries."

No one said anything for a few minutes.

Justin pulled out his cell phone while still upside down and put it to his ear. He was on for quite a while before whoever was on the other side answered.

"So, where am I meeting you?"

There was a pause as the person answered him.

Justin snorted. "Don't give me that. I'm supposed to be your watchdog tonight and I can't abandon my post. It will make me look bad in front of the other hounds."

Another pause as, Jack assumed, Lyra spoke.

"Don't make me hunt you down, girlie. You know I have the best nose in the pack."

Whatever Lyra said made Justin lose his playful expression.

"Fine. Then I'll be at you're place in an hour, end of story." He hung up the phone and slid it back in his pocket. Justin folded his arms and closed his eyes but continued to sit with his head less than a foot from the floor.

Within the next hour, the pack dwindled down to Jack and Seth. Jack was still on his stool and Seth sat across from him in a leather chair. Seth had his arms crossed and the two of them were staring at each other.

"I don't like it, Jack."

Jack snorted. "Don't like what? There's quite a lot going on." Jack himself couldn't figure out half of it.

Seth shifted in his seat. "Any of it. Something's not right and it's affecting everything else. I mean, the project has all but left us alone for over a year and now all of a sudden they want to rearrange us. They start with Lyra, who's been not exactly lying to us but withholding quite a bit. I mean, I knew she was secretive, that's just who she is and I accept that about her but now we are getting into territory that could harm us all and she still keeps her mouth shut. What is she clinging to so badly?

“Then Mathew comes along with an almost too convenient solution. I admit it is a good idea, but part of me can't help wondering if this isn't some kind of test, set up without our knowledge to see how all of us react."

Jack hadn't thought of that last part. Were they playing right into the scientists' hands or doing the right thing to protect themselves?

"And what the hell is up with Ryan?" Seth sounded almost disgusted.

Jack went still, trying not to give away his suspicions. "What do you mean?"

Seth shifted again and gave Jack a sarcastic look. "You're kidding right? How could you miss it? The last week he's been agitated and antsy. Not to mention practically hanging off Lyra. I mean I understand he's been watching her the last few weeks, but Cole's not freaking out. Even accounting for how worried Ryan might be simply because of who he is, it doesn't account for all of it." Seth watched Jack, expecting him to agree.

"I'm sure it will be over as soon as this thing blows over. I'm more worried about Lyra and her family. I'm curious as to what exactly happened."

Seth grunted his agreement. The two of them sat there a while longer in silence, lost in their own thoughts. Jack had no idea what he was going to do to get his pack through this. There was too much going on and he didn't have all of the information. Somehow he knew this was going to be something that would make or break them as a community and he couldn't help but think the latter was more likely.

Chapter 6

Justin was getting impatient. He had been waiting in hallway outside Lyra's apartment for fifteen minutes. When he talked to her on the phone, she had been far too adamant about him not meeting her anywhere. Justin had met some of Lyra's family; it shouldn't have been that big of a deal. She had been so adamant he was tempted to follow her trail from the office just to see what she felt needed hiding. He hadn't, but she was now fifteen minutes later than when she knew he would be here. She knew he would sniff her out. If she wanted to hide so badly than she should have been here on time.

The door to the outside started to open. He knew it was his littermate before it opened enough for him to see her. When he did see her, he growled. She glowered back at his as she headed for her front door.

"Don't start with me, Justin."

She was covered in cuts and bruises. She had a long slash in her forehead that went down to her right temple. Justin could see a row of neat little stitches. There was a bruise forming on her left cheekbone and her lower lip had a small split. Justin looked down to see her knuckles were raw from use. Her jeans and college logo hoodie prevented him from seeing much else.

As she opened the front door, the boys came wiggling up to her, jumping up and down in their excitement. Lyra dropped her keys on the counter and flopped on to the floor so she was at the same level as the two squirming dogs. Justin shut the door and leaned against it watching her. They both knew she was avoiding him and he was determined to wait her out. She ignored him a good five minutes before she cracked. In any other situation Justin would have smiled, patience was not one of Lyra's strong suits.

"What, Justin?" She was talking to him but refused to look at him, burying her face in Fizgig's fur.

"What happened, Lyra? I know you weren't jumped again, or else you wouldn't have the stitches."

Justin swore he heard a sob bubble up from Fizgig's fur. That surprised him.

"I gave my word I wouldn't tell you, any of you." Lyra took her word much more seriously than most the people in the twenty-first century. That only worried him more.

"Lyra." His tone came out almost scared.

She finally looked up at him, her eyes were glossy. "It's nothing like that, I promise."

He was a little relieved but there was a twinge of jealousy. "Would you tell Hazel?"

She looked away from him, which was answer enough. "She already knows. It's kinda hard to keep secrets from the person you lived with for three years." Then she turned her attention back to her dogs.

Mogwai half crawled into her lap and was looking up at her. Fizgig was sitting in front her but facing Justin, so it was easier for her to play with his fur. Both of them could obviously sense Lyra was upset.

"I want to tell you I swear. I just...can't."

Her pain made Justin's heart ache. "Can I do anything? At least, have all of your injuries been taken care of?"

She nodded.

Justin knew he wouldn't get anywhere. There was only so far he could push her when it came to her family. They were like the mob "Then we're going to bed. Kick Mogwai off you so you can change into pjs."

She got up, patting both dogs on the head before walking back to her room. He gave her a few minutes before following her.

It was a secret Justin and Lyra kept. As far as he knew, she hadn't even told Hazel. Both of them were not the most social of creatures. Knowing that, they took solace in each other's company. After a bad or trying day it was not uncommon for Justin to sleep over at Lyra's or Lyra at his place. They would snuggle up in bed together and just sleep. There was nothing sexual about it, it was just physical contact.

Justin was worried about his littermate. He worried even more when he crawled into bed and she cuddled against his chest in the fetal position with her head resting under his chin. Justin wrapped his right arm around her, rubbing slow circles on her back. He couldn't help wondering how much worse things were going to get.

Chapter 7

Usually Kelly was into work at five AM. So it wasn't too big of a deal to be at Lyra's door at nine. He didn't know Lyra well, beyond the occasional threat to his manhood they didn't talk much. Kelly liked a challenge though, especially with women. Not that he wanted Lyra, or any of the girls in his pack for that matter. He just found the challenge women presented enjoyable.

Justin answered the door; another packmate he didn't know well. The other man didn't look like he had slept a full night.

"What happened? You look like hell."

Justin snorted but moved so Kelly could come in. Cole warned him about the dogs. They were huge and one was a Rottweiler. How did she get away with having one of those? Walking in, he bent down and patted both dogs. Apparently they were not appeased because as he stood, the furry dog nudged Kelly so hard he lost his balance. Luckily, he got his arm out fast enough to catch himself on the wall.

"Geez."

Justin was laughing at him as the other dog head butted him in the knee.

"They don't like when you don't give them enough attention."

Kelly looked down as the furry panting beast who started leaning on him. Thankfully, Lyra came walking down the hallway and both dogs bolted over to her. She smiled and patted each on the head, and they were wiggling like crazy. But they didn't accost her as she moved past them and into the kitchen.

As she was getting her coffee, Kelly got a good look at her face, as well as some very large scratches across both her upper arm. It looked like she had stitches in both arms and her face. Kelly frowned and felt his anger surge.

"What? Are we pretending she's not all banged up?" He looked at Justin.

Kelly knew Justin hadn't caused the damage but that didn't mean he couldn't get angry at the other man.

Justin's eyes flashed. "Yes."

Kelly folded his arms and flexed as he turned to Lyra. She watched him over her mug.

"And why would we do a stupid thing like that?"

She lowered her mug, eyes narrowing. "Because my face will be mostly healed by tomorrow and the rest will follow Thursday. If I'd known you were going to be here so early, I'd have put a sweatshirt on."

Kelly flexed again, "And why are we not telling anyone?"

He hated secrets in the pack.

She put her mug on the counter. "Because it doesn't have anything to do with the pack. I can't give them the answers they'll want. Either deal with it, Kelly, or leave." She sounded bitter.

She spun around and stormed down the hallway. She came back before he could say anything to Justin. She put on a thin long sleeved v-neck that covered everything but the bruise on her face and the cut in her forehead.

She grabbed her mug and glared at him. "There, better? Out of sight, out of mind."

Justin walked over to stand next to her. He put his hand under her chin and moved it delicately into the light and began inspecting her face. She glared at him, but he ignored it.

"You heal fast, Lyra. The stitches are gone."

Kelly didn't miss the panic that flew through her eyes.

"Weres heal faster, period, Justin. They're quick dissolving stitches, they only last twelve hours."

Kelly couldn't read the look on Justin's face as he let Lyra's chin go.

Backing away he looked at Kelly. "All right she's all yours. You kids have a nice day."

With that Justin grabbed his bag off the floor and left.

Kelly kept his arms folded and watched Lyra. "Wow. You two have a fight?"

She didn't even look at him, busying herself about the kitchen. "Of sorts. Coffee?"

Kelly nodded and walked into the kitchen. He was standing right next to her when he sniffed and froze.

"You smell of Justin." Kelly couldn't hide his shock.

He might not have the best nose but it was still pretty good. Lyra had just showered, her hair was still wet. If the contact was casual the scent would have washed off in the shower. He never would have suspected Justin and Lyra as a couple. Now that he was thinking about it, he supposed it could make sense.

She finally looked at him as she handed him a latte from her machine. Lyra's tone was so level he could have balanced on it.

"So, what's your point?"

Kelly took the cup. "What do you mean so? You smell of him, after you've taken a shower. Do you know what that means?"

She moved toward the table with a heaping bowl of Corn Pops. "I know what YOU think it means." She started eating, as if nothing was out of the ordinary.

Kelly sat down across from her trying to keep the shock from his voice. "Okay then, enlighten me."

For a moment he wasn't sure she was going to, then she sighed. "Don't say anything to anyone. Justin and I like to keep it between us. I mean it." She glared at him.

Kelly took a sip for the foamy mug. "Fine."

He hated secrets, but Lyra seemed just agitated enough to pique his interest.

She inhaled deeply. "We just sleep together from time to time. Nothing else, literally just sleeping."

Kelly could believe that but he was still surprised. Letting her off the hook, he changed the subject. "So, what's on the agenda today?"

Lyra drained her mug. "Work. We'll be heading out quarter to noon and won't be back until three-thirty."

Kelly raised his eyebrows. "You work at home. Where are we going?"

Kelly racked his brain for anything that could possibly take that amount of time.

She gave him a mischievous grin. "My other job."

Kelly instantly didn't like it. He didn't like the look on her face or the idea of a job he never heard of.

She spoke as she got a second cup of coffee. "Don't worry, Kelly, no one will make you join in." She smiled at him again.

The next two and a half hours were spent with her reading a manuscript and him reading a new fitness text, a hobby Kelly got a lot of flack for. He constantly read books on fitness and health. It wasn't just his job, he loved studying it.

Every once in a while he would try and coax hints out of Lyra about her other job. Lyra just smiled and would go back to reading. It wasn't until she came back from changing that he started to put two and two together.

"Don't take this the wrong way but you've got a great body." Kelly couldn't stop the words once they came out.

Lyra gave him a weird look. "And how am I *supposed* to take that?"

Kelly concentrated on using the right words. "You're very well proportioned and toned. I didn't mean it as a come-on, just as a fact."

He held his breath waiting to see if she took offense.

She didn't, she just nodded and grabbed a mat bag from behind the couch.

Kelly folded his arms again before following her to the door. "Should I have brought workout gear?"

Lyra waved her hand at him. "No you're cool. You can hang out in class or down on the main floor."

They had been walking a few minutes before Kelly caved. "Okay so what do you teach?"

He was dying to know. He kept imagining some kind of combat class.

She snorted. "Normally I only teach on weekends, mainly yoga. Today I'm covering for an instructor who was just fired. It's a lunchtime step class and an afternoon step class."

Kelly started laughing. "What are you certified to teach exactly?"

She gave him a look. "I'm glad this is so funny for you. I'm certified for the basics: several levels and types of yoga, step, cycling, kickboxing, dance aerobics..."

He burst out laughing. "What? You're a dance aerobics instructor? Are you kidding me? How did that happen?"

She shrugged. "One of the other instructors was hosting the training. It was only a hundred bucks, so I thought, why not?"

Kelly thought for a second. "You know my gym is hiring group instructors. You could do that full time and make a pretty good living."

She smiled. "I make decent money now. Plus I love both my jobs I don't want to do anything else."

After seeing her in class and interacting with her coworkers, Kelly agreed with her. He never saw Lyra that comfortable, content, and secure. He was happy for her, everyone should have something they love. They got out around five because a couple of students convinced her to do a spur of the moment yoga session. It was a whole new side of Lyra Kelly had never seen before, almost cheery. She was practically beaming when she walked over to him after the yoga class.

"Hey, so what do you want for dinner? We have two hours until the next macho man shows up."

Kelly chuckled as he stood up. "Yeah, tell Cole he's a macho man. I want to see that."

She grinned. "Seriously though, I don't feel like cooking, what do you want?"

He shrugged, he didn't know the area too well. "Pizza."

Lyra nodded. "Okay, let's go."

Kelly was glad he was walking behind her, then he didn't have to hide his smile as Lyra waved to about a dozen people on their way out. An older lady behind the front counter made some comment about attractive men that he didn't quite hear, but Lyra rolled her eyes.

Kelly was surprised by how well he and Lyra got along. She was perfectly relaxed and the two of them talked over a loaded pizza for quite a while. He couldn't believe how easy she was to talk to. She wasn't quite as gruff as she wanted everyone to think she was. Though he wouldn't dare tell her that. After a while they devoured the large pizza and were just talking when her phone rang. Kelly started laughing when 'Hungry Like the Wolf' started playing.

Lyra was laughing with him as she pulled out her phone. "What? You try finding a song involving wolves."

She looked down at the phone, giving a confused look before answering. "Hey Ryan, what's up?"

Kelly knew all the packmates swapped phone numbers a while ago, but he wouldn't have felt comfortable calling more than half of them. He watched as her eyebrows scrunched together.

"What are you talking about? Cole's staying with me tonight."

Kelly watched her stiffen and her voice took on a wary tone. Kelly stiffened as well; he didn't hear Ryan's response but he could tell he would not like it.

"We're at the pizza parlor down the street from the community center. What's your problem?"

Kelly could tell she was getting angry and it only increased as she listened.

"You have issues." Her eyes narrowed and she hung up.

Lyra looked up at Kelly. She was pissed. "Ryan has taken not only Cole's shift but just about every night shift for the next week. He's pissed because we're not at my apartment and now he's on his way down here. We have about ten minutes before Mr. Crazy rains his insanity all over us." As she finished she began scrolling through her contacts.

After a few seconds she became more agitated, and Kelly was guessing it went to voicemail. She was growling into the phone. Kelly was glad there were no other customers near them.

"You better call me as soon as you get this or I'll rip you a new one." She slammed the phone onto the table.

Kelly could see she was shaking with anger.

"What can I do?"

She blinked at him for a few seconds before standing up. "I need to run."

Kelly stood up with her. He waited as she swiped up all her stuff and followed her as she stalked out of the restaurant. If she was as fast as Jack made her out to be, Kelly wasn't sure how good of an idea this would be.

"Where are we going?"

She glanced at him as he came up next to her.

"Dog park. It's off leash."

Kelly knew his eyes widened. "You want me to take you to a dog park? Isn't that dangerous?"

Lyra gave a jerky shrug. "I've don't it before. The locals will recognize my wolf. They think I belong to Hazel."

Kelly was so shocked he couldn't think of anything to say. Lyra was letting people take her to a dog park, as if she was a family pet. Suddenly she stopped walking.

"We need to get a collar and a leash, crap. That means the boys will want to come." She turned to Kelly. "How do you feel about pretending to walk three dogs?"

Kelly was just about as shocked as he could get. "Yeah sure, are you telling me you have your own collar?"

Lyra nodded. "Yeah, my neck is smaller than my dogs are. It has a fake I.D. tag and everything." Then she turned left and sped up.

When Kelly was in step with her again her phone was playing 'Leader of the Pack' which seemed to be a song from the 1950s. Kelly swore as she pulled out her phone. If Jack was calling, someone was in trouble.

She looked over at him. "No, it's okay I called him first." Then the anger was back in her eyes. "Jack! Control your Second!"

Kelly was close enough to hear Jack's response. "Why? What did he do?"

"Are you at the office?"

Kelly was pretty sure she meant the pack office since Jack worked at a local TV station.

"No, should I be?"

Kelly didn't know how Jack did it. If Lyra was talking to him like that Kelly would have given her attitude but Jack sounded calm.

"Your Second has somehow swapped for every evening shift on your little schedule, except the nights I'm with littermates. The man is insane. He threw a fit when he showed up at my apartment and Kelly and I weren't there, and I mean threw a fit. I told him where we were but I'm too furious with the prick to stay put. So Kelly, the boys, and I will be at the dog park."

There was a pause for several long seconds. "I'll be right there." Then he hung up.

She didn't turn to look at Kelly as she put her phone away. "You don't have to stay, you know. Technically your time is up. After we get to the park you're more than welcome to leave."

Kelly snorted as their pace picked up again. "Not going to happen. I'm not leaving until after Jack gets here and things are settled. If Ryan really has lost it, I'm not leaving you with him."

Lyra stopped so suddenly Kelly bumped her shoulder. Before he knew it, she was hugging him. Her voice was so soft he could barely hear it. But he could hear the gratefulness in her tone loud and clear.

"Thank you!" She let go and started off again.

Kelly's thoughts were a whirlwind; he couldn't figure out where to start. Making the decision, he stowed all of it and concentrated on the moment. He didn't want anyone coming up on them without him knowing about it.

Within twenty minutes they were at the park. Lyra and her two dogs, or should he say 'Luna', were running like mad. Kelly had taken up a spot under a tree where he could see the whole park. He watched as Lyra ran full out across the park and her two dogs fought to keep up with her. She stayed within Kelly's line of sight but she wasn't staying still.

"Luna! Luna come here girl."

Kelly's attention shot to a group of tween girls walking a pack of tiny dogs. One of them moved slightly away from the rest and was patting her thigh and calling Lyra. To Kelly's complete surprise, Lyra came to her alter-ego's name. Lyra slowed her pace, started wagging her tail and letting her tongue loll. Making herself look as non-threatening as a wolf could. The girl didn't have to bend far, as Lyra's wolf form was a little over two-and-a-half feet tall. The girl was crooning down at Lyra when two other girls came and joined in.

Kelly stood up and walked over. The two 'real' dogs had no interest in the girls and flopped down on the grass ten feet away. When Kelly was a few feet closer than the dogs, Lyra wagged her tail a little harder and trotted over to him. The girls looked at him and giggled. Great, the tweens thought he was cute. Just what he needed. Kelly looked down at Lyra. He knew she found the girls' reaction priceless.

Kelly rolled his eyes. "Come on, *Luna*, let the girls walk their dogs." Kelly gave extra emphasis to the name.

There was more giggling before the one petting Lyra spoke. "Oh it's okay. We see her often enough to not be bothered by her. It's just so cool, you know, to be able to pet a real wolf. Even if she is domesticated."

Kelly bit back his laugh and the string of comments that went with it. He just patted Lyra's side and she wandered off.

"Yeah, it's pretty incredible." He gave them a tight-lipped smile before turning to follow Lyra.

Lyra was trotting toward the same hill Kelly had been sitting on earlier. Kelly looked up and saw why.

Coming over the hill was Jack, flanked on one side by Cole and Syrus, with Seth and Justin on the other. All five of them made a very intimidating image.

Their expressions were all dead serious. Seeing them made Kelly wonder why the scientists would want to go against them.

Kelly watched as Lyra froze mid-step, her furry head cocked to the side for a split second. Then her head whipped to the left. Hearing and smell were better in wolf form so it was a few seconds before Kelly and the other men saw what she was looking at.

The edge of the park had a nature trail and out of one clump of bushes Ryan, in wolf form, burst out into the park at a run. Kelly was close enough to hear his packmates' curses. They began turning to face the black wolf as he bee-lined for Lyra.

She put her front paw down and turned to stare at him with her lip pulled back. Kelly ran up to stand next to Justin. From there he could hear Lyra growling. When Ryan was about three yards away, he seemed to speed up. More cursing.

Kelly could hear Seth talking under his breath. "Did we have to do this in public?"

Kelly agreed. Ryan was being downright stupid. Ryan was maybe ten feet away when Lyra made a break for it. She shot past Ryan and straight for the nature trail, with her dogs coming out of nowhere to trail behind her. Ryan couldn't switch direction that easily and caught one of his own legs as he tried to turn mid-stride. Jack took advantage of the slip and grabbed the back of Ryan's furry neck. Ryan growled but before he could wiggle out of the grip, Seth was there with a leash and choke collar.

Syrus looked up at the people watching the scene with one of his charming smiles.

"Don't worry, folks. We members of the Wolf Owners League got our parks crossed. Our girl over there is in heat and by total mistake my friend here--" Syrus thumped Cole on the back as Seth handed the larger man the leash. "--forgot his dates and took this poor male wolfie to the wrong park."

Cole inclined his head apologetically and there were several comments by men nearby commiserating with the male wolf's plight.

As the group of them started after Lyra, Kelly could see why Seth handed off the leash. Cole and Ryan were the pack's strongest members, and Cole's grip on the leash was so tight Kelly wasn't sure how Ryan hadn't passed out yet.

The entire time they were strolling toward the woods, both Jack and Justin were calling 'Luna'. They were crooning and scolding, just like you'd expect an owner to do. They had been walking on the empty trail for about five minutes before Lyra's dogs came trotting up to Lyra's three littermates, giving Ryan a wide berth.

Seth was petting the furrier dog when he reached out for Kelly to hand him the leash. Once the bigger dog was on-leash, the same thing was done with the Rottweiler. Jack and Justin continued walking and calling for Lyra. The rest of them hadn't caught up yet when Justin stopped everyone with the wave of his hand. He motioned for everyone to stay put and stay silent as he took a step off the trail. Justin had the nose of the group and was probably pinpointing Lyra. Kelly chanced a glance down at Ryan. The wolf was seated on the cement, tail wrapped around his feet, completely still. Kelly didn't like it; he wanted to pummel Ryan.

Looking back he saw Justin hip deep in the bushes, looking down.

"Hey there, girlie. You're okay. We've got him on a leash and Cole's holding on real tight. Aren't you, Cole?"

The last part was louder, but he didn't look away.

Cole's voice rumbled loudly. "Hell yes I am, moron."

Cole gave the leash a yank so Ryan would know the insult was aimed at him. The wolf merely shifted his head to glance at Cole before turning back to watch Justin.

There was a second or two before Lyra appeared through the bushes, with Justin right on her tail. Ryan sat up and would have moved forward if Cole hadn't given a swift yank. Lyra bolted right behind Jack. Everyone seemed equally surprised. The Weres in human form all exchanged glances and Justin moved to stand beside Jack, giving Lyra more cover. Kelly wanted to move too, but he knew that would look too much like drawing lines in the sand, which was the last thing they needed.

Jack recovered, folded him arms and gave Ryan the meanest look Kelly had ever seen on Jack's face.

"What the hell do you think you're doing? Scratch that, Cole volunteered his apartment as a quiet place to settle this nonsense." His eyes shifted to Seth. "Seth, you have keys to Lyra's apartment, so you and Kelly drop off Fizgig and Mogwai, please."

Seth didn't answer, just nodded and turned with the dogs. Kelly gave the group one more glance before heading after him.

Chapter 8

Jack felt as if his heart was going to break. He preferred the overriding anger from earlier. But when the group spilt up, Jack, Lyra, and Justin climbed into Jack's dark blue Forrester. They originally put Lyra in the backseat. But as Justin closed the door after her, Lyra began to whine. Once Justin slid onto the seat and buckled up, Lyra climbed into his lap. She curled up into the tightest ball she could, but only about two-thirds of her fit in Justin's lap. Justin buried his hands in Lyra's fur. Neither Jack or Justin spoke the entire ride to Cole's apartment.

Cole's door was slightly open. Jack scanned the room before walking in. Both Lyra's and Cole's apartment complexes were owned by the same company, so the layouts were similar. The main difference was that the floor plans were flipped. Cole's kitchen was to the left side. It was also about a hundred square feet bigger.

Syrus was pacing back and forth between the kitchen and the couch. His hands in his pockets and his head was down.

Cole tied one end of Ryan's leash to his fridge. Jack had his doubts that would hold Ryan if the wolf really made an effort.

"Do you think that will hold him?"

Cole shrugged as he finished the complicated knot. "It will slow him the hell down."

Jack sighed. He did not need whatever this was right now. They were just lucky there wasn't a pack meet and greet tonight. Leaning out the door, Jack motioned to Justin it was safe to come in. Lyra stayed plastered to Justin's side the entire walk through the complex and still had not strayed. When Jack asked about it, Justin simply shrugged.

The pair of them walked in and Jack shut the door behind them. At least Ryan seemed to have calmed down. He was now lying on the floor but kept his eyes on Lyra. She did the same but from the safe distance of Justin's far side. Jack jumped as his phone rang and pulled it out. He didn't know the number but answered anyway, keeping one eye on Lyra and the other on Ryan.

"Hello?"

"What's wrong with my cousin?"

Jack pulled the phone from his ear. It was Graham and he sounded pissed. How did he have Jack's number? How had he known something was wrong?

Jack debated lying to the other man but pushed the idea away, it would take too long and he needed to deal with the problem at hand.

"She's going to be okay. I'm handling it."

There was a pause. "She's not answering her phone. I need to talk to her."

Jack tossed around a few answers. "She can't exactly talk on the phone right now."

There was panic and suspicion. "Why?"

Jack rubbed his face. "She doesn't have human vocal cords at the moment and I don't think she's shifting any time soon."

"Is she in the room with you?"

"Yes."

"Put me on speaker phone."

Jack did as the other man asked. "All right."

"Lyra? Can you hear me?" He sounded worried.

Lyra gave a quick high bark from the living room.

"Okay then." There was a heavy, relieved sigh. "I expect you to call me tonight." Then he hung up.

Lyra gave a small whimper and huddled in closer to Justin. Ryan lifted his head and began to growl. Before Jack knew what was happening, Lyra launched herself at Ryan and the two of them were growling and tumbling in the kitchen. There was a second of shocked silence before the room filled with swear words and the four of them rushed to the kitchen.

The two wolves were moving too fast to grab one of them. Jack knew as Alpha he had to do something. He rolled up his sleeves.

"Damn it, this is going to hurt."

Then he dove his arms into the fray and clamped on to the first sizable grip and pulled. There was some resistance, but after a few steps back Jack was relieved to see his arms were around a snarling Lyra. She was still trying to lunge for Ryan, but Jack's grip was too strong.

"Justin, sit on the couch!" It was an order Jack knew would be obeyed.

He slowly made his way back to the couch and plopped the fussing wolf onto Justin's lap. "Grab on to her and make you have a good grip."

After a few seconds, Justin nodded at Jack, telling him to let go. Jack's arms only had minor scratches. He shoved his face right up to Lyra's nose, making it impossible for her to look anywhere else. Her eyes snapped from the kitchen to Jack. Though she stopped snarling, her eyes still overflowed with anger.

"You stay right here until you calm the hell down. I mean it don't move." Jack knew he was growling at his littermate, but he was terrified out of his mind.

What was she thinking? Ryan was bigger and stronger than she was. She could have been seriously injured. She snapped her jaws at him as he moved away. It wasn't a threat, just to show she was unhappy with him.

"Hey Jack, you're gonna wanna see this." Syrus's tone brought Jack back toward the kitchen.

Syrus sounded confused and surprised. When Jack stood next to Cole and Syrus, he could see why. The wolf was licking a gash in his paw. Ryan had slashes and bites all over. None of them were fatal or close to it. Jack glanced back at Lyra who watched him, panting.

Ryan hadn't harmed a hair on Lyra's head. Jack couldn't see one scratch. Yet she managed to get Ryan wherever she could. What was going on?

Cole snapped his fingers to get Ryan's attention. The wolf looked up with his tongue still out.

"Ryan, man, change already so you can stop bleeding on my floor."

The wolf stood up and Ryan started changing. Jack was glad Ryan could change with boxers on. He had no idea where they would get clothing for him otherwise.

The shifting would hurry along the Were's already speedy healing process.

Around the time Ryan finished, there was a knock at the door.

"It's open," Cole bellowed.

Seth and Kelly walked in, both scanning the room. Seth's eyes landed on Ryan and narrowed in anger. Then he seemed to notice the claw marks across Ryan's back because he walked over and ruffled the fur on Lyra's head.

"Good girl."

Jack rolled his eyes and returned his gaze to Ryan. "Explain now and explain fast."

Ryan cracked his neck and reached around to unclip the collar before dropping it to the floor. "I got to Lyra's and I smelled her with Kelly. I figured they were out for dinner, no big deal. As I was pulling out my phone to see if I could meet them, I got a better whiff of Lyra's scent."

Ryan's hands became fists and his teeth clenched. Jack snuck a glance at Lyra. She was simply sitting on Justin's lap, her head towering above his. Both were watching Ryan.

"She reeked of Justin."

Jack's head snapped back to Ryan. "What?"

"Justin's scent was all over her and not in a casual way. That would have come off in the shower."

Both Lyra and Justin began growling.

Jack didn't even look at them. "Justin, Lyra stop it!"

The sound ceased. Jack knew how threatening he sounded.

Ryan was struggling to stay on topic, Jack could see it in his face.

"I smelled it as the phone was ringing and I went berserk. I'm not quite sure what I said exactly, but once I got their location I bolted from the complex. When I got to the pizza place I could smell them going in the opposite direction and I saw red. Before I knew it I tracked them to the dog park. I could smell Lyra in wolf form so I changed. Then I saw her. I just headed straight for her. I can't explain it. I just went nuts."

Complete silence filled the room for a full minute before Syrus moved toward the couch.

"No way. No. Way."

He stopped directly in front of Lyra, who looked up at him curiously. Syrus bent down and buried his face in Lyra's fur.

That gained growls from Ryan, Justin, and Seth. Lyra surprisingly stayed calm.

Syrus crouched down so he was at Lyra's eye level. "He's right. Now my sister's going to kill me." He stood back up and took a huge step away from the couch.

Lyra was off the couch so fast Jack barely saw her move. She was circling Syrus fast enough to keep him in one place, barking and snapping at him. Syrus looked down at her sadly, then sighing, he ignored her entirely.

Jack got a creeping feeling he didn't want to know what Syrus was about to say. Syrus looked at him, and Jack realized he must have sworn out loud. Lyra took the distraction to start changing.

Syrus side-stepped her and looked right at Ryan. "This isn't your fault. Not entirely anyway. You've been around Lyra almost every day for the past week or so right?"

Ryan nodded cautiously.

Before Syrus could open his mouth again, Lyra's long fingered hand was covering it. She looked so sad Jack hurt for her.

"Stop."

Syrus looked at her.

"If someone's getting thrown under the bus for this, it's going to be me."

Syrus gave Lyra a look Jack couldn't fully understand but when she removed her hand he let her be the one to continue.

She was refusing to look at anyone in the room. "Since the first few months in training, the girls noticed something the doctors did not and we've tried to keep it that way. We don't tell anyone who doesn't need to know. Which means you can't go sharing this. It isn't just the females of our pack, it's all of us."

Lyra took a slow deep breath and Jack knew he wasn't going to like this.

"We go into heat just like real wolves do."

There were several strong reactions but Lyra made a cutting motion with her hand and everyone quieted down.

"We noticed two hormonal reactions to the heat. The first is obvious. The second is less common. We call it the 'big brother' response. This is when the male does whatever he can to fight off males with the first reaction. Most males become aggressive. We try to keep to ourselves when in heat. The thing is, we can't smell it on ourselves, so generally someone else has to tell you." She trailed off.

Syrus waited a beat before cutting in; apparently he didn't want Lyra to be the only one going out on this limb.

He looked directly at Ryan. "You've been exposed to the hormone with little to no relief for the entire heat cycle. That's bound to make you out of your mind."

Cole folded his arms. "Then why am I not in the same place?"

Ryan answered him. "I spent most of the nights on her couch. The last couple of days it was just you and me and I was there for the nights. During the days there was more time spent in the fresh air." Ryan was keeping his voice and face perfectly blank, but his fists gave him away.

Syrus nodded. "Too much exposure is really bad. I can't even be around Sadie for more than five hours without twitching with violence."

The room was quiet for a few beats, then Justin stood. "Maybe it's the hormones, but I'm not comfortable leaving Lyra in Ryan's care."

Jack watched Ryan stiffen.

"Fine." Ryan strode straight out of the apartment, only partially slamming the door on his way out.

Lyra rubbed her face. "No one needs to watch me."

As the others started to make sounds of disagreement, Lyra narrowed her eyes.

"Enough!" She said it loud enough to be heard over everyone. "I'm packing up the dogs and myself and staying with family for the rest of the week. I'm needed there anyway. There are enough overbearing people there to see that I'm okay."

She walked over to Kelly and held out her hand. Kelly's eyes flickered to Jack before he pulled Lyra's keys and phone from his front pockets.

"They've been fed," Seth mentioned as she headed for the door.

Lyra nodded on her way out.

Jack scrubbed his face and grunted in aggravation. "This is just great. What the hell is going on around here? Suddenly there are overpowering hormones, mad scientists kidnapping people, secret alliances, threats from Pack L. Seriously, someone explain all this to me."

Jack knew no one had the answers, so he wasn't surprised when no one said anything. They were even past the point of sarcastic remarks.

"Fine, everyone go home. Seth, you're on call for the meet and greet if Ryan can't get himself together."

Seth nodded and a few minutes later, Seth, Jack, Justin, and Kelly were out the door.

Chapter 9

Cole and Syrus stared at each other for a few moments. Cole rubbed his hand back and forth over his very short hair, he missed his braids.

"Okay Sy, you know Ryan better than I do. That was pretty off behavior, even when you include the hormone stuff."

Syrus shifted his weight. "Yeah, but Ryan's got a thing for her. He doesn't say it, but I've seen him watch her interacting with her male littermates with jealousy. He wants that kind of connection with her and up until now, I thought he was finally getting there, but this is going to throw him way back. I think part of him realizes it and that's killing him. Plus, Ryan doesn't just lose control like that, ever. I'm sure that's a factor too. I'm thinking we should buy some booze and pay him a visit. Today he needs it."

Cole nodded. "I'm in. I'll split the bill with you."

Since becoming Weres, it took more alcohol to impair them than before. However it didn't prevent the hangover the next day, which was usually a killer.

Syrus snorted. "I'm getting stuff from the Fred Meyer down the street and raiding the pack office." He yanked the front door open.

Cole snatched his keys off the counter and followed Syrus out. This was going to be a long night.

Chapter 10

Jack sat in the pack office, waiting. He had been assured by Ryan that the other man would be there by six forty-five. Ryan still had five minutes but Jack was so agitated that every little thing was setting him off. He'd gotten a call at five from Lyra saying she was going to attend the meeting, but she would be arriving with her cousin Graham and his Alpha, Rachel. Jack told her they could meet him and Ryan in the Pack F office. That way they would know if it was safe for the entire group to attend Pack M's meet and greet. Jack was not looking forward to this. He really needed Ryan on good behavior and Lyra at the top of her game.

Jack heard the door and looked up from where he sat at the bar. Ryan walked in with heavily tinted sunglasses and slight stubble. He was wearing all black, a leather jacket, black T-shirt, and black jeans. It looked like he was trying for a more muscled James Dean look. He also looked like he hadn't slept. Ryan headed straight for the fridge and pulled out a beer.

"You look like crap. Are you going to be able to do this?"

Ryan drained the bottle and tossed it in the recycling bin. "Yeah, I'm fine, just hungover."

Jack groaned. That was just fantastic, his second was hungover and looked it.

“This is going to be real great.”

Ryan tilted his glasses down so he could look at Jack over the rims. "Jack, it will be fine. Just as long as there's no screaming or sudden movements." He moved the shades back over his eyes.

Jack rubbed his face. "That might be hard. Lyra's coming."

Ryan opened the fridge and popped open another beer. "Yeah I know. She sent me a text warning me and asking me if that would be a problem." He tipped the bottle back and downed half the contents. "I told her it wouldn't."

There was a knock at the door. Two seconds later it opened. Jack sighed. Lyra's way of warning them. When she stepped in though, Jack growled, as did Ryan. Her face had fresh scratches and bruises. Plus she was wearing a thin turtleneck so there was no way of knowing the extent of her injuries. She held up her hands as Graham stepped in behind her. He looked like he fared better, with only one long gash across his left cheek. He was favoring his left arm. Rachel came in after them, looking peeved but unharmed.

Jack growled as he turned to Lyra. "Explain."

There was a command in his voice that surprised him as much as Lyra, but he didn't show it.

She lowered her head a little, but still looked him in the eyes. "Family crap. I told you this when we were still in school. My family plays rough. It took me a long time to be accepted and I'm sure not going to back out now just because it pisses you off. Don't worry, I'm going to the meeting in wolf form, so no one will know."

Jack knew Lyra was hiding something. But he couldn't figure out where the missing information fit. He didn't say anything else, but he reminded himself to look into it later.

"Shall we head upstairs then?"

There where nods from the others in the room. Ryan finished his beer and Lyra began to change. It was not lost on Jack that she winced several times and her change took longer than usual.
He and Ryan exchanged glances. That answered the question of whether there were more injuries.

After she finished, they headed out the door and up the stairs.

Ryan spoke about halfway up. "Just tell me you had nothing to do with that and we can continue on just fine."

Lyra growled at him, but Ryan ignored her. Truth be told Jack had been wondering the same thing.

Graham kept moving but looked over his shoulder at Ryan. "You think that doesn't piss me off? That I wouldn't stop it if I could? She wouldn't have any more injuries if she hadn't crashed at my dad's last night."

The snap in Graham's voice kept everyone quiet until they were at the door of the Pack M office.

Victor answered with a grin until he saw the group and their expressions, then it dropped. "Whoa! What happened? Why is Lyra in wolf form?"

He dropped his voice so the Weres behind him wouldn't hear.

Rachel moved to walk past him. "Trust me I don't even know half of it and I don't want to know."

Victor gave a curious look but moved so they could walk in.

When they walked through the door, each of them were greeted by Bishop. As he and Rachel were speaking, Jack looked around the room. There were a good number of chairs that had probably been brought in just for the meeting. There was a kitchen but all it had was water and booze.

Pack M sat in a cluster.

The only female member was in the middle of eight men, all in suits. Her arms were folded and she wore jeans and a long-sleeved black shirt with white letters that read 'Bite Me!'. Jack chuckled. Poor woman, trying desperately to be independent amongst all the testosterone.

Bishop turned to follow Jack's gaze, then turned back, rolling his eyes.

"She wasn't wearing that when she got here. Must have hidden it under her clothes. Miriam tends to be like that. How are you, Jack?"

Bishop was trying to sound upset about his packmate's attire but there was a thread of amusement.

Jack reached out to shake the other man's hand. "I've been better. You?"

Bishop nodded. "Same."

He turned to shake Ryan's hand. There was only a minor glimmer in his eyes that said Bishop noted Ryan's change in appearance.

Then he raised an eyebrow at Lyra before bending down and holding a hand out for her paw. To Jack's surprise Lyra sat down and placed her right front paw in his hand. Bishop bent down even more and laid a kiss on her paw before straightening.

Jack glanced down at Lyra. He hadn't known a wolf could look surprised, but Lyra did as she looked up a Bishop's knowing smile. They seemed to be holding their own conversation. Lyra tilted her head up at him and Bishop nodded. Jack was really confused as Lyra moved her paws out a bit so she could do what looked like a bow. Not very low but low enough to get the idea across.

Bishop laughed. "No, no absolutely not. Just go take a seat."

Lyra gave Bishop one more curious glance before moving up beside Jack so they could join the rest of the room.

Jack had no idea what was going on. Again he had the feeling no one was going to tell him. He and Ryan sat down in two folding chairs. Lyra curled herself around Jack's feet so she could see the rest of the room.

Jack leaned into Ryan. "Did you understand any of that?"

Ryan shrugged. "Inside joke?"

Jack moved away but he didn't agree. Though it was possible, Jack didn't find it likely. After a few seconds of brooding, Jack's thoughts were interrupted by a wolf squirming his way from the circle of Pack M and wiggling his way over to Lyra.

Jack recognized the wolf belly-crawling across the floor and smiled. It was like Taylor thought the crawling was stealthy. When Taylor was nose to nose with Lyra, he gave a thump of his tail. Jack looked around and no one seemed to be watching the two wolves but Ryan and himself.

Lyra raised her head and swatted Taylor's nose. Taylor immediately rolled over as if mortally wounded. Jack felt Lyra sigh against his feet before she lay her head back down, away from Taylor so she could watch the room. When Taylor realized he wasn't getting a wolfy playmate, he rolled back on his stomach. Very quickly he licked Lyra's snout and ran off back to Pack M. Jack could see her narrow her eyes after him but she didn't have any other reaction. He was surprised she didn't do more.

The meeting when almost identical to the last one, but with one major difference. The seven Weres the scientist were after were all in wolf form, except Graham. No one mentioned it until the meeting was winding down.

Grant sat forward on his folding chair. "Does anyone know why six of them are wolves? It would be more helpful if we could talk to them."

All six of them shifted so they could stare Grant down. It was a little eerie.

Graham shrugged, since part of the room looked to him.

"How should I know? One of them was in wolf form, so the others did it too so no one is singled out? I don't know. If any of you can read minds, then you can tell the rest of us."

When people started mingling and leaving, one of the three wolves Jack didn't know came up to them and sat down about two feet in front of Lyra. She turned to look at him. He pawed at the floor between them. Lyra shifted herself into a seated position, her tail covering the tips of Jack's shoes and cocked her head. The peppered wolf did the same. For several seconds the two of them just stared at each other. Then the unknown wolf trotted off. Jack watched as the wolf returned to the two rocker Weres from SWU. He looked down at Lyra. She craned her neck to watch Jack from where she sat. Not for the first time, Jack wished he could see inside Lyra's head. Sighing, Jack stood up and looked from one packmate to the other.

"Are we ready to go?"

Ryan nodded and Lyra opened her mouth, making a face of wolfy excitement.

Ryan snorted. "It's creepy when you do that. It makes you look like a harmless house pet when you're anything but."

Lyra's tail thumped.

Jack just rolled his eye, inclining his head to Bishop as they walked out the door. Jack called the elevator and Lyra moved away to sit next to the far wall.

Jack folded his arms. "Are you really going to wait there until your cousin comes out?"

Lyra's tail thumped.

Ryan moved in to stand next to Jack. "One of us can take you home, or wherever you're staying."

Jack didn't like the idea of Ryan taking Lyra anywhere but he kept that to himself.

They were prevented from further discussion by Rachel and Graham exiting the office. Graham looked relieved to see his cousin still there. With her tail swaying a little, Lyra moved up beside him. He patted her side.

Rachel lifted her hands and moved next to Ryan to wait for the dinging elevator. "I don't want to know," was all she said as the doors opened and the five of them stepped in.

Chapter 11

"Penny for your thoughts, cuz," Graham drawled as they entered the I-5 on ramp. He had a pretty good idea what was swirling around in that head of hers.

Lyra snorted and turned so she was looking at him instead of out the car window. She had changed forms before getting into his car. "Graham, I don't care how many times you say it, 'cuz' is never going to sound cool coming out of your mouth."

Graham chuckled but didn't respond. He knew if he didn't rise to her jab she was more likely to answer his question.

She sighed. "I'm scared out of my wits. I'm worried Jack and the pack will do something stupid. I'm scared for the family because I have a sneaking suspicion the attacks on our family are because of us. How far up does this project go? I don't want to be forced from Pack F, but I wonder whether it would be in their best interest if I left. Or maybe I should just disappear for a while. I feel terrible about poor Ryan going completely batty just because he was trying to help me. Did you see him? He looked like crap."

Graham snorted. "He looked hungover."

Lyra waved the comment away. "But I told the females' biggest secret to six guys. That alone is going to get me in trouble. I didn't want any of this, Hammy. I just wanted a plain, simple, quiet life. This is a mess. I'm just moving from one problem to the next and I'm sick of it."

Graham felt for his cousin and felt the same angry frustration she did. He gave her a second before responding. "First off, none of us asked for this. It was one cruel scientist and a bunch of misguided students. As for the family, they are holding their own. There are enough of us to deal with whatever comes. Don't you dare think about disappearing on me. I don't care if you think it's the best idea. I will hunt you down, drag you back and dump you in front our family. Then I'll tell them about your brilliant plan to flee at the sign of trouble and leave yourself defenseless. That will go over real well. And if you really feel going to the scientists will solve this problem then we will go together." It was the absolutely last thing Graham wanted to do, but he was not trusting those wack-jobs with his cousins ever again.

Lyra sighed. "You're not leaving me much choice here, Hammy."

He glanced at her. "I'm not trying to."

Lyra went back to staring out the window. She looked so lost, Graham wanted to help her but he knew she saw herself as alone in the world most of the time and any help he offered would automatically be denied.

"You never told me exactly what happened with Ryan. I know you were in heat, I could smell it. What did he do exactly to make Jack so wary of him?"

Lyra seemed to curl in on herself more. "I don't want to talk about it. I just want pretend it didn't happen and move on."

Graham knew enough about the other male to know nothing truly bad happened and he trusted Jack to stop things from getting to a point where people were getting their throats ripped out.

"Ryan looked like he feels the same way. I'm guessing it's Jack, looking out for all of you that's going to keep it lurking around for a while."

Lyra didn't say anything. She continued to stare out the window, not really seeing the world as it passed by.

About ten minutes later, Lyra's voice barely reached the driver's seat. "I wish we didn't have to come back here."

Graham couldn't have agreed more as he looked at the looming buildings ahead of them on the private road. The ten-foot iron gates looked menacing in the dark. Trees and shrubs lined the fence, not too close though, because it was electric. The roofs were the only parts of the buildings visible once the car turned on to the gravel road.

"It makes me wonder where my allegiances are, coming from that meeting straight here. I feel like the wolf in sheep's clothing."

Graham knew Lyra was much closer to Pack F than he was to Pack C. They were his friends, his good friends but for Lyra Pack F was like family. He didn't think any of Pack F knew how important they were to her. He kneaded the steering wheel as he slowed the car toward the gate.

"Your allegiance is to us, to your family first. After that it doesn't matter."

Lyra shifted in her seat as Graham unrolled his window to press the call button on the box next to the gate.

"You don't truly believe that. That's your father talking and you know it."

Graham didn't answer her as the face of a security guard popped up on the tiny screen.

Chapter 12

The next three days were blur of names and faces. So far all the packs agreed to the alliance. Jack was becoming unnerved by Saturday. He had not spoken with Lyra in person, since Tuesday. He spoke to her on the phone, finally, earlier that day and Jack flat out asked her why she was changing before meeting him and Ryan. She told him she was avoiding human form as much as possible because it just made things easier. Jack asked what her family thought about that, since she was still staying with them. She went quiet before telling him she was avoiding them as well.

But every night, Graham had shown up with different bruises, which made Jack suspect why Lyra really insisted on wolf form. She hadn't been the only one, though. After Tuesday's meeting the six non-Alphas/Seconds started showing up in wolf form. Jack noticed if any of them were the host pack they always welcomed the other wolves, standing next to their Alpha as the wolves came in. It was odd. The Weres seemed to be developing new customs for inter-pack relations. Jack also noticed the peppery wolf always came over and did the same pawing at the ground he had done on Tuesday. Jack didn't know what it meant, but Lyra seemed to.

He knew today was going to be a struggle because it was the first soccer game of the season. It could only go one of two ways: it could be an utter disaster, or Lyra could pretend nothing was wrong. Jack was putting money on the second one and hoping he was right.

As Jack swung his car into the gravel parking lot, he could barely make out Pack F's pale brown jerseys. From what he could see it looked like Cole, Ryan, Liam, Bruce, and Felix were already here. They all seemed to be acting normally. Which was a plus, but Cole and Ryan were the only ones who knew what had been going on.

Jack nodded to all of them before dropping his duffel and sitting down to start stretching.

Liam followed suit and when he spoke it was quiet. "So, what exactly is going on? Did the meetings go bad or something?"

Jack didn't even look up. "Why do you ask?"

He wanted to know exactly what he missed.

Liam snorted. "I was the first one here. You'll notice Lyra's bag is over there. She came with her cousin and we chatted for a couple of minutes, until out of the blue she looked up at him and asked if he wanted to go for a warm up run. Then they took off. Within two seconds, Ryan and Cole walked up. She saw them coming and we all knew it. So I ask again, what's going on?" He was looking Jack in the eyes as he finished.

Jack sighed. "It's a really long story that I had been hoping was over."

He was interrupted by Graham and Lyra jogging around the corner field and heading back. When they reached Pack F, Graham nodded to Jack. As Jack nodded back, he understood what was happening. Graham didn't want Lyra with Ryan, but he was trusting Jack to handle things.

"Okay cuz, I'll meet you at the car after the games, but make sure someone's with you until then, got it?" He gave her a stern look.

Lyra curled her lip. "Yes, sir."

Graham narrowed his eyes before scooping up his own bag and jogging off to join the rest of the pale blue jerseys.

Lyra bent down and started angrily searching through her duffel. Jack tensed as Ryan came to stand beside her. Jack noted he wasn't the only one as Cole's back straightened.

Lyra looked up as Ryan. "What?"

It came out angry and biting, but Jack was positive Ryan wasn't the cause.

Ryan continued to look down at her, completely blank faced. "You're looking for your shin guards. In a second when you find them you're going to be asking for someone to lean on so you can put them on." Then he shrugged. "I was closest, just trying to make things easier."

Lyra seemed to blush. "Oh, thanks." Then she went back to rooting through her bag.

Both Jack and Cole relaxed. Cole turned around to exchange glances with Jack before shrugging.

Jack finished his stretches, stood up and went to stand in front of Lyra. She was doing her regular balancing act while pulling on her shin guards and socks. Ryan stood there, propping her up and watching the game going on before them.

"Lyra, are things okay with your family?" Jack struggled with a neutral tone. He knew Lyra's family was difficult, to say the least.

She looked up at him as she put her first cleat on. “Okay as they ever get.”

She said it in such a blasé tone that Ryan turned his attention from the field to her.

“Should we be stopping you from staying with them?” Ryan’s face held concern.

It was all Jack could do not to yell, ‘Hell Yes!’

Lyra snorted. “Although I know Jack disagrees with me, no you don’t, I’ll be fine. Thank you for the thought though, big guy.” Then she smiled at Ryan and patted his arm with the hand she was leaning with.

Ryan watched her for a second before looking back out to the field.

Jack couldn’t let it go that easily. “Would you tell us if we should?”

Lyra didn’t even look up. “Nope.”

He heard Ryan snort. But Jack was prevented from showing his anger by the arrival of Seth and Hazel.

Seth gave Jack a questioning look and glanced at Lyra and Ryan. Since Jack didn’t really have an answer, he shrugged.

As Lyra slid her second cleat on, the field was clearing. A red shirt jogged across the field toward them. Jack knew it was Taylor but still tensed as the other man approached.

When he was about three feet from Lyra, he bowed at the waist.

Lyra just put her hands on her hips.

“My lady, I have a challenge for you.” Taylor gave her a mischievous grin.

Jack watched Lyra’s interest pique. “Oh do you now?”

His smile grew. “Since the cat is out of the bag, so to speak, I just want you to know I’m gunning for you.” Taylor winked, blew her a kiss and jogged back to his team.

Lyra laughed before turning to smile at Jack. “Oh Jack?”

Jack wasn’t sure he would like where this was going. “Yes, littermate?”

“What are the odds that I play mid-field today?” She actually batted her eyes at him.

Jack looked at her suspiciously. “Better if you stop doing that.”

The batting stopped. Interesting.

"I think we can arrange it if you can tell me why you want it so bad."

Lyra lips twitched into a devilish grin. "I was just challenged. Taylor was telling me he wasn't going to hold back now that everyone knows how fast we are. I want to give him a run for his money."

Jack heard Seth chuckling from his left. "Oh this should be fun."

Jack had to agree, this game was definitely going to be interesting.

The game had definitely been interesting. Taylor and Lyra were neck and neck at most points in the game. The two of them blew past everyone. But F had Syrus, which ultimately tilted the scales in their favor. Pack F won five to three.

At half time, Syrus scolded Lyra for not using her speed earlier. She just rolled her eyes. Jack had been glad to see the pack dynamic get back to almost normal. Maybe Bishop and Mathew were right. Their packs were stable because their packmates wanted stability.

Jack's after game thoughts were interrupted by Hazel's worried face appearing in front of him. "Jack, where's Lyra?"

Jack's attention shot out, scanning the area. Damn it, he didn't see her.

"She went to the restroom but that was a while ago. Justin!"

Their littermate snapped to attention at Jack's tone, so did the remainder of the pack.

"Everyone else stay put. Justin, I need you to track Lyra."

There were several curses as Justin took a deep breath and took off toward the restrooms. Both Jack and Seth headed off after him.

"Seth, I said stay put," Jack growled as they passed two playing fields.

Seth snorted. "Not a chance in hell, Jack."

They stayed silent as Justin guided them past the restrooms and curved off the right into the wooded area. Jack's feeling of panic rose a little further.

Then Justin stopped and Seth and Jack followed suit. They could hear voices. Jack could smell Ryan with Lyra and he felt marginally better, but he was worried about the other four males with them. He motioned for Justin and Seth to stay there and made his expression hard enough that they would.

"What Ryan, is Lyra not allowed to talk to males outside her own pack?"

Jack heard Ryan growl before answering. "Of course she is, just not with anyone from either of your packs."

The voice Jack didn't know spoke again. "See Lyra, you should join us. We don't keep our females bound up like that."

The tone made Jack's hackles rise.

Jack stepped through the bushes. "Is there a problem here?"

All six of them looked at him. Neither Lyra or Ryan seemed surprised. They must have smelled him coming.

One of the males in the middle smiled at Jack and when he spoke it was the same voice from before. "Not at all, Jack." There was emphasis on his name. "We were just pointing out that some packs are more open to independence than others."

Anger filled Jack as he memorized all four men. "I think it's time for you to turn around and walk away."

He really wanted to beat the crap out of all four of them but he knew that wasn't a good idea. They would have information on how to fight Pack F and that was the last thing Jack wanted to give them.

For a moment it looked like they would press the issue but all four of them turned and left without another word.

Justin and Seth came through the bushes. "They're gone, I can't even smell them anymore."

At Justin's words, Lyra turned and before Jack knew what was happening, she buried herself against his chest. As he put his arms around her, he noticed she was shaking, not crying, shaking. His littermate was terrified.

Jack exchanged looks with Justin and Seth before turning to Ryan. "What happened?"

Ryan's face was blank but his eyes were furious. "They grabbed her coming out of the bathroom. I had followed her, figuring I had to go so I might as well go now. I thought I was being a little paranoid but then I saw them grab her. They had chloroform on a cloth and were putting it over her mouth when I came up and ripped her from the two bigger guys. I beat the crap out of them, but those four pricks came out of nowhere faking worry, claiming Lyra could go with them and be better protected. But I know all six of them were together."

Jack didn't doubt it. He kept making soothing noises and rubbing Lyra's back. Her shaking started to calm down. Then he heard more people coming around the bushes. He turned so they wouldn't see Lyra. Seth and Justin got the hint and moved to cover Jack.

He relaxed when Bishop, Taylor, and Graham appeared.

Graham grunted for Seth and Justin to move out of his way, then stood directly in front of Jack. His face seemed to break as he saw his cousin shaking. Jack started to understand how close they were. Graham gave Jack a look that told him he was taking his cousin.

Jack wasn't about to argue and make things worse. He kissed the top of Lyra's head and whispered to her. "Lyra, your cousin's asking for you."

Lyra looked up at him with glassy eyes before she unlatched herself from him and turning, latched onto Graham. Her cousin's arms wrapped around her like a vise, but Lyra didn't seem to mind.

"Jack, what has happened?" Bishop asked.

Jack tore his gaze from Lyra to look at Bishop. The other Alpha's face was full of worry.

"They tried to kidnap her as she left the bathroom. They had chloroform. Ryan was able to save her, but four more guys showed up pretending to be worried and told Lyra that joining their pack would ensure her safety and independence."

"So the six of them were working together?"

Jack nodded. "We think so."

Bishop didn't particularly like that answer.

Suddenly there was growling from Graham and Ryan. Everyone turned their attention to the two men. But Graham was looking at the top of his cousin's head.

"Don't be stupid. They would hurt you."

There was more growling as Lyra said something else only Graham and Ryan could hear.

"No, they wouldn't, and if you're going to talk like that I'll keep you locked up at the estate."

Ryan chimed in. "And don't think we wouldn't help him."

Jack figured it out then. Lyra was volunteering to go to Pack L. If she thought that was happening, she had another thing coming.

Bishop cleared his throat to gain their attention. “On account of these circumstances I think it’s in everyone’s best interest if the soccer games are postponed until this matter is fixed. Would you agree, Jack?”

Jack couldn’t have agreed more. He nodded once.

Bishop took a deep breath. “All right then, I will contact Finn and let him know what is going on. If he does not think games should be canceled, I can think of seven teams that will be forfeiting their games this season.” Then he inclined his head to the group and headed back to the fields.

Taylor glanced at Lyra before following his Alpha.

Jack looked back at Graham. “I take it you’ll be driving her straight back to your families place?”

Graham snorted. “I sure as hell will be now.”

Jack rubbed his face. Things just kept getting worse and he had no idea how to stop them.

As Sunday rolled around, Jack was ready for these meetings to be over, but there were still five left. Finn canceled the games until further notice. Jack received the email that morning. All it told the Alphas was Finn was canceling the season due to ‘extenuating circumstances’.

Jack was preparing himself for the meeting with Pack X. Cassandra already warned everybody to bring their own seats since they only had enough chairs for their pack and there wasn't enough time to find more. She said there were loads of pillows and beanbag chairs should anyone want those.

So here Jack and Ryan were, waiting outside the SWU Pack C office for Graham or Rachel to open the door.

Rachel's face appeared in the cracked doorway. She looked angry and resigned. The door only cracked enough for her head to peek out and nothing more. That worried Jack.

"I want no violence in my office, Jack."

Adrenaline shot through Jack's body and Ryan stiffened next to him.

"What happened to Lyra? Let us in, damn it!"

He was growling and probably looked downright frightening but Rachel held her own.

She shook her head. "I want the promise of no violence in my space."

Both Jack and Ryan were growling in the back of their throats.

"Fine," Jack bit out.

Rachel looked at Ryan.

"Only if it's due," he rumbled.

She seemed to think about that before giving a quick nod and opening the door wide enough for them to rush in. Then she closed it again.

Jack knew Ryan was with him in seeing red. Lyra was in wolf form. She was on the floor half in Graham's lap, half out. Her fur was matted with blood in places and the eye Jack could see was swollen shut. There was a large wrap around her side and another around her right hind leg, which was obviously broken. Her breathing was shallow and she stayed perfectly still.

Jack grabbed Ryan's arm as the other man moved, squeezing hard enough to be convincing.

"Graham." Jack was shaking from fury so bad he couldn't get out anything else.

Graham looked up at him. His eyes were filled with anger and anguish. "They jumped her. I have no idea how or who. We were getting into my car, same as every night, and Lyra was changing forms before getting in, only this time I heard her make a strange noise. I ran around the car and there were three huge guys surrounding her. They caught us both by surprise. I hadn't heard them, seem them, or smelled them approaching. Lyra collapsed as I watched from a hit in the leg. They were using bats and knives. Who the hell uses weapons! I knocked one of them out before they saw me. I managed the second, but the third ran off. I was too worried about Lyra to go after him.

“She changed forms and I got her into the car. It took her five minutes to change, Jack! FIVE DAMN MINUTES! I couldn't take her to a hospital or a vet. The only place I thought of was here. She kept blacking out on the way, and I could feel it. They had maybe a minute tops. I don't know how they could have done so much damage in so little a time. I swear to you I was paying attention. I don't know where they came from." Graham sounded like he was one swift move from jumping off the sanity cliff. He was curled around Lyra's body and petting behind her ear.

Jack tried to push as much of his emotions back as he could. He could dwell on this later, when he could afford to rage. Now he needed to do what was best for Lyra.

"Grant has med students in his pack. I'll call and get him to send them over."

Rachel jumped in from where she stood about ten feet away. "No need. I'm an ER nurse. I made my way through nursing school by being a part-time EMT. As soon as Graham told me what happened, I drove straight here. I examined her and really it looks worse than it is. Her leg is broken and the other ankle is sprained. They broke three of her ribs, but she changed fast enough prevent further damage. Several other ribs are bruised. She has a knife wound in her chest, and that's where all the blood is coming from. That whole side of her face is swollen, not just the eye. There doesn't seem to be any internal bleeding, currently, or anything life threatening. But I won't know anything else until she can change forms. Which I don't think is going to happen in the next twenty-four hours. She should be in okay condition by the middle of the week and unless anything else happens, she'll be completely healed by Friday. That's if she doesn't move around too much."

Jack crossed his arms. "How do you know her healing time?"

Rachel shrugged. "Educated guessing, mostly from watching my own pack healing from various wounds."

Jack looked down at Lyra again. He couldn't believe he had been stupid enough to let her go stay with her family where the pack couldn't look out for her. He needed to get her some place quiet where she could heal. Some place she would be comfortable. Jack pulled out his cell to call Hazel. Sure she would freak out initially, but Hazel's would still be the best place.

As he flipped it open, Jack turned to Ryan. "Go up to Pack X's office and apologize for our absence due to a pack emergency."

No sooner had Ryan turned, did Jack hear a growl. Both men looked at Lyra, who was growling and trying to stand up. Graham was holding her down, but Jack knew Lyra would keep struggling until she really did some damage.

Jack took the extra two steps and squatted down in front of her. "Lyra, calm down. You're going to cause damage."

She actually snapped at him, like she meant to hurt him.

Jack looked at her in shock until Graham got his attention. "She doesn't want to miss the meeting." The other man's tone said he disagreed with his cousin's decision, but wasn't about to outright say it.

Jack looked at both of them. "What?"

Graham sighed. "She wouldn't change forms until I promised her I would convince you to not only attend the meeting but take her with you."

Ryan was suddenly next to Jack. "What in the world made her think we'd agree to that?"

Graham resumed petting the now motionless Lyra. Jack sincerely hoped she had stopped moving by choice instead of making her injuries worse.

"She said the display would help the cause more than anything anyone could say. Her being there would prove Pack F's loyalty by letting others see a weakness. It would urge those on the fence to move to our side. That once the story got out it could flush out some of the people working with Pack L."

Jack knew politically it could be a very good move, but he hated the idea of putting his littermate's pain on display.

Ryan didn't seem to find the idea appealing either. "Isn't that a little cheesy? Won't they think it's a set-up?"

Graham shook his head. "No. Anyone with a decent nose could smell the difference. She doesn't smell like she was attacked by any of us."

Jack took the idea out of debate. "Lyra, I need you to concentrate on me."

She twitched a little but she was slowly able to see him out of her good eye. That image was going to haunt Jack for a while. He wanted to kill the men who did this to her.

"Are you absolutely sure about this? Move your right front foot for yes, left for no."

It took a second but her right paw moved, folding at the lowest joint.

Jack stood up. "Okay then. We will do this your way, but afterwards you're going to do what I tell you until this is over. Are we clear? Otherwise I'm calling Hazel."

There was an even longer pause this time. Jack knew she was against following Jack's orders, but if she believed in her idea enough she would do it. Finally her right paw moved and Jack nodded.

"All right. Ryan, you're carrying her up since it doesn't look like Graham's arms can support her weight."

Ryan nodded and leaned in so he could get his arms under Lyra.

Rachel moved in. "Tell them we will be up as soon as I attend to Graham. He wouldn't let me touch him until after Lyra was taken care of."

She didn't seem too thrilled with that, but kept her thoughts to herself.

Jack nodded and called a different number from his phonebook.

"Jack? Is something wrong?" Bishop's tone was blank.

"Are you in the X office?" Jack deliberately ignored the question.

"Yes. Should we not be?" Jack could hear the worry began to spill into Bishop's voice.

"I need a favor." Jack tried to keep his voice blank as he and Ryan moved out the C office door.

Bishop paused. "And you know I will not ask you for repayment. All right, what is it you need?"

Jack took a deep breath. "I want my pack sitting next to you today. I need you and Victor to clear that space."

Bishop interrupted. "Done, no one is next to us."

"And I need you two to find as many pillows as you can and put them in a pile four feet around...in the next two minutes."

Jack heard Bishop relay the request to Victor and Taylor. "You and one other pack are the only ones not here, Jack, that might not be the easiest request."

"I need it done, Bishop." Jack winced at how clipped he sounded.

"It will be." Then Bishop hung up.

Jack knew once Bishop saw Lyra's condition he would understand. As they stepped into the elevator, Jack felt a tongue on his arm. When he looked down he saw Lyra licking him.

He smiled at her. "You're welcome, littermate."

She stopped and her good eye closed. Jack watched her side to make sure her breathing hadn't changed. Then he looked over at Ryan. The other man's face was stone, except for the fury burning in his eyes.

"I need you to monitor her, just in case anything changes."

Ryan continued to look straight ahead and spoke through clenched teeth. "Of course."

Jack took a deep breath before knocking on Pack X's door. When Cassandra opened it she glared at him, until she saw Lyra then several choice swear words slipped from her mouth.

“Okay, I am definitely all right with the pillow confiscation now." The she moved back so they could walk in.

The room went dead silent as all eyes snapped to Lyra. Victor even dropped the pillow he had been holding. The moment was broken by a pained howl coming from Taylor's wolfy throat. He was soon followed by the other wolves in the room. Through the chorus, Jack and Ryan moved to where the pillows were piled. Ryan laid her down as slowly and gently as he could.

Jack turned to face Cassandra. "I'm sorry we're late. Pack C is right behind us. Rachel is taking care of Graham's injuries now that Lyra has been taken care of."

She was holding on to her necklace, as if it was a talisman. "Is he as bad as that?" She sounded like she wasn’t sure she wanted to know.

Jack shook his head. Then he felt something brush past him. He looked down to see Taylor moving past Ryan. Taylor gingerly lay down next to Lyra's back so their bodies were touching. He laid his head on his paws, facing forward as if he were some kind of bodyguard. Lyra didn't seem to mind, so Jack let it be. But within the next minute, the other wolves were there as well, in a haphazard circle around the injured female.

There was a knock at the door and as Cassandra opened it, a black wolf brushed past her and headed for his cousin. He was still favoring his front leg, with a very obvious limp. The wolves shifted so Graham could lay opposite Taylor against Lyra's paws.

Everyone in the room sat in silence watching the seven of them. There could be no doubt in anyone's mind that if Lyra hadn't fought the scientists, their plan would have worked perfectly. The wolves were showing a level of loyalty that transcended pack lines. It made the exact kind of statement Lyra said it would.

"How did this happen?" Mathew's voice was barely audible and filled with disbelief.

Jack looked at Mathew and shook his head. "I'm not exactly sure. I wasn't there. Lyra was jumped by three men with weapons while she and Graham were on their way here."

"Weapons? What kind of weapons? No one's ever used weapons before." Gina asked from where she sat on the other side of her Co-Alpha.

Jack shrugged. "I have no idea. I don't think Graham got a good look and Lyra is not in any condition to tell us."

"Tell me Graham at least maimed one of them." This was from Charlie.

Jack nodded. "Yeah, he told us he was able to knock two of them out. The third ran away, but he didn't want to leave Lyra unattended."

"How are we to find these men?" Grant asked. He seemed almost as pissed as Jack. "Did anyone get their scents? What do they look like?"

Jack shook his head. "No, Graham said it was as if the men had no scent. They didn't see or hear them coming. I have no idea how to find them. Believe me I wish I did." Jack's fingers curled into fists as he spoke.

Ryan sat on the ground next to the pile of wolves and pillows. "Can we get on with the meeting please? I would like to get her some place she can rest. Then when she's well enough we can decide what, if anything the alliance wants to do about this."

The room was silent for a second.

"Ryan is right. I'll start. Pack X, I am Bishop, Alpha of Pack M. This is my Second, Victor, and with us is the wolf at Lyra's back, Taylor."

Jack noticed throughout the meeting none of the wolves moved beyond the occasional shift of weight. The Alphas kept shifting their gaze curiously over to the layer of fur. The meeting was shorter than most, but that was fine with Jack. As soon as it ended, he had his phone out and was calling Hazel. While it rang, he watched his packmates.

Ryan was on his knees in front of wolves, looking down at them. "Please, I need to move her now." The wolves very reluctantly slid out of Ryan's way so he could get his arms around her body.

Lyra made a small pained sound as he initially moved her. Only those nearby heard it. Ryan stopped mid-movement. Both Bishop and Victor froze in their conversation. Rachel got a tense expression on her face. Jack turned away; he couldn't watch and break the news to Hazel.

Hazel picked up her cell after four rings. "Hey Jack, what's up?"

Her voice was cheery and expectant. Jack winced.

"Hazel, sit down." Jack scolded himself for sounding so harsh.

After a moment she responded, sounding guarded. "Okay."

Jack took a deep breath so he could spit it all out before Hazel could start in with hysterics. "Lyra's been hurt, badly but if she rests she'll be okay. I want to put her somewhere she can rest but I don't want her at her place."

Just like Jack hoped, Hazel jumped on that last sentence.

"Bring her here, she can stay in my extra bedroom. I'll call her family and tell them to look after the dogs. How far out are you?"

Jack took a second to incline his head to Cassandra as they walked out of the office. "About fifteen minutes."

"Okay, I'll get everything ready." She hung up. Jack knew Hazel would spend the next fifteen minutes keeping herself as busy as she could until she could see Lyra for herself.

As they waited for the elevator, Ryan cleared his throat to get Jack's attention. He waited until Jack was looking at him to speak.

"We seem to have some stowaways." Then he looked blatantly at the floor.

Jack followed his second's gaze. Graham and Taylor stood with them.

"I take it you two are coming with us?"

Both of the wolves looked up at him. Their faces were unreadable, but Jack knew he was probably stuck with them.

The ride to Hazel's was in the top five quietest car rides Jack had ever been on. The silence only gave him time to fuel his anger. Ryan put Lyra in the back seat. Taylor and Graham lay on either side, like furry bookends. Jack guessed they were trying to stop her from jarring too much. By the time they reached Hazel's fourth floor apartment, Jack was angry enough to beat something to a pulp. Once Lyra was settled in that was exactly what he would do.

Jack didn't even knock, Hazel was in the doorway when they reached her floor. She didn't seem fazed by the two wolves with them. As they entered her well-lit apartment, Hazel scrutinized Lyra, seeing every injury in detail before she took a step back.

"They're here."

She yelled as Justin and Seth came jogging down the hallway leading to the extra bedroom and second bathroom. They stopped when they got a look at their littermate. Seth started growling and Justin brought his hands out to cup Lyra's face. He gave her a kiss on the forehead before taking a step back.

Ryan turned to Hazel. His voice still held a growl from earlier. "Where am I taking her?"

Hazel blinked and looked up at Ryan as if she had forgotten he had never been there before. "The left hallway, second door."

Ryan brushed past them and headed down the hall, trailed by the two wolves.

Justin looked at the two wolves, then Jack. "Who are they?"

Hazel answered before Jack could. "The big black one is Graham, her cousin. The mostly white one is Taylor, and he's one of Bishop's wolves."

Justin nodded then headed after them.

Seth looked at Hazel curiously. Jack could tell he was trying to distract himself from his anger. "Why do you know that?"

Hazel shrugged then followed Justin. "Why wouldn't I know that?"

Seth caught Jack with his gaze. When he spoke, his tone told Jack the other man was barely keeping his anger in check.

"What happened?"

Jack folded his arms. He was starting to get sick of that question. "I wasn't there, I only heard about it from Graham. Three guys jumped her on their way to the meet-and-greet tonight. He said they had weapons and neither he or Lyra could sense them coming. He knocked two of them unconscious but the third got away. I'll bet when they wake up they'll be right back to planning. I haven't figured out a plan of action yet. I'm waiting to hear Lyra's take before making any definite plans."

Seth folded his arms. "At least two of us at any given time."

Jack had been thinking along the same lines.

Hazel walked in while they were talking. She went straight into her kitchen and started rummaging around on top of the fridge.

Seth strode over to her. "Can I grab something for you, Hazel?"

She shook her head and kept feeling around. "Aha!" She pulled her arm down and in her hand was a bottle.

Seth leaned over her and snorted. "Good luck getting her to take that."

Hazel just gave him a look then turned back toward the extra bedroom. This time Jack and Seth followed her in.

Lyra was in the middle of the queen-sized bed, on top of the blankets. Both Taylor and Graham were stretched out on either side of her. Hazel shook a pill out of the bottle and held her palm out in front of Lyra's face.

"Take this, Lyra."

Lyra didn't budge. She hated pain killers, something about being wussy.

"Lyra, take the damn pill!" Hazel never swore. "It will make you sleep."

Jack watched his two littermates have a staring contest before Lyra's tongue finally flipped out and the pill disappeared.

Hazel seemed to relax marginally. "Okay, all two-leggeds out." Hazel started shooing everybody.

Once the door was closed behind her she turned to Jack. "Tell everyone only four-legged visitors for the next two days."

Seth folded his arms again. He was not a fan of staying in wolf form. "Why?"

"Because they make less noise."

Jack knew Hazel wouldn't budge on her new rule, so he didn't even try to argue otherwise.

"Okay, since things are under control for the moment. Ryan, I want you to brief the pack about Lyra's condition and Hazel's rules about her care. Hazel, I only want Were medical people in there."

She nodded.

"Good, now excuse me because I need to go beat things for a while until I can think straight again."

When no one questioned him, Jack let himself out and headed for his car, knowing full well he wasn't going to get any sleep tonight.

Chapter 13

The world was really fuzzy, not just around the edges, and dark, really dark. Lyra kept her eyes closed as she assessed her surroundings. It was hard because whatever Hazel had given her had knocked Lyra out. She had no idea how long she slept. Her mind assaulted her with nightmares, but finally she was able to wake herself up, though she was still so groggy. Even now she could feel her body pulling her back to sleep.

Warm, it was really warm where she was...Hazel, she was at Hazel's place. Lyra could smell others in the room with her. Graham and Taylor were the strongest. She moved her back a little, snuggling closer to her cousin. There was a small push back telling her he was awake...She could smell Justin somewhere...and Ryan. There was the faint scent of Dylan, but not like he was there now...no he must have left...The room smelled of pack. It was comforting and not at the same time.

The pull to sleep was too strong for her...she gave in, hoping there wouldn't be nightmares this time.

Lyra woke to feel warmth on her fur. She was so stiff she knew she must not have moved for a long time. Lyra had a sneaking suspicion Hazel had given her more than just the one pill. She could vaguely remember Hazel waking her up to give her water. Now she remembered the pills. She was going to yell at Hazel just on principle.

Lyra felt groggy but one thought came through loud and clear. She really had to pee. Shifting her weight, Lyra started to get up. There were noises of protest from the other wolves on the bed. It smelled like Cole, Taylor, and Dylan. As she continued to struggle up on the mattress, Taylor swatted at her and shifted so his head was on the part of her chest that was not bandaged. She seriously had to pee. Lyra whined at him, hoping he'd get the message. He did, and Lyra had never been more thankful. She couldn't help but wonder, had Taylor ever left? Every time she had woken up, she remembered him being there.

It took two tries, but she was able to stand. Being as careful as she could with her hind legs, Lyra made her way to the end of the bed. She knew it would hurt and was contemplating the best way to jump off when she was scooped off the bed. Lyra was so surprised she let out a yelp. All she got in response was a chuckle. Taylor, Taylor must have shifted while she was trying to stand. He acted as if she weighed nothing, which she knew wasn't true. Were strength came in handy, but in this case it was just weird.

"Okay, I'll be right down the hall. Need me, give a shout." Then he gingerly put her down in the spare bathroom and closed her in.

Lyra didn't waste any time, she started shifting as soon as she heard the door click. It was painful. Her shifts had not been painful in over a year. When she finally finished, she panted like crazy. What should have taken a minute, max, had taken three. She was exhausted. Leaning on the counter until she regained her balance, Lyra looked in the mirror. She healed somewhat since she was last fully conscious. She still only looked about two steps up from death warmed over. Lyra was just grateful the wounds appeared more superficial now. Just heavy bruising.

She was still in the jeans and long-sleeved grey shirt she had been in before, but now they were blood spattered. In fact, most of her was. Hazel's poor sheets. Sighing, Lyra gave in to her screaming bladder. When she finished, she stuck her head out the door.

"Haz, could I have a change of clothes please?"

"Sure, hold on a sec." Hazel's voice came from down the hall.

A few seconds later a masculine arm entered the bathroom holding one of Lyra's duffel bags.

Lyra snatched the bag. "You're not Hazel and this is from my place."

Taylor's voice came from behind the door. "No I'm not, and your other female packmate volunteered to gather some clothes for you." He sounded amused.

Lyra was touched Sadie did that for her. "Where are my dogs?"

Taylor laughed. "Where you left them. Graham made sure they were being taken care of."

Lyra's curiosity got to her. "How long have I been here?"

Taylor hesitated and his voice took on a serious tone. "Three days."

Lyra was shocked. Normally healing didn't take that long, and she wasn't even fully healed.

"And how long have you been here?"

She wasn't sure he was going to answer and since he was on the other side of the door Lyra couldn't see his expression.

"Three days."

"Taylor..."

"Get cleaned up, my lady. We can talk about it later. Unless you want some help." Then he closed the door.

She glared after him. "Jerk."

Lyra swore she heard a masculine chuckle through the door.

It took her a lot of time to unwrap everything. Rachel had done a good job. After that, Lyra stepped into the shower. The shower stung but felt amazing. It stung more, but she sucked it up and got clean. It took longer than Lyra would have liked but she finally got dressed in a ribbed black tank top and a black broom skirt, since she couldn't get any of the jeans on without ripping them, due to a swollen knee.

Slinging the bag over her shoulder, Lyra winced as it hit one of the healing scratches. She carefully bent down and picked up the bloody clothes. Her legs were stiff and it was difficult to walk but she made her way to the front of the apartment.

Hazel was in the kitchen keeping herself busy.

Taylor sat at the counter, shirtless. Lyra rolled her eyes. Taylor liked to pretend he couldn't shift with his shirt on. Poor Dylan, who looked up to Taylor, had started doing it as well. Lyra tried to knock him of that habit.

Dylan was sitting on the stool next to Taylor, grinning as Lyra walked into the room.

Cole was still in wolf form. When he saw her, he leapt off the couch and came over to rub his head on her uninjured side. Cole was moderately scary in wolf form. He was three and a half feet tall and all grey and black patches. It was hard to reconcile his appearance with his attitude. Lyra scratched behind his ear. He gave her a wolfy grin before snatching her bag in his mouth and walking back toward the couch with it.

Lyra went to put her hands on her hips but one was so heavily bruised she couldn't, so she wrapped that hand around the other wrist.

"Stealing is wrong, Cole."

He looked at her open mouthed, with his tongue hanging to the side. He was laughing at her.

Hazel spoke from behind Lyra. "He's right. You shouldn't be lugging that thing around. I'd put money on you already hitting one of your injuries with it." When Lyra didn't answer, Hazel laughed. "Oh wow, you did. Just sit down so I can feed you."

Lyra heard her move away. She turned around and sat on the empty stool to Taylor's right. Both he and Dylan gave her amused smiles.

Lyra narrowed her eyes. "Oh just shut up. And you're not that attractive, put a shirt on."

Taylor laughed. "Actually I don't have one. The one I was wearing has your blood all over it."

That reminded Lyra that she was still holding her bloody clothes. "Could I have a trash bag please?" Hazel nodded and pulled one out of a drawer, passing it over the counter. Lyra shoved her clothes in it before dropping the bag next to her.

A light bulb went off in her head. "I wasn't bleeding when I got here. How did your shirt get messy?"

The room went really quiet and Hazel faked interest in whatever she was doing. Lyra looked Taylor in the eyes. His face blanked.

"You had nightmares the first night. You thrashed around a lot and managed to reopen some of your wounds. I just happened to be facing that side. It took Graham and me about five minutes to calm you down."

Lyra didn't remember this. She remembered the nightmares, but not the thrashing. She watched Taylor's face for some hint he was joking. She had practically grown up with Taylor because their families were so closely tied. She could read his face better than anyone. There were no signs of jest. Lyra didn't know what to say.

"I'm sorry."

Taylor laughed. "Don't apologize to me, my lady. Graham's the one you whacked in the chin with your back. You jarred him pretty good."

Lyra rolled her eyes. "I feel no pity for him."

Hazel cut in by putting a plate of scrambled eggs in front of Lyra. They were stuffed with chives, sour cream, bits of bacon, cheese and potato bits. There wasn't a much better way to distract Lyra than food. A large cup of coffee was set down next to it a moment later.

Lyra looked up at her ex-roommate. "I love you." She grinned, knowing her voice dripped with sugary sweetness.

Hazel chuckled before turning back to the stove. "I know. I love you too."

Lyra dove into her food and didn't come up for air until two platefuls later. When she finished, Hazel was leaning against the opposite counter smiling at her. Lyra glanced at the digital clock on the microwave. By the amount of light coming in through Hazel's open shades, Lyra guessed it was nine AM not PM.

"I've already called Jack and told him you're up."

Lyra's attention snapped to Hazel.

"He'll be by after he gets off work tonight. So at about seven-thirty, I'm guessing."

Lyra's mind immediately jumped to escape plans.

"Don't even think about it. There's myself and two others here at all times. You're still too wounded to get past all of us."

Lyra altered her plans. She could get out a window.

"I said stop it. I will send Taylor and Justin out to hunt you down. You know they'll find you anywhere."

Lyra narrowed her eyes at her friend. "I take it back. I hate you."

Hazel shrugged. "I know."

Lyra gave Hazel a meaningful look. They both knew Lyra couldn't tell Jack the whole truth. In fact, everyone in that room but Cole knew Lyra couldn't tell Jack what was truly going on. Her family might actually kill her for that. Hazel gave Lyra a sad smile. She knew what Lyra was worried about.

Taking a deep breath, Lyra moved on. "Did anyone call in to work for me?"

Everyone but Hazel looked confused.

"I did. I told them you caught a very bad flu and you couldn't be in public until Friday. So it shouldn't interfere with your classes, but just in case you didn't get back until Saturday, I thought they should know. Then I was told that you have two classes on Tuesday as well as Thursday." Hazel lifted her eyebrows at Lyra.

Lyra squirmed a little bit. She and Hazel didn't keep secrets.

"I just forgot, I promise. I'm replacing Ms. ‘I don't show up for work for the rest of the term’."

Lyra actually felt bad. She wasn't too good at the full disclosure thing, but with Hazel she made a real effort. Hazel seemed to accept that because she nodded before continuing.

"They said since it was Monday, they could find replacements for the week. But you would have to negotiate your deal. Whatever that means."

Lyra's eyes narrowed. "Who'd you talk to? Mother or Daughter?"

"Mother."

"Damn it." Lyra didn't want to teach cycling. In her opinion, cycling sucked.

Hazel continued with a wave of her arm. "And I didn't call your other job because I knew your next due date wasn't until next Tuesday, and if you weren't out of the woods by then we had bigger things to worry about. I had Sadie and Syrus grab all the work you had on your table, though, so you'd have something to do."

Lyra slumped on her stool. That was not good to hear. "You let Syrus in my apartment. Aw man, come on."

He had probably moved all sorts of things.

Hazel laughed. "No, I gave Sadie your keys. Syrus just happened to be with her."

Lyra glared. Her friend was enjoying this too much.

Before she could answer, Taylor interjected. "How many jobs do you have? As far as I know, you read manuscripts from a slush pile. What is this other job you two are talking about? Are they letting you teach children?" He sounded genuinely surprised and a little worried.

Lyra rolled her eyes. "I have just the two. No, for the most part I don't teach children."

Taylor waited for her to continue. Lyra had no intention of telling him. She felt as if too many people knew about her second job already. She wanted to keep it separate from the Were world and keep part of her life to herself. She hadn't minded telling Ryan. She actually liked having him there. He was a different person at the center, more relaxed and fun to be around. Hazel knew because Hazel knew everything. Now Jack and Kelly knew. Lyra could handle that. She didn't particularly like it, but as long as they didn't intrude on it she could handle it.

"You're not going to tell us are you?" Dylan asked.

Lyra smiled and rose to take her dishes to the sink. "Point me in the right direction of my stack of work, please."

When Hazel pointed to the small, square table in her living room, Lyra walked over to dive in to the latest manuscript.

Chapter 13

Jack was at Hazel's door at eight PM, with Ryan next to him. Traffic had been bad, which made him slightly irritated. He used the time it took Ryan to meet him at Hazel's complex to calm down. Lyra had been right. When word of her injuries got out people were clamoring to join the alliance. Every group petitioning to join, had. The whole situation still wasn't settling well for Jack and he was hoping Lyra's account of what happened would clear some of it up.

When he received the call from Hazel, Jack had been so relieved. Lyra's healing had been a struggle and was taking longer than anyone expected. Jack had been surprised Taylor never left her side. Graham stuck around most of the time, as had Dylan. Both Ryan and Justin took turns being there, and both had become extremely quiet the last few days.

The three other wolves didn't let them get too close to her. It was all very strange and Jack wanted answers.

He knocked on the door a little too hard, which caused Ryan to look at him with a raised eyebrow. Jack ignored his Second and listened to the footsteps coming up to the door. Jack only became more irritated when he saw who answered it.

"Yes." Lyra said holding onto the 'e' sound for several beats. She stood in the doorway, one hip leaning on the frame. She didn't look as well as Jack hoped.

"Why the hell are you the one answering the door?" Jack growled and pushed the door open so he could get them all inside and the door shut.

Lyra shrugged at him. "I knew it was you."

Her attention moved to Ryan and she went from mysterious smile to happy grin. "Thank you so much, Ryan. That was so sweet!"

She gingerly leaned over, as if it hurt, and gave him a hug. Jack had no idea what was going on. Everyone else in the room apparently did, which made Jack more irritated. Ryan was being very carful where he put his hands as he hugged her back. Jack didn't really blame him, none of them knew the extent of her injuries.

"Yeah, suck up!" hollered Justin from where he perched on the side of Hazel's red couch.

Ryan grinned at him as Lyra pulled away.

She was the one to respond. "You're just upset you didn't think of it first."

Justin laughed.

Jack was grateful when Taylor, who was on one of the bar stools without a shirt, let him into the loop.

"A basket arrived today with fruit cut up in the shapes of flowers. With it was a wolf stuffed animal that looks surprisingly a lot like Lyra. It was named Wolfington."

Jack heard Ryan snort. "You're joking, right?"

Lyra shook her head. "No, that's what the tag says."

Ryan shook his head. Jack renewed his suspicion that Ryan had feelings for Lyra. He was going to have to sit down and have a talk with his Second. Now was not a good time for them to be drawing attention to themselves.

Jack looked around the room but didn't see either gift. He raised an eyebrow at Lyra, who giggled. "Are you kidding? That thing is completely gone and the wolf is in the bedroom. It was giving Hazel the creeps."

Hazel interjected. "It was not. It's just weird to see you holding a doll of yourself. That's all." She sounded like she had been picked on about it for several hours now.

Jack laughed and took one good look around the room. Everyone appeared to be doing okay. Sighing Jack broke the pleasant mood.

"Okay, I need to hear Lyra's version of events. She, Ryan and I are heading back to the extra bedroom. I seriously expect everyone else to stay out of hearing range." Jack looked at each one of them individually.

Graham and Taylor seemed displeased by his statement. Jack didn't comment, he just motioned for the now solemn Lyra to take the lead down the hall. She did, but not before exchanging looks with her cousin.

Ryan flopped on to the light brown chair that sat on the opposite wall from the matching chair Jack was in. Lyra opted for the bed, since there were no other chairs in the room. She changed positions several times before finding one that seemed to cause the least discomfort. Now she was cross-legged near the foot of the bed. The one and a half foot stuffed wolf sat in her lap. The stuffed animal had been on the bed next to her and she automatically dragged it to her and now was playing absently with its right ear.

Jack agreed with Hazel, the toy did bear a remarkable resemblance to Lyra's wolf form.

Jack cleared his throat to get her attention from the floor. She looked at him with a sad nervousness Jack was not used to seeing from Lyra.

"Start from the beginning."

She blinked at him. "The beginning of what? There has been quite a lot in the last few days."

Jack knew she was being sincere in her confusion but it wasn't helping his irritation any. "Tell me what's been happening while you stayed with your family. I thought you meant you were going to stay with your parents, but Graham made it sound like you were staying with his."

Lyra sighed and she unconsciously hugged the little wolf. "Jack...I...." She was looking at the floor again, as if sifting through her thoughts trying to find the right one. "You never came to my parents' house did you?"

Jack opened his mouth to say of course he had. He met her parents and two little brothers on multiple occasions. But then he shut it again. He had never been to the house. He only met them when they came to visit Lyra. Jack didn't bother to say anything since it seemed Lyra already knew the answer.

"My father's side of the family is extremely well off. My Dad and Graham's are brothers. Both of them, along with the younger brother, all live on the same ginormous family estate. So in a way, staying with one family is staying with all of them." She went quiet, still looking at the floor.

Jack had to recalculate what he knew of Lyra. He had known the family was well off but not enough so to be considered upper class. He set it aside to chew on later. "So what's been happening over there?"

Again she gave a searching expression. "The company the three brothers run helps them make lots of enemies so there is lots of security. But they are not equipped to handle OUR type of intruders. There were two nights where they got in and there was some fighting, but in the long run we came out on top. That night I was attacked, I was off the family property. Graham was just swinging by from work so I could jump in the car and go. I think that's why we didn't hear them. We were being sloppy. Graham was in the car and I started changing. It left me vulnerable until Graham heard me yell. Then he basically kicked the crap out of them. From there on out, it's really fuzzy. The world just kept going in and out."

Ryan cut in. "Do you remember what the guys looked like, smelled like?"

Lyra began to shake her head but stopped. "Maybe. They had something covering their scent but not very well, I might recognize one if I was near them again, but I can't guarantee anything."

Jack thought she seemed better than when they first entered the room, less nervous.

She finally looked him in the eyes. "Jack, I'd like to see my dogs."

For a second Jack had no idea why she would say that. Then it clicked. She promised to do things his way until whatever this was blew over.

"Not by yourself you won't."

Lyra rolled her eyes. "Do you seriously think anyone is going to let me be alone any time soon? Even for a second." She sounded a little irritated. "I'd take Graham and Taylor with me. That way Graham's paranoid father isn't being subjected to anybody new."

That got Jack's attention. "I understand Graham would be extra careful after the last time, but why is Taylor not new to your family?"

Lyra got a look on her face that said she clearly hadn't meant to share that little bit. "Taylor's dad works for my uncle as one of his trusted people so Taylor hung out with Graham and me a lot growing up."

This was news to Jack. "Why is Taylor not part of our pack then?"

Lyra snorted. "I don't know. I didn't organize the packs. At the time I was just trying to keep Hazel from losing it. When Taylor and I saw each other he started heading over but he didn't get there soon enough to get lumped in with us.

“Bishop is a good leader though. Taylor and I discussed it and if he was not contented with his pack we would find a way to switch him. But as luck would have it, Taylor cares for his pack so there was nothing to be done."

Jack almost couldn't process all that information. How could he not already have known this? This was a long term thing, not just recent.

Ryan interrupted Jack's thoughts. "You guys know Dylan as well don't you?" Ryan sounded sure of the answer.

Lyra swung her attention to the other man, looking a little surprised. "Yes, though nowhere near as well as Taylor. Dylan's father works with my younger uncle, Deidrick, and his mother works with Deidrick's wife. That's how they met." She smiled, then tilted her head. "How did you know?"

Jack looked at Ryan, and the other man shrugged. "He was here a lot of the time you were out. I figured he would only do that if he knew you well."

Lyra nodded in understanding and went back to playing with the wolf's ear.

Jack folded his arms. "Exactly how many others in the project have family that work for yours?" Ha was not thrilled about these coincidences.

Lyra shrugged. "I have no idea. Taylor, Dylan, and Graham are the ones I know because I grew up around them. There are about a dozen others around our age I know just as well from growing up. They just are not part of the project."

Lyra's social circle was much wider than Jack thought. It seemed somewhat at odds with what he knew of her. Jack really didn't like where this was going. He liked to know everything in his world and Lyra ran in and moved everything around.

"What if I get Dylan to come with us as well? That way there's three of them."

It took Jack a second to figure out that Lyra changed subjects on him. He knew how Lyra felt about her dogs but Jack would have been much more comfortable if someone he knew he could trust was going with her.

Flexing his arms, Jack nodded. "Fine, but only if all three are with you and you call me if you end up going anywhere else and when you get back." Jack could almost feel himself about to regret that, but he didn't want to say no.

Lyra beamed, and making a small happy sound, slid off the bed, almost taking the wolf with her before she remembered she was holding it and set it on the bed before leaving the room.

Jack sighed and turned to Ryan, who mirrored him. Jack did not want to have this discussion. He wanted nothing to do with the pack's love lives but he had to put his foot down now before things progressed.

"You can't pursue her."

Ryan's blank face became stone but his gaze sharpened.

Jack went in head first now that he started. "I'm not talking as her littermate. I'm talking as your Alpha."

Ryan straightened in his chair but remained silent.

"The last thing we need right now is to give the scientists another reason to pay attention to us. Especially Lyra. They already have an unhealthy interest in her. Being part of a Were couple would only made them more interested. And they would find out. They followed her home, Ryan, it would be nothing for them to find out who she is seeing. Even if she doesn't feel the same way you do, your interest alone will draw attention. We don't need that right now. We need to find out what's going on and solidify the alliance. If things ever stabilize...then you'll just have to deal with me as a protective littermate. Until then, as your Alpha, I'm telling you to drop it."

Ryan was furious. Though his face was stone, his eyes blazed, his jaw and fists were clenched. "And if I don't?"

Jack matched Ryan's stony expression with his own. "Don't try me, Ryan. I will protect my pack from this threat, doing whatever it takes."

Ryan stood up slowly, glaring down at Jack the whole time. "Fine, Jack. We'll do it your way." His tone was a lethal growl as Ryan stalked from the room.

There was no doubt in Jack's mind that Ryan could challenge him for position as Alpha. Jack wasn't sure who would win. It was Ryan's desire for pack stability that kept the challenge from ever coming up. Things worked well as they were and no one wanted to rock the boat. But Lyra was fast becoming a major weakness for Ryan. Jack would have noticed if Ryan had always been like this. No, it was definitely recent. Something else Jack would have to watch. Just what he needed: more complications.

A few hours later, Jack was sitting at his desk at home when his cell went off. Reaching over, Jack read Lyra's name flashing on the screen. Figuring she must be at Hazel's, Jack answered. "Hey, Lyra."

"Oh good, you're still awake. Look, we are stopping as Shari's for food. The backseat is getting whiny. We may be another hour or two. Do you still want me to call you when I get to Hazel's?" Lyra sounded happy.

Despite his mood, Jack smiled. "Duh, just because you're going to eat cheap food doesn't mean I no longer care about your safety."

Lyra gave a small laugh. "Okay, Jack, I'll talk to you later."

There were several male voices in the background imitating Lyra's goodbye.

He chuckled. "Bye, Lyra." Shaking his head, Jack set down his phone.

Chapter 14

"Lyra, you're not lying. We are grabbing food at Shari's." Dylan said soothingly as the four of them walked up to the diner.

"Yeah and the baby here was whining in the back seat." Taylor added as he grabbed Dylan in a headlock and rubbed his knuckles on the younger guy's scalp.

Lyra sighed. She still felt dishonest. "It's a lie by omission. And you know me, I hate lying, period. Even if I am good at it. Jack is trusting me and I don't deserve it."

That quieted them for a moment. She knew the guys felt similarly, though not as strongly as she did. None of them liked hiding so much from their packs. But all of their hands were tied until they could convince the right people otherwise.

Graham swung his arm around her shoulders. "Hey Little Luna, everything will be fine. You have us. The four of us are our own mini-pack."

Dylan gave a noise of enthusiastic agreement. "Yeah, like those little packets of cookies."

There was a thud. Lyra was sure Taylor smacked Dylan.

"We know you. You know us, we can settle for that. Hey and you never know, maybe we'll be adding three more to our little troupe tonight." Graham said the last part as if trying to drum up more excitement from an audience.

Taylor snorted. "Please don't call us a troupe. I want to be associated with actors as little as possible." As they approached the doors, he let go of Dylan.

Graham nodded to the hostess as they scanned the restaurant looking for the rest of their group. Lyra mumbled so only the other three Weres would hear her.

"I can't help but see the irony that we are meeting with the three guys the scientists wanted to pair us with. Does anyone else feel as if we are doing their job for them?"

There were several answers of half-hearted agreement. Then her brain clicked off for a split-second before clicking back on again. She had never seen the 'rocker wolf', as she and Hazel had been calling him, in his human form. He stood so the four of them could find the booth. He was very nice to look at. He had shaggy black hair and pale green eyes. He was tall, which was always a plus. Lean without being intimidating. He was definitely worth looking at.

Graham growled next to her ear as the walked toward the booth. None of them were taking their eyes off the Were watching them. "Easy, Lyra. I don't want to have to kill the guy, just on principle." Lyra knew he was only half-joking.

Lyra made a noise in the back of her throat. "Deal with it, Hammy. I know I'm the closest thing to a sister you have, but you need to get used to it."

Graham grumbled.

Lyra knew if Graham could sense her interest in the guy, then everyone would in the close quarters of the booth. So she concentrated on the task at hand: form a plan to stop the attacks on them before it started to reach beyond just the seven of them.

Boone, Kipling, and Reed were already taking up one side of the booth. Taylor half shoved Dylan into the opposite side first, then stood back so Lyra could go next. She rolled her eyes. Lyra hated sitting in the middle but she knew why they were doing it, so she kept her mouth shut. Taylor slid in beside her. Graham grabbed a nearby chair and swung it around to the head of the table. That was Graham, putting himself in the most danger while maintaining a position of power.

Boone broke the silence first. "You look much better than when we last saw you, girl." He had a slight southern accent.

Lyra wasn't sure how she felt about being called girl, so she decided to leave it alone.

Kipling shifted in a little. "Yeah, it's definitely good to not see blood all over."

There was a general murmur of agreement.

The waitress, a peroxide blonde about five-foot-two, stepped up to the table. Lyra was mildly amused the woman couldn't decide who to ogle first.

"They're all single." She grinned at the waitress.

The other woman laughed, looking slightly embarrassed, but comfortable enough in her own skin to laugh about it. Lyra was starting to like her.

After the waitress left, Taylor playfully smacked Lyra's arm. "Come on, Little Luna. Now she's not going to go for any of us."

Lyra rolled her eyes. "Oh please, like you'd ever let a little thing like me stop you from getting in to a woman's pants."

Dylan laughed next to her and Taylor pretended offense.

"Speak for yourself, Yankee boy. Women rarely turn down us southern gentlemen," Boone drawled, his accent suddenly prevalent.

Lyra cackled. "Oh Taylor, he's got you beat."

Taylor looked genuinely offended. "Hey!"

Dylan just about lost it.

Lyra shrugged. "I'm sorry, dude, but women are suckers for accents."

"Are they now?"

It was so quiet Lyra wasn't sure who else heard Kipling. She chanced a look. He was looking right at her, smirking. It was all Lyra could do not to react.

Graham cleared his throat to get the table's attention as their drinks came. "Could we maybe stick to the task at hand for a bit?"

Reed jumped in as soon as the waitress was back out of earshot and Boone and Taylor stopped flirting with her.

"Do we have any way to track them? Any of them? I know your Pack L is involved but I do not believe they are of any real importance. Lyra's Alpha said they were not traceable, but I do not believe that. There has to be a way to find these people."

Lyra looked at Graham, having a silent discussion over how to proceed. Lyra looked away first. "Graham did not tell Jack the entire truth. Neither did I when he questioned me later."

The three on the other side of the table exchanged glances.

Boone spoke, his accent back to its normal faint whisper. "Then what did happen?"

Lyra looked at Graham again. It was more his story than hers.

He took a deep breath before looking at the three men. "Lyra and I were staying on the family estate. For obvious reasons."

The three men nodded solemnly.

Lyra felt a pang of guilt. Taylor's left hand slid to her leg under the table, he must have sensed her feelings. She had told Jack a lie of omission about these three Weres. She didn't know them personally, but they still fell under the umbrella of Graham's dad. She knew they could be trusted and could with minimal effort find out a great deal about any of them. They knew the justifiably paranoid things her family did.

Graham continued, as if oblivious to Lyra's guilt, but she knew he wasn't. He just wouldn't make a scene.

"I picked her up outside the grounds. I was in the car when she was jumped. I did not knock anyone unconscious. I killed both of them and the third didn't get far. My older brothers were nearby and heard the fighting. They shot him in the leg. My father is now interrogating the man. We don't actually know whether they were sent by enemies of my father or by enemies of ours. Either way, we won't need to track them. If they turn out to be our enemies, my father will turn over whatever information he gets to me."

In the meantime Pack L, as insignificant as they may be, are our best bet. We might want to try working with them until we find out what exactly is going on. Find out who is pulling the strings, so we can rid ourselves of them. My father has offered to help us, as long as it's under the table. His board of trustees can't find out about it."

The group sat silently for several minutes as the food came.

Lyra took advantage of the silence. "I am our best bet, whether you like it or not. I particularly don't like it, but I'm willing to do it. They already think less of me, so I'm more likely to sweep under their radar. Since I'm the only girl, they will think convincing me means convincing you. I don't care how any of you feel about it. It's the best idea we've got. Don't make me run with it without all of you."

Dylan sounded so quiet next to her. "What about Jack? Didn't you promise him you would do what he said?"

Lyra sighed. "Yes, but Jack doesn't always think out every possibility. I'm a pro at finding loopholes when it comes to Jack. The only problem will be when my..." She raised her arms to give air quotes. "Guard detail has Pack F males in it. They wouldn't go along with the idea. Even if we could tell them about it. But since this could be hostility toward the family, we can't tell them."

Lyra hated speaking in code but her paranoid uncle demanded it.

Boone chimed in thoughtfully. "We could get ourselves on the detail. There are six of us and what, eleven males in Pack F. The first chance we get to double up you can contact them. I'm sure more than one of us has their contact information."

Graham interjected before anyone else could be swayed. "NO! Absolutely no way are we using Luna as bait!" He growled low enough only their table would hear it.

Taylor squeezed Lyra's leg to drag her attention from her cousin. When she was looking at him he gave her a sad smile.

"Little Luna, you don't have to do this. It is not your job to put yourself in harm's way."

Lyra was getting frustrated now. "Can we stop with the Luna now please? It's getting irritating. Let's just settle this. Who's going to help me spy on the enemy?"

She was done having this discussion. The sooner they finished, the sooner she could spy and be done with this whole mess.

Everyone at the table but Graham raised their hands.

Graham growled. "Fine, but if anything starts to look fishy, I'm yanking you whether you like it or not."

Lyra nodded and they slowly moved into lighter topics. About an hour later, they paid and were lingering out in the parking lot finalizing their plans. As she started to head for the car, Kipling grabbed her wrist and spun her as if they were dancing. Then he started to foxtrot with her.

When she faced him he smiled down at her. "I'd like to take you out some time. Just us, no guards or family. What do think?"

Lyra grinned up at him. "That would be great."

He grinned back. "Great." He spun her again before letting go. "I'll give you a call." Kipling started to pivot then stopped and gave her an embarrassed grin. "This is totally going to ruin my coolness moment, but I don't have your number."

Lyra laughed, then held her hand out for his phone.

He reached into one of his front pockets and pulled out his phone. Instead of putting it in her hand, he held it just out of reach so she would have to grab it.

Lyra narrowed her eyes but continued smiling as she grabbed the phone and dialed her own cell. After a second, the theme from Ghostbusters started. Lyra canceled the call and handed him back his phone. "There, two birds with one stone."

Kipling grinned down at her, but before he could say anything Dylan came bounding up beside her and looped his arm around her waist. Both of them looked at Dylan's huge grin.

"I've been sent to fetch you away from the Were flirting with you before Taylor or Graham have to maim him." He grinned widely as he spoke.

Kipling laughed. Lyra rolled her eyes, but looked at Kipling as she spoke to Dylan.

"Let me guess. They figure I'm less likely to hurt you for coming over here than either of them so you got volunteered?"

Dylan grinned wider. "Pretty much."

Lyra couldn't help but laugh. Dylan was only twenty-two and sometimes it was a young twenty-two. She had a sneaking suspicion as an only child Dylan just loved being part of a group. In this particular group he was the younger brother and he relished that role.

"All right, all right." She looked up at Kipling. "It was really great to meet you, outside of wolf form."

Kipling grinned back at her. "Yeah, you too. I'll talk to you later." With that, they split ways.

Dylan kept his arm around Lyra's waist as they walked. She let him. Lyra knew Dylan didn't mean it as a possessive gesture, the way Taylor or Graham would have. Dylan was just being companionable.

"I like him."

Lyra smiled. "I'm glad you approve, Dylan." She didn't want to insult him by laughing.

"I like the other guy better for you, though. I think in the long run he would work better."

That got Lyra's attention. "Who are you talking about, Dylan?"

Dylan shook his head. "No." Then he looked at her, smiling. "You're cute when you're oblivious, Lyra."

She almost stopped walking. He was using her own saying against her, as she used it on him all the time. What was it he thought she was missing?

As they reached the car, Graham and Taylor stood watching them.

"Did you just give him your number?" Graham actually seemed distressed.

Lyra rolled her eyes. "Yeah, Graham, I did. As I said earlier, deal with it." Then she unhooked herself from Dylan and walked to the passenger seat.

Graham didn't speak until he was pulling out of the parking lot. "I don't like the idea of you dating a Werewolf."

Lyra couldn't stop it, she burst out laughing. "You're a little behind the times there, Hammy. I've dated Weres before."

Graham shot up in his seat and almost missed the turn onto the freeway. "What?!"

He looked at Taylor in his rearview mirror. "Did you know about this?"

Lyra turned to see Taylor shaking his head with a surprised expression. "No, I had no idea."

Lyra started laughing again. The shock was priceless.

Graham gripped the steering wheel. "Who?"

Lyra snorted. "I am not about to give you names."

Then she heard Dylan from the back seat. "She was dating Grant for a while. They seemed very on-again-off-again."

That even surprised Lyra.

She turned in her seat. Dylan smiled at her.

"How did you know that, Dylan? I thought no one but Hazel knew?"

Dylan grinned. "I'm more observant than I get credit for. It's in the way he looks at you and in the way you used to look at him. I'll bet you broke it off the last time, right?"

Lyra just nodded.

Dylan looked from Taylor to Graham, who both appeared distressed. "They were one of the three couples at the beginning of the project. But I'm guessing you were off again at the time of the accident."

Lyra nodded again.

Dylan tapped his chin. "I would say the whole thing went for about ten months, a year tops."

Lyra turned to face forward. Dylan was right on the dot. From their first date to the last break up, it had been two weeks short of a year. She hadn't known it had been that obvious.

Dylan seemed to be reading her thoughts. "It wasn't obvious. If it had been, Taylor and Graham would not be suffering this stunned silence right now. I always wondered what you saw in him. The two of you were an odd match."

Graham's knuckles were white but he stayed silent. That worried Lyra.

Taylor finally found his voice. "Just so I'm clear, we are talking about the same guy who got into a yelling match with his wealthy father while in quarantine?"

Lyra sighed. "Yes."

Taylor was quiet a moment. "Yeah, I don't see it either."

Lyra folded her arms. "We did break up, guys."

Graham looked like a mix of horror and anger. "I need us to change the subject. I can't listen to this anymore." He sounded pained.

Lyra laughed. Graham had never been able to handle her dating very well. The only time she ever had her heart broken, Graham trashed the guy's car. She had a sneaking suspicion he had help, since the car ended up in a tree.

"So, how 'bout them Mariners?" Dylan chimed from the backseat.

Lyra groaned. She liked baseball, but she grew up with a bunch of guys who just took it too far. The rest of the ride home was going to be filled with baseball facts no one really needed to know.

Lyra and Taylor were dropped off at Hazel's with some argument. Taylor refused to leave her 'alone'. He worked for her father and when Taylor told him of the situation, he was instructed not to leave Lyra unguarded. Apparently he was going to take that far too seriously.

Once they were inside Lyra flipped open her phone to call Jack. Taylor started shifting next to her.

Jack picked up after the first ring. "Hey Lyra, you back safe?"

Lyra smiled. He sounded like she interrupted him working. He had a distracted quality to his voice.

"Yeah, and I've got Taylor with me, though he's changing forms at the moment. He's refusing to leave me alone."

Jack snorted. "I figured as much. Syrus should be there somewhere."

Just as that sentence reached her ear, an inky black wolf made his way from the back of the apartment. Syrus's wolf form always looked like he was stalking instead of walking.

"I see him. Hey Jack, I'd like to go in to work tomorrow. See if they need me. You know, to get back in their good graces."

There was a long pause. "It's fine by me, if you run it by Ryan. I do ask that you shift before bed so you are more healed before work."

Lyra let out the breath she had been holding. "Deal. Good night, Jack."

"Good night, Lyra, sleep well."

They both hung up and Lyra emptied her pockets before changing forms. It took her a normal amount of time, for which she was grateful.

Chapter 15

Within minutes of hanging up with Lyra, Jack's phone rang again. This time he didn't know the number, and he was tempted not to pick up. But just in case it was important, Jack answered.

"Hello?" Jack made it a question, hoping it wouldn't be a telemarketer this late.

"Hey Jack, this is Graham. As in Lyra's Graham."

Jack had no idea why the other man felt the need to add the last part but he didn't say anything. "What can I do for you Graham?"

"Me and the other six guys the scientists were after want on the guard rotation."

Jack waited a second to respond so he could get past his initial feelings of surprise, anger, and frustration. "No."

Graham seemed to do the same thing. "Why not?"

Jack didn't much feel like being diplomatic. "Because I know none of you as well as I know my pack. The most I'm willing to concede is you and Taylor. That's it."

There was an angry silence.

"Not even Dylan?"

Jack could feel the test of wills. Alpha males always clashed.

"I don't know Dylan or the other three. You're her cousin and Taylor apparently is the next closest thing. Lyra would kill me if I didn't put you on the detail. So for her I will, but not at the same time and I'll let my guys know not to swap with you."

Jack knew he was treading dangerous waters but he wanted this pissing contest out of the way.

Graham's voice held a small growl. "You do not trust us to protect her."

Jack was careful to keep his tone flat. "You didn't the last time."

A roar, or the closest thing Jack ever heard human vocal cords make, blasted through the phone.

Jack felt his own anger rise in response. "It's my detail. I make the rules. If you're on said detail, you answer to me."

The growl was so low if Jack hadn't possessed Were hearing he might not have made out the words.

"I could take her from you, Jack. Keep her safe from the world better than you ever could. She would come with me willingly. Walk away from your detail. Family comes first Jack, you know that."

Jack finally let his temper show. "Either you do things by my terms or you don't play at all. Lyra gave me her word, and to Lyra her word is a contract."

There was shuffling on the other end of the phone and several growls. Jack was positive they came from more than one person. After a beat or two, a different voice came over the phone.

"Hi Jack, sorry about that. Had to save Graham from himself. Lyra would be really upset if he managed to get himself on her detail only to get himself kicked off thirty seconds later."

Jack recognized the voice but couldn't put a name with it.

"Oh sorry, this is Dylan."

Jack didn't want to deal with the young wolf at the moment either. But before he could get a sound out, Dylan pressed on.

"I know, I get it. Your detail, your way. I'm cool with that. I just want to know if you're going to stop me from visiting her or vice versa. I kinda like having lunch with her twice a month. The date is supposed to be tomorrow. I'm guessing that's canceled, though. I would like to call her and reschedule, but I won't if you're won't let her."

Jack sat puzzled for a second. He was trying to shift from anger to level-headed faster than was possible for him.

"Why would I stop you from visiting her?"

Dylan made a sound. "I just wanna make sure I knew the rules."

Jack wanted to clarify for the young guy. "No, I won't stop her from hanging out with you, but I don't want you on her detail."

Dylan was quiet for a moment. "I understand. Can't say I'm not disappointed,, but I respect the decision."

To Jack's surprise the other man sounded like he meant it.

"Well, it was nice talking to you, Jack. I'm going to hang up the phone now because I think it's better for all of us if I don't hand it back to Graham. Just call Taylor with their shifts. He's more...personable. Do you have his number?"

Jack couldn't figure out how he felt about Dylan. "No."

The young wolf shot off the number, as if he had it committed to memory, then hung up.

Jack was still angry at Graham, but he was amusingly confused about Dylan. Instead of thinking too much about it, Jack turned back to his work. He would rearrange the schedule in the morning.

Chapter 16

When Saturday rolled around, Ryan was glad Jack agreed Lyra could go back to staying in her own place. He could tell she was antsy to get back home. He wasn't sure Taylor was helping anything. The other man rarely left Lyra. The only times were when he ran by his own apartment to get clothes.

At first it bothered him that Lyra and Taylor were so close. Ryan had only seen them interact a handful of times before, and he never knew why they got along as well as they did. Thanks to Jack, now he knew and he couldn't help but be a little jealous of the friendship.

Ryan though he was as close as he could get to Lyra, short of her littermates. He had been so wrong. To make matters worse, the three of them were headed to lunch with Dylan, which apparently Lyra did regularly. Ryan was not looking forward to being the odd man out.

Adding to Ryan's dim mood, Jack was no closer to figuring out the attacks on Lyra. The Alphas in the alliance were pooling their resources, but very little was getting to them. The only intel they received stated that Pack L was socializing heavily with the other two lab assistant groups. There were also rumors they were acting on behalf of someone higher up the food chain.

The pack couldn't trade off playing guard dogs for much longer. It had been a week since Jack found out about the attacks on Lyra and more than three since Ryan and Cole began watching her. Patience was wearing thin and Ryan knew if Lyra didn't get some alone time soon, she would start snapping at people.

He wasn’t sure why, but Lyra appeared to dread taking Taylor with them to the fitness center that morning. He found that both interesting and flattering. Ryan knew he was the only one she actually invited into that part of her world. It was made plain the moment Taylor stepped into the center. The other man stayed absolutely quiet the entire time. Ryan could tell Taylor hadn’t liked not knowing about Lyra teaching, and he liked that Ryan knew about it even less.

Ryan was rousted from his thoughts as Taylor parked his green Grand Cherokee in the parking lot of a diner with a 1950s theme. He slid out of the car and automatically scanned the lot. He smelled Lyra moving in step with him before he saw her out of the corner of his eye.

"You going to light up and start yelling 'Danger, Will Robinson, danger' if you see anything?" She was smiling at him.

Ryan snorted as he finished his scan. "You do know you watch far too much TV right?"

She just shrugged as they walked into the restaurant.

It took them a second to hunt down Dylan, since the other man had been on the phone and not paying attention. Once they were at the booth, Taylor moved to get in after Lyra. She stopped halfway in to turn and glare at him.

"Don't even think about it. That would be so rude. You're friends with Dylan, Ryan is not."

Then she reached around the other man, grabbed a handful of Ryan's shirt and tugged.

Ryan just about jumped her, but stopped himself. Remembering Jack's words, Ryan kept his mouth shut as he moved into the booth next to Lyra. That didn't stop his mind from wandering though, and there wasn't too much he could do about the tiny smile that curled onto his face.

Dylan smiled at them when they sat down but went back to listening to whoever was on the phone. Lyra and Taylor exchanged glances, then Taylor shrugged. It was good to know they didn't have a clue either.

The waiter came by and took drink orders from them. Dylan already had a Sprite sitting in front of him.

They sat in silence until it seemed to get to Lyra. Before anyone could move she whipped her torso forward and snatched the phone from Dylan's hand.

She put the phone to her ear. "He's going to have to call you back because I want actual interpersonal interaction, dang it."

Then she tapped the screen and handed it back to the slightly stunned Dylan.

Ryan tried not to laugh. He would be ticked if it was his phone. But then he wouldn't have been on his phone, so he didn't feel bad for Dylan.

Dylan slipped the phone under the table, into a pocket. "You know I hate it when you do that, woman."

Lyra didn't look up from her menu. "Then get the hint."

Dylan was trying to glare at her, but with no effect, he soon gave up and looked at the menu.

The lack of conversation continued until after they ordered. Ryan knew something was off because he could feel Lyra's nervousness coming off her in waves. Ryan glanced at the other two men, but he didn't know either of them well enough to know if they were the cause.

Then Lyra's voice came softly from beside him. When he looked down at her, Lyra was staring at the table.

"Ryan, I have a very large favor to ask. Please before you respond, let me get the whole idea out."

Ryan straightened. He had the feeling he was not going to like where this was going.

"Some of us have been talking and we think maybe it would be in everyone's best interest if I turned myself over to Pack L."

Ryan saw a flash of red. He didn't know he was growling until Lyra's hand clasped over his in a calming gesture.

"Ryan, let me finish. This way I could spy on them. We could use the opportunity to find out who Pack L is working with. Jack's plan isn't working. This is a better option. But you and I both know Jack would never see it that way. It would have to be kept from him. I trust your judgment, if you say there is another packmate we can trust with this, I'll believe you. But it needs to be done."

Ryan sat there a moment. Too much was going on. Lyra's hand on his and her scent surrounding him made it hard enough to think straight and now she was asking him to lie to their Alpha and work behind his back.

Ryan spouted off the first question he could think of. "Who is ‘we’?"

He felt her hand tense. "Me and the other six Pack L are after."

Ryan felt a pang of angry jealousy but shoved it out of the way. "When did you meet with them? I'm assuming Jack doesn't know about it."

Lyra shook her head but still stared at the table. "Wednesday night."

Ryan thought back, there would have been plenty of time. He didn't want her doing this, and he adamantly disagreed with Lyra turning herself over. But he was smart enough to see the merits and a tiny voice in his head argued that Lyra was fully capable of taking care of herself. The idea went against all of Ryan's instincts.

"What guarantee do you have that I won't go tell Jack your plan?"

Ryan watched the two other men stiffen and their eyes narrow. He could tell neither of them wanted him involved in the first place. It made him wonder why Lyra picked him.

Lyra gave a heavy sigh. "You won't. You're too smart. You understand why this is our best bet. You might not want to be a part of it but you won't sabotage it, either."

Normally Ryan would have taken enjoyment out of the fact that Lyra knew him so well. In light of how little he seemed to know about her though it didn't have the same effect.

"What is it you're asking me to do, Lyra?"

She shifted her weight. "I'll need to make contact with them. Since Jack won't put Taylor and Graham on guard duty together, we'll need you to help us. I'll make contact, have meetings and such while you and one of them are on duty. That way it won't cause suspicion."

Ryan looked at the two other men. He could tell neither of them was too fond of the plan either but both accepted it as their best option. Ryan wondered how they convinced Graham. He ran his hand through his hair.

"Lyra, if you can look me in the eye and tell me you think this is the only way we'll beat this and give me your word that you will be as carful as you possibly can be, then I'll agree to help you. Within reason, if things get out of hand, I'll carry you out myself."

The other two men exchanged a look, but Ryan was paying too much attention to Lyra to know what the look meant.

Lyra finally looked up at him, slowly. She gave him direct eye contact.

"Ryan, I see no better way to get things resolved and I would really appreciate your help with this. I give my word that I'll be careful and I'll try not to kick you in the crotch should you ever be stupid enough to carry me anywhere."

He watched a small amused flicker flash in her eyes as she said the last part.

Ryan gave her a small smile and nodded his agreement as their food came. He knew he wasn't imagining things when Ryan saw Lyra's shoulders slump in relief.

About five minutes of awkward silence, Dylan reached across the table and snagged a handful of Lyra's fries.

She looked like she couldn't decide whether to laugh or be shocked. "Dude!"

Dylan shoved half the fries in his mouth and gave her a wide grin as he swallowed. "Yes?"

She gestured to his plate. "You have your own fries."

Dylan shoved the other half into his mouth and continued to grin. "So?"

Lyra glared at him but Ryan could see the sides of her mouth twitching. "Stick to your own plate, fur boy."

Dylan started laughing. "Oh please, Taylor and I could so take you."

Taylor paused with his triple cheese burger inches from his face and shifted his eyes to Dylan. "Boy, don't get me involved. You forget I grew up with her. There's no way I'd be stupid enough to get into a fight with her...again." Then he took a huge bite of his burger.

Ryan watched Dylan's face flip to worry. Ryan snuck looks at both Lyra and Taylor. To him it was obvious they were messing with Dylan. But the young Were wasn't so sure.

Taylor started laughing. "Oh man, you are so gullible. Seriously Dylan."

Dylan gave a relieved grin and began reaching for Lyra's fries again. This time she was prepared and smacked his hand hard enough to hit the table. Ryan had a feeling that would convince Dylan to stick to his own plate.

Ryan bumped Lyra's arm to get her attention. She gave Dylan one last warning glare before turning her head.

"So, how are you going to go about this plan of yours?"

Lyra swallowed her food. "Pack L gave their contact info to all of us, so I'm just going to call and set up a meeting, hoping I sound convincing. And so Graham doesn't have a coronary, you guys will be hiding nearby in case things go wrong."

To Ryan, it sounded simple and broad enough for any number of things to go wrong, but that was probably the point.

"When are you going to contact them?"

Lyra took another bite of her chicken wrap before answering. "As soon as we finish eating. I'll try for later tonight. I'll claim it will be easier to give you guys the slip." She smiled at him, before returning to her food.

Ryan heard Taylor snort. "Oh please, Ryan and I are two of the four hardest Weres for you to give the slip to."

Lyra popped a fry in her mouth and looked at her friend. "Oh yeah? Who are the other two?"

Taylor shook his head as if scolding her for asking such an obvious question. "That would be Graham and your littermate Justin. That guy is the best nose there is, or so I'm told."

Ryan wasn't sure how he felt about being included in that company. He was not a good tracker, but he made up for it in strength, speed, and aggression. Why would Taylor include him?

Lyra rolled her eyes. "That is so a challenge."

Taylor put his burger down and glowered at Lyra. It was very convincing and Ryan had no doubt almost anyone else would have caved, but Lyra just popped more fries in her mouth and looked back at him.

"You will not take that as a challenge."

Lyra gave a non-committal shrug, which seemed to frustrate Taylor.

Ryan watched the other man and couldn't help the question forming in his mind. "Taylor, why aren't you an Alpha? Or barring that, a Second. You seem much more dominant than Victor."

Taylor shrugged and picked up his burger. "I am, but I have absolutely no urge for power. I don't really want to be in charge of making decisions for anybody but myself."

Ryan thought about that for a second. He didn't think there were any dominant Weres in their pack other than him and Jack. He wondered what it would be like if there were.

Lunch went by faster than Ryan expected. By the time they paid and were standing out in the parking lot, more than an hour had passed. Lyra was getting slightly fidgety, playing with the end of her braid.

After a few moments of silence she gave a sigh. "All right, everybody stay quiet so I can get this over with."

Then she pulled out her phone and a business card, one Ryan assumed must belong to someone from Pack L. She finished dialing and put the phone to her ear.

Dylan swooped in and came up behind her, clasping his arms around her waist, standing flush against her back. Ryan was downright shocked that all Lyra did was stiffen as the younger man laid his head on top of hers. Even more surprisingly, Lyra relaxed after a moment, even leaning back a little. Ryan chanced a look at Taylor, but the other man only looked a little.

Then someone must have picked up the other end because Lyra spoke.

"Hi, this is Lyra from Pack F." There was silence for a moment. "I've been considering your proposal and I must decline."

That made both Ryan and Taylor stiffen and exchange worried glances. Dylan didn't seem fazed.

"Well, on the grounds that your people attacked me and mine on several occasions. I have no guarantee that if I join you I will be unharmed. In fact it seems to be quite the opposite."

There was another pause as the person on the other end of the line spoke.

"Yes I'll be sure to ask their names next time they jump me." Lyra's voice oozed sarcasm.

After another pause, her expression became curious. "Really? You would schedule a meeting and let me bring someone with me? Do I get to pick that someone? How do I know you won't just outnumber me?"

Another pause and Lyra looked at Ryan in surprise. He wasn't sure he wanted to know.

"Let me get this straight. You'll let me bring however many people I want, whoever I want as long as they are all Were and none are Alpha. Why would you agree to this?"

There was a much longer pause this time. Ryan made eye contact with Lyra. He was glad to know they were on the same page, neither of them liked where this was going.

"And where would I meet you?"

She stiffened momentarily and Dylan made a small soothing noise in the back of his throat.

"All right, fine. Be there just after dusk. That way the families are gone and the drug dealers are not out yet." Then she tapped her phone.

Instead of putting it away and disengaging from Dylan, Lyra seemed to shake a little and her arms curled around where his encircled her waist. Dylan just continued to make that noise in the back of his throat. Lyra turned her to the side and up, to dislodge Dylan's chin so she could look at his face.

"You heard all that, didn't you?" She sounded hopeful.

Ryan watched Dylan nod. The other man's eyes were closed and he had a peaceful expression on his face. Lyra turned back and stared at the ground. Dylan seemed to know she couldn't see his expression because his eyes snapped open and he looked from Taylor to Ryan. The younger man was furious. He had the perfect vantage point to hear whatever it was the other person had said.

Lyra didn't appear to want to talk. She looked more fragile than Ryan had ever seen her. Even when injured, she stood her ground and stayed strong. Now she looked like she was struggling to hang on by a thread. Ryan wanted nothing more than to wrap himself around Lyra and be strong for her. But Jack was right, that was not a possibility. Mentally shaking himself, Ryan looked directly at Dylan.

"What did they say?"

Dylan looked at him, not trying to hide his anger. "It was not the exact wording. It was more his tone and what he didn't say. He told Lyra the perfect place to meet would be Crystal Park, and since Lyra was allowed to go home today, it would be closer to her apartment. He or his associates have been watching her. He simply hinted here and there. He said the other six of us were more than welcome to join her since we all seem so close."

Ryan couldn't help it. He scanned the parking lot around them. He caught Taylor doing the same thing. Neither found anything.

"Do you think he knows our plan?" Lyra's voice was so quiet Ryan barely heard it.

Dylan laid his chin on her head again. "I don't know. I don't think they know everything, but I think it's safe to assume they know something. And this meeting is a trap."

Before Ryan or Taylor could say anything, Lyra straightened up and before their eyes, collected herself into a core of strength.

"That's why I need to go alone."

They started to protest but she glared and shifted her weight to push against Dylan's hands until he let go. She took three steps away from him and looked at all three men.

"At the very least I need to appear alone. I want to endanger as few people as possible. I'm going to go to the restroom. I'll be back in about five minutes. In that time you guys need to decide how you want to do this because when I get back we are not discussing it. I need to know nothing about it. Are we clear?" Then she drilled Taylor with a look. "And we are not to involve my family in any circumstances, understand."

Taylor slowly closed his eyes and nodded. "Yes, my lady."

Once she got her answer, Lyra turned and strode back into the restaurant.

Taylor pulled his phone out of his pocket and began flipping it. "We'll need eight for a decent perimeter, but six will do." He continued to flip his phone, thinking, with a grim expression on his face.

Dylan shuffled his feet. "You're not going to call Graham, are you?"

The way he said it made him sound younger again.

Taylor's hand paused. "No."

Ryan wanted to ask why Lyra's cousin wouldn't be called but somehow he knew he wouldn't like the answer. He asked his other question instead. "What is the plan?"

The phone flipping started up again. "I want to set up a perimeter around that park. Eight would be a good number but we could probably make due with six. I assume you will be helping us." Taylor looked questioningly at Ryan.

Ryan nodded. There was no way he was letting Lyra walk into this without him. He didn't know these other Weres well enough to trust them at her back.

"Good, than we only need to find three more Weres to go behind Graham's and Jack's backs to do this. I believe strongly I could get Bishop and Victor to help us. If so, then we are still one short."

Dylan shuffled his feet then moved a step closer. "Boone. Boone is the best tracker we know."

Ryan sifted through his memory until he got a picture of the Were Dylan spoke of. He had no idea why the two of them would know each other, yet Ryan wasn't surprised.

Taylor nodded his approval. "You're right. As long as he's having a good day, Boone would be perfect. You call him and see what kind of day it is."

Dylan nodded. Pulling out his phone, he walked out of earshot.

Ryan couldn't help but worry. Was Boone unstable? If so, he didn't trust the man with Lyra's safety.

"What do you mean by 'good day', Taylor?" Ryan knew there was an edge to his voice.

Taylor straightened and looked Ryan in the eyes. "Boone had a bad adolescence. Understandably that still comes back to haunt him. Lyra's always been nice to him, though. In her way."

Ryan folded his arms. "I wasn't aware they knew each other."

Taylor shrugged. "They don't. They knew of each other. When Boone started working for her family, knowing he was one of us, she sent him a kind of welcome basket and stuff like that. You can trust him to take care of her. It would take the worst of days to make him decline an act of chivalry."

Ryan thought on that for a second. He wanted more people he could trust involved in this. "You want eight, right?"

Taylor folded his arms. "That would be ideal. Why?"

Ryan pulled out his phone. He knew Syrus and Cole would jump in to help their packmate without needing to tell Jack.

"I might have two packmates that could help."

Taylor gave the same suspicious look Ryan must have given him about Boone. "Fine, give them a call and see." Then he hit some buttons and turned away.

Ryan hoped this worked the way Lyra wanted. Otherwise it was going to be a huge mess.

Chapter 17

Dylan shifted his weight for what seemed like the millionth time. The tree Taylor had him perched in was not exactly comfortable, but it gave him the perfect vantage point to look down and beyond Lyra's left shoulder. Dylan knew Bishop was somewhere off to his left and a Were named Syrus was positioned to his right. But he couldn't see or smell either of them. Dylan couldn't imagine how Lyra must feel.

They had 'dropped her off' at the park an hour before dusk. Then parked four streets down and met the other five men before taking positions around the park. But she didn't know that. Lyra was probably hoping they were out there, but she wasn't counting on it.

She could be too self-reliant for her own good. That was why he went out of his way to touch and hug her as much as he could throughout the day. His scent would be with her as she stood there alone. That friendly familial scent could make all the difference in the world sometimes. In the last twenty minutes he had seen her take in several deep breaths and he knew she was breathing him in, trying to calm herself down.

Dylan found himself wishing for the tenth time that their Little Luna didn't have to put herself in this position. He knew it was a good idea, agreed with it even, but he hated it. If something were to happen to her, Dylan knew a number of people would lose it.

Among them was her packmate Ryan. Dylan had a gift for reading people. He didn't really need it to see the strong attachment the male felt for Lyra. She didn't reciprocate. He would be good for her, though. It had been Ryan Dylan had been teasing. He loved Lyra like an older sister, but when it came to her own personal life, she was blind.

Shaking his head, Dylan scanned the park again. His vantage point meant he saw the four Weres a spilt second before Lyra did. She smelled them though, because she knew exactly where to look for their appearance.

They were all male, but that wasn't a surprise to Dylan. Every time he was approached, it had been by all men. It was what made the multi-pack meeting even more strange. A woman had asked for Lyra.

The man in the middle was shorter than the others, maybe five-foot-eight. He possessed a leader's presence, though. Dylan couldn't catch their scents from so far away, but something about them had Lyra spooked. He could tell by the way her weight shifted so she could more easily turn and run.

When the men were about fifteen feet from her they stopped. Even from yards away, Dylan could hear the leader's voice clearly. It was the man from the phone.

"Could you really be trusting enough to come on your own?"

Lyra knew there was a possibility these men could sense a lie. It was why she demanded to stay out of the loop for Taylor's plan.

"I was dropped off." She folded her arms. "I can convince them of anything. I told them I needed time alone. They'll be back in fifteen minutes. So talk fast. What is your interest in me?"

The guy got a smile on his face Dylan really didn't like. The man snapped his fingers and two dozen men came jogging from the same direction the other men came from. Dylan got ready to pounce. Was that Cole guy or Victor sleeping on the job to not notice that many people wandering in the parking lot?

"You're bait. Don't think it has escaped us that you seem to be an important person in some circles. What is it they call you? Ah yes, Little Luna."

Dylan's blood ran cold. It was a nickname given to her by Graham's oldest brother. A lot of people they grew up with used it. Whoever this guy was, if he knew her nick-name then this wasn't anything a multi-pack alliance could help with. This had to do with the family. Dylan let out a curse and jumped from the limb he squatted on and hit the ground at a run, but the dozen men were closer to Lyra.

Boone got to the group first and started tearing into the men closest to him. He was obviously trying to pull some off Lyra. It worked well as three men pulled away and focused just on Boone.

Dylan did the same thing, getting as many as the element of surprise would allow. Now he was close enough he should smell them, but it was almost as if they were scentless. Dylan shut off his brain as it started to wrap around that thought. He needed to concentrate on fighting. Three of them came at him in the chaos, and Dylan quickly noticed the blades in their hands. He leapt in and out as fast as he could, trying to get shots in before they could cut him. It didn't always work. The men were faster than they should have been. But Dylan kept going, attacking until he got the better of one and the guy fell. Since he was no longer much of a threat, Dylan concentrated on the other two.

It seemed to be over in minutes and yet it took eons until Dylan finally knocked his third opponent unconscious. Taking a deep breath, he felt one broken rib. He looked around and saw Syrus still had two guys on him and was bleeding badly from a gash on the inside of his leg. Without hesitation, Dylan ran into the fighting and took out one of them before anyone knew he was there. It didn't take much to finish off the last one.

Dylan took a good look at Syrus's leg. The cut was deep. If the other man didn't shift, he was going to pass out from blood loss.

"Change, it will stop the bleeding."

Syrus gave his a look that said he had no intention of doing so.

Dylan growled. "Change, damn it! I'll watch out for you. We don't need you passing out."

Syrus gave him another look but started changing.

As he waited for the other man to change, Dylan looked around. Everyone was wrapping up. Cole was dropping an unconscious man. Victor and Bishop were scanning the park back-to-back. Everyone's attention was yanked by a loud, inhuman roar.

Dylan's eyes ripped to Ryan who stood growling loudly, looking down at the men on the ground. "They got Lyra. How the hell did they get by all of us and drag her off!"

There was a loud long string of curses.

Dylan's heart stopped as he scanned the park. "Boone's missing too."

Before anyone could stop him, Ryan shot off in the direction of the parking lot. There was more cursing and Cole ran after him. Victor and Bishop exchanged glances before Victor joined the chase.

Dylan's instincts tugged at him to follow, but he needed to check Syrus's leg first. Dylan turned back to the wolf. Syrus was looking at him impatiently. He was not happy to be out of the action. Dylan bent down and examined the leg, wincing over his rib. The bleeding had slowed a great deal but it would still take a day or two to heal. Lyra had always been the one to handle the injuries when they were growing up. Dylan couldn't stop the whine that slithered out of his throat but he struggled to pull himself together and tie off the leg.

As he stood back up, both Bishop and Taylor were standing next to him exchanging glances. Taylor looked down at Syrus. "He going to be okay?"

Dylan nodded. "Yes, he changed in time but it will still take two full days to heal. Taylor, how could they have taken her? And Boone?"

Dylan wanted Taylor to have an answer more than anything. Some kind of plan that would fix everything. He and Graham had always been good at that.

Taylor looked in the direction Ryan and the others had taken off. "I don't know. It doesn't make sense. Unless she went with them willingly, but that would have been really hard to miss."

Bishop slid his hands in his pockets. Dylan thought it was strange to see the Alpha not taking the dominant position. But as he explained when he and Victor arrived, Bishop was aware he did not have all of the information, so there was no reason for him to take the lead. Dylan had been impressed.

"May I make a suggestion?"

Taylor just nodded.

"I think they didn't get past everyone. I believe they got to Lyra and managed to sedate her in some fashion and carry her off. We were too busy fighting armed men to see it. I believe Boone saw it though, and did one of two things. One, he followed and is stalking them as we speak. Or two, he ran after them and managed to get himself sedated as well. I do not know Boone well enough to know which option he is more likely to take."

Taylor glanced at Dylan. "It could go either way depending on his state of mind."

Bishop nodded. "I see." Then he pulled out his phone, pressed a few buttons and soon ringing came loudly from the speaker.

"Not a good time, boss." Victor's voice came over the line after four rings.

"Victor, where are you and where are you headed?" Bishop asked in a calm, authoritative tone.

There was a pause. "Hell if I know where we are. I'm just trying to keep up. Ryan's freaking fast. Wait, there's a street sign coming up. Fifty-first and Kent. Don't tell me how far we are. I don't want to know. Cole is about two blocks behind us, he's just not fast enough to bridge the gap. I'm guessing he'll probably last another mile or two before the gap is just too big and he turns around. As for where we're going, I'm not sure. We're headed out of the residential area. I can still smell Lyra and what I think is Boone. But it's faint. Ryan's nose has got to be better than his legs to be tracking at this speed."

Bishop took advantage of the pause. "Can you tell if Lyra is sedated or if Boone is with her versus outside the car?"

There was a snort. "Not at this speed I can't and I don't think Ryan would answer me if I asked. The scent I think is Boone's is stronger though, so I'm guessing he's outside the vehicle. But I'm thinking their head start is going to be too much once we hit the freeway, which at this rate will be in the next five minutes. Hopefully Ryan's not planning on running along the shoulder of I-5. It's gonna hurt like hell to tackle him if he tries."

Bishop sighed. "All right, keep me informed about where he goes and call it anything changes."

"Will do." Victor hung up.

Bishop slid his phone back in his pocket and looked at Taylor. "So what is your plan now that Lyra is missing, as is Boone, and Ryan seems to have lost his senses and is running for the freeway?"

Taylor's head fell back on his shoulders and he let out an angry, frustrated sound. Dylan wasn't sure he ever heard Taylor do that before. It just make Dylan worry even more about Lyra. It meant no one had a real plan.

"Well, at least we know as long as Boone stays solid he's watching out for Lyra. So for the moment I'm not too worried about her. They are in transit, so there is very little that could happen. Some of these guys are just unconscious so I think we are going to have to tell Graham's father. He should be able to get information out of them. That will tell us where they were planning to take Lyra. Which means Graham will find out. Boone's pack are too close not to notice his absence and we could only keep this from Jack until morning when the next shift comes to take over.

"Ryan hasn't lost his mind. It's just hard to explain. He has feelings for her, being a Were intensifies things." Taylor sighed and reached for his phone. "I'm not looking forward to this call."

Dylan knew Taylor was calling Graham's father and requesting a clean up, so he tapped Bishop's arm and motioned for him and Syrus to follow him out of hearing range. When they stopped, Bishop shook his head.

"It amazes me how much this family is like the mob."

Syrus barked in agreement.

Dylan sighed. "You have no idea."

Bishop raised an eyebrow but Dylan wasn't about to share.

There was about five minutes of silence in which Dylan became more and more worried about Lyra. He kept sneaking glances at Taylor, who clenched his jaw at whoever answered the phone.

Bishop's phone rang and they all jumped.

He pulled it out of his pocket. "What news, Victor?" He then pressed a button so it was on speakerphone again.

"We got about half a mile onto the freeway and Ryan lost the scent. I convinced him to head back to you, but it took a while to get through. Cole finally punched Ryan in the face, hard. They tumbled into the bushes at the side of the freeway and beat the crap out of each other for a while. That seemed to calm Ryan down enough to actually use his brain cells."

There was growling from the other end of the line.

"What? It's true. Anyway, we are headed back but at a much slower pace. I'd say maybe ten."

Bishop nodded. "We'll be here. Cleaning up the mess."

There was some swearing and Victor hung up again.

Taylor came over to join them halfway through the call and now everyone, including the wolf, was looking at him for news.

Taylor rocked on his feet. "So Graham was with his father."

Dylan let a few curses fly. Graham would be beyond pissed. He and Taylor were in deep trouble.

"Yeah, that about covers Graham's reaction. They are sending a clean up crew who will take care of the survivors and the non-survivors. He seemed pretty sure they would find Lyra. He mentioned they already had a lead on where they could be taking her. But he wouldn't say how or where. It was made very clear to me that Graham was coming and we were all to go with him to clean up the mess on our end. Which apparently means telling the missing Weres' Alphas."

Bishop grunted. "Jack will be thrilled. He is likely to attack us all. He is very protective of his littermates."

Dylan wanted to make a comment about how Jack couldn't be any worse than Graham, but kept his mouth shut.

"So are we calling Jack or will Graham?" He asked Taylor.

Taylor gave an angry smile. "He said he would tell the Alphas to meet him but we get to give them the news because it was our own damn faults."

Bishop sighed. "How pleasant."

Taylor looked down at Syrus. "That means you need to be in human form for this. Sorry."

There was a small wolfy whine and Dylan looked down at Syrus.

"Can you not change and maintain clothing?"

The wolf shook his head and Dylan saw the pile of clothes on the ground a few yards away.

"Fine, change over there. We won't peek."

The wolf gave him an unhappy look before slowly walking toward his clothes. The three of them turned away and stared out into the night. Dylan wanted answers so bad he could hit something. He couldn't believe even with eight of them there to protect her she had still been kidnapped. Something just seemed wrong.

No one said anything for a few minutes until Syrus came to stand next to Dylan.

"So do we know when we're going to have to break the news to Jack?"

Taylor turned and shook his head. "No, my guess is within the next two hours."

Syrus ran a hand through his long hair; apparently the hair tie had gone missing. "Man, I do have to be at work tomorrow morning."

Bishop snorted. "Are you telling me you're not worried about your packmate?"

Syrus grinned, but he obviously didn't have any feeling behind it. "Not at all. I have full confidence Lyra will either beat or annoy the crap out of whoever took her. We have someone tracking her. He most likely has a cell phone and can tell us where they are."

Dylan and Taylor exchanged astonished looks. Dylan couldn't believe neither of them had thought of that. Dylan ripped his phone out of his pocket and scrolled until he got to Boone's number and put the phone to his ear.

Boone picked up after almost a dozen rings. His voice was a harsh whisper. "WHAT!"

Dylan exhaled the breath he had been holding. "Where are you, dude?"

"Watching Luna. They drugged her. For the moment she is lying on a mattress, unconscious. But they left her alone with two guards outside her door."

Dylan shook with relief and moved the phone away from his mouth so he could speak to the group. "He can see her. She's okay."

Shoulders slumped all around him.

He turned his attention back to the phone. "But where are you?"

There was a long pause and Dylan strained to hear anything. Several minutes crept by.

"Sorry, guard patrol came by. It seems to be every ten minutes, since this is the second time I've seen them. Graham's gonna want to kill the blond, he thinks Lyra's real pretty. Poor soul."

Dylan wanted to yell, but he knew how Boone's mind operated so he asked again. "Where is the building? How long have you been there?" Dylan quickly moved the phone so he could see the time on the screen the moved it back before Boone could answer. It had been about a half hour since he had been hiding up in a tree, but it felt like ten minutes.

"We're outside SeaTac. The city, not the airport. We've been here about fifteen minutes, maybe."

Dylan couldn't help the surprise. "You ran all the way to SeaTac?" He knew the disbelief was plain in voice.

Boone gave a gruff laugh. "Shoot, Dylan. Hell no, I didn't run all the way here. Have you ever tried running on the freeway. Good way to get yourself killed. I hitched a ride on an open-bedded semi for most of it." There was another pause. "So when's the assault on these pricks?"

Dylan hesitated a second. "I don't know. Graham inadvertently found out and he's going to haul us off to tell your and Lyra's Alphas."

There was another gruff laugh. "Boy, I don't envy you. Tell 'em I can stake out for about a day. Any longer than that and I won't be too reliable, you know."

Dylan nodded.

Taylor cut in, obviously wanting to know how the conversation was going. "Can he smell them? Are they Were or not?"

"None of us could pick up their scents. Can you?"

There was a pause. "Yeah, I couldn't pick any of them up until I got here. Some of the men milling around have scents. They are all regular people but even they smell kinda off, you know. I can't really explain it. But I’m signing off so I can pay full attention to what’s going on” Boone hung up.

Dylan wasn’t surprised but he was a little frustrated as he put the phone back in his pocket and addressed the group. “Boone’s watching her and she’s fine, but he says he can only give us a day.”

Taylor cursed.

Bishop looked from one of them to the other. “What exactly does that mean?”

Taylor sighed and jammed his hands in his pockets. "Boone’s a little unstable. He has to be able to go off on his own for periods of time. I know him and he’ll stay put as long as he can but he might not be at his best here soon.”

Bishop was quiet. They were saved from further conversation as six large black vans pulled into the parking lot. Dylan was really not looking forward to what came next as he watched Graham exit the first van. To say the Were was furious would have been like calling the Grand Canyon a pothole.

Chapter 18

"YOU DID WHAT!" Jack had never been more furious in his life. Before he knew what he was doing his fist was buried halfway through the wall inches from Ryan's head. The other man didn't flinch.

"Jack..." Bishop's voice came calmly from somewhere beyond Jack's left shoulder.

Without even looking Jack sliced the air in a silencing motion. "Keep quiet, Bishop. I'll deal with you later. Right now I am dealing with my Second."

Jack could see the anger flowing in Ryan's eyes but the other man kept the rest of his face completely blank. It was taking all of Jack's self-control not to rip his fist from the wall and pummel Ryan. That was usually the biggest difference between the two of them. Jack had better control of his temper.

Jack took a deep breath and shot daggers at Ryan from inches away. "Let me guess whose fine idea this was."

There was a momentary shift in Ryan's eyes. It was only a split second but enough to know his suspicions were correct. Lyra planned this herself and convinced everyone else to go along.

"It is my job to protect her, Ryan. Aiding her idiotic schemes does not help me do that."

Ryan finally snarled down at Jack. "At least she was willing to do something instead of just waiting around for the alliance council to arbitrarily pick something."

Growling, Jack withdrew his fist from the wall and shoved Ryan as hard as he could. "Damn it, Ryan, think with your big head on this one."

Then both of them were on the floor throwing punches. Ryan was stronger than Jack, but Jack could be more cunning. All Jack saw was red as Ryan managed to get two good shots into Jack's ribs and Jack felt something snap. Jack got one solid punch to Ryan's face and knew on impact he broke the other man's nose. Jack rolled to deflect Ryan's next shot, but it never came.

Jack rolled to his feet to see Cole gripping Ryan in a bear hug with Syrus on one arm and Taylor on the other.

Bishop was looking at Jack warily, wondering he would need to jump in front of Jack to prevent him from charging Ryan. Jack shook his head at the other Alpha. He had no intention of continuing a physical fight with Ryan, though a small primal part of him wanted to. Physical aggression always seemed to calm Jack down, level out his head. Ryan had the opposite reaction.

Jack watched as the three men held the snarling Ryan. Cole was saying something to his friend, but Jack doubted anyone else could hear it and it didn't seem to be getting through to Ryan. After about a minute, Cole sighed and reached into one of Ryan's front pockets. The Samoan pulled out a piece of thin dark blue fabric, roughly the size of his palm. Cole waved it in front of Ryan's face, more directly under his nose. Ryan's eyes snapped to that piece of fabric and the arm Syrus had let go of shot out and snatched it from Cole and held it closer to his face. Inhaling deeply, Ryan put it back in his pocket, but his hand remained holding it.

Cole turned to Taylor. "You can let go."

Taylor had been watching Ryan with wide eyes, then he turned to Cole. "Is that what I think it is?" His voice full of shocked disbelief.

Jack couldn't see Cole's face, but whatever Taylor found in the other man's expression had him cursing, dropping Ryan's arm and bee-lining for Dylan and Graham. Graham looked equally stunned, but also like he was entertaining ideas of beating Ryan himself. Dylan's expression was peacefully blank. Jack still wasn't sure how he felt about the younger man.

Jack looked at all nine of the other men in turn. Both Bishop and Victor shrugged, but the other six wouldn't meet Jack's eyes. In all fairness, Ryan was staring at the ground trying to gain control so Jack really hadn't expected too much from him.

"Is anyone going to tell me what the hell is going on?"

Dylan actually chuckled and jammed his hands into the pockets of his jeans. Jack wasn't the only one who looked at the young wolf like he was nuts.

Dylan didn't even seem to notice. He smiled at Jack. "Trust me Jack, that is a long, unrelated and relatively pointless story. We can tell you all about it later after everyone is tucked safely back in their beds."

There was a momentary silence as everyone but Ryan stared at Dylan.

Charlie, Boone's Alpha, shook it off first. "Anyway, so Boone is watching this base camp where they are keeping Lyra, right?"

There were several nods.

"Do we know if he is injured?"

There was silence and Jack mentally started swearing.

At least Dylan's smile disappeared. "We didn't think to ask."

Then he pulled out his phone and hit some buttons. Within a few seconds there was a ringing over speaker phone.

"DAMN IT, STOP CALLING ME! You are so lucky none of these soldiers walking patrol are Weres or they would hear my phone. You're damn lucky I keep the stupid thing on vibrate."

Boone's accent was stronger than Jack remembered.

Boone's Alpha exchanged worried glances with Taylor and Dylan before he spoke to his packmate in a calm voice. "Boone, are you injured?"

There was some shuffling before Boone's voice came back over the phone. "Mildly. Several cuts to the legs. Only one or two are anything serious. I tied them so the bleeding has slowed down. If we could get someone down here to switch with me in the next few hours so I could change, it would be much obliged."

There were more worried glanced. Dylan closed his eyes. "What happened to having a day?"

More shuffling. "I hadn't noticed the extent of the bleeding at that point."

There were several curses and Charlie snatched the phone.

"If I call Trevor, will you be able to give him your general location?"

There was a long silence and Jack wasn't sure if Boone would answer.

"Maybe."

Charlie looked over at Jack. The other Alpha was worried about something far beyond Boone's physical injures. That thought was less than comforting to Jack.

"Okay, Boone. He should be there within two hours."

"Not a problem. I'll call him this time, though. I'll give it about ten minutes." Boone hung up the phone.

There were more curses and Charlie yanked his own phone out of his pocket. He rubbed between his eyebrows as he put the phone to his ear.

"Trevor, we have a problem."

There was a pause as Trevor responded.

"I don't have time for all of it. Boone is injured and needs to change, but he's spying on some people that abducted a Were female."

There was another pause and from Charlie's expression, Jack guessed Trevor was spouting expletives.

"Look, he is going to call you from where he is in SeaTac. Just get there ASAP and see that he changes. You know how he can get and this is not the best time for that." Charlie gave a weary sigh. "Let me know when it's done." Then he snapped his phone shut.

Jack must have been showing his anger because Charlie looked over at him and held up his hands. "Trevor is the best at handling Boone. Plus he lives in Northern Burien, so he'll get there a hell of a lot faster than anyone else."

Jack glared at the other man before glaring at the room as a whole. "Is she or is she not still in my pack?" He wasn't even trying to muffle the growl.

Bishop took a step forward but the look Jack gave him made the other man stop.

"Lyra is my responsibility and mine alone. Yet I seem to be the only one not involved in this ridiculous operation."

Out of the corner of his eye, Jack saw Ryan prepare to speak.

"Don't get me started on your unstable behavior recently."

Ryan's mouth shut.

Jack swung back to Bishop but encompassed Graham as well. "Neither of you saw fit to tell me Lyra was going to endanger herself or try to stop her from doing so. She is mine, damn it! How dare you step in and try to run my pack."

Jack knew he was growling louder but did nothing to hamper it and swung his gaze to Charlie. "And you are calling some Were I do not even know to protect what is mine, because apparently Boone is not in stable enough condition to watch out for her. How the hell is this alliance supposed to work if I can't trust a single person in it?"

No one said anything.

Charlie folded his arms and glared back at Jack. "Don't give me that crap. I knew nothing about any of this. My third is bleeding out in the woods somewhere trying to protect YOUR female. I called in back up for him to give us time to think of something. I'm looking out for my people and there was no way I was leaving Boone out there alone for how ever long this is going to take."

Jack could tell Charlie was pissed, not as far gone as he was, but still pissed enough to join a fight if it came to that.

Graham's movement got Jack's attention. The other man was practically seething. When he spoke, Jack imagined his tone was the same one Jack just used.

"I have been protecting her for far longer than you. From worse things than you possibly could imagine. She was mine before you even met her."

Graham was stalking toward Jack, arms flexing when Taylor jumped in front of him and stood between the two of them.

"ENOUGH! First off, Lyra would be far beyond pissed if she heard you two talking like this and you know Dylan is going to tell her."

Jack glanced at Dylan to see the other man give a sheepish grin and shrug. Jack cursed under his breath. If they got through this, Lyra was going to kill him. But then if they got through this he might just kill her.

Taylor continued. "Second, this pissing contest blame game is not going to help us get Lyra back. We need to form a plan first and that's only if the family hasn't already started their own."

That got Graham's attention. He snapped his gaze to Taylor and started swearing. Then took several steps back and ran his hands through his hair. "He's right. My dad might already be on this." There were a few more curse words.

Dylan folded his arms only to jam them in his pockets again. "He would be within his rights to do so."

Graham swung around to Dylan. "What do you mean?"

Dylan shifted under Graham's stare and looked down at the ground. "The guys Lyra met. The talker, he mentioned following her and he mentioned knowing we called her 'Little Luna' and how she was important in some circles."

Both Graham and Taylor exploded.

Taylor began pacing. "This is bad. This is really, really bad."

Graham growled at the other man. "You think I don't know that."

Jack started to get a feel of foreboding that replaced some of his anger. "What, what don't I know?"

Graham and Taylor exchanged looks and Taylor held up his hands.

"Hey, they're your family."

Graham gave Taylor a less than friendly look before turning to Jack. "If my father decides this is his business, which considering what Dylan just said, it probably is, then there is no way we will have any part of saving Lyra. My father will go in, guns blazing, so to speak, and get rid of the problem. He won't question or try to get information out of anyone. When it comes to his family, dad has a scorched earth policy. If we want any information on what is going on and how Pack L is involved, we have to beat him to it. That means we have to move fast because odds are he already has a plan in place."

Charlie's phone started twanging some country song and the entire room jumped. Charlie looked down at his hand for a moment as if trying to figure out if he ever put the phone back in his pocket. Then he shook his head and flipped it open.

"Yeah."

He listened for a few seconds before speaking to the group.

"Trevor found Boone and got him to change. He says Boone toned down the severity of the injuries but in a few days he should be okay. He also says he knows exactly where they are and can text me directions. He says they are about five minutes from the airport."

Charlie paused again, this time his face became stony.

"He's telling me they are going to move her at dawn. He and Boone overheard some smokers. They are expecting a few more people then the whole group is moving out. That gives us ten hours to come up with a plan."

Charlie turned his attention back to the phone. "Yeah, Trevor shoot me those directions, and be careful." Then he flipped his phone shut.

Jack had no idea how to go about this kind of operation. The scientists hinted they wanted to train the Weres for these kinds of operations but at some point that plan fell through. Jack felt panic fly through him. He had no idea how to save his littermate. Then an idea formed in his mind, he almost dismissed it just on principle but then he thought about Lyra and opened his mouth.

"We're going to have to ask your father for help. Ten hours isn't long enough for us to create a plan of our own."

Graham gave Jack full eye contact before looking away. He didn't like the idea either. "Yeah, I know." Then the other man pulled out his phone again and walked across the room to call his father.

Jack couldn't help but think they were wasting time. He wanted to head south and beat the crap out of everyone involved but he knew that wasn't an option.

"No, Dad, that isn't fair!"

The room went dead silent as Graham put his palm over the phone and walked back to the group, looking at no one but Jack.

"He says he can handle the entire situation. He says the only thing he was waiting on is the address. Which we have?"

Graham glanced at Charlie who nodded. Then Graham's gaze swung back to Jack.

"His condition is the only people involved are family."

Jack saw red. His heartbeat sped up, causing a 'whooshing' in his ears. He fought the urge to yell his objection. Jack knew he was growling loudly but there was nothing he could do about it. He slowly started counting and forced himself to take deep breaths, finally stopping at thirty-two. He knew it was the best bet for Lyra's safety. He had to do what was best for her. Jack looked Graham in the eyes. The other man was completely stone-faced.

"Fine, but only if I get her as soon as she's safe and he lets you collect some intel so we can hunt these maniacs down."

Approval and relief flickered in Graham's eyes before he uncovered the phone. "Did you get all of that?"

There was a pause.

"No, I want your word that as soon as we have taken control of this base, or whatever it is, Lyra is placed in Jack's custody."

There was a very long pause.

"Fine, give us fifteen and we will be there. Just so you can't renege, I'll have the directions on me."

There was another pause before Graham hung up the phone. Then he turned to Charlie, flipping his phone so he could type.

"GO."

Charlie rattled off directions and Graham typed them in, then nodded to Taylor and Dylan.

"Let's go."

The three of them headed solemnly for the door.

Jack moved over to slide into one of the leather chairs. None of the furniture had been moved since they housed the meet and greet last week. It showed how distracted Hazel was. Ryan who broke the silence as he slid into the chair to the left of Jack.

Ryan seemed to have calmed considerably. "Should I be calling the rest of the pack?"

Jack just shook his head.

Syrus moved so he could gingerly sit down in front of Jack. "Are you serious? We're not going to tell anyone?"

Jack shook his head again. "No. What would we say? Lyra's been kidnapped because of some stupid scheme but don't worry because we will have nothing to do with her rescue? Can you imagine how up the wall Hazel would go? She would lose her mind. We'll keep our mouths shut now and beg forgiveness later."

Jack looked over when Ryan snorted. "Just like Lyra did. I don't remember you being so fond of the idea at the time."

Jack refrained from making a snarky comment. Ryan was right, Jack was doing exactly what Lyra had.

"Let's just hope she's around to make fun of me for it."

There were several mumbles of agreement before the room lapsed back into silence. Slowly, the other men took seats. It was as if no one wanted to leave until the situation had been handled. Not even Victor tried to break the tension. Jack was left with his thoughts. He didn't like the way events were going. He didn't know how he was to protect his pack in this new world forming around them.

Chapter 19

Taylor remained completely silent during the entire ride to where Lyra was being held. She had been captive for two hours now. Those responsible had done almost nothing to cover their tracks. That didn't sit well with Taylor, and it hadn't with Graham either. They brought it up to Graham's father, and he agreed but stated they were going in to get her anyway.

When they finally left the estate, there were seven black vans total, all of them filled to capacity. That meant more than sixty men and women had volunteered to rescue Lyra. There were more, but that many people would have gotten it the way.

In Taylor's van were his father and uncle, as well as all four of his male cousins. There were Dylan and his parents, both of them. Dylan's mother had threatened her way onto the van. Dylan had been glowing with pride. Driving the van was Vance, one of the guys who had grown up with Them.

The van was eerily silent as everyone concentrated on their part of the mission. Graham's father had broken them into teams and given everyone very explicit instructions that no one involved was to be spared. Taylor knew Jack would have been adamantly against it, but when someone grew up in the world Taylor, Dylan, Graham, and Lyra had people didn't even blink. Taylor took a deep breath as they made the last turn in Graham's directions. He just kept praying they would get Lyra out of there before anything else happened to her.

Chapter 20

Lyra knew there was something strange about the drugs she had been injected with. She was groggy and she already decided it must be some kind of hallucinogen because human voices just didn't sound like the voices she kept hearing. That and the walls kept moving. They had put her on the mattress, after what seemed like the longest car ride of her life, Lyra decided things were not as bad if she stayed as still as possible. Her legs were starting to cramp and she was afraid to move them.

Then she heard shouting. She couldn't tell what was being said, just the shock and anger behind it. She felt her eyes close again and hoped they continued to leave her alone. When the door opened, she left her lids down. Arms scooped her up and began lifting her. Lyra started to struggle, she was not going anywhere.

She heard a voice, but didn't recognize it. "…Stop struggling…What can…"

"Justin, She needs to be taken…Justin."

Lyra was pretty sure she knew that name, but her brain wasn't functioning well enough to make the connection. The talking continued, but she didn't know for how long. Lyra continued to struggle, but more arms came around her. She felt herself blacking out again and she fought it as much as she could, but felt herself slipping into darkness as whoever was carrying her started to move.

Lyra woke groggily. She began to panic. They had moved her. She had no idea what happened or where she was. The only plus was the hallucinogens must have worn off. She opened her eyes a crack, then slammed them shut. The world was still spinning. She would have to do this using her other senses. Lyra could tell her nose still wasn't working properly, but she had to get out of here. She took advantage and used her adrenaline to shoot off the mattress she was on. She couldn't tell if there was anybody else in the room, but she hoped the quick movement caught them off guard if there were. Arms shot out from all directions and yanked her back down. She began struggling, scratching, biting. But nothing seemed to work.

"Lyra." The voice was distorted but she could make out the word.

It made her pause for just a second. Just enough for a wrist to suddenly appear right in front of her nose. She almost bit through it, but halfway through the movement, she registered the scent.

"Justin?" It sounded like a cry even to her distorted hearing.

"Yes. Lyra, I need you to calm down. I'm right next to you."

She felt the weight of the mattress shift as Justin sat to her left.

Relief flooded her and before she could put thought in action she already wrapped herself around him, sobbing into his chest. She could feel him curl around her, no doubt making soothing noises. Finally, this time she let herself relax and get the sleep her body needed. If Justin was here, then she was safe. They were all safe.

Chapter 21

Ryan's heart had been ripped out of his chest as he heard Lyra crying her littermate's name. Dylan had been so sure Justin would be the only one who could reach Lyra past whatever drugs had been pumped into her system. No one understood it, but since no one had any other ideas they went with that one. An hour ago Justin shoved his wrist under Lyra's nose and she recognized him.

She hadn't even recognized Graham, who carried her in the ride over to Justin's. Taylor called Jack and informed him they needed to get to Justin. Jack gave them directions and called Justin. The four members of Pack F piled into Cole's SUV and broke every speed limit to get them to Justin's.

When they brought Lyra in she had been whimpering like crazy, the noise only broken by the occasional scream. She didn't quiet down until they laid her on Justin's bed. Then she managed to stir herself awake. It had taken all of them holding her to keep her on the bed. Ryan himself had slashes up him right arm, but they would heal within a day. Lyra was finally sleeping and Justin refused to leave her alone. The two of them lay facing each other, Lyra's forehead against Justin's chest. Both of Lyra's hands were curled in her littermate's shirt and Justin had slung his top leg over both of Lyra's. It was so intimate a position the rest of them exchanged glances and left the room. Dylan covered them in a blanket before following everyone else out and shutting the door.

The rest of the group made their way downstairs to the opposite corner of Justin's rented townhouse. No one spoke for several minutes as the seven of them stood around the island in Justin's kitchen. Syrus rummaged through the kitchen until he found whiskey and rum, then placed glasses on the table before filling one eight ounce glass with rum and downing it.

"Did anyone else know they were involved?" Syrus asked as he poured himself another glass.

Ryan didn't say anything. Up until a week ago he thought he knew everything about Lyra. That thought had him filling a glass with whiskey.

Everyone but Jack took some alcohol. For some reason Ryan couldn't figure out, Jack just didn't drink.

Jack laid his hands flat on the island and shook his head. "They aren't. I know they're not." He didn't sound fully convinced.

Cole snorted and took a swig of rum. “They sure as hell look it.” Cole looked at Dylan. “How did you know, man?”

Dylan shook his head as he took a sip of rum. “I’m pretty sure they aren’t together, but she smells like him a lot. Not all the time but often enough to notice. I didn’t even know who the scent belonged to until that Pack F meeting. I went out of my way to find him and remember his name. Lyra’s sense of smell has always been her strongest sense. I figured she would recognize his scent or no one’s. Just be glad I was right. Who knows how long those drugs will be in her system, we got through to her and that’s what matters.”

Ryan knew the younger man was right, but he still wanted to know how Justin and Lyra hid this from everyone. Even Jack had been surprised. He looked Jack. “Did you know they were that close?”

Jack shook his head. “No, but I’m starting to think I know nothing about Lyra.”

Ryan felt the same way, but it bothered him more to hear Jack say it. There was silence for a moment before Jack tapped the counter.

“Okay, so tell me about the rescue. What intel did you manage to get?”

Graham sighed and finished off his rum. “Not a hell of a lot. There were scribbled notes here and there. Turns out they were waiting on their group leader, whatever the guy is, and he had not shown up yet. They had taken Lyra without planning or consent from above. We did find some of what we think they shot Lyra full of, but our labs won’t have anything for us for another twenty-four hours.

“It seemed so spur of the moment no one had a real plan, which is scary because that means there’s more of them then we thought there were. Their leader is supposed to show up tomorrow so we are going to try to ambush him and get information from him. And before you ask, no, my father won’t let you help.

“Someone needs to be monitoring Lyra anyway. We need to make sure whatever drug this is clears her system. All her senses seem affected.”

Jack gave Ryan a disbelieving look before turning back to Graham. "Let me get this straight. You're telling me you really didn't find anything, mainly because no one of any importance was there. How stupid do you think I am?"

Ryan could tell Jack was getting angry again. Not that Ryan blamed him. As Alpha, Jack had the right to know what was going on. Ryan was more frustrated than angry. Though he did want to know what happened, he was pacified by the fact that Lyra was relatively safe upstairs. The drugs were bad, but she didn't seem to be at risk. At this point that was more than enough for Ryan.

Graham folded his arms over his chest. "Look, Jack, yeah there was some stuff there. But most of it was referencing the family. As much as it royally pisses me off, my father and his people are going through all the information we found and then will give you filtered copies. Yeah I know it sucks, especially considering they were just going to destroy everything, but my hands are tied. I may be his son, but as the youngest I don't have enough clout to go up against him. I'm sorry, but honestly I'm surprised he gave you Lyra. Anything else would border on a miracle."

Ryan was pretty sure Graham was being completely honest with them and that worried him about the kind of world he and Lyra grew up in.

Taylor downed what was left of his drink and pushed the glass away. "And your best bargaining chip is upstairs cuddled up with some guy I don't know."

Ryan tried to stop his lip from twitching at the distaste in Taylor's voice. Ryan felt better that he was at least one up on the other man.

Jack's eyes narrowed on Taylor, and his words came out slow and precise. "I would never, ever, use Lyra or any of my pack as a bargaining chip. Do you understand me?"

Dylan started coughing, which gained everyone's attention. He had whiskey in his cup and he pushed it away.

"Eck! How do you guys drink this stuff, seriously? Why does Lyra like this?"

After a few watery blinks he looked at Jack. "Though that way might work too, that's not how Taylor meant it."

He pause to give his attention to Graham and Taylor. "I feel as if I'm always interpreting for you guys."

Then he turned back to Jack. "Lyra can get away with just about anything in her family. She was the only girl until seven years ago. Her father and uncles enjoy spoiling her when they can. I mean, come on! They let her live farther away than any of the other children and she lives alone. If anyone could finesse Graham's dad into giving you information, it would be Lyra. Unfortunately, for obvious reasons, she's not at the top of her game at the moment and probably won't be until after the fact."

Ryan couldn't help his curiosity, even if it wasn't the best time for it. "What exactly does she get away with?"

Dylan grinned wildly. "Almost anything she wants. Lyra is smart enough to use it sparingly for maximum results."

Taylor was glaring at Dylan. "I still hate you for that by the way."

If anything Dylan's grin grew bigger. "I know."

Ryan exchanged glances with the others from Pack F. None of them seemed to know what the two other men were talking about.

Graham rolled his eyes. "Anyway, to get back on track. My father informed me to ask you, Jack, if after tomorrow Lyra was not improved if he could send the family doctor to check her out."

Ryan watched Jack turn the idea over in his mind. Ryan knew what his Alpha was thinking. The doctor could help Lyra, but it would make her uncle one up on Jack. It would also be giving her uncle more say in Lyra's care.

Jack tapped the island. "Does this doctor know what she is?"

Graham didn't even hesitate. "Yes and she's been looking after us since we were born. She's an every freckle, every scar kind of lady."

Ryan knew he wasn't the only one to notice the affection in Graham's voice.

Jack watched Graham for a few moments. "Fine, if she's not better by dusk, then the doctor and only the doctor can visit her."

Dylan's hand shot up in the air.

Taylor gave Dylan a dry look. "Really?!"

Dylan just looked at Jack until he nodded.

Dylan lowered his hand. "So we can't come to see her tomorrow?" He sounded like he was desperately trying to hide his hurt.

Jack scrubbed at his face. "I want to say you can, but one, it's not my house, and two, where would I draw the line? Pack F and you three doesn't seem all that fair to the rest of her family, which is huge. I'll leave it up to Justin's discretion but I don't like the idea of people I don't know in the house."

Dylan nodded. "Everyone in the known world except Franklin. He's a douche."

Taylor snorted. "He wouldn't come anyway."

Jack looked at both men. "Who?"

Ryan didn't recognize the name either.

Graham sighed. "One of my older brothers."

Ryan knew they were all wondering why Graham wasn't taking Dylan out.

Graham shrugged. "What? I know I should defend him, being blood and all, but he really is a prick."

Jack shook his head. "Like I said, I'll leave it up to Justin. Everyone has to have his okay and I'm maintaining a detail while she's here." Jack turned to Cole, Syrus and Ryan. "Look I know we can only keep this so long from Hazel, but everyone else stays out of the loop. Do you understand me?"

The three of them nodded.

"Good, now I want at least one of us here at all times. More would be better, but we just don't have the numbers." Ryan could hear Jack's frustration.

Ryan downed the rest of his alcohol. This was not getting any better. If his last bout with crazy was any indication, Ryan knew he couldn't spend much more time babysitting Lyra. Something about the proximity was making him slip. Hormones just did not seem like a good enough reason, especially for this long a time period. Ryan was afraid of losing it again.

Taylor cleared his throat to gain their attention. "Look, for what it's worth, I've been ordered not to leave Lyra until this whole situation is handled. So I will always be here, unless Justin doesn't want me here. Then I'll be out on the front curb."

Under normal circumstances, Ryan would have thought the other man was joking, but somehow he knew Taylor wasn't.

Jack nodded. "Okay then. I'm going to okay all of this with Justin and remember this has to stay between those of us that already know. I do not want any of this getting out in the general public, and Syrus, go home and rest, you look like crap." With that, Jack headed upstairs.

Cole turned to Ryan. "I assume you're sticking around."

Ryan nodded. There was no way he was leaving until that doctor came and checked Lyra out. He needed to know she would be okay.

Cole turned to Syrus. "All right then, 'mister looks like crap', I'll give you a lift home."

He nudged Syrus and the two of them headed toward the front door.

Graham hit Dylan in the arm from across Taylor. "Come on, let's get back to the estate and see if we can help with that intel."

Dylan looked between Taylor and Ryan before answering Graham. "No, I'd like to stay put for the night." Both Graham and Taylor looked at the younger man in surprise.

Ryan guessed Dylan didn't often voice against either of them.

"All right. I'll swing by and grab you in the morning." With an incline of his head to Ryan, Graham followed the route Syrus and Cole had taken.

The three of them stood in mildly awkward silence until Jack came back down the stairs a few minutes later, looking put out.

Dylan jammed his hands in his pockets. "So, what's the verdict?"

Jack grunted. "Justin said anyone here tonight is okay and anyone else Lyra wants."

Ryan snorted but managed to hold back his laugh. "I take it you don't approve."

Jack gave Ryan a bland look. "No, I don't. Look, I have to be at work in two hours. I need you to keep things under control."

Though Jack's words pricked Ryan's anger, he just nodded.

Jack headed out the front door. "Good Night."

Dylan's eyes lit up and a mischievous grin appeared on his face. He looked directly at Ryan. "You have feelings for her, don't you?"

Ryan's blood ran cold and he felt his face turn to stone. "Why do you say that?"

Before Dylan could answer, Taylor threw up his hands. "I can't listen to this." He walked straight out of the room and appeared to be going as far across the house as he could get.

Ryan didn't know how he felt about that level of avoidance, but at that moment he really wanted to follow.

Dylan's grin grew bigger. "Don't mind him. He just recently realized the concept that Lyra dates. It's hard for him and Graham and probably a few others we know."

Ryan raised an eyebrow. He knew this was his chance to get information about Lyra and her background. "And it isn't for you?"

Dylan shook his head. "Nope. I pay too much attention not to notice things like that."

Dylan watched Ryan, grinning, and Ryan lost his nerve.

Sure, he could get information, but he had the feeling he would be giving up more than he got out of it. So instead of answering, Ryan turned and followed wherever Taylor had gone. Ryan swore he heard the word 'chicken' follow him down the hallway.

Taylor sat on the floor with his back propped up by the wall to the left of the bathroom door. Ryan slid down the wall adjacent to Taylor and the other man held up one hand.

"Look, I don't know what Dylan told you but I don't want anything to do with what you two were talking about."

Ryan snorted and leaned his head against the wall. "And you think I do?"

Taylor gave him an appraising look. "Fair enough."

They sat in silence for several minutes before Ryan's curiosity got the better of him. "Why didn't she ever talk about you?"

Taylor had closed his eyes but at Ryan's question he opened them and looked up at the ceiling. "Multiple reasons, I would guess." Pausing he took a deep breath. "She and I are not as close as you think. Graham and Lyra yeah, they are actually six months apart to the day. Graham was one of my best friends growing up, so naturally I became friends with her. When it turned out we were at the same college, the two of us hung out more and became friends in our own right."

Then shifted his head so he could keep eye contact with Ryan. "After the experiment, in quarantine I saw her trying to calm down Hazel. Lyra didn't see me right away, I think she was just so stunned. As she was hugging Hazel, to hide the other woman's crying, she saw me. The relief and sorrow and fear on her face called to me. She was just as terrified as Hazel but was hanging on by a thread. I bee-lined for her."

Taylor turned his face up again. Ryan could tell the other man felt horrible about not reaching his friend in time to make the same pack.

"Afterward, I mean immediately after we got out of quarantine, she saw me outside and broke with you guys to catch me. I was checking voicemail on my phone and had a message from Graham asking me about how us and Dylan were. He apologized for not checking sooner because he had been in quarantine. The look on my face must have told Lyra what happened because our eyes met and she stopped walking. Just stopped, in the middle of the crowd and stared at me. Her eyes filled up and her hands went to her mouth. As long as I live, I will never forget that moment. I ran at her and swept her up. She was barely breathing until I got Graham on the phone and she could hear his voice. He had to convince her he was unharmed. At about that point Dylan found us completely by accident. He grabbed on to Lyra's back and we stood there for maybe ten minutes.

"In that moment, our friendship became much more solid than before. Stuff like that stays with you. She's like family to Dylan and I now." Taylor paused for a long moment, then smiled up at the ceiling. "Maybe she just doesn't want anyone thinking she's that social. Hard to keep up appearances if too many people are close to you." He chuckled to himself.

Ryan hadn't known most of that. He remembered Lyra disappearing into the crowd after she deposited Hazel onto Jack's arm. Ryan remembered asking where she had gone.

Justin had answer. "She needs more alone time than most people. She'll be back sooner or later." None of her littermates had worried, let alone been phased by Lyra's disappearance. Ryan had but kept it to himself, after all they knew her better. Now he was glad he hadn't pushed it.

"Why did you or Dylan never visit our office before the meeting? You acted as if the three of you barely knew each other." Ryan's curiosity was in full swing now. He wanted all the information he could get.

"Man, that seems like so long ago. This has been the month from Hell. You know that meeting was the first Dylan and I heard Pack L was attacking Lyra. I was pissed. I called Graham to yell at him about not telling me." There was that chuckle again.

Ryan's lips twitched. "I take it Graham hadn't known either."

Taylor shook his head. "Nope. Those two can get into gold medal yelling matches. But yeah, Bishop picked up on that. He said I was too friendly for a stranger and Victor said Lyra was too nonhomicidal for us to not know each other." Taylor smiled and glanced at Ryan.

Ryan hadn't noticed much difference in behavior, but then his mind had been on other things at the time.

"We didn't visit because there was no need to. Dylan has a key to my place and he uses it a hell of a lot and we both know how to find Lyra. The pack offices may be pack territories, but they are still pretty neutral ground. We just don't need neutral ground. We could hang out anywhere. Plus, Lyra likes things compartmentalized. No mixing relationship groups."

Ryan knew he had no right to feel hurt about his false sense of knowledge when it came to Lyra, but that didn't stop the feeling from creeping in.

The two of them sat in silence for a few minutes, each in their own thoughts. Both shot off the ground the moment they heard Dylan running down the stairs.

They met him halfway down the hall. The younger man skidded to a halt inches from them. The fear and panic were coming off him in waves. Dylan's eyes were wide, he was white as a sheet and shaking uncontrollably.

His voice shook as he stared at Taylor. "Call the Luna."

Ryan didn't know what that meant but Taylor picked it up immediately. His eyes widened and his phone was out of his pocket before Ryan could blink. Someone must have answered right off the bat because Taylor burst into a monologue. Then he paused and turned to Dylan, realizing he had no idea what was going on. He jerked the phone from his ear and thrust it at Dylan.

The younger man snatched it and put it to his ear. "Greetings, Luna." Dylan’s voice was panicky but it must have been some kind of formality. There was a pause before words started tumbling from his mouth. "I was upstairs checking on her and Justin, the man she is with, noticed bruises appearing on her body. But they aren't bruises. It's internal bleeding pooling under her skin. Her eyes are crying blood. And there is blood coming out of her ears, nose, and mouth."

His voice was full of panic, but he was silenced by the person on the other end of the phone.

Ryan was in shock, but couldn't get past Dylan to get to the stairs without knocking the other man over.

"It's a slow dribble." There was another pause and Dylan's face filled with a new level of panic. "No, I don't know the address."

Then he turned and sprinted down the hall with Ryan and Taylor on his heels.

They reached the bedroom and circled the bed. Justin was sitting up and had Lyra cradled to his chest. He was using his thumbs to hold thick green towels over her ears and the rest of his fingers to hold a matching towel under her nose and mouth. He had it over the lower half of her face to catch the bloody streams coming from her eyes. Justin was ghostly white as he watched them come into the room. Even in his state of shock Ryan moved in and grabbed the towels over Lyra's ears.

His packmate looked at him with sickening worry. "She won't wake up. I've been trying to wake her for five minutes." With his hands more available Justin started dabbing her eyes.

Dylan practically shouted in his panic. "We need your address."

Taylor put a hand on the other man's shoulder, trying to steady Dylan as well as himself.

Justin rattled off his address without looking away from Lyra and Dylan repeated it just as fast. When Dylan finished he hung up the phone. His hands were shaking bad enough that he was having trouble getting the phone into his pocket. After several tries he realized it wasn't his phone and shakily handed it back to Taylor.

"Luna says she will be here in fifteen minutes."

Taylor nodded and the two of them continued to watch helplessly as Ryan and Justin tried to cover the bleeding. Ryan felt numb. His body had gone from shock to auto-pilot. He couldn't handle the situation at hand. He knew as Second of his pack he had to be strong for Justin, who seemed only a step or two from falling apart.

Ryan looked directly at the other man. "Justin!" He knew the sharp tone would gain Justin's attention. When Justin looked up he continued. "I need you to stay with me on this, okay? Now tell me exactly what happened."

Justin visibly pulled his shredded control together as he deliberately only looked at Ryan. "I was holding her. Then she whimpered and shifted her weight. I moved to check out what happened, and…" Justin stopped in mid-sentence to shift Lyra's weight so he could lift the left side of her shirt.

Ryan's shifted slightly so he could see around Lyra's prone body to where Justin was gingerly pulling up her shirt. Ryan felt his heart stop momentarily as a nearly black discoloration appeared on her hip and waist that was the same size as one of his hands. Ryan deliberately kept his breathing steady and his face blank, even though he was panicking inside. He had no idea what could have done that.

Justin lowered Lyra's shirt again, being careful to brush her skin as little as possible. Once she was covered, Justin looked back to Ryan.

"That was when Dylan came in. I started to lift her and try to wake her, but she wouldn't move. I can hear her breathing and her heart. I shook her shoulders. I was careful not to shake her torso. When that didn't work, I asked Dylan what he thought we should do. Then I felt dripping on my hands and we both smelled blood. I turned to see her bleeding from her ears and eyes. I told Dylan to get some towels, by the time he came back her mouth and nose started to bleed. Once we got the towels in place as best we could, he ran down to get you two."

Ryan could hear the barely contained panic in the other man's voice. He knew it was his job to keep the other man calm but had no idea what to do. Instead he looked over at Taylor. The other man, much like Ryan, was keeping himself blank, but Ryan could see the anger in Taylor's eyes as the other man made eye contact.

"I need you to come here and hold these towels. I have to call Jack. The last thing we need at this point is him exploding at us over this."

Taylor nodded and started to move toward the bed but Dylan grabbed his arm. The younger man looked worried. "Are you sure that's a good idea?"

The other man snarled a growl and ripped his arm from Dylan's grip. He was still rumbling a little when he gently moved his hands to replace Ryan's.

Ryan headed downstairs so he wouldn't be overheard. Pulling out his phone, Ryan sighed as Jack's frustrated voice came over the line.

"What?" It sounded like he was in his car.

"You might want to come back here. Lyra is having a severe reaction to the drug they gave her and is now bleeding from her ears, nose, mouth, and eyes. There's also some internal bleeding in her side."

Jack repeated a choice word over and over, increasing in volume each time. "I'm turning around. I'll be there in fifteen."

Ryan interjected before Jack could hang up. "They called that doctor. She's on her way. She might beat you here, but just barely."

There was silence for a few seconds. "Good." Jack hung up.

Ryan leaned his forehead against the wall and concentrated on taking deep breaths. His mind was moving so fast. This was bad, very bad. He couldn't lose Lyra, none of them could. Losing one of their own would devastate all of the Weres. Worse of all, he couldn't see an end in sight. He had no idea what they were going to do and if his growing hunch was right, they were in much deeper trouble than Jack thought.

Chapter 22

Jack sped the entire way to Justin's. His mind was an angry, frightened whirlwind. He didn't know what to think, what to do, to save his littermate. Justin's front door was unlocked when Jack got there. Not that he was entirely surprised, but Jack was too overwhelmed at the moment to work up agitation at the lack of safety.

The Were hearing made it possible for him to hear the conversation going on as he made his way upstairs. It was just the voices he could make out, not the words. There was Ryan, Taylor, Dylan, and another male voice Jack didn't know. They didn't sound like they were in the bedroom and as he turned the corner, the four men appeared across the hall from the closed bedroom door. For some reason that made Jack panic more.

There was a scream from the other side of the bedroom door. All Jack could think about was getting to Lyra. He made it halfway before he was tackled to the ground. His senses burned with anger as he lashed out at the man on top of him. He was an Alpha, he could go where he wanted. Then a large hand closed over his throat, slowly squeezing and Jack stilled.

As his eyes focused on the face belonging to the hand, its grip loosened. It was the man he didn't know holding him down. The other man was large with very little body fat. He had a dark tan that looked natural. He looked calm but his eyes blazed down at Jack.

"Will you stay calm then?"

Jack glared up at the larger man. He was fully aware this man could kill him if he so chose and that didn't make him any less angry.

As if the bulk of a man could read Jack's mind, he tightened his grip a little as he spoke. "'Tis my woman in there you plan to barge in on. She wanted no one going in there and I'll be damned if I'm goin' to let anyone defy her wishes." He gestured with his other hand toward Ryan. "This one already tried it, but I set him right. You're the Alpha, yes?"

He lessened his grip enough for Jack to nod.

"Good, then you damn well better act like it." The giant hand moved about two inches away from Jack's throat.

Jack was careful to not let the relief show as he inhaled deeply.

"We'll be explaining things to ya then, eh?"

Jack wasn't positive if that was a question or a statement. But something in his face much have shown the other man what he wanted to see because the man slowly stood up and offered Jack his hand.

Jack didn't want to take it. However, something about the older man told him if he didn't it would be taken as an insult. Gripping the outstretched hand, Jack scanned the other men to get a quick sense of the situation.

Both Taylor and Dylan stood very still. They looked pained but resigned. If Lyra put her trust in these men as deeply as Jack thought she did, then he could trust they would have stopped anything worse from happening to her.

The new man seemed to be sizing Jack up. The man was the same height as Ryan but a good bit bulkier, while managing not to look too big for his frame. He was impressive, more so when Jack included the fact that the man looked fifty.

Another scream rang from the bedroom, but this time it was quieter, more desperate. Jack stiffened, his heart breaking.

The older man pointed one beefy finger past Jack to Ryan. Jack turned as the man's voice because a stern growl again.

"You better not move from that spot, Boy-o or we'll be having another disagreement."

Jack turned to look over his shoulder at Ryan. His Second was giving the new man a murderous look, but he didn't move. His hands were digging into his upper arms, and Jack wasn't entirely sure Ryan hadn't drawn blood.

That snapped Jack's control into place. One of them had to remain level headed for Lyra's sake and it obviously wasn't going to be Ryan.

He turned to face his Second. "Ryan!"

The other man's eyes snapped to Jack, but the anger didn't lessen.

"Should I be fighting them about this? Is Lyra being harmed?"

He already knew the answer, but he needed Ryan to admit it.

The other man started to growl with every exhale and his breaths came faster. "No, they may cause her pain but they aren't harming her."

Jack nodded and felt a weight lift off his chest, but he kept his face stern. "Then snap the hell out of it. When this is all over, you and I are going to be having a discussion."

The voice he used would have made any other packmate submit, including Lyra. As it was, both Taylor and Dylan slouched their shoulders.

Ryan maintained eye contact but blanked his face. All that was left were those murderous eyes and a very faint growl. They stared at each other for a few seconds before Jack looked away, not in submission, but in dismissal. Knowing that would get to Ryan better than anything else.

The older man was watching Jack when he turned back. He had the distinct impression the other man was impressed. Once again a hand was held out to Jack.

"You can call me The Scotsman. It's nice to finally meet you, Jack."

Jack stopped halfway to shaking The Scotsman's hand. "How did you know who I am?"

The other man let out a belly laugh, odd under the circumstances. "You're Alpha, correct?"

Jack just nodded.

"Then who else would ya be? The Lass in there speaks very highly of you. Was always curious what you looked like."

Jack was starting to become curious himself, despite the terrible circumstances. "Why is it everyone I come across lately seems to know Lyra on some level?"

He meant it to be rhetorical, but The Scotsman gave another hearty laugh. "How could you not? Precocious young thing like that, with some very strong strapping young bucks wrapped around her little finger. She's a tad hard to miss."

Jack could accept that. He wanted to know more but the matter at hand was more pressing. "So what exactly is going on?"

The Scotsman's smile died. "I don't know. I only got a glimpse of the wee lass before I had to set myself to dragging your man there out into the hall." He didn't do more than glance at Ryan before continuing. "By the time we settled our differences in opinion these two already left the room and shut the door behind them."

Jack looked from Dylan to Taylor. They were solemn, but Taylor made eye contact.

"The Luna, our medical specialist, told us if we could not prevent ourselves from interfering, then we had to leave. Justin was the only one strong-willed enough to stay."

There was silence for a long time. It was broken by a wolf's whimpers. None of them spoke, they simply watched the door. Jack knew those whimpers hadn't been Lyra, they were Justin. Dread settled in his stomach. There was one more panic and pain-filled scream. This one was longer and warped. Jack's heart leapt to his throat. Lyra was stuck between forms, the scream couldn't be made by human, or wolf lungs.

Jack felt more than saw Ryan move. Before Jack could fully turn and stop him, Ryan was at the door. Jack watched as Ryan's hand shook an inch from the knob before making a fist and sliding on the door. He slid down to curl into a crouch next to the frame, head resting against the wood. It was heart-wrenching and in that moment, Jack knew there was no way he could convince Ryan to leave Lyra alone.

There were unknown curses coming from behind Jack. He turned in time to see The Scotsman elbow Taylor.

The older man looked shocked and surprised as he watched Ryan. "Why didn't 'cha tell me this?"

Taylor didn't take his eyes off Ryan. "I only just realized it."

The older man did some more cursing. "Poor sod. Her father'll kill him."

Jack was just about to ask what exactly the other man meant when Ryan suddenly leapt to his feet and the bedroom door opened.

The Luna was short maybe five-foot-three. She was delicate but Jack could plainly see a core of steel. This woman appeared soft on first glance but she held a lot of power in her position. She carried it more like she was royalty than as if it was a burden.

Her eyes went straight for the Scotsman. Jack chanced a look at the other man, whose face appeared close to a worried, overprotective father. It made Jack wonder if the man was of any relation to Lyra. The Luna spoke rapidly in another language. The Scotsman answered in the same language. The two seemed to be discussing Lyra's condition and what exactly to share with the others.

Taylor finally stepped forward to get both their attention. "With all due respect, we would like to hear it in English, please."

Taylor was clearly irritated but trying desperately to remain respectful.

The Luna inclined her head. "You'll have to excuse me, Taylor, but you know how you boys get when it comes to Lyra. Overreacting does not do the behavior justice."

Taylor ground his teeth. Jack noticed he was looking just over the woman's shoulder instead of making eye contact with her.

"Again with all due respect, Luna, she was drugged and bleeding, hallucinating and did not recognize anyone but her packmate in there." Taylor's breathing sped up as he spoke. "I think overreacting fits the bill right now."

The Scotsman seemed to growl in warning. "Watch yourself, pup."

Taylor's head jerked to the Scotsman, the anger rolling off of him.

The Luna raised a hand. "Stand down, my love."

Amazingly, the Scotsman did what she said and took a deep breath before flushing the anger from his face.

The Luna seemed to realize Ryan standing next to her. She looked up at him and waited for him to switch his gaze to her from where he had been looking in the room. She gave him a sad smile. "Hello there, I do not believe we have met."

Ryan seemed to be fighting his way back from the more primitive part of his mind as he answered her. "Ryan."

Her smile sweetened a little. "Ryan. Well, I'll give you the option of going in there to be with her or to stay out here and hear my diagnosis." She watched him, and behind that sweet calm persona, Jack could see a sharp mind working, waiting for Ryan's answer.

Ryan took a deep shaky breath, then took a step away from the bedroom.

Luna simply watched him a beat before stepping into the hall and shutting the door behind her.

"Smart man."

It had been so soft Jack wasn't even sure he heard her say it. Then she moved to be closer to the rest of them. After a moment's hesitation, Ryan followed her.

She nodded to Jack before speaking to the group, quietly enough she wouldn't be heard in the next room. "I want to start by saying I don't know what's wrong with her."

She held up her hand again as Taylor and Dylan began to stir.

"I do know the drug in her system is the cause. However, I do not know what drug it is. I will need to get her blood tested in the hopes of identifying it. But I don't hold out a lot of hope, the best we can do is to figure out a way to counter its attack on her system until we either stop it or flush it from her system. I've managed to stop the bleeding, both internal and external, as well as drain the blood pooling in her side. She still does not recognize me, so I would guess she will not know any of you either."

Her voice faltered with that last statement. The Scotsman move to her and wrapped himself behind her, as if trying to physically shield her from the pain.

Luna took two deep breaths. "We won't know what the drug's next step is until it makes it. I'm not sure how long it will take me to come up with a more permanent treatment. I've only just received the notes retrieved with her and I don't know how helpful they will be. Right now she is very heavily sedated. I've instructed Justin how and when to give her the shots. I want to keep her that way for at least two days. I will be back here tomorrow evening to check on her. But call me if anything happens." Her last sentence was more plea than command. She inclined her head and walked down the hall.

Both the Scotsman and Dylan followed her.

There was barely a pause before Ryan began stripping. He didn't even look up as he shucked his pants. "She's in wolf form."

Taylor nodded and started changing himself.

Jack watched both men change. A tiny voice in his head that sounded an awful lot like Lyra made fun of the fact that neither man thought to open the door before changing. Instead of finding that voice comforting, it made Jack choke up. Doing his best to ignore it, Jack walked over and opened the door.

He saw Lyra's prone form on the bed, lying on her stomach facing the foot of the bed. Justin was lying against her left side, as close as he could get, with his head and front paws on her back. The wolf that was Justin looked up at Jack. Jack could see the raw pain and worry in his littermate's eyes, but what scared him was the desperation and hopelessness he saw there too. Jack looked away. He didn't have an answer for his littermate. He was their Alpha and yet there was nothing he could do to protect them or make the situation better.

Ryan brushed past him and Jack leaned down to tap his furry back. Ryan stopped and looked up at him. Ryan's eyes were the exact opposite of Justin's. Ryan had a furious will in his eyes. He told Jack there was no way he was letting this happen without a fight. That steadied Jack, they had to fight this. Gaining resolve, he spoke to Ryan. "I need to get to work. I'll be back as soon as my shift is over, but call me should anything happen."

Ryan nodded his shaggy head before turning back to the bed.

Jack couldn't stand there another second. He spun on his heels and whipped out his phone. Somewhere in the midst of this he had forgotten Graham hadn't been there. It seemed to Jack that someone should let Lyra's overprotective cousin know what was going on.

Jack got Graham's voicemail for the second time as he reached the front door. He found himself getting angry. As he shut the door behind him, he noticed Dylan standing on the porch, staring off into the sky.

Jack ended the call and used that as an opportunity. "Why isn't Graham here?"

The younger man jumped. He had to have been out of it not to hear Jack coming. When he turned Dylan's eyes were shining as he blinked back tears.

"Um, around the time the Luna got here, Graham got a call from his dad. He was telling Graham to get himself to the family compound. Graham argued but whatever his dad said convinced him to go. He didn't even stick around until Luna was working on Lyra. Graham just turned right back around. But I left him a message. Told him what the Luna said. He's not going to be happy. Which means he and the Scotsman are going to have a fist fight. The Scotsman doesn't let anyone question his wife." Dylan turned his body back to face outward again.

Jack wasn't entirely sure how to handle this situation. Everything seemed way above his head. He was trusting people he didn't know with the lives of those in his charge. Jack wanted more than anything to get a handle on this situation. He shook his head, that wasn't true, he wanted Lyra well more than anything else.

Jack nodded his thanks to Dylan before heading for his car, but halfway there, he pulled out his phone and called Bishop. The Alphas needed to meet, now.

Chapter 24

Lyra felt like she was going to vomit. The world seemed to be spinning, even with her eyes closed. It was like having a really bad hangover. At least she was coherent now. Or she thought she was coherent. Lyra could smell Justin, and feel him, which went a long way to calm her nerves. She thought she could smell Ryan and Taylor too. Opening her eyes to find them, the world began to tilt. She let out a whimper and slammed her eyes shut.

Within seconds, her nose filled with Ryan’s scent and Lyra felt his muzzle against hers. He gave her face a gentle nuzzle before moving a few inches away, but Lyra could still feel the heat from his body.

Right after, she smelled Taylor on her other side. He was careful not to touch her, but she knew he was there.

It was a huge comfort to be coherent again, to know for a fact she was safe. Even if it felt as if her head and stomach were going to explode. Lyra wondered for a second what woke her up. Then it dawned on her how cold it was in the room. Justin was a lot like her, he preferred lower temperatures, but this was pushing it. She moved in closer to Justin in an effort to absorb some of his furry warmth. It wasn't enough though. Her body grew colder, Lyra began to curl herself into a ball to maintain warmth. She realized then it wasn't the room that was cold, it was her, no doubt another side effect of that drug.

As if he could read her mind, Ryan hopped onto the bed. The mattress shook a little, but Lyra was too cold to feel nauseous. He stood over her for a second, positioning himself before slowly laying down on her legs, so they were face to face. Even with her eyes shut, Lyra could tell he was trying to hide his worry. He had been so careful to make sure he wasn't putting too much weight on her.

After a few seconds, she felt Justin curl around her lower back. He was mostly on top of her, but again he was taking most his weight off of her. Lyra hadn't realized she was shaking until she felt her body stop. The she heard Taylor exit the room but she didn't bother wondering where he went, she was just too cold.

When Lyra came to again, she felt warmer, not a comfortable temperature but not unbearable. That was probably due to the pile of wolves on and around her. She could smell at least six different wolves, all of whom she knew. Ryan was still positioned where he had been the last time she lost consciousness. Which was not a surprise, as Ryan could be stubborn when he wanted.

"There now, lass, good to see you still in the land of the living." It was Scotty, and if he was here than so was Luna. If they had called Luna, then things had gone really bad.

Lyra opened one eye, and the world shifted a little but it was nothing unbeareable. As she opened her other eye, Scotty stepped into her line of sight. He was giving her that nervously worried smile he gave her every time she was in Luna's care.

"You've got quite the show of friends here, lass. I only know three of them. The house is almost full. Neighbors probably think there is some kind of gathering."

Lyra did her best to give Scotty a stern look. She wanted an explanation, not a distraction. She was sure however her wolfy expression lacked any real emphasis, but Scotty would get it, he always did.

"I would tell ya love but I was not here for most of the ruckus. All that were are now on the bed, not exactly in the position to talk." Scotty smiled down at her. "I'm gonna get Lu, she'll wanna know you're awake." Then he left her line of sight.

Lyra let out a sigh. She wanted to know want was going on. She wanted to get caught up. She wanted to know why she was the only female on the bed. Ryan nipped at her nose. Lyra focused in on his face. His eyes were closed, but Lyra could tell he was amused by her attitude. So she did the only thing she could think of, she kicked him. Not that it would hurt him, as he was on her legs, but it was the principle that mattered. Her movement causes several others to move. She heard a growl that was distinctly Graham. He had to be the one wrapped around her head. She growled back. Lyra felt him move right before he nipped at her ear. There was more warning and less play to Graham's nip that Ryan's. Lyra growled back; normally she would retaliate, but at the moment she was covered in wolves, each of whom outweighed her.

When she laid her head back to its original place, Ryan was watching her. Lyra could see the amusement on his face and she narrowed her eyes. If it had been anyone else, she would have taken revenge for getting her in trouble with Graham, but Ryan was so rarely amused that she let it be. Ryan had such a heavy chip on his shoulder she was always glad to see him let go of it, even for a second. Lyra closed her eyes and tilted her head forward so her snout playfully hit him in the nose. He sneezed, just like he always did. Ryan glared at her, but they both knew he didn't mean it.

Luna's voice carried down the hall. "She's awake? And she knew who you were?"

She could hear Scotty's deep laugh. "I assume so, it's not like she can talk and there are quite a bit of young bucks preventing her movements."

There was a light smack, and Lyra figured Luna's hand slapped against Scotty's forearm. It was a habitual gesture she had seen hundreds of times. A heartbeat later, Lyra knew the couple was it the room. Then Luna appeared above Ryan's head. Her smile was full of relief.

"Hey there, Lyra. Are you feeling better?"

Lyra had been treated enough by Luna in the last two years to know the routine, one blink for no, two for yes. She blinked twice.

Luna smiled. "Good. Are you still cold?"

Lyra hesitated a second before blinking twice again.

The smile dropped and she gained her look of concentration. "As cold as before?"

Lyra quickly blinked once.

She was rewarded when Luna gave a sigh of relief. "I'm glad to hear that. You gave us quite a scare. In fact, it's been quite a roller coaster since you were brought here."

Lyra looked from Luna to Scotty. She knew Luna wouldn't tell her exactly what that meant, but later she would be able to convince Scotty to. Lyra knew her aunt's husband had a soft spot for her and some times that came in handy.

A voice came from the doorway. Lyra didn't have to look to know it was Jack standing there, but she was a little worried she hadn't been able to smell him coming. She really should have smelled him.

"You didn't recognize us, any of us, except Justin." There was hurt and anger in Jack's voice, but she also heard the fear.

There was a shove on her butt that let her know the weight down there was Justin. Odds were he was just as uncomfortable with their sleeping habit being outed as she was. Lyra made a mental note to apologize to him later.

Luna shifted her weight toward her husband so Jack could step into Lyra's view. He didn't just step in, though. Before she knew it, his face was buried in the fur on the back of her neck. Lyra was so surprised, she jumped. When Jack spoke it was so quiet no one else heard him but her, and Lyra wasn't entirely sure she was supposed to.

"You had me so scared. Don't you every do that to me again. It killed me to see you like that, knowing there was nothing I could do."

One of his hands was wrapped in the fur on her side, as if he was trying to get the closest thing to a hug he could. Jack was there several moments and no one said anything. When he finally stood, his face was determined, and Lyra wasn't exactly sure how she felt about that.

"I've been talking to the other Alphas and when you're moderately better, you and I are going to have a talk." There was the anger.

Lyra felt herself automatically begin to rebel. She didn't follow anyone. Then she felt pressure from three different places on her body. She knew two were from Ryan and Graham, but she would put money on the third being Taylor, all of them telling her to hold herself in check.

Scotty laughed and Lyra felt her muscles relax, which earned her an open eye from Ryan. Something about Scotty's laugh always mellowed her out, even as a little girl with nightmares. If Scotty laughed, everything would be all right.

"Boy-o you don't know my girl too well if you think she'll be doin' anything she doesn't wish to do." Then Scotty made eye contact with her and though his face was smiling, his eyes weren't. Coming from him, the effect was creepy. "Sometimes I wonder if she only goes along with things simply to humor us." Then he shook his head.

Jack wasn't deterred, he faced Scotty full of pent-up rage. "I am her Alpha and as such, she will listen to me."

Lyra swore everyone in the room stiffened. She barely noticed herself growling.

"You shouldn't talk that way to him. It will only piss Lyra off. She doesn't need the agitation." Heads turned toward the door, toward Hazel's worried voice.

Jack seemed to only get more frustrated. "I don't care, it's true and it's about time she realized it."

Lyra's felt the rumble in her chest grow louder in outrage and she began struggling to get up. No one showed such blatant disrespect to her and her family, no one.

"Damn it, Jack, apologize, she's going to hurt herself."

Lyra knew better. She felt Taylor, Graham, and she assumed Dylan give way. They wouldn't try to stop her. They knew better. Ryan looked confused, but got up once he saw the others do it. The last two wolves followed suit. She was struggling to get to her feet, but her legs just wouldn't hold her weight.

Jack watched her in angry surprise. He actually seemed surprised she was upset. In that moment she wanted to hurt him. She may want her freedom and knew Jack would fight her on that, but no one spoke to her family that way. He uncle deserved respect.

"Jack, apologize." Hazel's worry increased.

Lyra just about gained her balance when she was scooped up by large Scottish arms and wrapped against her uncle's chest. Scotty was just holding her, her legs dangling. He started speaking Gaelic. Lyra didn't know much of the language, just enough to know he was trying to soothe her. She felt awkward with her legs just hanging, but Scotty had done this enough times that Lyra knew she wasn't going anywhere. The sigh of defeat was more of a subconscious reaction, but Scotty chuckled anyway.

"There now, lass. Let's not be undoing all your aunt's hard work."

Everyone but Hazel, Taylor, Graham, Dylan, and of course her aunt, seemed to go wide-eyes at Scotty's words. Lyra's eyes narrowed, and she knew he said that on purpose. It was his way of telling Jack they were family, explaining to the others why Lyra would be so defensive of him, without actually saying it. Even though he couldn't see her face, Lyra was sure her uncle knew she was glaring at him. Jack let out a curse and moved to make eye contact with Lyra.

"Really, can we find someone you're not related to?"

Lyra felt her chest start to rumble again.

Scotty bounced her once, and she stopped growling simply from the shock. "Let's not be getting her agitated. Or I'll be removin' ya from the premises."

Jack started to open his mouth but her uncle cut him off. "You aren't my Alpha, I don't have to listen to a word you say. You're here out of courtesy to the patient, but if you can't play nice, then ya won't be playing t'all. You understand me?"

Jack seemed to get angrier and Lyra found herself wanting him to try her uncle. She wanted to see Jack fall flat on his back. But her littermate kept his mouth shut.

Since the fight seemed to have died down, Lyra leaned her head on her uncle's arm. She was getting cold again. Until that moment she hadn't realized how much of her strength had been a front. She was getting cold fast, and Lyra snuggled in closer to her uncle. Then her right front paw twitched. Only she and her uncle seemed to have caught it.

Scotty's voice was solemn. "Tell me that was on purpose, lass."

Lyra whined as a shooting pain arched up that leg and into her chest. Her leg curled in of its own accord. Lyra became terrified as the pain bounced around her system, never settling in one place, but wherever it hit became numb. The pain was blinding but the numbness was much worse. Then her brain was jolted and all she could do was let out an inhuman scream before the world went black.

She was dreaming, Lyra knew it right away. It wasn't a dream as much as it was a memory. She was in the Pack F office. She wasn't sure how long ago it was but it was definitely a ways back because the foosball table was still there, though no one was playing it. There were only four of them there and it was calming and peaceful. Lyra was sitting on one of the leather chairs facing a side table. This furniture incarnation Hazel put all the chairs into two rows, facing each other.

In the chair opposite her, sat Bruce. They were playing chess; they had done that a lot for a while. On Bruce's right was Felix. He was curled around a thick manual of some kind, appearing totally engrossed but Lyra saw him sneaking glances at the game through the curtain of his hair.

To her right sat Ryan. He was stretched out, watching the game and lazily nursing a bottle of water. Lyra wasn't sure where the memory came from but she had a sneaking suspicion her subconscious was trying to calm her down. This memory represented a calming, comforting period for her. It was from when they began to gel as a pack. She was vaguely aware of Bruce telling Ryan to stop distracting him from the game with whatever they were talking about.

Lyra took in the sense of belonging attached to the moment. She could smell all three of them, but Ryan's cologne was the strongest since he was so close. Lyra secretly loved Ryan's cologne. It mingled well with his natural scent and reminded her of that period right before it rained. She'd never told anyone how much she enjoyed it, but of course Hazel picked up on it and teased Lyra about it.

The memory began to fade around the edges and Lyra reluctantly let it go. She was in the pack office again. It was night this time and it was Justin, Hazel, Seth and her. Lyra had no idea where Jack was or why he wasn't in the office, but she quickly let that go as Justin and Seth raced each other to the foosball table, shoving each other all the way. Hazel was laughing and Lyra couldn't stop the smile creeping onto her face at watching her littermates tumble to the floor. This time the memory faded sooner and the black seemed to last longer in between.

Lyra was in the bleachers on the side of a soccer field. She was bundled up and her right arm was looped with Taylor's. They were using each other's body heat to keep warm in the unusually cold November air. Scanning the field, Lyra saw a gangly teenage Dylan running toward the goal. A second later she and Taylor were on their feet screaming as the ball hit the net. Dylan had been a star player at his high school.

This time when the memory went fuzzy, Lyra held on. Somehow she knew there wouldn't be another comforting memory after this one. When the world went black it was going to stay that way. She didn't want it to stay that way. Despite popular belief, Lyra loved her life and was not ready give it up yet. When she lost and the dark hit, she struggled, tugging at her consciousness as if to wake herself from a nightmare, but she could feel herself slowly losing. It hurt, but she wasn't about to give up.

Chapter 25

This time Ryan refused to go anywhere when Luna cleared the room. It was him and Justin in wolf form with Lyra's aunt and uncle. The Luna had the two of them clear the bed. Ryan's heart was racing so hard he could hear it in his ears. Both he and Justin jumped onto each of the room's two armchairs so they could see Lyra's prone body.

Justin made the occasional whining noise, but other than that neither of them drew attention to themselves. Luna bent over Lyra, listening to her breathing before speaking to her husband in another language. He went to the large black doctor's bag by the closed door, on the other side of which, Ryan could hear Hazel crying. After some rummaging The Scotsman pulled out a syringe filled with an amber liquid. The other man's expression was grim, but resigned.

Ryan knew whatever was in that syringe was going to be painful. He fought the almost overwhelming urge to jump over Lyra's body and guard her from whatever they would stick her with. Ryan watched Luna over the last day. He knew the woman would not harm Lyra, but the more primitive part of his brain was struggling with that.

The Luna held her hand out for the syringe, her expression pained. Her husband shook his head and gently moved her out of the way. With a steadying breath, he poked the syringe into his niece's neck.

When the syringe was empty, he removed it and both he and he wife stood watching Lyra. They waited for a long minute before Luna's eyes swam with tears and she buried her face against her husband's chest.

Justin let out a confused whine.

Ryan made eye contact with the stoic man holding the syringe. The cold look on the other man's face filled Ryan with dread. Something very bad just happened. He and Justin simply didn't know it yet.

The Scotsman maintained eye contact with Ryan as he spoke. "She's in a coma. We only had one way to get her out. The notes we received from the raid were incomplete. She had to guess and with your body chemistry, it had maybe a seventy percent chance of waking her up. Whether it worked or not, it is extremely painful, which would be worth it if she woke up."

Ryan felt the horror hit. He and Justin looked at each other. Lyra was now in pain with no way to relieve it. Ryan hopped from the chair onto the bed, curling himself protectively around Lyra and promised himself he wasn't moving until she woke up.

Chapter 26

Jack strained to keep hold of his anger. He was holding on for dear life as the other Alphas in the alliance debated on the best form of action to take out this threat. All Jack wanted was to tear every person he came across apart until someone gave him the antidote for what was killing Lyra. She was in a coma and her body was slowly shutting down and there wasn't a damn thing they could do about it.

Her aunt was working around the clock with scientists from their family in a lab they owned, trying desperately to break down the drug given to his littermate. As far as Jack was concerned, nothing was moving fast enough.

Ryan hadn't left Lyra's side, and neither had Taylor. So now Jack was at an alliance meeting without his Second. At least Seth was there with him to be another set of eyes and ears.

They were stunned by this drastic change in behavior from those running the project. Mathew's intel finally came through for them and the Weres now knew some of the scientists from the original project had broken off and wanted to experiment on the Weres. They narrowed down the possible places that might be used for their headquarters. The Weres were at a definite disadvantage because the scientists knew where the pack office buildings were and could probably break in at any time.

Now they discussed how to eliminate three of the four possible locations. Boone suggested scouting them, but that was quickly rejected when Bishop pointed out if they found the right place the Weres could be playing right into the scientists' hands. No one came up with a better idea and that was driving Jack crazy.

Most of his pack were camped out at Justin's, on top of Dylan, Graham, Boone, and Taylor, the last of whom never left. The townhouse was overcrowded. They were taking turns sitting in the room. Jack figured Justin would have joined Taylor and Ryan in the around-the-clock watch if he hadn't been so busy playing host.

Hazel insisted Lyra could hear them talk to her and their voices would be what brought her back. Jack didn't have any such hope, but he didn't have it in him to burst his littermate's bubble.

There seemed to be several others clinging to the same hope as Hazel. Dylan came in and sat for hours reading Aesop's fables, and he barely even looked at the book, as if he memorized them.

After three hours, he closed the book and said, "Good night, elephant child" before letting Jack relieve him. Jack had no idea what it meant, but he could tell it meant a great deal to the younger man.

Lyra had been out for two days now and Luna only gave her three more doses. Not that she told Jack, he overheard her tell Graham the day before. Graham appeared half dead. Jack wasn't sure if the other man was sleeping or eating; he was supposedly working with his father to gain information that might help the Weres, but every time Jack saw him the man looked worse. One Were in danger and they were all breaking at the seams. What would happen if these scientists got hold of more of them? Were they doomed to break after working so hard for what little stability they had?

Jack shook his head and moved his attention back to the meeting. Mathew was saying something about a stake-out. Jack leaned in toward Seth.

"What is he talking about?"

Seth's stoic face melted around the eyes to show momentary worry before answering. "He wants to invite outsiders to check out the locations for us. Lyra's family was suggested."

Seth seemed about as unhappy with that idea as Jack was.

"And why can't we just do this ourselves?" Boone sounded irritated. "Don't give me that crap about the scientists catching us. If, after training, we're not damn sneaky enough than that's our own fault." He stood up and scanned the room.

Charlie was giving his packmate a wary look.

"I say we do this ourselves. We can't just rely on others to do this for us. If you don't sanction this, then I say screw you all I'll do it by my damn self. She doesn't have time for your diplomacy. Geez, you're like the government. I'll put money down that says I could get a dozen guys with me by the end of the night." He glared at each Alpha individually.

To Jack's surprise, Seth stood up. "I'm with you."

There was a moment of surprised silence from the room before Charlie, Victor, and Bishop stood. Reed and Kipling followed shortly after.

Grant pushed off his seat. "What the hell, Lyra'd do it if she was conscious."

Seth and Jack exchanged glances. Jack was pretty sure Grant and Lyra didn't know each other, but at this point Jack wasn't sure of much he thought he knew about Lyra.

Mathew sat back in his chair and made eye contact with Jack. "Why do I have a sneaking suspicion if we don't okay this we are going to have another half-planned scheme that might just muck things up more than they already are?"

Mathew shot a pointed look at Bishop, whose calm expression remained in place. When Mathew turned back to Jack, he was shaking his head.

"They are not going to give us a choice in this."

Jack knew the other Alpha was right. This was the plan to go with, even if it was stupid. Sighing, he stood up.

"All right, scouting it is then. Everyone who doesn't want to be involved, leave now so you can plead ignorance later."

Jack wasn't surprised when no one left. It made him feel more confidence in the decision to join together.

"Our next step is to get as many people here as possible to help out. I want everyone in teams of two. No one is going off on their own on this one, is that clear?"

There were several nods and murmurs of agreement.

Jack pulled out his phone. "We'll regroup in ten. Use that time to call your packs and get anyone capable of doing this. Don't worry about hurt feelings, only contact those who won't be a liability. The last thing we need is one of us getting kidnapped." With that, he started dialing, and heard several others do the same.

Jack knew in that moment this would be a turning point for the Were community. They couldn't afford to play fair anymore. They were willingly stepping into a grey area. Jack sincerely hoped this didn't backfire on them.

Chapter 27

Justin wished like hell life could go back to the way it was a month ago. Since then everything had turned upside down. Lyra was dying, he knew it. Luna didn't say anything but Justin could feel Lyra fading. Her presence wasn't there when he snuggled up next to her. Justin knew exactly what he would be losing if none of them could save her. Ryan didn't.

Justin had seen the way the other man watched Lyra. The way he inhaled deeply when she entered a room. Justin waited months for Jack's Second to make his move, but it never happened. That always baffled him, and Justin knew if he was in Ryan's place, nothing could stop him. Recently Ryan had been teetering the line of stability and Justin knew Lyra was to blame. Justin knew how deeply he would mourn Lyra, but the other man might lose it entirely. If this plan of Jack's failed, they wouldn't just be losing one packmate, they'd lose two.

When Jack called him two hours ago, Justin rounded up a sizable majority of the people at his house. At first, Ryan hadn't budged. Oddly enough, Hazel convinced him to come. A part of Justin wanted to know exactly what she had said.

Justin scrubbed his face before looking at Seth. The two of them were leaning against the wall watching the Weres organize. A few feet away stood Syrus, Cole, Ryan, and Sadie. She walked in with her brother and glared at Jack before the other man could say a word.

Seth remained his calm, stoic self. Usually he and Ryan had that in common, but at the moment Ryan only looked about half a step better than Graham, who looked as if he had been hit by a bus.

"You think this is going to work?" Justin tried to keep his voice steady as he spoke to his littermate.

Seth turned to give Justin his full attention. "Don't ask questions you don't want the answer to, Jus."

Justin felt his dread solidify and drop like a rock in his stomach. "I want the answer."

"No, I don't think this will get us the cure for Lyra."

Justin stared at his best friend in shock. "Then why did you volunteer so fast?"

Seth turned back to the room at large. "Because if we find them, we can get information we don't have. Information about us. It also takes out part of the threat to us."

Justin felt his anxiety rise. "And what about Lyra?"

Seth glanced at him out of the corner of his eye for a second and Justin saw his jaw clench.

"I've already accepted we are going to lose her."

Justin felt his eyes go wide. "What do you mean you've accepted? How do you accept something like that?"

He knew his voice grew louder as their packmates shifted their attention.

Seth shifted so his right shoulder leaned against the wall instead of his back. He looked Justin in the eye, speaking too quiet for anyone else to hear. "I've lost loved ones before. I know that sinking into the pain is the worst thing I can do. No, I don't think what we are doing will help, but at least we are doing something."

Justin couldn't understand his friend's logic. "How can you give up hope like that? This is Lyra. The only person alive to every knock you off your feet."

Justin saw the smallest shift in Seth's eyes, but it was barely noticeable before in was gone.

"Don't kid yourself, Jus. She's dying and you know it. I know it. Taylor and Dylan know it. Hazel knows it, that's why she was so fanatical about talking to Lyra. And Ryan, Ryan sure as hell knows it. I'm sure someone's told her cousin. I knew she was leaving us. I could feel it when I was watching over her yesterday morning. You've spent more time cuddled up next to her than I have. If I could feel it across the room, then you sure as hell can feel it from inches away." Seth gave him one more long look before leaning back against the wall.

Justin didn't say anything. He knew Seth was right. Lyra's chances were miles past slim. He went back to watching the room. There were maybe forty people there, all of them itching to leave.

Mathew stuck his thumb and forefinger in his mouth and let out a loud whistle. Justin wasn't the only one to wince at the noise.

One guy with dark brown hair and eyes growled. "Damn it, Mathew, give some warning when you're gonna do that. Some of us have sensitive ears."

Mathew inclined his head in apology before motioning for Jack to take the floor. Seth looked as struck by that as Justin felt.

Mathew was a talker, it was strange for him to give the spotlight to someone else.

"Thank you everyone for coming on such short notice. We have reliable intel that has given us four possible locations for the headquarters of these ex-project scientists. Tonight we are going to split into four teams. From there, you will be paired up. Do not, I repeat, do not leave your partner. Each group will have one pair of Alphas as lead. This will prevent favoritism and you will not be put under the authority of your pack Alpha."

There were several murmurs throughout the room.

"You will, however, be partnered with someone from your pack. Your pack Alpha picked your partner, so if you have a problem bring it up with him or her."

Jack seemed to wait a beat just in case there were protests. "Okay then, we'll break you up now and head out. You'll get more direction from your Alphas."

Justin hoped this plan was well thought out or else they were screwed. But he kept his thoughts to himself as names were called out and people were organized. Justin was grateful to be paired with Seth but he wasn't quite sure about the rest of his group. Their Alphas were Mathew and Grant. Justin didn't have a problem with either of them but Taylor seemed to. Taylor was paired with Victor. Even Victor seemed to notice Taylor's aversion to Grant. Justin was pretty sure the other man was as much in the dark as Justin and Seth were. The twins were with them. Syrus was uncharacteristically silent as the group rode in a van to their destination in Everett. The last team were two men Justin didn't know. They were from Graham's pack, two bulky guys Justin was told worked as bouncers in Seattle, named Tomas and Greg. No one seemed to be in the mood for talking. The tension in the van was thick. Finally someone picked an argument. It had been inevitable but Justin had been hoping against it.

Grant turned in the front passenger seat to glare at Taylor, who sat directly behind him. "What?"

Apparently he noticed Taylor's snubbing too. Justin was across the row, so there wasn't a lot he could do to help the situation.

Taylor glared back. "You know what."

Justin felt totally out of the loop. He looked over his shoulder at Seth, but the other man shrugged.

Grant shifted in his seat to get a better angle. "I don't, actually. I don't know you. Why the hell are you giving me attitude? And is this going to continue all night because it won't help us any?"

Taylor seemed to grow angrier. "Lyra."

The look of surprise on Grant's face was almost comical. Justin looked at Seth, and Seth looked just as confused as Justin felt. He turned in time to see surprise leave Grant's face replaced by amused anger.

"You're joking, right?" When Taylor didn't respond, Grant let out an angry laugh and faced forward again. "Get your facts straight, Taylor. She broke up with me last time."

Justin felt shock fill his body. He whipped around to exchange wide-eyed looks with Seth. He couldn't believe neither of them knew that.

Seth leaned to the right so he could see Grant's back. "Care to repeat that for the lady in question's littermates?"

Justin heard cursing from both Alphas in the front seat.

Grant turned around again, this time with a blank face. "Your littermate and I dated on and off for about a year. Before and after the accident."

Justin's surprise overwhelmed everything else. It was the only time Lyra ever had flowers in her apartment. He never knew who was giving them to her, but they were always on display.

"You're the flower guy?"

Amusement and a flash of hurt passed through Grant's expression before he turned around again. "If that's what she was calling me."

Justin sat in surprised silence.

After a full minute, Tomas spoke from the back seat. "No offense, I do not know this Lyra, but how would her littermates not know who she was seeing? Me and G have one female littermate and we know damn near everything about every guy she sees. And why is the other guy upset about this?"

No one answered him right away.

Taylor cleared his throat. "We grew up together. I've known her since she was born. I had no idea she was seeing anyone, let alone another Were."

There was silence again before Tomas answered. "Yeah, I hear that. No one wants their littermates seeing a Were. Angry dudes."

Seth spoke up from the backseat. "Our Lyra is a very private person. With now two exceptions, I've only known who she was seeing after the fact."

That surprised Justin. He always knew when Lyra was seeing someone. He might not know who the guys were but he knew when she was seeing someone.

"Really? Who was the other?" he asked as he leaned back in his seat.

Seth grunted. "Casey Norton."

Justin bit his lip as he heard Taylor growl from across Victor, who looked at his packmate, confused. No one had liked Casey to begin with. Then the guy cheated on Lyra the summer after high school. He was pretty sure that guy didn't get a good night's sleep for the rest of the summer. That was how Justin first met Graham. He and Seth ran into Graham and his gang as they headed down the block to take revenge on the unsuspecting Casey. Justin didn't remember seeing Taylor, though.

It wasn't until Seth spoke again Justin realized there was a silence.

"Prick cheated on her."

There were sounds of angry sympathy from the others in the van.

Taylor's voice was a heavy growl threaded with a menacing satisfaction. "Between all of us, we made him regret it."

Justin snorted. "Yeah, I don't think Lyra realized what we were doing to that guy. I mean there was more than a dozen of us tormenting him for months."

Taylor gave a dark chuckle. "Dylan still stares the guy down when he sees him. Just on principle. Scares the crap out of Casey, even now."

Grant's voice was low from the front seat. "She knew."

Justin's attention slid to Grant, as he was sure Seth's and Taylor's did as well.

"What?"

Grant's lips curled into a smile. "She knew. Just because she didn't tell you about me doesn't mean she didn't tell me about all of you. She thought it was sweet. All of her 'Avenging Angels' was how she put it."

Justin figured Seth and Taylor were with him in wondering what exactly Lyra said, but Greg interrupted his thoughts.

"Shoot, does everybody but T and I know this chick?"

Justin refrained from commenting that some days it felt like it.

For the first time, Mathew piped up from the front seat. "She's Graham's little cousin. Dark hair, pale. Calls him a rather emasculating nickname." The last was said with some amusement.

Recognition dawned on both Tomas and Greg's faces at the same time, before they dimmed and they exchanged looks.

"She's dying, isn't she?" Tomas's voice was barely audible.

Justin jumped in before anyone else could. "Why do you ask?"

The two men exchanged glances again before Tomas answered. "We do not think Graham has eaten or slept in days, and there are few things that would cause that."

That effectively stalled the conversation and the silence continued until Mathew parked the van four blocks from the location in question.

Justin wasn't quite sure what they were looking for as he and Seth slowly made their way toward the north side of the old brick warehouse that had been neglected for quite some time. Weeds were everywhere and the white paint peeled off in large chips.

The two of them dropped to the ground in the tall grass when they heard voices approaching. When the first man came into view, Justin's adrenaline spiked. Both men wore fatigues with a sidearm strapped to their right sides.

Justin and Seth were downwind so he could smell the two men were human, not Were. Justin moved his left hand to click the talk button on his mic, the first man spoke loud enough for them to hear.

"Not a bad gig? Are you kidding? This is pretty cushy. All we do is walk the perimeter on the lookout for some dumb college kids who fancy themselves activists. It couldn't get much easier."

Justin exchanged looks with Seth. Neither spoke as the two guards reminisced about past jobs and turned the far corner of the building. Once they were out of sight, Seth clicked his mic.

"We got ourselves a live site. I repeat, this is a live site."

Syrus got on the radio. "Yeeeeehaw."

Mathew clicked on to prevent further chatter. "I'll let the other three groups know. We might need the backup."

Justin and Seth squatted in the bushes in silence.

After a few seconds Grant came over the radio, his tone was not happy. “We have a problem.”

Justin exchanged worried glances with Seth.

“It seems we are not the only live site.”

Justin felt adrenaline speed through his system. Things were about to get worse.

“We are getting backup from Bishop and Cassandra’s team. They will be here in fifteen. Get as much recognizance as you can in the next five minutes, then meet up back at the van.”

Justin cracked his neck and made eye contact with Seth, silently agreeing to move forward.

In that moment, Justin finally understood where Seth was coming from. The pain in Justin’s chest solidified as he accepted that he was going to lose Lyra. The pain made him more determined to get these rogue scientists for causing it.

Chapter 28

Jack couldn't help the sneaking feeling they had been set up. The dread spread through him like tar when he heard the second call for back-up on the radio. Jack knew all his packmates involved were now at the other site. He and Rachel already committed to the site in Shoreline when Mathew came over the radio. It was one of the hardest things Jack had ever done not to head straight to his pack. He was dead set against losing any more of them. The rest of Pack F was going to stay intact through this. Jack was determined to keep them all together and alive.

"Jack. JACK!" Rachel's voice cut through the fog of Jack's thoughts a moment before her shove registered on his shoulder.

Jack turned to the attractive woman driving their van. She was quite striking and under a normal set of circumstances he would pursue her. But fate was against him and that wouldn't change any time soon.

"Yeah?"

Worry flitted across her face. "We're here, Jack. It's time to meet up with the others."

Jack nodded and stepped out of the van. He could see Dylan a few feet away, watching Jack and his team approach. Beside him was a man Jack didn't know, but he looked as young as Dylan. Dylan moved in beside Jack as he passed them. The other man scrambled in step beside him.

Dylan didn't wait for Jack to speak. "There are ten guards in all. I'm not quite sure how he managed it, but Boone has a case of tranquilizer darts. Charlie offered to bring more if we want them."

Charlie and his wife had been expressly barred from joining any of the groups. The idea being if Lyra was valuable, the married couple would be priceless. Charlie understood, but he had been pissed.

Jack glanced at Dylan. "You told him no, right?"

Dylan gave him an angry look. "Of course we did."

He sped up as they reached the group and headed straight to the pacing Boone.

Jack and Rachel broke off from their own group to speak to Fin, Rafael, Gina, and Reggie, who were standing in a small circle away from the rest of their team. Jack nodded to each of them as they made room for him and Rachel.

"So, do we have anything resembling a plan?" he asked the other Alphas. He knew his voice came out a little sharp.

They all exchanged glanced before Fin spoke.

"This is what we were thinking. Boone, for one reason or another has a dozen tranqs on his person. We count ten guards. So every shot will have to count. If we take out the guards and tie them to some out of the way trees, they should not be a problem.

"The people inside are going to cause difficulty. We already decided we are not going to kill them, period, but we don't want them floating around to cause problems later. This means all we have is stealth. Boone and his partner, as well as two others from their pack, are ex-military. All four claim to be able to 'cure people of their consciousness' is how it was put. That only works for us if there are a small number of people inside."

Rachel jammed her hands in her pockets and looked at each alpha individually.

"How about we take out the guards and tie them up as you said, but we do the same with anyone inside. We can send in the teams of military guys while we tie the guards up. That building doesn't look too active, and I'd say fifty people are in there max. If the military guys can knock people out and we can get them out of the building, then we can look around in peace and torch the place when we are done."

Jack could see dozens of holes in that plan, but he knew they were working with a limited amount of time and odds of them getting a better plan in the next hour were slim. The Alphas already decided things were to be handled tonight. Jack saw burning the building as a major flaw. It needed to be done, but they couldn't just leave a fire in a place as populated as Shoreline.

Rafael seemed to be thinking the same thing as his thinly accented voice once again filled the night air. "I can call the fire department from farther downtown at a payphone. That way the fire will not have the chance to spread too far."

With that statement, it appeared they were agreeing to the plan. Jack couldn't help feeling something would go wrong but he kept it to himself because he had no doubt the other Alphas felt the same way.

Chapter 29

Justin hadn't liked waiting for the other group to show up or having to wait for the four alphas to huddle together and come up with a plan. He and Seth stood a little away from the others but Graham made his way over to them after having a few words with Bishop. Both Taylor and Victor followed suit and the five of them were now huddled in their own clump. Oddly enough, Cole, Ryan and the twins didn't join them, but broke off on their own.

Graham looked even worse close up. The other man's packmates were right. It looked like he hadn't slept or eaten in days. Taylor watched Graham like he half-expected the other man to collapse.

Graham looked straight at Justin and spoke directly to him. "I know you are closer to my cousin than the others and other than Taylor, who is suspiciously silent on the subject--" Graham paused to glare at the man in question before continuing. "--You are the one who would be spending the most time with her. I need to know how she is doing."

Justin knew good and well why Taylor would stay silent. No one would want to tell Graham his cousin was dying, Graham already looked like he suspected as much, but that didn't mean Justin wanted to be the one to confirm it.

Seth stepped in and took the bullet for Justin. Seth always did that. If he could take the heat for a friend, he would without question.

"She's dying and you know this, or else you wouldn't be asking. You just want someone to blame it on other than Lyra. You can't even bring yourself to say her name, can you?"

Justin looked at Seth. His littermate was genuinely angry and disgusted with Graham. That surprised Justin, and he had no idea why Seth would be picking Graham of all people to pick a fight with.

Graham bristled, but Taylor's hand on the other man's chest stopped him from pummeling Seth. "And you blame me for this, do you? You claim I am looking for someone to blame but you have already found who's at fault, haven't you?"

Seth folded his arms over his chest. "Yes, I say it's between you, Jack, and Lyra. All three of you are too stubborn to do anything anybody else's way. Lyra was going to be contrary to be contrary, that's who she is. Instead of accepting that, you and Jack try to force her into this little box. Granted, you're better at it than Jack, but you still don't see that Lyra needs her space.

"And Lyra doesn't compromise to save her life. Though she's getting better at it she still doesn't see how her actions affect others. She simply does what she thinks is best, and is only right about seventy percent of the time. Mainly because she's the only one that knows what's going on because she's so damn secretive.

"You and Jack don't like each other because you both see the other trying to box Lyra in and see what damage it will cause. But for some reason, only you know you don't see that each of you is doing the same thing yourself. So yeah, I'd say the three of you had a hand in Lyra's current state."

There was a heavy. Justin wasn't sure he really agreed with Seth's assessment, but at the same time he didn't wholly disagree either.

They never found out what would have been said next because Bishop called over from where he and the other Alphas were standing.

"Graham, you're sure the tranquilizers you have will work?"

Graham fought to get himself together and to tear his gaze from Seth. He didn't say anything, just nodded at Bishop.

Bishop gave a look that said he clearly knew something was going on over there before turning back to the other Alphas and saying something too quiet for Justin to hear. Mathew stepped away and gestured for all of them to move in.

Justin's head was spinning with thoughts and he couldn't seem to latch onto just one. As he moved toward the Alphas, he pushed all the thoughts from his head and promised himself later, when they weren't all in jeopardy, he would take the time to figure out all of them.

"We only have four confirmed guards but we assume there are more. Graham has tranquilizer darts courtesy of his family, and two guns that work with said darts. We've decided we want four volunteers. Each pair will split up with a gun and take out the guards on their given side. That will give us about two hours to get in, gather and destroy any work we find. We will go in in pairs. Don't separate and don't kill unless it is absolutely necessary. Am I understood?"

There were nods and sounds of agreement.

Graham stepped forward. "With all due respect, Taylor and I both have experience using these guns. I would feel better if it was us and our partners that secure the perimeter."

Justin noticed out of the corner of his eye Ryan was about to protest, but both Cole and Syrus laid hands on his shoulders and he stayed quiet. Justin personally thought Graham and Taylor would be their best bet anyway.

"All right, we'll go with that. Get on the radio when the coast is clear, don't go in alone. I mean it," Mathew said.

The four men nodded before heading off toward the warehouse.

Justin turned to Seth. "So what, we just wait here until they're done?"

Seth shrugged. "I guess."

Justin was not sure this plan was going to succeed. But he didn't know the entire situation and he knew second-guessing was the last thing they needed right now. Justin's adrenaline and nervous energy was making it impossible for him to stand still so he folded his arms and drummed his fingers, figuring that would be the least irritating for everybody else.

The other four members of Pack F made their way over to Justin and Seth. The two of them exchanged glances. Under normal circumstances this wouldn't be a big deal, but recent events made it hard to trust anyone, even pack.

Ryan spoke after the four of them reached Justin and Seth. "I know neither of you are exactly happy with me right now." He paused and watched both of them.

Justin kept his mouth shut. He wasn't unhappy with his pack's Second. He didn't trust the other man to be thinking rationally. Seth didn't answer either, just folded his arms and watched Ryan.

Ryan sighed. "Fair enough. That aside, we are still pack and I was thinking…"

"WE, WE were thinking." This from Syrus.

Ryan looked at his friend and gave him a sad smile.

Justin understood. Syrus was trying to cover for his best friend. Seth and Justin would do the same thing.

Ryan turned back to them. "I was thinking the six of us should go in together. I know it means we cover less ground, but as a group we are safer. I'm not losing another packmate to these scientists." Ryan's expression was more like his old self, a force to be reckoned with.

Justin felt for the guy. Ryan saw what happened to Lyra as his fault.

Seth must have felt the same way because he dropped his arms. "Yeah, I agree. Let's keep this pack as intact as we can."

An emotion flashed across Ryan's face before it blanked, almost too fast for Justin to catch.

"Okay, I'll let the Alphas know." He strode off toward the leaders.

They watched him with almost identical expressions on their faces.

Seth shifted his weight. "How worried should we be about him? He's almost completely lost it. I mean Jack is bad, but Ryan's way past that. Do I need to step in as Second?"

That was Justin thought exactly. It was somehow worse when someone else said it, as it meant it wasn't all in Justin's head.

Syrus jammed his hands in his pockets.

"There are some extenuating circumstances Ryan would kill us for telling you. It explains a hell of a lot. But yeah, to be completely honest, you might have to step in and take his place."

Both Cole and Sadie looked at Syrus in surprise, but he kept going.

"I'm not saying do it now. Wait until this blows over. Now just isn't the best timing, and if…if we lose Lyra then yeah, don't hesitate because he'll lose what little stability he has."

Pain and sorrow filled the air around them. Seth and Justin exchanged looks. Justin knew that was not what Seth wanted to hear. Any further conversation ceased as the radios crackled to life and Graham's voice gave them the all clear.

Chapter 30

Jack didn't like this. It didn't make any sense. Once they took out the guards, Boone came over the radio giving them the all clear. Then he said it really was all clear. There were only two lab personnel in the entire building. There should have been near fifty. Both teams fanned out and were searching through the stacks of papers for anything useful, but there wasn't much.

Rachel came to stand next to him from one cubicle over. "Are you catching how much of this crap is blank?"

Jack nodded. About ninety percent of everything they found was blank: blank pages, blank files, and no computers. It definitely appeared to be a set up.

Dylan's voice rose across the room. "I found something! Jack, I think this is about Lyra."

There was a slam of a door being opened all the way as Jack sprinted across the building. The adrenaline shot through his system. He hoped Dylan found something to save Lyra. Jack latched on to the hope as he skidded to a halt at a trapdoor hidden under one of the many desks. Dylan's head disappeared down a ladder. Then there was a shot from below and Dylan cried out, followed by a thud.

Before Jack could move, Boone leapt into the hole. Jack quickly followed suit. He landed and cursed; there were no lights anywhere except above him. Jack was perfectly illuminated and he rolled into the dark a second before he heard a bullet hit a wall behind where his head had been. Jack could hear Rachel up above yelling for everyone to stay put. Jack was grateful. The last thing they needed was for more people to climb into a dark hole with an unknown amount of guns.

The darkness was thick enough Jack couldn't make out anything beyond the trapdoor's box of light. Jack took a slow deep breath. His nose wasn't the best, but it was good enough. He could smell blood to his right, maybe twenty feet. It had to be Dylan. Boone was somewhere across the room, which was much bigger than Jack would have thought. There was a strange scent off to his left, like people but not quite. Jack never smelled it before. He knew that was where at least one sniper was. Jack had a choice, try to find the gun, or help Dylan.

He knew Boone had military training, but Jack didn't. He banked on Boone having better odds against the gun and slowly scooted back further into the dark, then toward where he could smell Dylan. It seemed to take forever, but he had to be sure he didn't make a sound. The last thing he wanted was to draw the attention of however many weapons were down there. His heartbeat thumped deafeningly in his ears. Instinct wanted to remove the threat, but his mind screamed at him to find Dylan. He was breathing hard and trying to keep in silent.

Just as he could smell Dylan right in front of him, Jack heard another shot and Boone growled. There were sounds of a struggle and another shot, then silence. Jack wanted to help but had no way of knowing where they were, so he just hoped Boone was okay.

A hand reached out and grabbed Jack's arm, and he jumped before he could stop himself. Dylan's face was inches away and his voice was so quiet Jack knew no one else could hear it.

"My sight is better than yours, he's fine. He got hit once in the side but the way he's moving makes me think it just grazed him. I need help though, I'm losing blood too fast. I need to change, but I might pass out in the process."

Jack nodded. "I've got you." Though he wasn't sure how he'd handle an unconscious Were stuck between forms.

Dylan exhaled and Jack felt him move away, closely followed by sounds of him slowly struggling to change. Jack never realized how much noise was made when they changed until now.

A gun went off from several feet away. It wasn't aimed at Jack, but the noise stopped. That scared Jack. He leaned over the struggling Dylan.

"I need to check on that."

There was no way for Dylan to respond, so Jack didn't stick around to find out. Instead he moved toward where the shot came from and strained his advanced hearing. The smell of Boone's blood hit Jack all at once and he fought not to gag. There was a lot of blood. Jack fought through the nausea and kept listening. Adrenaline raced through him so hard he knew he would have one hell of a headache afterward.

A few seconds later he was rewarded with a shuffle of a boot on the cement floor. It was faint and regular hearing wouldn't have picked it up. Jack recalculated his route to the left where the noise came from. The good news was that put them farther from Dylan. The bad news was they were closer to the smell of Boone. Whoever had the gun saw Boone as the most obvious threat and wanted to take him out first.

Jack stopped abruptly as the unknown man suddenly came into view. He wasn't facing Jack, but, if he turned, Jack would be in plain sight.

Jack didn't even think. He stood straight up and used all of his strength to snap the unknown man's neck. It made a disgusting cracking noise. Jack slowly lowered the body to the floor, so as not to alert anyone else as to what happened.

Once the body was secure on the floor, Jack controlled his nausea, hunched down and made his way to Boone.

Boone was a lot closer than Jack thought. He almost stumbled over him. The smell of blood had been too overpowering to pinpoint the other man's location. Another wave rolled through Jack's stomach as he squatted down near Boone's head. Jack could see Boone had a blood stain across his right side, but Dylan had been right, there was not enough for it to have been a fatal shot. The second shot seemed to have ripped through Boone's left shoulder. It didn't look fatal but it was more blood than Jack had ever seen.

"Boone, we need to get you out of here."

Boone shook his head. "Can't risk it, I got two of the three but the last guy, he has some kind of night vision goggles, the prick. But they do not seem it be working too well. We can't risk moving. Where's Dylan?"

Jack felt relief fill him. "You sure you got the rest of them?"

Boone nodded once and tightened the grip on his shoulder. "Damn sure."

Jack stood up and yelled toward the trapdoor. "Rachel, Boone and Dylan need medical attention, Boone's worse. Get some damn light down here!"

Rachel's voice came from above. "On it. "

Jack knelt back down to the confused Boone. "The last guy was heading toward you. He didn't see me. I snapped his neck."

Boone watched him for a moment. "That your first one?"

Jack knew what the other man was asking. "Yeah, it was."

Boone nodded. "I'm sorry."

Jack wasn't sure how to respond. He was holding all his emotions at bay, to prod at later.

Luckily he didn't have to respond because Rachel jumped down through the trapdoor holding two huge flashlights. A few seconds later after a sweep of the room her voice rang through the dark.

"EYES!"

Fluorescent lights flicked on from all directions. Apparently Rachel had found the light switch. Jack blinked repeatedly and Boone cursed. A moment later Rachel was beside them, looking down at Boone.

"I need the shirt off, so I hope it isn't a favorite." Then she started ripping the clothing with a small knife.

Jack stood up. "I'm checking on Dylan."

Rachel didn't answer, just nodded as she concentrated on Boone's shoulder.

Jack looked toward where he left Dylan. Sure enough there was a grey wolf panting on the floor. When Jack reached the wolf, he bent down and examined the injured leg. It wasn't bleeding anymore but he was pretty sure the muscles hadn't repaired enough for Dylan to walk. Jack looked into the furry face.

"I'm going to pick you up and carry you out to the main floor, okay?"

Dylan gave him a wolfy nod and Jack leaned down and gingerly scooped up the Were. Jack had an inward debate on how he was going to get both of them up the ten foot ladder. As he reached it, Jack settled on a fireman's carry and slowly slid Dylan onto his right shoulder.

It wasn't as hard as Jack thought it would be. Once they were up top Jack set Dylan down. The packmate Jack didn't know was there before Jack stood back up. Sure Dylan was going to be all right, Jack climbed back down the hole to join Rachel and Boone.

She was wrapping Boone's shoulder when Jack came to kneel beside her. She didn't even look at Jack as she spoke.

"How much can you lift?"

Jack thought about it. "Maybe three-fifty, why?"

She tied off the dressing and looked Jack in the face. "His best bet to stop the bleeding is to change, but that means someone needs to lift him out of here, and I know I can't do it."

Jack nodded. He could do it, though he might not be the strongest in his pack.

Rachel slapped her hands on her thighs and stood, looking down at Boone. "All right, you heard him. You need to change. Do you need help getting your clothes off?"

Boone snorted. "Not unless we are going to be doing something a little more fun than changing forms."

Jack saw Rachel roll her eyes and Boone started to shift. Both he and Rachel took a step back and she gave a low whistle. Jack looked over to see her impressed expression.

"Wow, the only Were I know that can do that is Graham. Hell, I'm lucky if I keep my panties on."

Jack struggled not to visualize the image that popped into his mind at her words. Instead he concentrated on the first part of her statement. Jack prided himself on being a gentleman.

"There are several I know. Lyra can do it. Ryan can, some of the time. Both Dylan and Taylor can, I've seen them do it."

Rachel looked away from Boone to stare at Jack. "What are the odds that all seven of them could do that?"

Jack actually hadn't thought of that. What if all seven of them could do that? That meant they wouldn't just be the fastest Weres. They were hiding something bigger than Lyra let on. Jack inwardly cursed. Secrets like this were going to get them all killed.

Boone was panting heavily when he finally finished. Jack cleared his head and concentrated on getting Boone up the ladder.

When he reached the top, Jack saw the other Alphas huddled together. Jack laid Boone down and moved to join them but was stopped by a hand on his right arm.

Jack turned to see a Were he couldn't place beyond a vague recollection. The guy was maybe three inches taller than Jack. He was pale with black spiky hair, and on the thin side. Once the other man was sure he had Jack's attention he let go of Jack's arm.

"I think I know what Dylan was talking about. I was just down the row." He motioned about four desks down before waving to the desk nearest to the trap door. He turned as if expecting Jack to follow.

Jack gave the other Alphas one more look before sighing and following the other man. When Jack stood beside him at the desk, the Were handed him a blue filing folder. There was only one word on the label. *INJECTIONS*. Jack opened the folder to somewhere in the middle. As he began to skim, his blood ran cold. There were notes on the drug that was probably in Lyra's system. The page he was reading mentioned possible side-effects. The list was almost a page long. Jack began flipping pages, looking for something that might mention an antidote. On a page toward the back there was mention of antidote work done in the lower lab. Jack assumed that was the room through the trapdoor. The paperwork said the best they had come across was a suppressant, but the work appeared promising. It stated live subjects were needed for the next phase of testing.

Jack shut the folder and headed back to the trapdoor. If something down there could help Lyra, he was damn well going to find it. He stopped in front of the door and turned back to the other man, surprised to see him standing two feet away. Jack hid his surprise and nodded.

"I really appreciate this. Thank you."

The taller man smiled and held out his hand. "Kipling Fuller, and you are Jack, Alpha of Pack F."

Jack shook Kipling's hand and tried not to be surprised that the other man knew who he was. "I take it you're going to help me find the paperwork about the antidote?"

Kipling nodded. "Yup."

Jack turned back to the trapdoor and headed down with Kipling not far behind. Once they were both in the lower room Jack pointed to the left work area.

"Go ahead and look through that half of the room. I hope you're not squeamish about the dead." Jack was trying hard not to be. The thought of Lyra was the only thing keeping him down here.

Kipling shook his head and strode to the first of three desks filled with lab equipment. "Nope, Grandpa's a mortician. Used to help out as an after school job."

Jack tried really hard not to find that creepy, but it was difficult. After a few minutes of the only sound being the rustling of papers. Jack heard Rachel's voice from the ceiling.

"Hey, Jack."

Jack turned from the notebook of calculations he was looking at to glance at the trapdoor, where Rachel's head was upside-down.

"What are you doing down there?"

Jack flipped the notebook closed. "There are notes about the drug they used on Lyra down here. I want to get as much of it as I can before we burn this place, but I don't understand most of it."

Rachel's head disappeared and a moment later she jumped through the hole and walked toward Jack. The rest of the Alphas climbed down after her. Rachel held her hand out for the notebook Jack was holding.

Jack handed it over and went back to the pile of papers in front of him. "You know you can take the ladder down, right?"

Rachel didn't look up from the pages. "Yeah, but my way is faster."

Rachel closed the notebook and shoved it into a backpack Jack hadn't seen before. Then she turned and spoke to the room at large.

"Okay, pack up everything with writing on it. I mean everything. Even if it's just a doodle, I want it taken with us. We need to get out of here. We can sort through it all later."

She started jamming papers and notebooks into her pack. Jack followed suit. It took seven of them ten minutes to grab every paper they could find.

It took another forty minutes to get everyone out and the fire blazing. Jack was quiet on the trip back to the pack offices. It was going to take time to decipher all the science and time was something Lyra didn't have.

An idea dawned on him. Luna mentioned the notes she had being incomplete. What if these notes could help her with the antidote she was working on? Hope filled Jack as he started rifling through the bag on the floor in front of him. When he found the notebook he was looking for, he spoke loudly over his shoulder, since Dylan chose to ride back with them.

"Dylan, I need you to change forms again if you can. I need to call Luna. I think you may have found something that could help with her research."

Rachel gave Jack an angry look. "He can't change back that fast. Even if he could, think of how draining that would be."

Jack knew normally Rachel was right, early on in training the Weres couldn't change form more than once in an hour time span, without being wounded. But Jack was counting on Dylan's love for Lyra to push things along. Jack had also seen both Lyra and Ryan do it, but Pack F kept that to themselves.

"It's ringing."

The shocked looked on Rachel's face told Jack she didn't have anyone in her pack that could make a quick change.

"How is that possible?" Rachel's voice was full of disbelief as she struggled to keep her eyes on the road.

"Hello Luna, Jack says he might have information for you."

Dylan's phone appeared between the front seats.

Jack grabbed it and put it to his ear. "Hello?"

"Jack, what have you found?"

The hope in Luna's voice made Jack's chest tighten. He hoped this was what she needed.

"I have a notebook with notes on the drug. There are two pages of notes on a suppressant. There is also mention of an antidote but it says those notes are elsewhere. We grabbed everything we could. How can I get these to you?"

There was quiet for a moment. "Does Dylan's phone have a camera?"

Jack glanced at the phone and saw the tiny lens. "Yeah."

She gave a relieved laugh. "Get photos of the pages mentioning the suppressants. Make them as clear as you can. If those notes are complete, I could have something as soon as tomorrow."

Jack felt himself smile for the first time in two days. "Done."

They hung up and Jack put all his concentration into getting the clearest pictures he could and texting them to Luna.

No sooner had he hit send on the last text, his own phone rang, making him jump. He handed Dylan back his phone and pulled out his own. Frowning, he saw it was Bishop.

"What's wrong, Bishop?"

"We need to talk. Your pack was not exactly careful in their part of the search. Our building set off a bomb."

Jack felt his entire body go still and his breathing stopped.

"No one is hurt beyond superficial wounds, but we were not able to gather much information from the site."

Jack let out a breath. His pack was okay, and to him that was what mattered. "Fine, Bishop, meet us as the F office."

"Why are you not upset by this, Jack?"

"We may have found an antidote to the drug."

"That is good news, I will let your people know." Jack could hear Bishop's relief as the other man hung up.

Jack laid his head back against the seat and closed his eyes. Thing might just be going their way, for the moment anyway.

Chapter 31

Justin was pissed and he knew he wasn't the only one. The group of them marched into the Pack F office to report to all the Alphas at both sites. Taylor, Graham, and Victor tagged along despite objections. Once Bishop gave a brief overview of events to Jack, their Alpha demanded his pack explain themselves. Bishop suggested all the Alphas involved meet to recap at the same time.

Justin could see Jack really didn't care about what happened at their site. He knew his littermate's mind was on Lyra and the hope she might be coming back to them. Justin knew Jack was just going through the motions.

Justin, Seth, Syrus, Sadie, Cole, and Ryan were banged up and standing in their pack's office looking furious and defiant. Justin was pretty sure it was one of the few things they had ever done as a team.

Jack gave them all a guarded glare. That was a good sign, it said he was willing to hear their side of the story first. What he was planning to do after however was probably not good. The way things were going, 'after' might not be for another week or so.

"Ryan, tell me exactly what happened."

Justin watched Ryan take a step forward. His face and body were completely blank. Since hearing the news about a possible antidote, Ryan seemed back to his old self. When he spoke, even his voice was flat. If their Second could still rein himself in, maybe there was hope for his sanity after all. Justin pushed that thought away and concentrated on the present.

"We decided to go in as a pack. We covered the same amount of space as everyone else. It just took us more time. Being together meant our pack was better protected. Should someone get hurt there would be more people around to have their back."

Jack raised his hands to cut Ryan off. "I don't care about any of that. I want to know how the bomb was set off and why."

Justin could hear the tension in Jack's voice. Not a good sign.

Ryan nodded. "Fine, no one was in the offices so once the guards were out of the picture we were able to take our time searching our side of the building. A section of ours over lapped with the group Graham and Dylan were in."

Jack cut him off again. “Why were they together? They are in different packs?”

Justin watched Ryan’s jaw twitch. “Once the idea was broached about exploring in larger groups, we split up into four teams and each took a corner of the building. We had the southwest. Graham, Dylan and their partners had the northwest.”

Ryan paused, as if waiting to be interrupted again. When Jack didn’t say anything he skipped ahead.

“Cole and I were in a large office when we heard noise in the next office over. We went to check it out. We bumped into Graham and his partner then entered the office in question. While searching, I opened a drawer. In said drawer was a bomb. Once the drawer was open, it set a five minute timer. I got on the radio and told everyone we needed an evacuation. We all got out of the building but obviously not far enough to avoid the blast and debris. No one received any injuries that won’t be healed tomorrow.”

Justin watched as Ryan and Jack stared each other down. There was no way Ryan could have known about the bomb, but having all of that information gone put everyone in a foul mood.

Jack looked away first, then turned to Bishop. “I am not seeing how this is their fault. We are not the bomb squad and you got everyone out of there.”

Bishop looked from Jack to Ryan. “It just appears too simple, a bomb in a desk.”

The silence was deafening. All Justin wanted to do was go home and curl up next to Lyra. He wanted all the time with her he could get right now, just in case.

Graham’s Alpha, whose name Justin couldn’t remember, shattered the silence. Though she spoke softly, there was no doubt she spoke to the entire room.

“That’s because they are toying with us.” She stared at the wall, tapping her fingers on her thigh.

“This was a test, to see how we do. Think about it. Minimal resistance until we reached that trap door, where we obviously were not supposed to go. Dylan’s partner told us if he hadn’t tripped on the mat under that cabinet, no one would have known about it.”

The room digested the implications of that statement. Justin couldn’t help the next thought that went through his head. Had the scientists really meant to kill Lyra? He pushed those thoughts back as the woman started talking again.

"We had almost no resistance until we found those notebooks. This was a test to see how we do in a pressure situation. We wouldn't come to training, so these scientists brought training to us."

The weight of that statement scared Justin. They were pawns in a game they didn't know the rules to.

He had forgotten about Graham and Taylor until Graham spoke from behind them.

"What notebooks?"

Suspicion saturated his voice as Graham looked from his Alpha to Jack.

Justin blinked. Had they really forgotten to mention the notes to Graham? The other man's expression confirmed it, and Justin felt guilty.

Jack ran his hand through his hair and sighed. "We found notebooks mentioning the drug given to Lyra..."

Graham was inches from Jack before Justin could blink. The move surprised most of the room.

He was growling loudly. "Give them to me." His fists were shaking at his sides.

Justin watched Jack become angry, more so because Graham towered over him.

"No." The word was quiet but pure steel.

Graham's growl became louder, the shaking more visible. The other man was slipping as they watched. "You will give them to me because my family has the scientists and resources to get the research not only done, but quickly. You will give them to me because you're not as stupid as you look and you know my world gives Lyra a better chance than yours does. You will give them to me because if you don't I will rip your throat out, as well as the throat of anyone else standing in the way of me saving my cousin."

The last sentence made Justin's blood run cold. The words and tone that went with it were the most menacing thing he ever heard in his life. Justin held his breath, his eyes glued to the two men. Jack slowly stood. Graham had several inches on Jack as the two of them stared each other down.

Dylan appeared next to them, laying a hand on Graham's shoulder. "Graham, it's okay…"

Graham shut the other man up by throwing him into the wall behind them.

Justin watched in horror as Graham's nails began to shift in to claws. Justin had never seen anything like it before. It happened so fast. Before he could get out a warning to Jack, Graham was on the floor.

It took Justin a second for his eyes to put together what he was seeing. Graham nicked Jack's throat, but before he could do real damage Taylor had come out of nowhere and ripped open Graham's back, tackling him to the floor. The whole room seemed to be in shock as they watched the two men fighting. There was snarling and growling. The two of them moved far too fast; an arm would move then suddenly there would be blood.

It went on for two minutes before both of them went perfectly still, Taylor squatting, Graham on the ground, each with their claws to the other's throat. The room held its breath. Taylor's voice rang in the air, and even with the thick growl he sounded calm.

"Be careful of the decision you make here, Graham. You are my family, in every way that counts, and my best friend. But I cannot let you do this. I understand what you are saying and I even agree with most of it. You know I would follow you into hell, especially for our sister, but this can not happen. If you save Lyra, by some miracle you save our sister, what then? What will you tell her about the cost of her survival? Yes, she lives, but at the cost of a life she cares deeply for. She will turn away from you. The girl who HAS walked with you through hell will walk away from you if you choose this path. Are you understanding me?"

All eyes focused on Graham, but it was as if he had forgotten any of them were in the room. Under any other circumstances Justin would have left. But drawing attention to himself sounded like a very bad idea at the moment.

"She would be alive." Graham's voice gained more intelligence. Not that the mindless anger wasn't still there, as Justin could still hear it but he also heard something that could be reasoned with. He was pretty sure that was a good sign.

"She would be alive and that is all that really matters."

Taylor searched the other man's face for a long moment. "Are you sure?"

Graham didn't hesitate. "Yes!"

Taylor closed his eyes and dropped his hand. Standing, he looked over at Jack. His expression was full of sadness and regret.

Jack seemed to have gained some composure but Justin could tell his Alpha was still pissed.

"I am sorry, Jack. I'm afraid there is only so much I can do. I will stand in his way but if he gets through me there will be no one to slow him down. I strongly suggest you give us the notebooks so Luna can work on the antidote. Really think about it. Yes, they are a secretive bunch of pricks but right now they are her best bet."

Justin watched as Graham stood up. Without taking his eyes from Jack, Taylor moved to stand between then. Justin could see Jack's anger clouding his judgment. There was no way they could help Lyra as well as her family could.

Seth shifted his weight to gain Jack's attention. When he spoke, his voice was like the one people used on those about to jump off a building.

"Jack, think about this rationally. I know you can do that. Until lately, you do rational thinking better than anyone I know. You don't have the resources or the knowledge to read whatever is in those journals. Even with Mathew's infinite connections, it will take us months. You and I both know she doesn't have that. If this really is a chance to save her, please let them do it. Damn it, Jack."

There was a spilt second where Justin thought Jack might lose it. He didn't know what it was about the more dominant Weres but all of them had trouble holding their tempers.

Jack took several deep breaths before looking only at Graham. "You have angered your cousin for no reason." Jack held up his hand before anyone could interrupt him again. "Personally I'm insulted you think me so selfish. Dylan was trying to tell you before you hit him."

Justin chanced a look at Dylan, The other man seemed more stunned and emotionally hurt then physically injured, though there was a dent in the wall.

"We already sent notes on the suppressant to your Luna. She told me if the notes are complete she would have it ready in a day."

He bent down and grabbed the plastic bag at the foot of his chair and threw it at Taylor, who looked at Jack in complete shock.

"You mean, Luna's been working on it this whole time?" Taylor's voice shook.

Jack nodded.

Justin saw the sadness and relief flood Taylor's face as he turned to Graham. "You have royally screwed up here, man." Then he walked over and offered Dylan a hand off the floor.

Graham stood there staring at Jack with too many emotions flying across his face.

"I am sorry, Jack."

He walked out of the office, grabbing the bag on his way out. Taylor and Dylan followed a few paces behind him.

Justin looked back to Jack, who slowly sat back down in his chair. Mathew cleared his throat.

"Well, we definitely need to set up some rules and procedures if this alliance is going to work, especially if these scientists are going to be playing games with us. We need a plan of action. We may need to train in the actual program. I know, that's insane but we might not have another choice. I'll fish around and see what I can find but we cannot continue to operate the way we have been. The rules have changed on us. We absolutely can't be fighting amongst ourselves."

Justin struggled to keep up with Mathew's change of topic.

"I won't go back into training."

Cassandra's voice was quiet and helpless, but it spoke volumes and Justin knew most of them agreed with her.

"I think blowing up the two buildings bought us some time."

The room looked at Bishop.

"I do not think we were expected to organize this well, or to dispose of so much of their work. Consider how few computers there were, I truly believe we set them back. How far I do not know. How they will respond, I do not know. But now they have to recalculate too."

"So what exactly are we saying? That we want to restructure the alliance? Or break out on our own? What exactly are we committing to here?"

It was the first time Justin heard Victor be completely serious. That seemed to make the situation more dire.

"I don't know," Mathew answered.

The stillness that followed let Justin know no one had a solution.

Chapter 32

They spent two hours in the Pack F office debating what could be done and in the end they weren't closer to an answer. Ryan was frustrated, but at least things seemed to be moving in a productive direction. What finally ended the meeting was Jack receiving a phone call telling him Luna was pretty sure she could replicate the suppressant mentioned in one of the notebooks. It wouldn't cure Lyra, but it should fend off the worst effects for a period of time. The only problem was it would take her about thirty hours to put the suppressant together, cutting Lyra's time very short if Luna was wrong.

They had all gone their separate ways. Jack had to be at the studio, so he didn't join Ryan and Justin as they drove back to be with Lyra. He said he would be there as soon as he was off work.

Dusk on Wednesday had Ryan standing in Justin's hall, feeling numb and watching Lyra's aunt putting a clear blue liquid into a syringe. The older woman walked over to her niece, appearing to be steadying herself. She took a deep breath and Ryan was pretty sure he saw her lips move in a silent prayer. Then she plunged the syringe into Lyra's neck. As the liquid disappeared, Ryan held his breath. One minute passed, then two.

"That's it? Nothing's happening?"

Ryan could feel the same panic he heard in Graham's voice as he started stripping so he could change. Luna turned to them. Her face was shadowed from lack of sleep and worry.

"The notes stated it could take up to seventy-two hours to take effect, depending on how strong the original dose was." She packed everything back into her bag and began to leave.

Graham grabbed her arm, not hard, but like a child would when they had a nightmare. "We just wait and see? How do we know it even works? She could still be dying! By the time we know for sure, she's dead."

Luna gave him a sad smile. "I am going to continue to study the notes to see if I can get more. But yes, all we can do is wait and pray."

Then she left, with her husband at her side.

Ryan stopped paying attention to the conversation at that point. What they were saying didn't matter. He climbed up on the bed and laid against Lyra's left side, since Dylan was on her right. He curled up so he would be nose to nose with her. He would wait. Ryan had absolute faith Lyra wouldn't leave them. He had to. The alternative would break him.

Chapter 33

She was in a memory again. Lyra's relief was overwhelming. The dark had been so overpowering. A memory was a good sign, she decided. A sign she was winning, and she ignored that little voice telling her she wasn't winning, that this was the last stop before the end.

She was curled up in one of the leather chairs with the ottoman in front of her untouched. She was wearing a bright orange skirt. She loved that skirt. In her lap lay a hard-bound book without its jacket. Across from her, stretched out in another leather chair was Ryan. He was grinning at her. They were the only two people in the office. There had been several times when that happened and they always had amazing conversations.

"So you have a big family, then?" he was asking her.

Lyra nodded. "Oh yes. Not just biologically either. There are people who work for my family that mean just as much to me. People I've grown up with. My chosen family. The family I picked."

She grinned back at him. She was always so comfortable with Ryan. It was like she could tell him anything.

His expression was confused, not that Lyra blamed him. Then his eyes widened and he blinked at her, as if seeing her for the first time. Then he seemed to recover.

"I like that about you. Your heart is much bigger than you want everyone to think it is."

Lyra glared and threw a pillow at him.

Ryan chuckled. "I rest my case."

The memory grew hazy around the edges as they laughed, before it blurred all together. This time the blackness wasn't bleak. It was warm and comforting and Lyra didn't struggle against it. If this was the end, it was a good note to end on.

About The Author

Gretchen happily lives in Seattle, Washington where she spends her time creating new characters and situations to put them in. She also enjoys cheering on her local sports teams, even though it sometimes seems they are allergic to winning (Except the Super Bowl!). She graduated from Central Washington University with a BA in History and a BA in Philosophy. She loves that Washington provides a large range of activities, from Shakespeare in the park to rodeos. At the end of her adventures she unwinds by curling up on the couch, knitting while catching up TV shows via Netflix.

If you enjoyed this book please feel free to leave a review on Amazon, Barnes & Noble, or Good Reads. Reviews are always appreciated.

You can find Gretchen at:

http://www.gretchensb.com/
https://twitter.com/GretchenSB
https://www.goodreads.com/author/show/7398184.Gretchen_S_B_
https://www.facebook.com/pages/Gretchen-S-B/540293959350712